The Blushing MBA

The Blushing MBA

(Secrets from Graduate School)

Feddy Pouideh

iUniverse, Inc.

New York Lincoln Shanghai

The Blushing MBA

(Secrets from Graduate School)

iUniverse books may be ordered through booksellers or by contacting:

iUniverse
2021 Pine Lake Road, Suite 100
Lincoln, NE 68512
www.iuniverse.com
1-800-Authors (1-800-288-4677)

ISBN-13: 978-0-595-37287-4 (pbk)
ISBN-13: 978-0-595-81683-5 (ebk)
ISBN-10: 0-595-37287-2 (pbk)
ISBN-10: 0-595-81683-5 (ebk)

Printed in the United States of America

To Julie and Mort, a.k.a. Mom & Dad, for not only lifting me over the sidewalk cracks during childhood, but for also making me laugh along the way.

And for Rick Marini, who always makes time for me...

Contents

▼

Chapter 1:   THE GREAT ACQUISITION
             (The Beginning: How on Earth Did I Get Here?) 1

Chapter 2:   INVESTING IN ME
             (The Admissions Interview: Hear No Evil, Speak No Evil,
             See No Evil) 14

Chapter 3:   THE LEVERAGED BUYOUT
             (Preparing to Leave: It's Going to Cost You Big!) 25

Chapter 4:   DIVERSIFYING YOUR PORTFOLIO
             (Orientation: Who Are You and Why Do I Need to Know
             You?) 50

Chapter 5:   COMPETITIVE POSITIONING
             (First Day of School: Classless Classroom Strategy) 68

Chapter 6:   MY NET WORTH
             (First Year: Go on, I Dare You) 97

Chapter 7:   ATTRACTIVE INDUSTRIES
             (The Social Life: Bulls, Bears, Sugar Daddies & Other
             Personal Assets) 126

Chapter 8:   TRICKS OF THE TRADE
             *(Recruiting Season: Cutthroat Criminals of Interviewing)*154

Chapter 9:   RISK VS. REWARD
             (Second Year Splendor) 190

Chapter 10: TAKING STOCK OF YOUR INVESTMENTS
             (The Final Stretch: Finding Meaning in It All) 221

Chapter 11: FORECASTING
             (Graduation) 260

Chapter 12: THE ANNUAL REPORT
             (Epilogue from the Author) 271

Acknowledgements

With true delusions of grandeur, I dreamed of this acknowledgements section in poignant "acceptance-speech" form before I even began writing the book, never expecting the first line to read:

Thank you to all the writers of the world.
I humbly bow to you with the greatest admiration and respect for both your profession and your intelligence. Writing this book has been the most difficult endeavor of my professional history; I will forever find myself declaring to skeptical, naive non-writers, "You have *no* idea."

Thank you to the admissions offices of the University of New Hampshire and Dartmouth College for taking a chance on me; I'm eternally grateful to all professors and teachers who put up with me throughout my academia.

My life would not be the same without: Amy Holt, my friendship soul mate; Nicole Rivera, my truest and dearest friend for 20+ years and a lifetime; and Lisa Girard-Bouvier, one of the wisest voices of reason on earth. And to the ladies of business school—the strongest, smartest champions I know: Leslie Fong, who understands the true meaning of the phrase, "I carried a watermelon"; Ramona Walker, my savior; Daphne Streeter; Potoula Chresomales; and to Mr. Jeff Stern and Susie. Look closely, all of you, because you were the inspiration behind every positive character trait in the book—I could not have done it without you.

Special thanks to those who supported me with love, professional input, enthusiasm, and friendship: Jennifer Tibbetts Young; Alyse Fox Townsend; Francesca Wodtke; Carmine and Erica Ciampi; the Rivera's; the Holt's; the Marini's; Jeff Soto; the Dovalis family; the Tietz's; Ruth Chris & staff for making me smile; and the entire Blue Cross Blue Shield clan—Jeff Howard, Jeanne King, Gary Kelly, Lou Lombardo, Dale Carriger, Gina Foley, Donna Julian, Claire Hangen, Josef Aukee, Gaye Clark, and Bonnie Woodruff.

I applaud all the women of the world who have boldly contributed to academic and business communities; in doing so, you have enriched our lives and inspired thousands of women to reach for the stars.
This is my star.

Thank you.

Introduction

"It's never too late—in truth or fiction—to revise." ~ Nancy Thayer

What a wonderful concept! The chance to rewrite our personal histories? And that's exactly what I did with *The Blushing MBA*. I wrote this book for two very simple reasons: 1.) to provide a woman's perspective of business school, and 2.) to expand our horizons of the great opportunities awarded to all people who pursue business education.

What you are about to read is humorous (I hope) fiction loosely based on my experiences. The characters are not real (no lawsuits necessary, folks), but rather a crafty conglomerate of several quirky and lovable personalities in my life, or figments of my wild imagination. Yes, the main character is based on *moi*—but for obvious reasons I made myself much more likeable (easy to do on paper!) and witty. In fact, in my next book, I may just make myself a rocket scientist super-mom with X-ray vision and a body to die for. But on a note that will make your spine shiver, most of the events in *The Blushing MBA* actually happened...but not always to me (except the interview with the blow-up doll), not always at business school, and not always with the personalities described.

The book you are holding in your hands (presumably *The Blushing MBA*) is unlike anything you have ever read about business school. It is a sincere, gritty, honest, raw, emotional ride of trying times and magnificent triumphs in graduate school told from a woman's point of view. It is not, however, a clinical "How to" MBA book. If you're interested in Business 101, business cases, frameworks, or magical "getting in" formulas, I can assure you that there are many wonderful books already on the market for that sole purpose.

However, if you want a candid, sometimes startling, behind-the-scenes look at the life of a girl figuratively thrown to the wolves at a competitive Ivy League business school, and you actually get a perverse pleasure out of those sorts of things...well then, you've come to the right place.

And I thank you for being here.

"If you educate a man you educate a person, but if you educate a woman you educate a family." —Ruby Manikan

CHAPTER 1

---- ❋ ----

THE GREAT ACQUISITION

(The Beginning: How on Earth Did I Get Here?)

Decision Science Class, 8:15 a.m.

"Plug $4,221,848 into the formula because it's more profitable," the professor barks.

What in the world is he talking about?

I'm trembling in my seat.

"Look at your objective function. You know your variable constraints, now calculate your feasible region," he orders from over his shoulder while feverishly scribbling a frenzy of complex equations and running a hand through his Einstein hair.

For 15 minutes, he's lost in a mathematical stupor on a planet far, far away...

Without warning, he stops and manically spins toward the class with his crazed, glassy eyes piercing the room like laser beams.

My God, he's gone mad!

"Okay," he says, devilishly clapping his hands. "Enough about Barnett Lumber. Let's move on."

Oh no.

No no no no no.

There's not a student out there who doesn't know the simple equation: [infamous clapping of the hands gesture] + [lame "let's move on" comment] = complete classroom annihilation.

Step right up folks and witness the oldest and scariest teaching tactic known to man, the interrogation method of torture loved by professors and mobsters every-where—the dreaded cold-call!

I instinctively sink lower into my chair, expertly slouching my shoulders so that only my forehead is visible over my laptop computer.

"Please take out your homework assignments," he commands.

Absolutely, positively, DO NOT—under any circumstance known to man—make eye contact with him.

"You should have used Excel Solver in last night's homework," he continues, shrewdly moving toward the class while his beady eyes slowly search the classroom for student prey.

Be still!

Any sudden movement might catch his shrewd Velociraptor vision…

Look nonchalantly at my computer and nowhere else. Not at the ceiling. Not at my neighbor. Pretend to look distracted, deep in thought, hang up the 'Do Not Disturb" sign with furrowed eyebrows.

DANGER, Will Robinson, DANGER!

The professor is approaching at full speed.

He's four feet away from me.

Three feet…

Two feet…

"Let's see…" he continues carefully, stopping in front of me.

Do NOT make eye contact. Ground control to Major Tom, repeat, do not make eye contact. Do NOT look at him. Steady. Keep it steady, girl.

"Who was brave enough to attempt last night's assignment?" he asks.

We just made eye contact.

"Pull up your spreadsheets," he instructs the class, casually drumming his fingers on my desk.

We have breaking news at eleven: I'm doomed.

"Any volunteers?" he dares, looking directly at me but smugly knowing that he'd have more volunteers at the guillotine during the French Revolution. I'm no Charles Darnay, so I keep shut.

"Feddy!" he says to me as if we're old friends. "Come up to the front! Let's take a look at your spreadsheet model!"

Put a fork in me and call me <u>done</u>.

I know from previous experience that for the next hour I will endure pure humiliation (my own, just in case that wasn't clear) guaranteed to brand me with embarrassing memories not only perfectly suited to fuel a sizzling memoir, but also just awkward enough to haunt me (and my future offspring) for many years to come. There is an audible, collective sigh of relief from the class. Oh sure, now they can relax behind the safety of their new cold-call-repelling shield—moi. Frighteningly, this protection always seems to shrink their sympathetic bones and simultaneously fuel their most critical tendencies. I've been sacrificed so that they can sit back and check email, periodically impressing the professor by verbally critiquing my spreadsheet. Doesn't the expression, "taking one for the team," mean anything to these people? 120 penetrating eyes hit me like darts flying toward a bulls-eye. I can't focus and my body is numb. (Three hours of sleep will do that to a person.) I begin a rapid, irreversible descent into mental paralysis as everything moves into silent, slow motion.

I trudge to the front of the room. The only thoughts I can manage are a quick plea to God for a painless (but ultimately distracting) heart attack, and then the thought that has entered my mind at least 100 times since breakfast, *How on sweet earth did I get here?*

THE BEGINNING

Business first knocked me down with the sheer force of a raging bull. It had nothing to do with the state of the economy, or the unemployment rate, or my investments. It had to do with a paper route. I was just a child, and newspapers were my first chance to earn cold, hard cash for the greatest motivator known to a kid—ice cream sundaes at Kresge's Restaurant. Rain or shine, there I was rolling 36 papers into my canvas sack before diligently patrolling my Ohio neighborhood with a smile. My mom still has the original letter sent by the newspaper to my new customers (mothers of only children will do things like that):

> *Dear Customers:*
>
> *We are pleased to introduce our newest Business Associate!*
> *Please welcome Feddy, a 4th grader at Washington Elementary School, our newest, loyal Daily Jeffersonian carrier, by taking a minute to say hello today…*

That's me—a proud businesswoman in the fourth grade! At least until I crumbled. Literally. It was raining and I slipped on the Donald family's dangerously dilapidated front steps. I walked right into an excruciatingly painful ankle sprain, but thank God, Robin, my best childhood friend, was with me as I lay sprawled on the ground with my melodrama.

"Robin…I can't…go…on…"

Robin pulled my sock down to look at my ankle.

"Wow—it's huge!" she said.

"You…must…finish…my…route…" I croaked out a plea. I had money to collect, papers to deliver, and receipts to write.

"It's raining!" she protested.

"Please?" I begged.

She looked at me with skepticism.

"You can keep the cash," I offered desperately.

She smiled. "Can I eat dinner at your house tonight?" she asked.

Hmm...obviously a ruthless negotiator.

"Okay, I'll ask my mom."

After the shrewd dinner negotiations, she gladly accepted the offer; and she did a wonderful job. Unfortunately, I was laid up for several days, *sans* cash and (worse) *sans* ice cream. But I never said anything. I didn't know about insurance, or lawsuits, or workers' rights. The newspaper sent me a standard "Get Well, Hang in There!" card (cuddly kittens caught in a basket of yarn motif).

And the Donalds never did fix the steps.

The hairs on the back of my neck get a little prickly when I think about how the paper route was an eerie omen of my lifetime commitment to laborious professional work. They get even pricklier when I realize this was only one of many omens I would face throughout the years. The paper route started my adventures in business and foreshadowed basic business principles I would learn repeatedly for the next 20 years: negotiation, management, customer service, cash and collections, crisis control, insurance (or lack thereof), employee rights, incentives and teamwork.

Of course, the paper route happened many years before I understood that the sustainability of our nation's economic growth actually *depended* on women. Details like women owning 50% of our private businesses, the majority of consumers being female, and the number of women-owned businesses growing faster than the rate of all other firms—well, those statistics were of little significance to me at the time. Like any other kid, I was blissfully oblivious to business politics, and likewise to the true understanding of what my future had waiting for me beyond two scoops of vanilla ice cream drowning in rich chocolate fudge syrup.

Unbeknownst to me, my destiny had arrived.

Through the years, my business interests wavered, but only temporarily. My family moved from the Midwest to New England, and inevitably (against my will) I got older. I progressed from injured Paper-Girl to perky Grocery Store Clerk and then to Professional Babysitter before the age of 18. (Note: Never underestimate the importance of professional babysitting skills in today's management world.) These were the average jobs for a teenage girl at the time—along with marathon phone talking—but work always took a backseat to academics. School ruled in our household, and I submerged myself into a qualitative and quantitative academic world strongly supported by my family. For example, Dad encouraged me to take computer courses in high school at a time when 'high-tech' was a TV remote control and computers weren't…well…*cool.*

"I can't come over."

"Why not?" my best friend, Kim, demanded over the phone.

I could hardly hear her above Madonna's classic "Material Girl" blaring from her stereo, but she had raised a good point.

"I have to finish my reports on Iran and Iceland for Sociology," I countered into the mouthpiece, fighting Madonna for her attention. "And I still have computers."

"Oh…rrrright…*computers.*" Kim said, emphasizing "computers" the way a debutante mutters "bargain basement."

"It's not that bad, it just takes a long time," I explained weakly. *Had I actually sunk so low as to defend homework?*

"Whatever," she said, giving up. "I'll see you tomorrow at the bus stop."

Later…taking out teenage angst on my dad:

"Dad, I don't even understand the names of these courses."

He was an engineer who dedicated his life to science, but I had never heard of anything as frightening as Pascal programming.

"You'll thank me later. Trust me," he assured me.

"Dad, I'm the only GIRL in these classes!"

"You're a pioneer."

"I'm a nerd."

He championed me through the courses and only wavered once—the night he stayed up until 1:00 a.m. struggling with one of my complex computer assignments (I had gone to bed at 10). My parents were my biggest cheerleaders and always—usually against my teenage dream to live a life free of embarrassment—deeply involved in my life. I put my heart into school and was one of those studious kids who always did my homework, received decent grades in high level courses, and then lay in bed at night growing an ulcer, worrying that the quadratic equation I solved on page two of my homework wasn't perfect. *Please God, I promise to be good for the rest of the year if you let #4 slide—just this once.*

My dad continued to push computers while my mother introduced me to her love of literature. It was an academic tug-o-war but I credit them with giving me this admirable balance of math and literature in my life. I was probably the only

17-year-old who alternated between Jane Austen's *Emma* and *Computer Programming for Beginners* for bedside reading.

Then I read *Sybil*, the true story of a woman with Multiple Personality Disorder, and my life changed. Well, actually, I was fascinated by Sally Field's Emmy-award-winning performance in the TV adaptation, but I really did read the book, too. I truly thought I wanted to be Sybil's psychiatrist. (Or maybe I just wanted to be an actress—who knows?) I entered college as a psychology major to find out.

During college, my right brain and left brain continued their torrid affair while I worked as a Computer Consultant and as a full-time Resident Assistant for the university. I spent my time battling computers (hardware and software), counseling freshman (emotional development and dirty bathrooms), and studying Freud (cigars and term papers). Inevitably, my mind drifted back to business and I found myself asking taboo questions in psych class. *How do I raise money for a private practice? How is psychology used in advertising? How is that pharmaceutical stock doing?* I quickly learned that a person had absolutely no business (no pun intended) talking about profits in a psych class. Junior year, I came full circle and declared business administration as my new major.

Home at last.

GOOD MORNING, CORPORATE AMERICA!

During my senior year of college, marketing landed on my mental doorstep as the perfect combination of my two loves: psychology and business. (Looking back, my third love of TV and commercial products—an *addiction*, really—may have also played an integral role.) I just knew that I could not wait to start doing whatever in the world it was that marketers did!

You have to start somewhere, and my first job after college was at the ground level (subterranean worm-infested earth, if you prefer) working as a Marketing Assistant for a patriarchal, old-school commercial bank. Good ideas took a backseat to seniority at the bank, which wasn't super for me because I was about 40 years younger than the average employee. My days were filled with media planning, public relations, market research, and advertising. I also spent a fortune on stuffy, conservative business suits trying to assimilate.

After a year, I grew tired of press releases (faxing them), trade shows (hauling heavy equipment), and business planning (answering phones). I plotted my escape.

First, I made lists.

Reasons to stay at the bank:

1. Two wonderful managers
2. Valuable marketing experience
3. Short commute

Reasons to LEAVE the bank:

1. "Ground-level" shouldn't be a long-term professional goal
2. Have to wait 15–20 years for someone to "pass-on" before I'm promoted
3. Grad school
4. Lecherous old men

Lecherous old men! The harassment! I lost track after the 50th time, but there was one instance, in particular, that strengthened my desire to acquire power (albeit to crush the harassers) by climbing the corporate ladder in the future. It's in my "Working Girl Moments Hall of Fame" and it feels like it happened just yesterday.

It was a Saturday informational interview with the owner of a prominent advertising agency recommended to me by a VP at the bank. The owner of the agency—affectionately nicknamed "Libidinous Ogre"—proceeded to use the F-word five times during the interview. He was kind enough to explain that he always swears during an interview to measure a candidate's threshold. *Threshold for what? Idiocy tolerance?* Then, he told me that his staff bought him a plastic blow-up doll for his birthday.

"Would you like to see the doll?"

"See it?" I asked, confused.

"Yes, it's right in my closet, I'd be happy to get it for you," the Ogre offered.

"No!" I blushed. *A blow-up doll sex toy!?*

"All of my employees are female and sometimes I call them 'My Angels.' That doesn't bother you, does it?"

Yes, Bosley, it does.

"And sometimes," the Ogre continued, "I hug them."

Hugs what? His "angels" or his "plastic dolls"? Both images are equally gross.

"My angels…we hug hello, good-bye, whatever. We're like family here so everyone's comfortable with it. I have to screen new employees to make sure they're okay with the…*hugging*." He grinned and my stomach flipped.

Heeeeelp! Where's the ejector seat button?

He didn't wait for me to comment and just continued talking about his agency, not having any clue that I was seconds away from making a dramatic escape through the window until I mentally calculated the number of feet I'd fall to the ground and decided the Ogre wasn't worth a broken leg. Finally, I just politely asked him if he knew of any *other* companies hiring. Then, I dismissed myself and ran like Florence Griffith Joyner to my car.

Looking back, I should have talked to an expert about it. Instead, I just vowed that I would work even harder to reach a new level of power on the corporate ladder. Surely, I would be treated with more respect if I held a different position, I thought. I just needed to get out of there—I desperately needed to leave the bank. And fast.

The opportunity came sooner than I expected.

Real reason I left the bank:

1.   Bank merger

The CEO cashed out, left us a thoughtless farewell note, and then ran off with the cute Human Resources Director and a million bucks. Like most employees, I wasn't quite so lucky. I was left with only an unclear future at the company. I shifted my career plans into high gear (pending unemployment worked like gasoline) and thanks to a referral I soon found myself working in the marketing department of one of the most well known brands in the world, BlueCross BlueShield (BCBS).

BCBS was a professional blessing. The bank's overbearing and omnipresent stodginess was as severe as BCBS's progressive flexibility was light (very surprising for insurance). People actually listened when I talked; the culture shock was staggering. They laughed me out of the office when I arrived in a business suit on my first day. I had never heard of business-casual, flex-hours, open cubicles, a circular org chart, team leaders, or employee benefits which included dry-cleaning, massages, and auto repairs. The years went by, coworkers turned into my closest friends, and my cubicle became my second home. Life was good.

Then I put the wheels into motion that would alter the course of my life forever. I blame restless ambition because although I felt comfortable with the account management tasks of my job, I needed the infamous "big picture." I wanted to understand strategy, frameworks, and the integration of all the departments. I wanted to learn, to make a change, to go as far as I could in business. A master's degree of business administration—an MBA—was the perfect answer.

Friends and family knew I had always dreamed of going to graduate school, and I decided to finally make the dream a reality.

That's when the *real* work started…

GRADUATE SCHOOL TRAINING

Question:	How long does it take to apply to grad school?
My answer then:	A few weeks?
My answer today:	A lifetime plus 10 months of intense training.

Preparing for business school—'B-school' as it's affectionately known—became my second job (unfortunately one without pay or benefits). It was a grueling training program that I awarded the highest priority. I spent my days working late, eating dinner at the office, and then studying for the business school entrance exam, the Graduate Management Admission Test (GMAT), into all hours of the night at my desk. I couldn't risk the possibility of not getting in (my mom already told all of the neighbors that I was applying to an Ivy League school). My friends were busy reading wedding magazines while I buried my nose into *Business Week* looking at the B-school rankings. In the beginning, the process consisted of five easy steps:

1. Choosing schools
2. Taking the GMAT
3. Completing the application
4. Interviewing
5. Waiting

Five easy steps into the refined world of the business elite? Yeah, right! Becoming the next Ukrainian presidential candidate would have been easier. It's a long process, applying to business school: GMAT in the spring, application and admissions interview in the fall, acceptance or rejection determined in the winter (or a gut-wrenching "waitlist" verdict), and if you're lucky, classes begin in the fall of the following year. Likewise, those five easy steps multiplied into a complex labor of love:

1. Researching schools and MBA programs
2. Talking to students and alumnae
3. Reading overstated school brochures
4. Visiting campuses
5. Preparing for the GMAT
6. Studying monotonous guidebooks and websites
7. Sacrificing weekends
8. Worrying endlessly
9. Writing essays for the application
10. Pondering any part of my life worth writing about—*what was my greatest success to date?* I had never thought about it!
11. Doing extra projects for my manager in hopes of earning a sparkling B-school recommendation
12. Preparing for interviews—*where do I want to be in five years, anyway?*
13. Revamping my resume to put a positive spin on reality
14. Working, eating, sleeping, spending time with loved ones…

I was like Rocky, training for the Russian fight, but without the boxing and without the sweat (but yes, *with* the "Eye of the Tiger" music). I even succumbed to silly superstitions—the only pencils and erasers I would use were part of my "lucky bunch" in a rubber band and I wore my lucky shirt. And don't laugh, but the night before the GMAT (after studying, of course), I watched the movie, *Rudy,* a true story about a boy who tries relentlessly to get into Notre Dame College, for inspiration.

My friends were supportive. Amy and Gary, my partners in crime, professional peers, and best friends at work, razzed me about moving up the corporate ladder. They were afraid I'd become one of those *Office Space* characters we made fun of at work—the ones who came in, revamped the org chart, and then fired people who were inevitably rehired the following year. My other friends, who worked in noble fields like medical technology and book editing, didn't really understand why I wanted to go back but loved me unconditionally anyway. Other people, usually friends of the family, marveled at the idea of an Ivy League MBA and were really impressed (sometimes I even let it go to my head—but only for a second).

Then there were those who weren't so impressed, especially friends who were embarking on important milestones of engagements, weddings, and babies. Some didn't understand why I spent time studying tricky GMAT questions like, "If X units are added to the length of the radius of a circle, what is the number of units by which the circumference is increased?" I think they saw business school as a way for me to delay "real life."

But I didn't see it that way at all. I wanted the same things they did.

Secret #1: I really wanted a family. I never really felt any heart-wrenching Sophie's Choice-like torment readily hyped by our media over the pressure of choosing only one: business or family. In fact, I never even knew the possibility for a dilemma existed until I *read* about it—these fears becoming contagious in the media, planting seeds of doubt in my head like spider veins, dark shadows on my face, smile-lines, or age spots. I never knew these unique, genetic marks of character were a problem until the innocent flip of 10 glossy pages of a fashion magazine attempted (unsuccessfully) to rob me of my self-esteem. Likewise, in regard to business—I certainly didn't want to create a problem that wasn't there. The natural, uncomplicated path for me was: school, marriage, and kids (overlapping allowed). Business school and family simply weren't mutually exclusive to me.

Ninety percent of the people I knew who went to graduate school eventually had a family. I loved hearing stories from women who said it was much better to have the degree than not. Of course everyone made sacrifices to some extent, but sometimes it was a personal choice. Not every businesswoman was on the CEO track—many used their degrees for low-pressure, mom-friendly careers; they became entrepreneurs with flexible careers or worked part-time. One of my best friends managed a small clothing-design business from home; and I heard stories all the time about women starting home-based catalog businesses, consulting on short-term projects, opening yoga studios—they used business skills to market everything from screenplays to cookies. Project maintenance, time management, public speaking, negotiation, and networking—all the skills you learned in business could be applied to almost any aspect of life, from launching a new idea to managing a chaotic household.

Secret #2: I wasn't Supergirl. I wasn't trying to tackle the world. And my friends would be the first to confirm (between laughs) that to confuse me with some unrelenting, maniacal over-achiever is ridiculous.

I just wanted to experience something great—do something I loved, create a better world. And I recognized business school as one of those incredible, life-altering opportunities for a fabulous future. (Plus, there was no telling when I would need to use the independence MBA ticket nestled safely in my back pocket.)

Most importantly, though, I just couldn't wait to get started on my life.

I remember running up the steps to my family's home the day my GMAT scores arrived. My parents had followed my saga and were just as anxious as I was to see my scores. My mom was glowing with excitement as I trampled into their house.

I ripped open the envelope for our special Academy Award moment. (My mom later confirmed that it was actually "*Better* than the Oscars, especially after the three-hour mark, what a snooze fest!") My eyes quickly scanned the sheet until I found the numbers.

95th percentile.

I didn't break any records, but I scored higher than 95% of the people who took the test! The prep worked! We screamed and hugged.

My mom showered me with, "I knew you could do it! I just knew it!" She's my mom, but I still relished the comments; plus I knew we could relive the glory when my dad came home from work. Meanwhile, I ran to the phone to call my boyfriend at his office. Rick worked in corporate finance as an Associate in the mergers & acquisitions group of a Fortune 500 company that prided itself on old-school grandeur of suspenders and slicked-backed hair. Rick spent 16-hour days working on deals and picking up sharp business skills while I secretly (and sometimes not-so-secretly) hoped he would never become as miserable and unhappy as some of his overworked superiors. Rick, an obvious underachiever (ahem), was recently accepted into Harvard Business School.

"Yes!" he cheered when I told him my scores. "Congratulations, honey!"

He was ecstatic but couldn't talk for long—someone in the background was yelling for him and he had to go. Most likely, the person yelling was Brann, who was prone to shouting, having tantrums, and physically throwing things at the staff when he was mad. No, Brann was not a toddler—he was a grown man, Rick's tyrannical boss. This infuriated me because Rick is the most decent person I have ever known. He never complained about Brann's tantrums, simply decided against a harassment lawsuit (lucky for them), and constantly remained nice and easy-going. A rock.

My rock, actually.

Rick and I started dating years ago as undergraduate business students in college. I sat next to him in Organizational Behavior and the professor instructed us to exchange phone numbers in case of an emergency. Given the ambiguity of the word "emergency" (technically, the professor never properly defined it), Rick and I soon began dating and that was the beginning of a beautiful thing. It turned out that we had a lot in common—we were raised in tight middle-class families, both of our dads were engineers, our families lived in neighboring towns in New

Hampshire, and we were both business majors with big business dreams. Of course, friends and family pestered us about "The Big Day"—which I think means marriage—and questioned our long-distance relationship (we live an hour away from each other), but it works for us, and why ruin a good thing?

Rick starts business school in January (the accelerated 18-month program); and then if all goes well and I'm accepted into B-school, I will be starting the following September (the standard two-year program). Granted I'm not applying to Harvard, we will be states apart for almost two years. We try not to stress about the future of our long-distance relationship too much—sometimes making a big deal out it makes it seem worse—but sometimes it's impossible not to.

There are so many things to think about when going back to school. Love, life, money, career, GMAT scores…why do I do it? I guess because I love business and I love school. I mean, I *really* love them. I'm one of those dorky people who leaves the grocery store calculating how the store could improve customer satisfaction by changing the operational queuing, upgrading their scanners for greater efficiency, improving the deli layout, negotiating discounts with produce brokers, encouraging loyalty through a frequent buyer program, and rethinking this week's couponing which paled next to the competition's.

I see almost every aspect of society touched by business. The act of business itself is not immoral—it's only when people become tainted, the transaction sours, and the end goal is no longer mutually beneficial to all parties that we have a problem. Business has been around since the beginning of time and I don't just mean before Microsoft, or circa Karl Marx, or even 7th century BC when possibly the first coin was minted. I mean way back to the first transaction between two hominoids, a buyer and a seller, exchanging sharp stones for plants. Since then, there are very few things untouched by business today—the subway you took this morning, the lunch you ate, the clothes you're wearing, the TV show you'll watch tonight, the newspaper you read this morning, the donation you made at the office, the place you call home, the toys that make your kids smile, the game you'll go to this weekend, the pet you adopted, the car you drive, the party favors you've selected for your best friend's wedding shower, the vacation you'll take, the volunteer work you'll do…all touched by business. We can't stop it. Nor do we have to. We can check and balance it, harness it, improve it, diversify it, purify it, and grow it—and I'll gladly take on that opportunity. I am applying to business school viewing business as such: *a challenge*. It's not lost on me that if you want to make a change, the best way to start is to learn.

How strange then, that the year I was so confident about my career path and decided to go back to school was also the year I began to doubt.

CHAPTER 2

———— ✳ ————

INVESTING IN ME

(The Admissions Interview: Hear No Evil, Speak No Evil, See No Evil)

A hardworking female executive meets a Saint on her way to heaven.

"During your life, you courageously made intelligent business decisions. Now, you must decide whether to spend eternity in Heaven or Hell," the Saint says to her.

She is confident that she will choose Heaven, but agrees to visit both. When she arrives at the pearly gates of Heaven, she is overwhelmed with the breathtaking beauty of true paradise. She spends the peaceful day enjoying the splendor of the tranquil blue skies, relaxing while watching the calming sunset, and strolling on the white sand beach.

The next day, she arrives in Hell.

Satan takes her to a power lunch given in her honor. Later, they join several of her former business associates on a private golf course before she indulges in a soothing massage and facial at a decadent spa. At night, Satan escorts her to a top French restaurant for dinner and a bottle of her favorite vintage Bordeaux before she dances the night away in a Narciso Rodriguez gown at a star-studded party. At the end of the evening, a limousine drives her to a five-star hotel where she falls asleep on the deluxe bed in her premium room.

"I choose Hell!" she tells the Saint the next morning.

"So be it," he says and leaves her at the fiery gates of Hell.

Once inside, she is shocked to see everyone in rags—fatigued, filthy, and diseased. They are scavengers fighting for food, shelter, and clothing, living in a barren environment.

"What happened?" she exclaims.

"Well," explains Satan. "Yesterday we were recruiting you. Today you're full-time."

—Author Unknown

THE LONGEST DRIVE

All of this leads to where I am today, 8:24 p.m. on November 20th. I am driving northwest on a deserted New Hampshire highway, all alone in the chilling 28° F darkness. I have no doubt there are urban legends about people who drive on these dark, creepy roads at night. It is just me, an occasional truck, and the glaring "Watch Out for Deer Crossing" road signs. Most of the radio stations have lost frequency, which stinks because I have only completed half of the three-hour drive. But I don't care—I have worked a lifetime to get here and I cannot remember wanting anything more than I want this: I'm on my way to the Ivy League campus of one of the most prestigious business schools in the world, where tomorrow morning I will embark on one of the greatest honors of my life—an MBA admissions interview.

Trying to fend off insanity, my mind wanders as I drive. I hope my gas tank gets me to the next stop, although I don't know what's scarier—being stranded without gas, or pulling into one of these spooky, remote gas stations which seem to appear every 17 miles. Now would be a good time to go over my stock interview answers, witty responses I plan to use to dazzle my interviewer tomorrow.

Focus. Focus. Focus.

But I can't.

I can't stop thinking about the janitor. He was from the cleaning crew that I befriended during my late hours at work (okay, the crew woke me up when I dozed at my desk late at night). But on that particular night in April, I was awake and studying my GMAT prep book when the janitor came to empty my trash. I looked up and smiled at him, but then sighed in exaggerated exasperation so he would know just how hard I had been working.

"Hi, working hard tonight?" he asked. He looked just like James Earl Jones.

"Yeah, well, just studying for *grad school.*" I dropped the bomb. "A little GMAT prep."

I waited for the usual reaction—a "wow," or buttery praise of admiration, or talk about his long lost dreams of pursuing a master's degree. I mentally prepared a short but polite response.

I never used it.

"Been there, done that," the janitor said and laughed.

Hold on.

"You've been to grad school?" I asked, confused.

"I was a corporate accountant." He reached for my trashcan. "It wasn't worth it. The stress made me miserable; the people were terrible. I wasn't happy."

Circuits overloaded. Can't compute.

"So I left and went to work for my brother's cleaning service," he continued as he emptied my trash. "Now, I work only when I want to, with no stress at all, and I've never been happier. It was the best thing I've ever done."

"Wow, that's great! Good for you!" I practically shouted as I smiled and nodded insincerely. My over-compensating animation and frozen smile almost gave me away.

An accountant who becomes a janitor? Is this a joke? No one could possibly be that happy throwing away such an opportunity! No way. No no no way.

But he is.

He paused at my desk and flashed me an all-knowing grin that seemed to say, "I know what you're thinking, but you'll understand someday."

Then he moved on.

Wait! What did he mean?

Funny, I can barely remember the 1,489 positive things that people said to me about a future in business, but I can't forget the janitor's single comment. In fact, I have to fight away this thought as I drive across New Hampshire. After all, there is no stopping me at this point. I force myself to think about the thrill. I love business—the power, the limitlessness, the opportunity, the history, the rush of a closed deal, the adrenaline caused by a fractional change of a stock, the birth of a new brand, a satisfied customer, a well-managed team, the big sale, meetings, schedules, the hustle-and-bustle, the *Wall Street Journal*...

I curse the janitor for not wanting this. You can do anything you want to do in this world. Business if full of opportunities.

Right?

As I drive my mind alternates between confident fantasies of nailing the upcoming interview and insecure thoughts of turning into a bumbling idiot and botching the opportunity of a lifetime thereby disappointing myself, my family, my friends, and the entire country of the United States of America.

Tomorrow, I head to the interview.

THE INTERVIEW

Saying there was tension in the admissions waiting room would be like saying that Bill Gates had a minor impact on the software industry. There are 10 of us sitting in the admissions waiting room and we average one breath per minute. Total. No one moves, no one talks. I am tempted to take the pulse of the guy next to me, but judging from his sour expression I don't think he would delight in the silliness. In fact, I don't think anyone in here delights in anything. I look around. Navy. Black. Black. Black. Navy. Everyone has the same outfit. *Funny how a "powersuit" no longer seems powerful when everyone is wearing one.*

Nothing seems right. The walls are closing in. I have to speak or I am going to die. I turn to the woman sitting next to me.

"Hi! Pretty nerve-racking, huh?" I rant.

She looks shocked that I have dared to speak and barely turns her stiff neck toward me.

"Yes," says the Ice Queen.

"Where are you coming from?" I ask. I think she's starting to melt.

"Boston," she replies coolly.

"Nice place, Boston," I say, nodding. "The snow probably wasn't bad until you hit the border?"

I pause for her to respond.

Then I pause a little longer.

Okay, now it's just awkward.

She finally turns away. *Game over.*

But hallelujah, it's time for the tour! A handsome student Admissions Guide corrals us for a preview of the facilities. We start in beautiful Dalton Hall, a meeting lounge area of old New England grandeur with large, brown leather chairs, mahogany tables, a fireplace, and dark-paneled walls with oil portraits of tight-lipped people (I'm certain they must be important). I picture people smoking cigars and drinking brandy in this room while discussing plans for world domination. The tour continues as we roam through the library, then to the corporate-sponsored Dining Hall (shamelessly named "Starbucks Dining Hall"), then to the tiny, student-run mailroom (*why is there so much undelivered mail on the floor?*), and then into the prestigious corporate-sponsored interviewing area (the "Kraft Recruiting Center") where recruiting season is in full swing. *Wait— I'm not sure, but I think I just saw a young, red-faced student with watery-eyes run out of an interviewing room?*

The Admissions Guide then sprints us through the fitness rooms and dorms, quickly explaining that they "need a lot of work." He's right. The housing quarters resemble the prison accommodations on Alcatraz. (I feel I can say this with some authority because I have actually toured Alcatraz in San Francisco three times.) But I don't care. I love everything.

I fell in love with this school when I visited last year; and now I affectionately, and respectfully, refer to it as "The School" in my deepest, most grandiose voice because this institution truly represents the pinnacle of business education. I had accompanied Rick on one of his company's recruiting trips to the campus—he was wining & dining potential new hires—and I learned more about The School than I ever imagined. It meets all of my criteria.

The School, founded in the early 1900's, is situated close to Boston and New York and boasts a strong general management curriculum among the following statistics:

- annual applications received: 10,000+

- students per graduating class: 200

- average admitted age: 27 years

- average admitted GPA: 3.5

- average admitted GMAT: 700

Then I looked at the other vitals: the ratio of faculty to students (high), percentage of women (27%), percentage of international students (25%), marketing curriculum, teamwork emphasis, field studies, international and technology focus, mentoring program, caliber of faculty, facilities, and rankings in the usual rags, *BusinessWeek, the Financial Times, The Wall Street Journal,* and *U.S. News and World Report* (the program consistently ranks in the top 10). The School also offers joint degrees with the medical, law, and engineering schools. And when I dug into The School's reputation, met some people, enjoyed the beautiful New England campus, and found out that it was a "collaborative school" with a smaller, more personalized program, I was sold. The School is now my first choice. It's a fantastic program, one reported to treat women well, and (bonus!) it's close to my family.

Our tour group continues on. A cell phone rings and the girl next to me fearlessly takes the call. *During the tour?*

I quickly try to distance myself from her so everyone knows it isn't my phone ringing. The girl, oblivious to the disapproving stares, yells something irate into the mouthpiece, hangs up, and then turns toward me (I'm the closest sounding board) and angrily says:

"This is absolutely ridiculous! I have to get back to the office! How much longer is this tour? I cannot believe this day is taking so long."

It's only 10 a.m.

I look left and right to verify that she is talking to me. Unfortunately, she is. She is mad in a spoiled Veruca Salt way and talking loudly (very bizarre behavior on an interview, if you ask me). Everyone looks at us. I blush and then smile at her.

Is she nuts? Why is she here? Will they accept someone like her? And why does she seem to be yelling at me?

I have a brief fantasy that the Admissions Guide will glance over, see her ridiculous whining, and then look at me and smile. I'll give him my "don't-ask-me" shoulder shrug and then point to the loud-mouthed phone-talker and nod as if to say, "Sheesh, the nerve of some people." And then, realizing what a nice, non-phone-answering person I am, the Admissions Guide will immediately proceed back to his office and proudly stamp "ACCEPT" on my file folder.

This fantasy keeps me happy until I realize that the Admissions Guide is too far ahead to notice anything.

The group halts at a classroom door. Mr. Admissions Guide says that we are now going to "sit in on a class." (It's all very Discovery Channel, isn't it? Watch closely as the pedigree MBAs struggle for survival in their natural habitat by devouring the weakest of egos with a single, unexpected, ferocious remark...) He opens the door and the 10 of us march inside.

The room is a grand coliseum with ascending rows of seats and a pit in the front where the professor stands. *Or where the gladiators fight to their death?* Most of the students have laptop computers in front of them. The professor erases a slightly annoyed look from his face and replaces it with a big smile before he speaks.

"Welcome to Decision Science. Have a seat, if you can find one. You caught us in the middle of a case analysis." He looks like a mad scientist. The students watch intently as we scramble to find seats. I quickly find a chair on the side of the classroom and sit with two other prospective students. I sit there silently, once again afraid to move or breathe.

The professor starts talking in Japanese.

Well, it's really English, but given the depth of what he is saying, it may as well be Japanese. *Is this business?* It looks like calculus, or quantum physics, or something equally intimidating with the title, "Evidence-based Forecasting Principles." I see an Excel spreadsheet model with formulas projected on the big screen, what looks like algebra on the chalkboard, and some kind of statistical curve drawn on a whiteboard. Normally, I like numbers, but not this much, and not right now. I remind myself that I *should* be confused—I don't know the homework assignment or the case. *How could I follow?* I turn around to look at the other candidate sitting behind me just to confirm that he is as lost as I am.

Not only is he not lost, but he is also totally engrossed in what the professor is saying. In fact, he is nodding and making "ah ha, yes, I see" comprehension noises. *He's a visitor, for Pete's sake. How can he possibly understand what is going on in this class? Surely someone who so shamelessly sucks up to a professor cannot become a student here. FAKER! FAKER! FAKER! I can't believe this guy.*

The Admissions Guide motions that it is time to go. Thank God. We slip out and forge full circle back to the admissions office to wait for our interviews. I try to move away from the Ice Queen, the Loud-Talker, and the Faker when this really nice guy starts talking to me. *Oh, hello, nice person!* He's a candidate, too, and his name is Ben. We chat briefly in the waiting room, make some jokes about this whole process, and laugh to ease the tension. I am delighted to talk with him. I don't mind that he is competition, except he silently reminds me that I'm not so special here. I do volunteer work. He runs a volunteer organization. I was a Resident Assistant in college. He was a Resident Director in college. I work in healthcare insurance. Guess what? He is VP of a healthcare company. *Wow, he's terrific!*

I look around the room. *Wow—they're all terrific.* Then, a thought hits me like a Mack truck passing through the room.

I'm not special.

I mean, I'm proud of who I am, but my accomplishments don't really seem all that great when everyone else has done the same thing. Relativity is humbling. Why do I have a feeling that everyone here has not only done the same things as I have, but that they have also done them much better? And why is my self-doubt growing like a tenacious rash? *Stop stop stop.* Now would be a good time to think about my resume. But now I can't remember anything on my resume. *Oh my God, I've gone blank—what am I doing here?* My pulse is racing, my throat is tight, and I'm sweating. *Move out of my way, I have to get out of here!*

"Feddy? We're ready for you now."

Not exactly music to my ears at this point.

Get a grip. Breathe in through the nose, hold it for six seconds, and slowly exhale through the mouth. Relax.

The receptionist leads me to an office and informs me that a student representative will interview me. *A volunteer rep? What? No hard-nosed Admissions Director?*

Thank God.

I enter the office to face my enemy.

It's the Admissions Guide! He's going to interview me!

The interview starts casually, but inevitably progresses to the brutal questions about my work experience, future plans in brand marketing, and my expectations. I can feel the blood rush to my cheeks. My prepared answers are long gone—my nervous mind couldn't hold them—and I am doing something rarely seen in this environment: I am desperately speaking the truth. My story, my business plan for the future, is simple: study general management with an emphasis on marketing, learn as much as I can, secure a Marketing Manager position, and eventually, who knows, maybe pursue entrepreneurship.

After 20 minutes, my nerves finally begin to calm (which would have been great if the interview hadn't finished in 10).

He finally concludes with, "How do you want to be remembered by your classmates?"

Remembered?

Because this program will surely be the death of me?

"Well," I begin, "I'd like to be remembered as someone who made a difference in the lives of the other students—someone who worked hard to succeed but who also helped others along the way…" I continue with a few thoughts about how I want to combine my personal and professional profiles to help others. It's easy for me to answer because the sentiments are true.

My answer gets a reaction from him.

"That's terrific! Usually, when I ask that question, people go on and on about how they want to be remembered as the smartest, greatest people in the universe." He leans toward me. "I appreciate your answer—that's what we're looking for." He seems genuinely happy as he smiles and scribbles on his pad.

Or is he laughing at my corny answers? It's hard to tell.

He hands me his card. "Call me if you have any questions."

The interview is over.

Over.

I am numb for a second as I leave his office. I can't believe it's over. I feel tremendous relief—but only for a few minutes until I begin to critique my performance. *For the love of God, why did I talk about that stupid project?* Like Ralphie in *A Christmas Story*, I want to desperately climb the slippery slide for just one more chance to tell Santa that I really want a Red Ryder Carbine-Action 200-shot Air Rifle. Or in this case, a coveted spot in their elitist MBA program.

And when my interviewer said, "It's over," was he referring to the interview, or to my future in business?

I continue these unhealthy, self-deprecating thoughts all the way to the Starbucks Dining Hall where I am meeting Melanie. I see her walking nearby, flag her down, and rush over to her.

"Hi! Thanks so much for meeting with me!" I say as we hug.

Melanie is a Second Year student at The School and a friend I met through Rick. She was kind enough to agree to meet with me for a few minutes to discuss the program.

"Welcome to The School! How did it go?" She is enthusiastic.

"Horrible," I say. "Like Shawshank, but without the redemption."

Melanie laughs. "It's scary, I remember. Let's grab a coffee."

The Starbucks Dining Hall is crowded with *Night of the Living Dead* zombie extras. Okay, they're just exhausted students—but I wouldn't be surprised if a few actually rose from their graves to feed. Vacant eyes and laptops are everywhere. We find a round table near the window and sit with our drinks to talk about life for a while. Inevitably, we talk about business school.

"I wish someone had *warned* me..." she says softly, pulling a small, plastic container of ziti with marinara sauce out of her bag.

"Warned you about what?" I ask innocently, still in my numb 'I-can't-believe-it's-over' daze.

"The School."

"*Warned* you?"

"You probably know that The School has a reputation for being...well...*rigorous?*" she asks carefully, taking a bite of her cold pasta.

I know exactly what she means. The brochures will only tell you so much about a graduate program. The most valuable information comes from talking to students and alumnae—that's how I discovered that each program has a different "personality." Some schools are amiable, some are ultra-competitive, some are more qualitative, some are softer, some focus on marketing, some focus on finance. Every MBA knows the "personalities" of the top B-schools. One thing I love about this school is that they interview every applicant; they want to see the whole picture. The School has a reputation for being "nice and team-oriented," but extremely challenging with an "incredibly heavy workload."

"Yes," I answer slowly.

"Well…I just wish someone had warned me about how hard it would be, that's all." *Are her eyes watering?*

"The School is an incredibly difficult program," she continues, shaking her head. "Especially First Year. It seemed much harder than what some of my friends were going though at other schools. And it's more quantitative than people realize…I didn't think I was going to make it." *Her eyes are definitely watering.* "There were times when I really thought about dropping out." She sputters, "I put my life on hold to keep up with the work. There's no time for anything else! It's completely overwhelming! And it's a fishbowl in here!"

What!?

"But it's worth it, *isn't it?*" I ask desperately, partially to soothe myself. "And you *did* make it, didn't you?" I put my hand on her arm to comfort her.

She sighs. "Yes. And you will, too. But I just wanted to warn you so you can prepare. It's horrible."

My rose-colored glasses won't allow me to be deterred. *No, no, no.* She's just tired and stressed, that's all. I just pray that I'll get in so that I, too, can be tired and stressed.

"Why do you stay?" I ask her.

"Sometimes I don't want to stay, but I don't want to quit either. I feel like I'd be letting too many people down if I left."

A Clare Boothe Luce quote pops into my head, 'Because I am a woman, I must take unusual efforts to succeed. If I fail, no one will say, *She doesn't have what it takes.* They will say, *Women don't have what it takes.*'

Melanie continues, "I just keeping reminding myself of my end goal and keep trudging away like a good little soldier."

"I think I understand," I say, but she looks at me the way the janitor did months ago, with doubt in regard to the depth of my empathy.

"You will." She smiles.

We discuss classes for 10 minutes before she jumps up from the table. She's late for a study group meeting and cannot even finish her dinner. After that meeting she has a class, and then another meeting after that. We hug good-bye and I head outside to my car.

The cold New England air feels incredibly refreshing…*for about 15 seconds.* I feel major relief mixed with that bittersweet feeling that often accompanies the completion of an unyielding project—maybe like a bride feels after her wedding. No more long nights of preparation, that part of my life is gone. After almost a year of planning, the admissions process is really over. I've completed the

GMAT, submitted my application, and interviewed. I can't believe it. I'm done. I want to scream into the night—it's over! It's finally over! Ahhhhh!

Of course, my face is frozen by the time I reach my car so there is no roaring victory cheer. I head out onto the highway with too many thoughts dancing in my head, fighting for attention—Melanie, the interview, Rick, my family, my coworkers, the people I met today, the janitor…all omens, perhaps? All I know right now is that it would be an honor of a lifetime to attend this elite business school. If I'm accepted, this will change my life for the better—an experience of a lifetime that I will never forget.

After two aching months of torturous waiting, my future will arrive in a sealed envelope.

I cannot wait.

Breathe.

CHAPTER 3

---- ❋ ----

THE LEVERAGED
BUYOUT

(Preparing to Leave: It's Going to Cost You Big)

"Dear Ms. Pouideh:

Congratulations! It is with great pleasure and honor that we extend to you an invitation from the Admissions Committee to join us in September…"

I'm in! I'm in! I'm in! Alert the media and ring the bells! I am perhaps the luckiest woman in the history of the world and don't you forget it, baby! I pass my acceptance letter around the office. *I could have sworn someone asked to see it.* Congratulations surround me as people crowd my desk. I am blushing with success and make an attempt to be humorously humble when I say, "Oh really, it was nothing…probably just a mix-up at the admissions office!" My coworkers laugh and then someone shouts, "Hey, Feddy, I didn't know you were smart!" Everyone laughs louder. *A little too loud, if you ask me. Who said that, anyway?*

Wait. Hold on a second…what's this?

There's a second sheet of paper in the envelope.

Is it a bill? Already?

I take another look. *No, phew—it's not a bill.* It's just something labeled "Estimate of Graduate School Costs." I fearlessly keep reading. I mean, it's not as though I haven't given the financing serious consideration at this point. "A single student should plan to have available approximately $50,000 per year." *Yikes.* Sweat breaks on my forehead when I calculate the cost for two years before shoving the letter back into the envelope. I remind myself that getting an MBA offers a 20% return on investment—even factoring in the lost wages during school—because of the significant salary increase it yields. *At least that's what someone told me.*

Okay, forget about it for now, I'll take care of that later. Somehow.

Right now, my friends, we've got some serious celebrating to do!

GOODBYE LIFE, HELLO B-SCHOOL!

"We're moving to Arizona."

"What?" I ask, stunned.

"Your dad and I are moving to Arizona!" my mom repeats.

Saying goodbye to my family, my friends, my coworkers, and to my *wonderful life as I know it* is proving to be just a teensy bit more difficult than I expected and it's only February. Simply put, I grossly underestimated the monstrous emotional aspect of this titanic, life-changing event. It's one bombshell after another.

"Your father has accepted a job near Phoenix!"

Phoenix? 2,735-miles-away-Phoenix?

"Oh, honey, it'll be okay," she says and pulls me into a hug. "You'll love visiting us in all that warm sunshine."

Why not just move to the Sahara? Same thing.

"But, Ma," I protest, "One thing I loved about this particular graduate school was that it was so close to you and dad."

"You'll be so busy, you won't even notice we're gone."

"When are you leaving?"

"In May."

❉   ❉   ❉   ❉

That spring, my family headed southwest. I stayed behind to close the house, telling them I would join them soon for a fun summer in Arizona. I didn't have to be on campus until September because I wasn't participating in the pre-enrollment summer program (a financial math camp that The School indicated wasn't necessary for me because I had majored in business during college). This allowed for more time with family, not to mention a few extra thousand dollars in my pocket.

How bittersweet, I thought, after the movers vacated our family home—I spent 15 years of my life in this house and soon another family unfamiliar with the creaky doors and secret coves would make it their new home. To make it worse, our beloved 13 year-old Doberman Pinscher, Flint, passed away in January; he ominously left us the same week I was accepted into graduate school. But I smiled with nostalgia as I swept the floor of my family's empty house, fondly remembering his random barking at three in the morning and that time he stole the Thanksgiving turkey right off the table. *Funny little guy.*

Finally, I said goodbye to my old home, said a prayer for Flint, and locked the front door for the last time.

WHAT COMES BEFORE PART B?

June has arrived faster than expected and tonight I'm planning to bid adieu to my coworkers with a raging party—a big shindig graciously planned by my coworker extraordinaire and closest confidante, Amy.

Fortunately for me, I mentally checked out of work weeks ago (no one noticed) so the corporate goodbyes should be quick.

Okay—in truth, I've been working extra hard to tie up any loose ends at work because we all know that the most recent "former employee" is often the brunt of blame when things like revenue or Post-It pads mysteriously disappear. I'm going out responsibly—but with a bang.

I plan to arrive at Sparky's restaurant ready to part-ay!

❉   ❉   ❉   ❉

"Cheers to the MBA!" one of my drunk coworkers slurs, holding up his beer bottle. I'm happy with the turnout: 15 of my coworkers, including my bosses, are here. We're nestled near the noisy bar, laughing and sharing small bowls of peanuts, cheddar crackers, and pretzels over the loud clinking of glasses and bottles.

Apparently, no one can resist the MBA jokes…

"So an eager MBA goes in for his first job interview demanding $150,000, eight weeks vacation, full medical, and a 100% company-matched retirement fund," Davey, our regional Sales Representative, shouts across the bar. "And the Human Resources Exec looks at the new MBA and says, 'Sure, and how about we throw in a company car—maybe a Porsche Boxster?' The MBA gets excited and stammers 'Are you kidding?' to which the HR exec replies, 'Well, yes…but you started it!'"

The bar thunders with laughter.

"Very funny." I smirk at him.

"Stereotyping an entire profession is as bad as stereotyping a religion or a race," Amy reprimands.

"But it's not fun to talk about the positive influence of business on society, where's the *sensation* in that?" Gary, carrying around his usual bag of strong opinions and impressively infinite knowledge, interjects. "The media bears some responsibility for creating the negative stereotype," he continues. "Charitable donations by business individuals are well into the 12-digit figures, but who cares about business philanthropy tackling large issues like vaccines, global relief efforts, or education, when you've got some minor corporate scandal making tabloid headlines?" he jokes, taking a drink of his beer.

"I'll see what I can do about that," I promise, trying to visualize an actual 12-digit number.

"Are you coming back to Blue Shield after school?" our Sales Director, Jeff, asks.

"I don't know," I respond honestly to this wildly popular question. BCBS isn't offering tuition reimbursement like many corporations do, so there's no contractual obligation, but I love working with these people. "I really want to work for a consumer products company…maybe I could just bring you guys with me?"

"Oh God, be careful what you wish for!" Amy jokes, taking a sip from her beer bottle.

"I'm *happy* that you're leaving," Gary says nonchalantly. "Now you can just teach me everything they teach you. You'll save me a hundred grand."

"Very funny."

Amy laughs. "Be nice, Gary. She'll be your boss if she comes back."

"Women make better managers, anyway," he says.

"It's in the genes?"

"It's in the brain." He taps his fingers on his forehead and then gulps his beer. "Have you heard that before? Men make better experts, but women make better general managers? Your brain is less specialized."

"Well, well, aren't you the arbitrator of gender roles?" Amy jokes.

"I said 'specialized,' not 'special.' There are documented differences in our brains. Certain functions, like language, are spread over more areas of a woman's brain. Balanced. In a man's brain, each function is more likely to be concentrated in just one area of the brain." He crunches his pretzels. "Women have more inter-action between the left and right hemispheres, more neuron activity. Maybe four times as much."

"Then maybe I should ask for a promotion," Amy kids.

"Of course, there *are* exceptions," Gary teases her. "I'm just talking in general-ities."

"Women will eventually be the most educated sex." I say, reaching for the pea-nuts. "In a couple of years, more women will be enrolled in college than men. Millions more."

Amy nods. "And only like 10% of graduate students were women back in the seventies, so that's nice progress if you ask me."

"Women receive better grades in school," Gary adds.

I shake my head. "I'm not sure about that."

"If it's true, then why do women earn less than men?" Amy asks.

"Because more men are studying math, science, and technology and we award greater monetary value to those labor markets," Gary rationalizes.

Darn, we're out of peanuts.

"And other reasons…pass me the crackers, please."

"I think it goes back to elementary and high school. If girls excel in quantita-tive subjects early, they'll have a stronger foundation for college, and then for later in life," Gary explains.

Amy dips a pretzel in mustard and shakes her head. "I don't think that teen girls think too highly of business. They still see it as male-dominated, boring, confined to number crunching."

"Everyone's responsible for that deficit to some extent," Gary says. "Schools play a big part. Businesses. The media. Role models. Parents…no one cooperates anymore."

"I guess now's not the time to mention the P.T. Powell lawsuit," Jeff slurs, referring to the investment bank. I think he's drunk.

"What happened?" I ask.

Gary orders another round of beer.

"Oh yeah…" Amy shakes her head. "I just heard about this."

"They just paid…like $50 million or something…to a group of women employees…for a sex…discrimination suit," Jeff stumbles drunkenly on the words.

Davey and Jeff laugh.

"What!?" I ask in disbelief.

"Yep. Guilty as charged. Strip club outings, groping the female employees, making lewd comments, higher pay for men, favoritism for promotions," Amy explains.

"All the good stuff," Davey jokes.

I frown at him.

"Banking can be tough on women," he says.

"*People* are tough on people," I remind him.

"It would be better if more women were in banking in the first place."

Amy circulates the Heinekens.

"By the way," I say to Gary, reaching for my drink. "Do I get thanks for saving you a hundred grand?"

"You'll be making the big MBA salary for many years to come—isn't that enough?"

I laugh. "Minimum wage would be big bucks for me at this point."

Amy reaches for the bar menu. "Then good thing you're not paying tonight," she says, opening the menu. "Do you want spicy wings or buffalo wings?"

"Can anyone truly tell the difference?" Gary demands, sparking a long and senseless debate about the zest of various poultry appetizers.

I love this group.

If you do the math, I spend more time with them than I do with anyone else in my life right now. So why didn't I foresee how difficult it would be to say goodbye? I must be an early bloomer because I've heard that most people don't miss their coworkers until several months into business school.

Looking around, I realize (against all *Dilbert* odds) there isn't a single person here I won't miss.

"Cheers to Hetty Green!" Gary bellows, raising his bottle.

Amy and I glare at him.

"What?" he asks slyly. "Technically, she *was* the richest woman in history..."

True, but her scandalous reputation precedes her.

"Okay, okay..." He pauses to consider a better toast. "Cheers to women and the future of business!" he yells.

"Cheers!" we bellow, smiling and clinking bottles for the toast, marking the beginning of a long, lively night.

HARVARD

The next day, with only a mild hangover, I head to Cambridge, Massachusetts. I know this route by heart because I've been going to visit Rick at Harvard every weekend since he started his 18-month program in January. He loves business school, and I love Harvard. It's one of those powerful, historical New England academic institutions, like Dartmouth College, whose opulence causes you to instinctively raise your head just a few notches higher the moment you enter its illustrious halls.

Plus, Rick and I have our favorite little hangouts now. We head across the Anderson Bridge to see movies or grab a pizza in Harvard Square. Sometimes we'll dine at John Harvard's or check out the House of Blues. Other times we'll meet his classmates for drinks at John Harvard's, Cask 'n Flagon, or Bow and Arrow. This weekend we'll jump on the "T" (the subway) to go watch a Red Sox game, one of our favorite things to do. We also spend a considerable amount of time on campus because it's simply hard to resist.

I turn left towards Rick's dormitory and weave through the magnificent 40-acre campus of 32 buildings and lush lawns—*no secret where the money went.* Rick once joked that Harvard only allows a leaf to remain on the ground for 10 seconds—that's how impeccable their lawn maintenance is.

I park my car on the leafless grounds and head toward his dorm.

Today—and I know you'll find this to be a shocker—I'm actually a teensy bit nervous.

Yes, it's true.

Moi.

I'm nervous because on this sunny Friday morning I will accompany Rick to his favorite finance class. At most B-schools, students can bring visitors to class—family, friends, prospective students—and since I'm technically unemployed, I've decided to visit and experience an official Harvard Business School class.

Rick mentioned that "everyone" has been waiting to meet me. Now, if "everyone" referred to the United States Presidential Cabinet, I wouldn't be nervous. But "everyone" in this case refers to the future leaders of the global business world: his closet, most savvy, Harvard cohorts—a potentially terrifying bunch with high expectations. *Great.*

At 11:30 we head to class.

Rick introduces me to a few students in his section as we enter the classroom. (The large graduating class of almost 900 is divided into sections of 80 students each.) He's impressed with his section, especially because a significant portion of learning at B-school revolves around learning from your peers. I already know most of his closest Harvard friends, but it's nice to meet the new faces.

"That guy you just met—Roberto?" Rick whispers to me as we take our seats. I nod. "He's the one I told you about who just invented that new software for your television."

"No way!"

"And there's Darien, who's planning the Priscilla Ball for October—that's HBS's annual and infamous drag ball," he explains. "And there's Ellen…"

"I love her website for women!"

"And you should talk to Jennifer Tibbetts, later. She was a Director of Marketing for Disney. She said she'd love to talk to you."

"Great!"

"And she just sold her digital music company last year…"

Wow.

Rick continues to give me the impressive histories of the businesswomen and men, the royalty, and the other legacies in his class. Rick is tight with the finance crowd of bankers that seem to heavily populate the class along with the consultants, but one of his closest friends works in strategic planning for Johnson & Johnson, and another is in publishing. Many others are trying to secure networks and funding for new ventures.

It's time!

Silence everyone.

Professor Moorehouse just entered the room.

"I command your respect, won't put up with your bullshit, and if you double-cross me, you'll never work in this town again," he says to the class.

Of course, he doesn't actually *say* those words. It's just non-verbally communicated through his regal posture and air of deserving superiority. He confidently stares at the audience before a smirk appears on his face.

"Okay, let's start with the Fidelity case on internet banking," he says.

I hear snickers from the class. "What's going on?" I whisper to Rick, confused.

He points to the front door, and I see a young man standing in the hallway peering through the little window on the classroom door. "Oh no," Rick says.

Oh no is right. The poor student is late to class, a major taboo in B-school. Rick warned me that Moorehouse is particularly offended by tardiness. Once he shuts the door, no one can gain admittance. If you try to enter, he will actually stop class and ask you to leave.

The hopeless student finally walks away after Moorehouse notices him and stares him down with the look of death.

Gulp.

Class continues and it's interesting to observe the rituals. The students know when to make hissing noises, applaud, laugh, and shout random words or nicknames. And they sometimes start class with a rugby song or the wave. They're jovial with one another and it's actually fun to watch. *(Note: It's easy to sit back and kick up your heels when you're not a student.)* During the last five minutes of class, Rick formally introduces me to the entire class and I'm greeted with a cheer and a round of applause.

That wasn't so bad, after all.

Rick heads to BGIE (Business, Government, and the International Economy), while I head back to his room to relax. That night, we attend a cocktail reception in his dorm lounge before we say our goodbyes the next morning, promising to see one another as much as possible during the summer.

"I'll visit you in Arizona," he promises, putting my bag into the car trunk. "And I just realized something," he continues, "the next time I see you on the East Coast,"—he slams the trunk shut—"you'll be a bona fide MBA student!"

Me?

"Watch out, world!" I warn mockingly, grabbing him for a hug.

He laughs, saying, "That's an understatement!" before we kiss goodbye for a long time.

MY MENTOR

Her name is Delilah Chatten-Warner according to the letter from The School. From what I understand, she's an alumna living in Massachusetts who graciously volunteered to be my mentor. Apparently, The School provides every new female student with an alumna mentor, and then later with a Second Year student mentor. According to The School, mentors represent the most important professional relationships for businesswomen.

We're meeting in 10 minutes at a Mexican restaurant. I'm nervous, of course.

"Delilah?" I ask the tall blonde in the lobby.

"Feddy?" She smiles at me.

We shake hands, sit in a large booth that is common in such restaurant chains and, after the usual assortment of pleasantries, order chicken tacos and French fries. My feet don't touch the ground and if I sit back, the table is a good two feet from me. I feel small. Fortunately, I also feel comfortable because Delilah's sweet and sincere. It's easy to talk with her; she's completely relaxed, but confident and intelligent. She reveals that she's currently working as a Business Development Manager at Sun Microsystems and is four months pregnant. Our conversation alternates naturally between recent corporate mergers and Diaper Genies.

Eventually, I talk about my B-school fears.

"It's overwhelming, but you'll be absolutely fine," Delilah assures me. "It's only two years. First Year is basically freshman year; Second Year is senior year."

"First Year students are called 'First Years,' right?"

She nods, swallowing a bite of tomato. "And Second Year students are called 'Second Years.' And each year is divided by terms, Term One and Term Two. So you might say 'Term One, Second Year' or 'Term Two, First Year.'"

"What's the toughest part?"

"Definitely Term One of First Year. You'll want to quit. First Year forces you to prioritize and pace yourself constantly. Even the b-school social calendar is beyond aggressive. But the faculty and students are great—they'll help you through it. It's a small school, so you'll find a lot of support if you need it." She takes a bite of her taco. "And it takes some time to get used to the alarming male to female ratio. It's a bit of a shock to see that at any given time you're one of only a handful of women in a classroom of 60. It can be intimidating. Just remember that you're human first, before gender, and so are they. And fight the suffocating urge to conform to a gender that isn't yours."

She pauses to take a bite of her taco. "The primary, attractive feature of a business school is its people, the community—followed by careers, alumni, faculty, location, and class size, pretty much in that order." She wipes her mouth.

"So how is the Career Services department?"

"Mmm…they're pretty good, but I didn't use them as much as other people did. I found my job through a friend. You can always use the alumni network, too—it's small but mighty. You're fine, though, because there's a lot of opportunity for someone who wants to be a Marketing Manager. Marketing is competitive, but it isn't as popular as investment banking or consulting there. And most companies want to hire one or two people from each top school regardless of the size of the school, and at a larger school there's more competition, but at a smaller school the odds are better." She smiles at me. "And you can always count on me, if you need help."

I know how important mentors are—I try to ask her the pertinent questions:

Classes to take? (*IT and Communications*)

Professors to avoid? (*Cold-callers*)

Clubs to join? (*Women in Business or career-specific*)

On-campus or off-campus housing? (*On-campus First Year*)

Semester abroad? (*Maybe Second Year*)

I also ask her about the competitive nature of most business schools. She doesn't deny it, but she tells me that the business competitiveness "calms down" dramatically after business school; as the years pass on, both men and women begin to think more about marriage, children, and life in general. Right now, she's focused on family but still does something she loves. Sun has a terrific program for moms, which is important to her, and she loves the project she's working on.

She doesn't aggressively sell The School to me, but she's positive and mentions the strong camaraderie of the alumni ("cult-like, really"). She also explains that the personality of each new, entering class alternates—good, bad, good, bad. She does the math, and unfortunately I'm with a nasty generation of "bad guys."

Penguin, Catwoman, the Joker, or Mr. Freeze type of bad?

She assures me it's fine and explains that The School is receptive to student feedback for improvement. "Business school is basically an experiment."

Guinea pigs, Pavlov's dogs, or mice in a maze type of experiment?

They've recently added a forum to address business ethics, and The School strongly supports the work/life balance with various programs. "It's an evolution," she explains.

"People attend business school for one of five reasons: a major career change, entrepreneurship, the network, the learning, or accelerated career advancement. Almost everyone has an agenda of sorts—either they're trying to find resources for a new venture, or they're trying to squeeze into a competitive company, among other things. That might be a little frustrating for you if your goal is simply to learn more about general management and marketing." She sips her raspberry iced-tea. "Sometimes, part-time programs are the better choice if you plan to stay in the same field or at the same company."

"I just want to get it over with—two years straight. Total immersion living and working with my class," I assure her. My other choice is the executive program, but I don't have enough experience under my belt. And there are programs that accept younger candidates immediately out of college (makes the early mommy-track easier), but I graduated four years ago.

"Oh!" she says, switching gears. "I almost forgot! This is for you." She hands me a sheet of paper.

Hot Tips for Female MBA Students

1.   Resist the urge to re-org your family into a vertical multidisciplinary business team.
2.   Expect to be single by Christmas if you weren't already.
3.   Stop girlfriends from referring to previous boyfriends as "sunk costs," or conducting extensive "test marketing" on new dates.
4.   Against your better judgment, you will play Beer Pong at least once.
5.   You will inevitably grow to loathe your study group which is guaranteed to have one control-freak-know-it-all, one brownnoser, one free-rider, and a couple of nuts.

I start laughing. "Is it true?"

"Partially...except sometimes a free-rider is called a passenger." She smiles. "The list floats around B-school every year. I don't know who wrote it, but I can send you the longer version." Then she introduces me to the delicacy of using ranch dressing as a dipping sauce for our French fries.

Obviously a girl after my own heart. If I turn out anything like Delilah after business school, I'll be happy.

A few days later, I head southwest to spend the summer with my family.

THE SUMMER BEFORE B-SCHOOL

Arizona is hot. I don't mean "sweltering, I can't breathe, somebody douse me with water before I spontaneously combust" hot.

It's much worse than that.

It's like having my own portable incinerator programmed to blast hot air onto my face whenever my body temperature drops below 101 degrees. But it's a "dry heat" as many affectionately describe it. Dry...*and hot.* What do you expect in mid-July? But I love Phoenix. I don't have a care in the world.

Until, of course, the paperwork begins to arrive.

I could start a bonfire.

Okay, that's a wicked thought I should banish from my head immediately, but don't blame me for thinking it. I'm sitting on the floor of my new (sunny) Arizona bedroom surrounded by at least three rainforests worth of paperwork sent to me from The School. I don't know where to begin.

There's a 200-page workbook, *Essentials of Accounting,* by Robert N. Anthony, recommended as "summer reading" by The School. (Normally, I would make a joke that I would rather drink a glass of Tab through my nose than read this cure-for-insomnia manual, but I'm really quite excited—it's been awhile since I've exercised my accounting muscles.) There's also a card from my new Second Year mentor, Nicole Rivera, explaining that she will be on exchange in Paris for Term One, but will contact me as soon as she returns, hopefully in time to help with my resume preparation.

And then there's *The Binder* filled with three inches of miscellaneous mail. I call it *The Binder* because it commands respect and has a life of its own. Plus, every time I receive something in the mail, or via email, from The School, I'm instructed to insert it into *The Binder* for future reference. *The Binder* is growing at a frightening, science-experiment-gone-terribly-wrong speed. By graduation I will have read all of the contents, but so far I'm just reading the most pertinent letters.

Date: June 4th
From: Tami Dimetti, Director of Student Affairs

Welcome First Years! I am delighted you will be joining us in September.

The Student Affairs Office is here to be of service and support to you. Our goal is to ensure that the next two years develop into a wonderful experience for you.

In the meantime, we've organized a binder for you with the following information:
- Health Services application
- Maps and other travel information
- Pre-enrollment Program application
- Class exemption forms

And welcome to our digital campus!
Don't forget to visit our website for the latest school news, the alumni directory, and for access to web broadcasts of our special Executive Lecture Series.

In the fall, you will be granted a personal homepage.
Through this customized portal, and via our wireless network, you will have daily access to the following downloadable information:
- Special announcements
- "Guess Who's Coming to Campus?" calendars
- Video archives of past speakers
- Course registration & class schedules
- Simulation games
- Cases
- Jobs
- Multimedia tutorials
- Career Services scheduling

Please add any special information to your binder for future reference.

We look forward to meeting you. Have a happy summer!
TAMI ☺

ACADEMIC CALENDAR

First Year and Second Year Students:

TERM ONE

Pre-enrollment program (optional)	August 29 (check-in)
International Students Welcome	September 12
Registration	September 13
First Year Orientation	September 13–18
Second Year Orientation	September 14
Second Year classes begin	September 15
Convocation ceremony	September 18
First Year classes begin	September 22
Second Year recruiting week	October 26–30
First Year pre-recruiting prep	October 26
Thanksgiving break	November 25–27
Second Year classes end	December 1
Second Year exams	December 2–7
First Year classes end	December 4
First Year exams	December 7–10
First Year project presentations	December 10

TERM TWO

Registration	January 3
First Year classes begin	January 4
Second Year classes begin	January 4
First Year recruiting begins (internships)	January 19
Millionaire Madness (simulation game)	February 10–13
First Year exams	March 6–10
Second Year exams	March 7–10
SPRING BREAK	
Classes resume (all years)	March 29
Second Year classes end	June 2
First Year classes end	June 4
Exams (all years)	June 5–8
Investiture (Second Years)	June 12
Commencement (Second Years)	June 13

Please add this calendar to the official academic binder; you will be notified of updates.

Date: July 1st
From: Jean-Pierre Suavaire, Director of Career Services
Re: Career Services Office
(Please attach letter to binder)

Congratulations on your acceptance. This year has been one of the most competitive in our history with a record number of applicants.

I am also confident that the job search will be rewarding this year. It is my objective to work with each of you individually to review the skills necessary to master a successful job search. Our work will include workshops, interview practice, career fairs and events, liaisons with alumni, company primers, resume writing sessions, and recruiting etiquette overviews. We will also spend time this autumn developing the resume that you will soon use to secure a summer internship.

　　This mailing includes:
- The Interviewing and Recruiting Calendar
- A Schedule of Company Briefings

The final version of your resume is due Oct. 19th.

In addition, I have read your application essay in which you describe your future career plans and this will serve as the topic of discussion for our first meeting.

I look forward to working with you.

Jean-Pierre "JP" Suavaire

The Women in Business Club

The Women in Business Club (WIBC) offers a variety of resources to you. You will soon find that our organization is both proactive and exciting as we help you to prepare for gender-related challenges.

WIBC can assist with career counseling, the work/life balance, sexual harassment, and family issues. Please visit our website for more information in regard to advancing women in business.

Stay tuned for an exciting year packed with events:
- Guest Speakers
- Entrepreneurship Seminar
- Brown Bag lunch series with professors
- Global conferences
- Networking roundtables

We look forward to meeting you and hope that you will consider joining WIBC as you become more involved in the academic and business communities.

Mark Your Calendars!

<u>Academic Forums:</u>
Leadership Track—9/23
Negotiations—9/24
CEO Leadership Exchange—9/25
International Field Study (program overview)—10/26
Corporate Citizenship & Ethics—10/26
Entrepreneurship and Venture Capital—10/28
Balancing Life & Work—11/23
International Corporate Governance—1/19
Global Business: Managing Corporate Crisis—3/4
Diversity Conference—3/30
Technology and Digital Media—4/3

IMPORTANT!

Please review the following dated information*:

BUDGET:
Tuition is expected to moderately increase each year, but the estimate for First Year tuition is **$35,000**. Course materials are estimated to be **$2,000**. Living expenses vary for each individual, but can be expected to reach **$14,000** for First Year. (Living expenses for married students should be estimated at $19,000 for First Year plus an estimated budget of **$3,500** per child, if needed.)

TECHNOLOGY REQUIREMENTS:
Our campus provides a progressive digital environment. Each student will be required to have a laptop computer and should expect to spend **$2,500–$4,000** for this system, which includes specific hardware and software requirements.

CASE STUDIES:
Case studies, often penned by our professors and based on actual corporate scenarios, are provided in electronic format and can be purchased through the Student Affairs Office for approximately **$500**. The foundation of knowledge at business school is created upon problem-based learning through real world case studies in lieu of simple memorization of facts. Case analysis provides a greater multi-faceted approach to creating business solutions.

*We suggest adding this financial reference to your academic binder.

MOVING DAY

Today is the big move into the dormitory room I will be calling "home" for the next 365 days: Butler Hall, room 121.

I can't help but smile as I drive up the long path to the picturesque business school. The lawns are lush and green, thriving in the humidity. The ivy-clad buildings—the Main House, the library, and the dormitories—are classic colonial-era brick mansions with elaborately carved white trim. The Currier & Ives scenery conjures up images of horse-drawn carriages rather than automobiles. It's all so perfect.

Just like a Hollywood movie set.

I reach the cul-de-sac and frantically scan the buildings for Butler Hall. *Ah, there it is!*

Hmm.

Butler Hall is a small, drab, 1970's-ish brick building with dark, steel molding. It's different from the other buildings in its cold, angular geometry. Not exactly what I pictured—business schools usually have beautiful tangibles—but it'll certainly do. I'm just lucky they offer on-campus housing.

I'm here!

I breathe the fresh air as I admire the quintessential New England campus, then I park the car and sprint to the Main House to pick up my dorm keys. I enter the white, oversized doors into a world of dark, late-19th-century oak paneling and make my way down a long, regal hallway decorated with framed pictures of previous classes. I swing open the old, creaky wooden door to the Student Affairs Office and see a young, peppy woman wearing thick, black-rimmed glasses.

"Feddy!" She jumps up from her desk. "I'm Tami!" she says, looking at me for recognition.

Do I know her? Think.

"Tami Dimetti?" she continues when I don't respond. "The Director of Student Affairs?"

Oh, that Tami. We've never met but I remember her letter from *The Binder*.

"Welcome to business school!" Tami cheers from her desk, beaming from ear to ear, shaking my hand.

"Hi…but…how did you know my name?" I ask, mostly impressed but slightly weirded-out.

"Oh, Feddy." She takes a soft, matter-of-fact tone. "*Everyone* here has been waiting for your arrival. The faculty and administration work all summer to review the face book, match your photo with your name, and then learn your background. You won't find *anyone* on staff who doesn't know who you are," she says proudly.

Cue the *Twilight Zone* theme song.

"Terrific!"

"Here." She hands me a large white envelope while talking a mile-a-minute. "It's your registration packet. There's a list of restaurants, movie theaters, spas, gyms, and hiking trails. There's a fantastic Indian restaurant, Curry's, on Main Street—you'll just love it, and there's a terrific little bakery with the best butterscotch cookies. You probably noticed that all of the business school buildings are clustered together in the cul-de-sac? You'll never have to travel far. Main Street is just a quarter of a mile away and you'll have a lot of free time—most of our students aren't arriving until the weekend. I hope you won't be bored?"

Business School is an all-inclusive resort!

"No, this is great," I assure her. "I'll read this tonight. Thanks."

"And you've probably discovered our tunnels?"

Just follow the light?

"Tunnels?"

"All of our dorms, classrooms, the Main House, the dining hall, and the mailroom are connected by underground tunnels. You never have to go outside!" She lowers her voice and leans in. "Legend has it one student went 73 days without going outside."

Now there's one for Guinness World Records.

"Must be great during the winter?" I ask.

"Absolutely! No sense in walking through 30 inches of snow if you don't have to."

"Absolutely!" I agree. *30 inches of snow?*

"Well, Feddy, good luck today. We're happy to have you here!"

"Thanks, Tami."

"And don't forget to add the new information to your binder!" she calls as I head out the door.

❋　　❋　　❋　　❋

It takes me an hour to unload my car. I'm exhausted. The 85-degree temperature with intense humidity is making me sweat like a butterball. Rick is hiking Mt. Washington with his classmates today, so I'm on my own.

I finally collapse on my new bed.

Bed?

Well, not exactly, now that I think about it. It's more like a cot than a bed, a thin flimsy mattress on a net of springy wires. The room is probably 10' X 9', but don't quote me. The carpeting is dark brown; the walls are gray. The furniture (a desk and a bookshelf) is dark plywood. I have a window overlooking a garbage dumpster in the back of the building and a thick forest. Everything is depressingly dark, but I'm in good spirits from the adrenaline rush of being here. I get up to go to the bathroom.

"Oh! Sorry!" I say when I open the door and almost have a heart attack because I see a woman standing in my bathroom.

A stranger in my bathroom? She's six feet tall and reminds me of that beautiful actress who plays Jackie Brown.

"Oh, hello," she says smoothly, sizing me up. "I'm Tempestt. I live next door—I guess we'll be sharing this disgusting, little bathroom for the next year?"

Ah, yes. At that point I realize that one door in the bathroom leads to her room, the other leads to mine. I take a quick peek into her room—the lights are dim, there are white candles glowing everywhere surrounding a little statue of Buddha in the corner. I can smell incense. It's a soothing, inviting oasis. *Wow.*

"Hi. It's great to meet you." I introduce myself.

Ouch! My fingers crack loudly from the weight of her powerful handshake. *Thank God we weren't thumb wrestling.*

"I was wondering when you'd get here," Tempestt addresses me in her slow, faint, southern drawl.

At least I think she's talking to me? It's hard to tell because she's staring at her reflection in the mirror while she talks. "I've been here for a week doing the horrid pre-enrollment thing. Tonight's our pre-enrollment graduation party. What do you think? The Yves Saint Laurent tortoise shell, or the black Chanel rims?" she asks, batting her eyelashes coyly as she models two different pairs of eyeglasses for me to judge.

"I'll go with basic black," she declares, not waiting for me to answer. "You can't go wrong with the classics, right?" She puts on the black glasses and looks admiringly into the mirror, confident that she's made the right choice. "Where are you coming from?" she asks, still looking at her reflection, adjusting her coif.

I'm suddenly amused by the fact that we're having this conversation in a dingy bathroom.

"Here. I mean…New Hampshire…not the bathroom."

Smooth. Real smooth.

"I've lived here for several years," I explain before giving her the condensed version of my professional background, a story I'll be repeating continuously this week.

In this case, make that ½ a story because Tempestt seems to have tuned me out before I can finish. She must be what Delilah described as an *MBA Prima Donna*.

"Well," she interrupts, only mildly amused with my story. "I'm from New York. Graduated with my MFA from Yale. And I've spent the last seven years working in publishing—I'm now Director of Book and Cover Designs at Doubleday."

A New Yorker with a weak southern drawl? Maybe I shouldn't be too surprised; she's also a Buddhist with a materialist streak? Confusing.

As if reading my mind, she quickly explains the accent, "I'm originally from Atlanta."

I nod.

"I'm here at business school simply because I can accomplish *anything* I put my mind to," she adds confidently.

Anything?

I'm tempted to throw out a variety of obviously impossible feats: *cure world famine? Travel back in time? Conduct brain surgery on an ant? Secure "Saturday Night Live" studio-audience tickets?*

Focus on me for three seconds?

"I'm sure you can do a lot when you put your mind to it," I finally say. "Great to meet you, Tempestt." I decide against curtseying to her royal majesty and make a speedy beeline back to my room.

That was seven minutes of my life I'll never get back.

I lie on my bed again. *What now? I still have to pee. My TV doesn't get any reception. There's a stranger in the can. The lounge is a mess. I don't really know anyone. It's been less than two hours since I've arrived on campus and I'm already lonely.*

Suddenly I remember my car.

Oh no! It's parked right outside the dorm, in the loading zone, the perfect spot to get a ticket if you're there for too long. I grab my keys and run outside. *Phew, it's still there.* It hasn't been towed.

This fact proves to be of great consolation after I find the $50 ticket plastered to the windshield.

Welcome to business school! I laugh and drive away.

I've been instructed by Tami to park my car 1.5 miles away in "Lot D" which becomes harder to find than the Holy Grail; I need a symbologist and an international code-cracker to navigate the map through the country.

35 minutes later I finally park my car and hoof it back to campus.

Fortunately, I've got all the time in the world.

FIRST YEAR

CHAPTER 4

DIVERSIFYING YOUR PORTFOLIO

(Orientation: Who Are You and Why Do I Need to Know You?)

"I spent the summer restructuring the Capital Asset Pricing Model."

"I single-handedly saved 130 children, won an Olympic gold medal, and I drive a BMW."

"Promoting global peace has been a plight of my family for 300 years. I scored an 800 on my GMAT."

"I earned my B.S. from Columbia, my J.D. from Harvard, and my M.D. from Yale."

All heads turn toward me as we stand in a circle at this awkward getting-to-know-you mixer.

"Uh...hi," I say. "I went to a public university, worked for a nonprofit, and I drive a Dodge Neon."

Silence.

I have the sudden urge to crawl under the table and hide until Thanksgiving.

On second thought, make that New Year's Day.

Okay, okay, these quotes are not verbatim. But they're close. This is truly how powerful some of these people are. And they are not afraid to show it or tell it. Why should they be? They are smart, athletic, and beautiful.

They are also terribly intimidating to mere mortals.

<u>ORIENTATION WEEK</u>

My first full day on campus went surprisingly well, meaning there weren't any natural disasters, arrests, or *National Enquirer* moments. I spent the day milling about (classes haven't started, yet) and the dorm was alive with the majority of new students moving in today. I decorated my room, walked around campus, and then met some of my new classmates in the dorm.

Chakira, from Mexico, was absolutely hilarious.

"This place is an absolute peeg sty," she yells to no one in particular as she carries her boxes past my door. "Worse than a peeg sty, a dirty peeg sty. Even a peeg would not stay here."

During one of her trips down the hall, she stops in my doorway. Unfortunately, my room is next to the front entrance and shares a wall with the dorm lounge meaning every single human being, cockroach, or mouse that enters the building must consequently walk past my room. I'm the first door on the left—the unofficial welcome wagon.

"Why is this dormitory so messy?" she asks. I'm sitting at my desk, fiddling with my laptop. I'm fairly certain she's referring to Butler Hall in general, and not specifically to my room, but I'm pretty messy so it's hard to be sure.

"There was a party here last night. The pre-enrollment group moved the graduation party to the lounge," I explain.

"It smells like rotten beer. And there's a keg in the lounge! The floor is all wet."

"Yeah, it got pretty rowdy. I heard it all night." I didn't add that the music was so loud that my room actually *vibrated* until 2 a.m. Or that one of our new classmates, in a drunken rage, had pushed an empty keg down the stairs, severely cracking the first step.

"It must be so loud for you—you share a wall with the lounge?"

"Yeah," I laugh. "They call it Club Butler. I'll have to invest in some ear plugs soon."

"Are you Feddy?" she asks. "I remember your face from the facebook."

Does everyone memorize that thing?

"Yeah, I'm Feddy, nice to meet you."

"I'm Chakira Davanas," she says energetically in her heavy accent.

"Where are you coming from?" I ask her.

"Mexico City, for the last two years. I was part of McKinsey's business analyst program there, working mostly on a project for an automotive supplier." McKinsey is a competitive, top-tiered consulting firm.

"Welcome to the States." I smile and give her my two-minute biography.

"I am going to call you Smiley," she laughs, walking away to continue unloading her belongings.

"Thanks, I think," I call to her, reaching for a stack of new business cases I received today: *Quaker Oats & the Ready-to-Eat Cereal Industry; Taco Bell: Evolution of a Superbrand,* and *The Organic Dynasty of Stonyfield Farm.* Each case appears as a mini-magazine containing the history of the company followed by a business problem for us to solve. After scanning the cases, I reach for *The Binder* and pull out the latest sheet from The School:

ORIENTATION ACTIVITIES

September 12

- Computer Configuration Session
- Class Social Mixer

September 13

- Student Affairs Welcome
- Registration
- Scavenger Hunt

September 14

- Outdoor Team Building Exercise

September 15

- Teamwork Session
- Ethics in Business
- Class BBQ
- International Communications

September 16

- Teamwork Session
- Introduction to Ethics in Business
- Computer Lab review

September 17

- Teamwork Session

- Code of Conduct review
- Mountain Hike/Chili Cook-off

September 18

- Career Services Presentation
- Career Panels
- CONVOCATION CEREMONY
- Resource Fair

The School is rolling out the red carpet. There's a social mixer tomorrow night? A chance to meet some new people in a relaxed and fun environment? Yah! I can't wait. I just hope it's not one of those corny events filled with awkward small talk over stale baked goods, artificially colored beverages, and dated music.

SHAKEN, NOT STIRRED

I'm at the social mixer right now, sipping neon-pink punch and eating sugar cookies in the Butler lounge with 50 other students while classic Bruce Springsteen blares from the stereo.

They've decorated the dorm lounge with streamers and a paper tablecloth to distract from the lingering scent of stale beer. I'm armed with my "Hello, my name is…" nametag and a bright smile. Neither is needed. Everyone here is a walking, talking resume—Ivy League bred, next-to-royalty, President of Global Enterprises, Venture Capital Partner, Marketing Manager of the Century, superheroes of the universe who enjoy playing squash, sailing, and driving in new BMWs; and they love telling me so. I'm tempted to remind them that they really don't have to impress me—I'm not the Admissions Director. And guess what guys? You've *already* been accepted into The School! Put your Stanford-Binet scores away, we know you're smart. Relax a little.

I hold my head up high among the overachievers and proudly recite my modest professional history. I receive faux-smiles before my audience inevitably migrates toward someone more impressive. Plus, I'm the only one here who hasn't (A.) climbed a mountain, or (B.) run a marathon. It's obvious the students find me as interesting as they find last year's laptop. (Which I've discovered is apparently a pretty bad insult with this techy crowd. Earlier today, at the "Computer Configuration Session," a snotty student next to me casually mentioned how "completely obsolete" my laptop was because it was (gasp) "last year's model." Gee, thanks for the status update but it worked fine for me, I politely informed him.)

The painful introductions continue at the mixer for the next hour while I witness an interesting name phenomenon at B-school.

"Hi, I'm Lin Yao, call me Christine," she says to me in perfect English with a British accent.

"Hi, I'm Natsuki Suzuki, call me Adam."

"Lawrence Peter J. Henley Bracher Nehman-Pantzer. Call me Henley."

"I'm Jonathan Ryan. Call me J.R."

"Nice to meet you. I'm Elizabeth Davies. Everyone calls me Sissy."

Undercover code names? What else are they hiding behind?

My grand plan is to mingle tonight. After all, these are well-educated adults, not children, and this is graduate school, not a John Hughes movie. Still, people have grouped together quicker than girls at the prom. They are already chummy having met at Admitted Students Weekend and at the pre-enrollment program, both of which I missed (*Note to self: next time attending B-school, absolutely, positively, do not miss critical social events*). They've also classed according to previous Ivy League affiliations or common work experience, neither of which I share. There are Princeton alumni reminiscing with one another in a corner by the window, investment bankers challenging each other near the fireplace, consultants from the same global firm sitting on the couch comparing the perks of their respective regional offices, and a growing group of Brazilians talking about I don't know what in Portuguese. I even try infiltrating the nonprofit group, breaking the ice by telling one of them that I like his "Don't Partially Hydrogenate Me," t-shirt.

So far, not so good.

I'm impressed though because I can't find an organization that isn't represented here:

"I'm an Associate Consultant at Bain in Sydney."

"I work for JP Morgan."

"KPMG/Peat Marwick."

"Proctor & Gamble, brand management."

"E-trade."

"World Wildlife Fund."

"ING."

"Tickle.com."

"Pfizer."

"Goldman Sachs."

"Beringer Winery."

"Public Broadcasting."

"New products at Colgate."

"Hasbro/Mattel."

"Kimberly-Clark, retail channels."

"The Red Cross."

"General Mills."

"Accenture, Boston."

The list of investment banks, consulting firms, brands, nonprofits, funds, and start-ups never ends; every industry from manufacturing to the service sector, in every corner of the globe, is covered. There's even a concert pianist and a plastic surgeon in the class.

Unfortunately, it's becoming quite clear that I lack the coveted protection of a "clique." My only hope is to remain a confident independent (read: socially challenged) and stay clear of the vicious rumor mill that is rapidly developing as I hover next to the cookies. Gossip is running rampant! Men talk about the physical attributes of the women. Women talk about the physical attributes of the women.

Later on, the gossip spoils, and the programmed events climax, allowing the nightlife to digress into outrageous drinking games reminiscent of those at college keg parties. Don't get me wrong, they were big fun the first time around in college, but right now there's something quite comical about a room full of academic thirty-somethings trying to funnel beer. I get the feeling that some of these folks may be making up for lost time. I tell the guy next to me, whose nametag reveals that he is Kevin Kernels, that I'd prefer not to do a keg stand right now, thank you very much. I just ate.

"Aw, come on! We don't have classes tomorrow. Live in the moment," he pressures me as he adjusts his unusually large glasses over his pale face, sweat dripping from his forehead while he vigorously pumps the keg.

"What's the matter? Can't spare a few brain cells?" he taunts and then laughs.

Great—the social peer pressure has thickened to paste.

I head back to my room at midnight, but don't worry…it's like I never really left the party.

My room vibrates from the music until 3 a.m.

<u>WELCOME TO YOUR LIFE</u>

The next day, I attend the brief welcome session in the auditorium hosted by perky Tami. I can't wait to get my new schedule and section assignment. Our class is divided into three sections (cleverly named Section 1, Section 2, and Section 3) of approximately 60 students each. Each section (sounds so *La Femme Nikita*, doesn't it?) will remain the same for the entire first term. We'll attend all of our classes together and have study groups together.

Your section becomes your family, so to speak. Each section is pretty much independent of the other sections, so there's not much interaction between the sections, except outside of the classroom. Each term you will be assigned to a new section, so you will eventually be in a section with almost every other student. I hope I'm in a good section, although at this point I'm not exactly sure what criteria makes for a good section. We already know everyone here is smart, so perhaps it would help if they were patient, open to sharing their knowledge, fine communicators, and respectful of one another. *Maybe that's too much to ask?*

I open the registration packet to find my new schedule for Term One.

I'm in Section 3!

And First Years are required to take the following core courses:

- Financial Accounting
- Decision Science
- Managerial Economics
- Marketing
- Corporate Communication
- Organizational Management
- General Management (two week course only)

Seven classes in three months? Yikes.

And classes run from 8:00 a.m. to 1:00 p.m. every weekday, sometimes Saturday (no!), but never Sunday.

In addition to taking final exams, we have a consulting project due at the end of Term One. Each study group will be matched with a local business to resolve an existing business issue from which the company has been suffering. Then, at the end of the term, each group will present their recommendations in a project thesis and deliver an oral presentation to a panel of professors and to the business owner. It's basically free consulting for the company, and great experience putting theory into action for the students.

Between courses and projects, I'll be spending a lot of time with my new *family*, my study group. I can't wait to find out who they are. Rick has an elective study group at HBS, but over here study groups are mandatory and assigned for Term One.

Rumor has it that The School decided to assign study group members because in previous years some students were left out when groups cliqued together as friends (flashback: choosing teams for kickball in 3rd grade). However, if the School assigns groups, then everyone is guaranteed placement and the groups have a nice blend of professional backgrounds and nationalities. Case closed.

Tami has just posted the new study group roster.

CIRCLE-OF-FIRE-POUND-ON-YOUR-CHEST KIND OF THING

I anxiously walk downstairs to the mailroom to read the list of study group assignments on the bulletin board. People are crowded around the board, buzzing with excitement, like in *Fame*—everyone waiting to see if they got "the part." I quickly picture myself seeing "chorus" next to my name, disappointed of course that I didn't get the lead.

Wait—there's my name!
It's on a list with four other names under the heading "Study Group #13."
Thirteen? Well, I guess it's better than Study Group 666.

Study Group #13
Bradley Berger IV
Aldo DiPaola
Nelly Nettor
Dean Kawe Whistler
Feddy Pouideh

Nelly?
There's another woman in my study group?
Hoorah!
Considering there are only about 50 women in our class, this is fantastic. We can share our experiences, maybe even hang out together, go to the movies, have dinner, join the Women in Business Club…

Suddenly, I'm aware of this tall, muscular guy standing next to me, staring. I look at him and he flashes me a wide, fraternity boy grin.

"Hey, I'm Bradley. I think you're in my study group?" He points to the nametag on my chest, his finger a little too close to my body.

"Yeah, um…that's me!" I stammer, marveling at my clever way with words.

"Cool, welcome aboard," he says, looking up and down my body with his perfect grin intact. "I met Nelly a few minutes ago. She's just upstairs in Dalton Hall, if you want to meet her? I'll take you up there." He's referring to the post-registration cocktail reception in Dalton Hall.

"Sure!" I say without evidence in my voice that I actually fear for my personal safety if I go anywhere with him. Instead, because it is a public place overflowing with people, I follow him to Dalton Hall which is already alive and bustling from the cocktail party.

Almost immediately, we find Nelly.

She's a young Joan Collins with wavy black hair and dark eyes. I briefly picture her bitch-slapping both Bradley and me as we approach, but then a shocking metamorphosis occurs when her severe scowl is replaced by a forced perma-smile.

"It's *sooo* great to meet you!" She charms with her confidence as we shake hands. "I was *sooo* worried about who was going to be in my study group. I'm chuffed to bits that it's you and Bradley so far." *Chuffed?*

Dean, the fourth member of Study Group 13, slithers over.

"Well," he interrupts politely, "this must be my new gang for Term One?" He's soft-spoken, but has a slight nasal whine to his voice, possibly caused by his nervousness.

We're still missing Aldo. Bradley takes charge to go find him, leaving me alone with Nelly, Dean, and the usual, awkward, getting-to-know-all-about-you banter.

Dean is a doctor from Michigan, an MD who desires an MBA to become a healthcare consultant, improving hospital operations and bottom lines everywhere he goes. Nelly is an Associate Consultant from a third-tiered management consulting firm in New York. She also reveals that Bradley is an Investment Banker from New York, but he's fairly new to the job. (An investment banker, a consultant, and a non-business professional? Hmm…unless Aldo is also a Marketing Manager, it looks like I'll be the token marketing gal in this assigned study group.)

Bradley returns with Aldo before we're forced to talk about the hors d'oeuvres.

"Look who I found! Everyone, this is Aldo," Bradley booms in his deafening sportscaster voice, gesturing to a tall, dark man joining the circle.

"And this is my wife, Colletta," says Aldo, stepping aside to reveal his beautiful wife. "Hello everyone," she whispers modestly with a sweet smile.

We conduct a round of handshakes with Aldo and Colletta DiPaola. They're from Milan, Italy, and Aldo is an engineer who briefly worked for Booz Allen Hamilton Italia LLC before moving to a smaller firm. Colletta is a teacher.

Well, it's official.

Study Group 13 is now complete with Aldo, Dean, Bradley, Nelly and me. We stand apprehensively in a circle, awkwardly sipping cocktails from plastic cups but not saying a word.

What now?

I half expect Mr. Roarke to step out, introduce himself as our host, and welcome us to *Fantasy Island.*

Fortunately, a loud, irritating cowbell rings.

It's Tami Dimetti. "Attention, everyone!" she yells from across the room. She's more excited than necessary, almost giddy. "It's time for the ice-breaker— Pass the Potato!"

Eeek!

Pass the Potato?

I have a short neck and boobs—it'll never work!

I quickly say good-bye, noticing an unusual number of people coincidentally racing to the bathroom.

"But you're going to miss Pass the Potato!" Bradley screams at me like I'm a corrupt referee during the NBA finals. "Noooo!" he wails. "You can't leave!"

"That's okay, Bradley." I try to soothe him. "Next time—I promise."

Then I quickly sneak away, secretly relieved to have escaped the potato.

MY NEW BEST FRIEND

The next two days of orientation are filled with barbeques, a scavenger hunt, an Outward Bound ropes course (I skipped that one because I've done it twice before in my life, and once was really enough), a Myers Briggs personality test and a KAI Measure of Creativity Test, another cocktail party, a business ethics session, and more drunken festivities.

Today we hiked at a nearby mountain and now we're winding down the day with a Chili Cook-off at a small cabin The School has rented. Right now, I'm sitting at one of the wooden tables enjoying a steaming bowl of spicy chili. *Mmm.*

The School has done a fantastic job of integrating the students during orientation week. In fact, I wonder if everyone is secretly thinking what I'm thinking: I wish that we could just go on eating and hiking like this for the next two years.

I make the grave error of saying this out loud only to be met with a mass of objections from my new classmates:

"What do you mean? I can't <u>wait</u> for classes to start."

"Don't you think you'd get bored just hiking and barbecuing all day?"

"I paid a lot of money to be here. Classes had better start soon!"

Okay, back off, Stepford students. It was just a joke.

I finish eating then join a group sitting on the floor waiting to hear the Second Year Class President give a welcome speech. I have to admit, I'm beginning to get a teensy bit discouraged. I don't always wear my confidence on my sleeve, but I know I deserve to be here. I'm just not *clicking* with any of the rusty business-bots here.

Then I see it.

A flash of bright color. A large letter "P," and then what looks like the top of Jennifer Lopez's head.

Could it be? Can it? Wait! Oh my God—it is!

It's *People* magazine! The girl sitting next to me, wearing a pink tank top with the word "Fempire" across the chest, is actually reading *People* magazine (a taboo topic of conversation at business school, especially this early in the game). But this means there's a warm-blooded human being here after all—someone else who gets a few cheap thrills from a small dose of entertainment news!

"Is that *People*?" I blurt out.

"Yeah." She smiles hopefully with large brown eyes that sit above a bridge of freckles. "You read *People*?"

"Oh, yeah."

A match made in Heaven.

"I'm Sookie Wong," she says, talking a mile-a-minute with what I think is caffeine-inspired energy. She's a curvy five feet, with black hair to her neck that she secures into a ponytail as she speaks. "And I'm so glad that someone else likes entertainment gossip. People have been teasing me mercilessly for reading it, but come on! It helps me relax—there's nothing better than reading about Sylvester Stallone's botox injections or the fall TV line-up. Kind of puts all this B-school chaos into perspective, doesn't it?" She giggles with contagious energy.

I laugh and introduce myself. "I'm lost without TV reception," I admit.

She feels my pain. "Me, too!"

We joke about the dorms for a few minutes and then she introduces me to Suresh Kumar, a handsome, svelte, international student from Mysore, India, who works at Lehman Brothers and happens to be sitting on her left.

"Ready for classes to begin?" I ask him.

"Get your fear on ladies," he jokes in perfect English. "It's gonna be nuts."

I'm not quite sure how to respond, but fortunately we're interrupted when the Second Year Class President, Paloma Bouvier, grabs the microphone and welcomes us to business school. She assures us that Second Year is better than First Year, urges us to "hang in there" (why does everyone keep saying that?), and reminds us that the Second Years, when they arrive, will support us like a family. Everyone cheers before Tami instructs us to head back to the buses. It's time to return to campus.

Sookie and I crack jokes all the way home on the bus.

"She's like Mr. Belvedere—always creeping around my door, lurking over my shoulder," Sookie moans about her dorm bathroom mate. "And I thought she was going to positively *explode* when I refused to divulge my Pre-enrollment finance grade to her. Classes haven't even started and she's already competitive? I told her the only way I'd get in the way of her precious Ivy Scholar status would be if I died during graduation and she had to literally walk over my corpse to get her diploma!"

Sookie also shares that she's a Tax Consultant and a CPA, but it's refreshing that she wasn't a walking resume the instant we met. She's two years younger than I am; and she came to business school to make an exciting career switch into showbiz, where she wants to produce movies and run a studio. Her idols are Sherry Lansing from Paramount, Gale Ann Hurd (the producer of *Aliens* and *Terminator*), Laura Zisken, and Sara Risher. She figures being in school will phenomenally expand her professional network, plus she has faith that her MBA skills will eventually be useful at a studio (albeit not always valued by Hollywood), and at the very least, it's an excellent degree to fall back on should she choose any other direction.

"Oh God, I hope I don't get 'Planked' next year!" Sookie rattles.

"Planked?"

"Professor Plank?" She looks for my comprehension and continues when I can't offer it. "My alumni mentor already warned me about him. Professor Plank teaches Managerial Accounting during Term Two of First Year. And boy is he a force to be reckoned with! Every single person in the class will be cold-called to the front of the room at least once and then drilled on that day's assignment. Like walking the plank? Professor Plank. Don't get 'planked,'" she explains.

"What!?" I'm horrified.

"Every night there's an impossibly complex homework assignment, and if you're selected in the class the next day, you have to teach the class—for ½ hour to an hour—on how to solve the problem…showing your answers and explaining the calculations, all while standing at the front. It wouldn't be so bad if these were solvable problems, but it's rocket science."

My mouth drops open.

"It gets worse," She says. "He's not easy. He'll fire difficult questions at you, ridicule you, and then force you to do calculations in your head while everyone watches."

I stare at her, shocked.

She shakes her head and confirms, "No mercy," as if I had any doubts.

Finally, I ask, "Does it work?"

"What?"

"His teaching method?"

She's confused. "I don't really know. Maybe on some people?"

"Who? Masochists?"

"I guess it forces everyone to do the homework assignment," she says.

"Yeah, and so would a gun."

"Hmm, it probably does produce some emotional scarring—I heard there was a guy who sued him a few years ago."

"For permanent emotional damage?" I ask.

"No, for defaming his famous family. Plank loved to pick on this guy's family in class—talked about how unscrupulous they were in acquiring their money. Complete slander. The guy sued, and I think The School settled but lost the respective endowment."

"Wow!"

Now she's whispering, leaning close to my ear. "And what do you think of the highfalutin people here?"

"Well, um, they're an interesting bunch," I say carefully. "Mid-life adolescence comes to mind. You know, they want to belong. They're very much aware of how others perceive them—like teenagers."

Sookie laughs for a long time. "Oh God, you're too nice." Then she whispers again, "It's like *Revenge of the Nerds*, isn't it, the people here, the social life?"

Now it's my turn to laugh.

"No! I'm serious! All of a sudden the dorkiest people seem to be the most domineering and popular people. But they're not even the nice, dorky people. They're the mean, dorky people! So there's no empathetic relief, or soothing sense of sweet justice, from onlookers. No one's cheering for them. And they're taking revenge on the wrong people." She leans back in her seat. "It's screwy!"

"Possibly worthy of its own movie?" I suggest. "Maybe a documentary?"

"More like a mockumentary, like *Best in Show* or something, but for business school."

The bus comes to a screeching halt at the dorm. Before we part, I tell Sookie that she can borrow any of my movies when needed. "Do you have *Animal House?*" she asks. "I heard that was based on this college."

"Of course!"

"Great, I'll swing by tomorrow night after convocation and we can veg out?"

"Sounds great!"

Sounds perfect, actually.

Sookie heads upstairs to her room on the second floor and I walk toward my door where I'm greeted by three students, one I recognize as Tempestt, camped on the floor in the hallway.

"Feddy! I was wondering what happened to you?"

"Howdy, Tempestt."

"This is Juliet Ann. And this is Steven," she says, pointing her diamond burdened fingers toward her new friends.

"Hey there," I say, squatting to shake hands. Juliet Ann, slender, toned, and wearing a starchy, blue Brooks Brothers Oxford Stripe shirt that perfectly complements her curly brown hair, offers a genuinely warm smile. The image of a supermodel masquerading as a librarian comes to mind as I take her hand. Steven barely acknowledges me.

"We were singing to relieve orientation stress," Juliet Ann offers, explaining the guitar and gracefully uncrossing her long legs into a stretch.

"Ahh." I nod.

"Have you done the homework, yet?" Tempestt asks me.

Homework?

Yikes, I almost forgot.

We received a syllabus for each class via email yesterday. That was only the beginning of the horror—according to each syllabus, I actually have an assignment due on day one for each class.

"No, I haven't even started," I confess.

"Neither have we," Juliet Ann says. "I've barely had time to unpack."

We talk for a few minutes and I learn that Juliet Ann was Vice President of Client Managed Small Business at Bank of America in New York. Steven was an Information and Technology Consultant for Boston Consulting Group.

"I'm not worried about it," says Steven confidently, referring to the homework while strumming his guitar. "Spreadsheets are easy for me. I could build them if I was in a coma."

Now there's a story for Dateline: Comatose MBA Fights Odds Building Financial Models Despite Lack of Brain Activity.

"Well, it's not easy for me," Juliet Ann admits humbly.

"I could probably give the professor a lesson or two." Steven turns toward Juliet Ann. "He's probably just as lost as you are."

And now back to our regularly scheduled programming: Lifestyles of the Young & Arrogant.

Juliet Ann rolls her eyes but maintains her natural, pleasant aura of sophistication. "I'm not going to dignify your ridiculous statement."

"You don't have to," he retorts with a laugh. "Your silence reeks of defeat."

Give me a break.

I don't want to engage in their conversation anymore. "Well, it sounds hard to me! See you folks at career services tomorrow," I say, quickly heading toward my room, glad to get away from Steven, especially when he starts to sing "All by Myself" as I walk away.

Jerk.

PASS = MBA

"Case interviews focus on a structured model to solve business problems," JP Suavaire, the Director of Career Services, explains with a sardonic edge as though he's somewhat bothered by our presence.

Or bored?

He's giving an overview of the Career Services department and the interviewing process. It's been a long day; I spent the first hour of this morning at the Club Fair. Delilah was right—I'll have to choose my time wisely. There's everything from a Brandy Club to the Christian Business Association and more:

- International Students Association
- Asian Business Association
- Junior Achievement
- Habitat for Humanity
- Toastmasters
- E-Commerce Club
- Hispanic and Latin Business Students
- Women in Business
- MBAs for the Environment

- Real Estate Association
- Equity Research Association
- Black Business Students Organization

Plus, several academic fraternities and various clubs for: consulting, wine, soccer, rugby, marketing, media/entertainment, venture capital, entrepreneurship, investments, healthcare, life sciences, energy, ethics, citizenship, organizational strategy, technology, gay/lesbian/bisexual, significant others and spouses, emerging markets, finance, and European Business, to name just a few. Everything but a stand-up comedy club (which wouldn't hurt, if you ask me). In the meantime, I've enlisted in the Marketing Club, the Media Club, Women in Business, and Junior Achievement to keep me busy until the next millennium.

"You must first define the case problem," JP continues the Career Services orientation. "If you can't clarify the central case problem, how can you structure the analysis? And more importantly, what are you doing here? You should pack your chic Louis Vuitton luggage and take the first jet home."

Louis Vuitton? I have an old L.L. Bean backpack.

"Or," he persists. "You can take advantage of the expert resources we have available to you. You can spend every day in the career services office with us—studying analytical frameworks, scouring sample cases, practicing interviews with my staff, and learning about case interviews. At the end of the recruiting season, there won't be a single question you can't answer, an interviewing process you can't master, or a feisty interviewer you can't tame. I wasn't hired by the school to sit on my firm tush waiting for Tom Cruise to win an Oscar. They hired me because I am the best in my field! They hired me to produce the strongest job candidates in the world!" He bangs his hand on the table. *Cue the lightning bolts, the dark castle, and the shrill hiss of electricity.* "And that's *exactly* what I intend to do."

Dr. Frankenstein?

JP continues, "This is a hostile *makeover*. If I have to knock on your door at midnight and pry your resume from your cold fingers, or whisper subliminal interview questions to you while you sleep, I will make it my last mission in life to hunt you down and mold each and every one of you into the ultimate job candidate."

Step back as he reveals his latest creation: Frankenstein MBA.

"How do we balance our respective course loads with the heavy demands of the upcoming recruiting season?" someone finally asks, changing the subject.

It's alive!

"Simple," JP answers. "If you are to remember one equation this year, let it be this." He then walks to the board and writes: PASS = MBA.

Pass equals MBA?

"If you want to become an Ivy Scholar (the top 1% of our class), ask yourself why you're choosing to commit suicide. It will bring you nothing but misery; and believe me, you will have enough of that without reaching for the Ivy Scholar stars. There are three grade levels here—High Pass, Pass, and Low Pass. Failures are rare and there is *no forced curved*, people. We don't terminate the bottom performers like other schools do. Therefore, if you are not seeking Ivy Scholar status, you do not have to strive for straight High Passes. All you need is a Pass. If you receive Passes in all of your courses, you will still receive—surprise, surprise—the *same MBA degree that someone with straight High passes receives!*" He feigns surprise. "Except you will not be suffering from an ulcer, popping antacids like bonbons. As the Second Years will remind you: *Straight P's = 100 G's.* However, I don't advise you to strive for Low Passes. You do, after all, want to learn something. And three Low Passes will certainly land you a front row seat with the Academic Board. Just aim for Passes in all your courses. Pass, people, that's all you have to do. And this will unleash valuable time needed for this recruiting season. Any other questions?"

This winter, we will begin the ruthless interviewing process for our upcoming summer internships.

CONVOCATION

"Please report to Holt Auditorium at 2 p.m. for the Convocation Ceremony."

If just hearing the term "Convocation Ceremony" conjures up images of *Animal House* rituals, you are not alone. I'm thinking the same thing. And as it turns out, we aren't too far off.

Everyone marches into Holt Auditorium, which has a very strange, eerie red glow to it. I'm horrified to see my old buddies, the Ice Queen and the Faker, sitting in the third row! Several gray-haired men wearing regal academic robes stand at the podium. *I wonder how much those robes weigh? With the heavy gold cord, and the shoulder pads, and the five layers of material…maybe a good 30 pounds?* I think I faintly hear the chant, "Thank you, brother, may I have another?" but I can't be sure. I don't actually see any paddles, which is a good sign.

I quickly slide into the closest available seat.

"You can't sit here!" says the girl next to me, giving me the Rosa Parks welcome.

Oh great! Yet *another* student confirming that I am a total social outcast! I've had just about enough of this. I can sit wherever I want to sit. I look at her with my 'back off I'm not moving' eyes.

"They're assigned seats," she whispers. "Alphabetical? Look right here, each seat has a name tag taped to it."

Oh. Oops. Ha ha.

I smile and thank her for pointing out the obvious, then I humbly find my assigned seat nestled between Kary Poler and Nanako Pun.

Suddenly the lights dim and a blinding spotlight shines brightly on a single man at the podium. Either it's Robert Plant back for a reunion Led Zeppelin laser show, or it's Dean Denton. I'm thinking the latter. *But what's with the lights?*

He speaks in a powerful, political voice:

"I am pleased to welcome our most robust class, yet. Look around this room at the 200 classmates you will have for the next two years. You will find not only a group of the finest scholars but also a class that boasts..." He rattles off the student body statistics, which are similar to those of the previous years, except minorities, international students, and women have increased by 1–3% points.

He continues the welcome speech and then introduces each professor individually—all 60 of them. Afterwards, each student is recognized by name and awarded a certificate (an official convocation ceremony document!) at the podium. I can't believe how giddy I feel.

It's official.

They even pronounced my name correctly! I'm a student here—and now I've got an *authentic document* to prove it! I blush with pride as I shake the dean's hand.

Now all I need is the diploma, of course. *Minor detail.*

I'm overwhelmed with pride. Rick told me about the convocation ceremony at Harvard. He said that the dean would tell us how wonderful we were, how we were the future leaders of the world, how we were the best of the best, yatta yatta yatta. I'm slightly disappointed that Dean Denton didn't butter us up like that, but at the same time I feel proud that our school is humble and grounded. *Keepin' it real, folks. Keepin' it real.*

Classes officially begin tomorrow.

CHAPTER 5

COMPETITIVE
POSITIONING

(First Day of School: Classless Classroom Strategy)

PIT DIVER—pit di•ver—noun (verb—to pit dive): Student who makes a shameless race to the professor's pulpit immediately following a lecture; resorts to embarrassing kissing-up tactics including dumb, meaningless and redundant questions or fake laughter. Subject may even stoop so low as to regurgitate the professor's words, claiming them as his own. Pit Diver is usually on a crusade to become a top scholar; warning: will stop at nothing. (also see: lonely brown-noser)

BACK TO SCHOOL

I shouldn't feel nervous, right? Technically, if you include kindergarten, this is actually my 18th first day of school. ("People get less for *murder!*" my mom liked to joke.) I'm prepared, I deserve this, and what more could a girl ask for in today's business world?

Unfortunately, I soon get an answer to what I thought was a rhetorical question: fancy pedigree, trendy technology toys, a resume to rival Greenspan's, an unrequited love of posh hobbies, and an almighty attitude with a stone exterior.

But at least my first class is marketing—thank God, something I can relate to first thing in the morning—with Professor Beatty.

I found his biography in the faculty catalog yesterday:

> **David Beatty**—BA, Dartmouth College, 1976; MBA, Columbia University, 1983; PhD, Stanford University, 1990. Assistant Professor, New York University, 1990–2005; at *The School* since 2005. Author: "Integrated Models of Asymmetric Reference Price Effects," *Journal of Marketing Research*, 1997; "Trajectories in the Overall Index of Product Quality," *Journal of Consumer Research*, 2000; "Retailer Pricing Heterogeneity," *Advances in Consumer Research*, 2001; "Coefficient Alpha Inflation," *Marketing Science*, 2004.

What? What? And what?

I forced myself to put the catalog away because although the impressive faculty credentials were one of the factors that initially drew me to The School, they were now psyching me out. I had never seen such a variety of nationalities, research credits, publications, honors, degrees and other distinguished, brilliant adornments in one catalog (Neiman Marcus Christmas Book excluded). It was an honor, I kept reminding myself, just to study with these professors.

THE BELL RINGS

I walk into the Stetter Classroom at 8 a.m. sharp on Monday morning. I've got my laptop (last year's model) in tow and although I'm a bit nervous, I'm excited in that nauseating roller coaster kind of way. The room is packed.

Where to sit? Where to sit?

It's like walking into a crowded movie theater with the pressure of only having a few precious seconds to find the perfect seat while 60 people watch your every move as you try to balance your popcorn and drink before someone yells, "Hey, siddown!" I don't know where to sit, but I have to play it cool.

Darn, I should have had a strategy.

On the one hand, I need to sit near the front because I will have trouble reading the board and overhead projections. On the other hand, I remember what Rick said—it could be dangerous to sit too close. He explained the nicknames assigned to each row (or deck) of seats in the coliseum classroom: *worm, garden, power* and *sky* decks, in ascending order. Worm and garden decks are the first and second rows, respectively—the professor can see everything you're doing. Ivy Scholar candidates often reside here. The power deck is eye-level with the professor so you had better know your stuff because there's a high risk of being tapped with a tricky cold-call. The sky deck is ideal for surfing the web and other distractions for the confident, seasoned professional of a certain superiority.

After attempting to cleverly rationalize the optimal seating choice, I simply take the first available seat I see which happens to be in the second row (garden deck) near the exit. All seats form a semi-circle around the professor's podium, so I figure I'm doomed no matter what.

There is an empty seat separating each person from the next, and I am at the end of my row, so no one is sitting next to me on either side. I pull the plastic name card out of my bag and place it on the table just like everyone else has done, facing it outward so the professor can identify me. These cards are just begging for trouble, if you ask me. My name in bold print? It's practically daring the professor to call on me. *Hey—look over here! Pick me!* I'm suddenly tempted to remove my card, or write a fake name on the other side.

He's here!

The Professor enters and we sit a few inches taller. Professor Beatty is very slight, with maybe only 115 pounds on his bones, with hunched shoulders, thinning blond hair, and small glasses that keep sliding down his nose. He's silent. He doesn't make eye contact as he slams his books on the small table near the podium. Then he shuffles his papers and unravels his computer cord, completely ignoring us, seemingly preoccupied with deep thought. This goes on for a good five minutes. Eventually, we begin to glance uneasily around the room at one another. *Does he know we're here?* It's pretty hard to miss an army of 60 students surrounding you, so I'm fairly certain he knows, but he hasn't made a noise except for his constant allergy-like sniffling. I mean, it's not like I expected him to arrive on a Rose Bowl parade float, but a simple "hello!" would have been appreciated.

No one knows **what** to do, so we keep mum and stare at him in silence. Finally, he speaks.

"Last night, you **met** with your study groups to discuss today's marketing case—General Mills, Inc: Speedy Potatoes."

What? Oh no! Our group didn't meet last night.

Immediately, Dean, Bradley, Nelly, Aldo and I exchange worried glances from across the room. *Oops!*

"The dry packaged potato market is segmented into only two potato product categories. Volume remains flat at only 11% of the total side dish category dollar volume. And dried potatoes are only 5% of total potato preparation. Retail dollar sales for last year were $250 million…" Professor Beatty continues.

What—no introductions? No roll call? No customary academic "free day" wasted on inefficient administrative procedures and greetings? Papers shuffle as students quickly scramble to pull out the case.

"What's the central case problem?" Beatty asks. "Jonathan?"

All heads turn toward Jonathan, a red-faced man sitting in the center of the third row. *Note to self: stay away from the third row center.* Jonathan looks surprised but manages to compose himself and answer.

"Uh, product placement...where to market this new product...shelf placement."

The professor hesitates. "Well, yes, I guess that's a *rudimentary* explanation for a complex marketing dilemma...and certainly the executives at General Mills can sleep better tonight knowing that you are—thankfully—*not* managing their product development. Any one else?"

Thirty hands go up.

"Cooper Allwin?"

"The key issue is one surrounding distribution and merchandising. One alternative places the product in jeopardy of product proliferation but drastically reduces the marketing and merchandising expenditures, thereby allowing for more budget dollars to be allocated to consumer spending. The other alternative considerably leverages the brand name and reduces advertising expenditures, but will be faced with possible objections from the retailers," Cooper rattles valiantly.

Wow.

"Look at Exhibit 5 in the case, the Consolidated Statement of Earnings, and at Exhibit 8, Revenue and Expense Information," Professor Beatty commands.

"When you calculated the equivalent case units, what did you get?" he asks.

Thirty hands go up, again.

"Andrew Shayes?"

Yikes. Andrew did not have his hand raised.

"Let's see," Andrew stammers, making it apparent that he does not have the calculation. "Last year...the deliveries...okay...in thousands...3,500."

Professor Beatty turns toward the board and grabs a stick of chalk. Andrew's calculation must have been correct, because Beatty has moved on.

I can't believe it. How could Andrew pull an answer out of thin air like that? God, that was good.

"Breakeven analysis is a precursor to the discounted cash flow analysis. In this case, the sales level in the P&L statement does not have strong justification, so another key issue is the accuracy of the volume forecast we will use to make a decision," Beatty continues.

Okay, I have to pay attention. He's talking about the Profit & Loss Statement.

"Capital expenditures, $850,000." He writes on the board. "Other fixed costs…$4 million, plus this number over here, and then another, and $900,000 (730 + 170). Total fixed costs = $5,750,000. And from the case, we know that contribution margin is 20%, and the proportion of sales is 60.5%. That means the weighted contribution is .605(.40)(460) + .395(.40)(260) = $152.40. So what is the breakeven volume?"

"37,729 units," someone shouts.

"5,750,000/152.40 = 37,729." The professor scribbles.

My eyes roll back in my head, which may soon start spinning. He's moving so fast, I barely have time to absorb it—and I was a business undergrad! The next hour is a blur. I can't retain any of the information because I'm worried that he's going to randomly call on me to perform a calculation. It's more science than qualitative marketing, which is interesting, but I'm not prepared right now; and if he calls on me, there's no way I'll be able to answer. I've got to meet with my study group tonight.

After class, Juliet Ann approaches me. Unbeknownst to me, she was sitting behind me the whole time.

"Unbelievable, huh?" she whispers to me as I pack up my computer.

"Yeah, pretty intense. I didn't have anything prepared. I just read the case, that was it."

"Our group met for a few minutes last night, but we didn't do any of these calculations." She adjusts her smart, black-rimmed glasses before securing her hair into a tight ponytail, not looking a day of her 35 years.

Tempestt saunters over, casually casting a silk scarf to one side of her neck. "Well, ladies, it looks like we're all in the same section this term?" She is wearing her leopard print sunglasses inside the classroom.

"Not for long—after this marketing class, I'm seriously thinking about dropping out," Juliet Ann jokes. *I think she's joking?*

"Ladies, ladies, ladies. Relax. All you have to do is raise your hand once, rattle off some rehearsed consultant-speak, and then you're guaranteed freedom for the rest of the class," Tempestt speaks matter-of-factly.

"What?!" Juliet Ann and I ask in unison.

"Simply speak before he *makes* you speak," Tempestt says. "Volunteer something—just say anything so he won't randomly call on you. He only calls on people who aren't participating, so say something first, before he calls on you, even if it's garbage. Watch, you'll notice everyone does it. And they do it *early*. The longer you wait, the more difficult the subject matter becomes and the harder it is to get in. So speak early—within the first 20 minutes of class, if possible," Tempestt continues assuredly. "By the way Feddy, do you think you could refrain from using the bathroom from nine to midnight tonight? I'm planning a spa night and I'll need the sink."

"Sure," I answer picturing her indulging in a night of nail polish and lavender oils while I slave over the homework.

"How in the world do you have time?" Juliet Ann asks bluntly.

"Simple. *Cooper Allwin* is in my study group. Take a look at this." Tempestt pulls out a sheet of paper with all of the calculations discussed in today's marketing class: the strategic analysis, the breakeven, the beta assessment, the cash flow projections, you name it, all meticulously printed on her sheet. "We prepared this last night in study group," she says triumphantly.

"*We?*" Juliet Ann asks. "Don't you mean *Cooper?*"

"Whatever." Tempestt laughs, knowing we're jealous. "I'll see you guys in accounting. Ta ta." She walks away.

Gee, I guess it's nice to have the most cutthroat, overachieving Investment Banker in the school in your study group. Cooper Allwin. Darn. Well, at least I have Bradley, Nelly, Aldo, and Dean.

Speak of the devil, Bradley walks past me as Juliet Ann and I are exiting the classroom.

"Study group. Tonight. 5 p.m. Dalton Hall," he barks and walks away in a huff, no doubt just as perturbed as I am that our group was not prepared.

"Who was *that?*" Juliet Ann asks.

"Bradley Berger. The fourth."

"He reminds me of that guy from *Seinfeld*…Putty. I can picture him smashing a beer can on his forehead."

"Yep. That's him."

Suddenly I wish I wasn't here. It's not that I want to be anywhere else in particular at this point—just not here.

Too late now.

Juliet Ann and I head to Accounting together.

WHAT DO YOU MEAN THE DAY ISN'T OVER?

Accounting inflicts less pain. Morteza (the professor insists we refer to him by his first name) is relaxed. He's a pleasantly gentle, seasoned professor who's uniform is a crisp, white shirt with slacks. He doesn't believe in cold-calling and will only select individuals who raise their hands, which means I may actually learn something. I even volunteered to be a Student Representative. For the rest of the term I'll be acting as a communication liaison between Morteza and my classmates. His teaching style is what I'm accustomed to—a homework assignment correlating to the assigned reading each night, review of the homework the next morning, discussion of new principles, and then a new assignment to start the cycle all over again. Perfect.

Unfortunately, I raise my hand to answer a question during our first accounting class and my answer is wrong.

Darn.

No one was able to answer, and I was one out of seven people who tried, so I don't think anyone noticed. But I sink lower into my seat, just in case. Morteza looked pained (like he needed to run to the bathroom) when he realized that no one could answer his simple question. He's got his work cut out for him this term.

I feel horrible that all of the material covered in *Essentials of Accounting* (my summer reading, if you remember) has already been fully discussed in class on day one. *So much for my accounting advantage.*

"Too bad your answer was wrong," Nelly says to me as we leave the classroom.

I guess someone did notice.

"I just wanted to give it a shot," I explain.

"Well, let me know how that goes for you." She laughs.

Hmm. That didn't sound very nice. Maybe I misunderstood what she meant? Too late.

She walks away before I can offer a clever, perfectly-timed rejoinder.

WHEN'S LUNCH?

I sit with Sookie, Juliet Ann, and Tempestt at lunch (my favorite part of the day) picking at my Szechuan peanut noodles while Sookie shares her Section 1 stories with us. So far, so good, she says, except for a "talker" who never shuts up in class. Tempestt explains that this could actually be a good thing because the more the "air hog" talks, the less time the professor has for cold-calling.

"Good point!" Sookie agrees enthusiastically.

"Keep'em talking," I joke. *Darn, why don't we have a talker in our section?*

"But if men do all the talking in class, then we're all just perpetuating the flawed stereotype that women are passive," Juliet Ann reminds us.

"At least you don't have *a shark* in your section, Sookie. Section 3 is full of them," Tempestt says and then looks at her plate and scowls. "This chicken piccata is absolutely offensive."

"A shark?" I ask her, not aware that we have a cartilaginous fish in our tank.

"Yeah, someone who not only attacks the professor's ideas, but also relishes in ripping apart the opinions of the other students? Aggressive. Grade-obsessed. Challenges everyone to make himself look smarter. You know. Like Gardner Elleson in our section? He's going to be a real shark. I can tell…"

Great, as if sharks aren't terrifying enough in the water, now we have our very own Great White in class.

"I mostly have fin-heads and quant jocks in my section," Sookie says.

"Finance majors and quantitative geniuses," Tempestt whispers to me patronizingly.

Is it that obvious I don't know the B-school lingo?

"But our section is filled with Pit-Divers," Juliet Ann tells Sookie.

"Mine, too! Romeo De La Carres was down at the professor's podium before class *and* after! He should just pitch a tent there!"

"No shame," Tempestt says in disgust.

"Bo Standish almost pulled a hamstring sprinting to Professor Beatty's podium. And Laura Heals left skid marks on her way," I add. "I don't think I'll ever go down to the pit. Unless someone pushes me into it."

"It's only if you want to be an Ivy Scholar. Then you have to schmooze," Sookie says. "Obviously these overachievers have already forgotten the 'Pass = MBA' equation."

"Well, I haven't," Juliet Ann says, closing the book that was on her lap and rising from the table. "But I do have to go read my cases for tomorrow. Anyone want the rest of my salad?"

We look at her wilted salad, a product of the university cafeteria, and unanimously declare no. Then we say our goodbyes and head in different directions.

My direction is back to my dorm room to read the cases. Tomorrow's classes are Decision Science (DecSci), Managerial Economics (ManEc)—which sounds comically close to "*manic*"—and Corporate Communication (CorComm). I decide to start with the Decision Science homework, a case about an electronics company. It's an easy read until I get to the questions on the last page forcing me to read the case for a second time, this time making some notes and underlining what I hope are key points.

I pull out my shiny, new $120 financial calculator with 250+ functions and an astonishing 37 buttons: the Hewlett Packard 17BII. Unfortunately, I don't have time to read the novella of an instruction manual. My head aches. *Where do I go from here? What's a decision tree?*

Fortunately, Rick interrupts me with a call of congratulations on my first day of classes. I find solace in knowing he is enjoying the lush life of a Second Year student—even planning a trip with his Harvard cohorts to Foxwoods Resort Casino in Connecticut for the weekend.

I describe my experiences thus far. "Everything at business school has a personality—the classes, the professors, the dorms, the classrooms, the recruiting companies, the industries, different professions, the administration, the students, the cliques, each school…even the rows of seats have distinct personalities!"

He laughs. "Personification is everywhere. And don't forget your study group—the strongest character of all."

"I know, I can't wait to meet *that* personality." *Just hope it's not the Three Faces of Eve.*

"Good luck tonight."

"Love ya."

"I love you, too. I'll call you tomorrow."

I've got to do something, so I switch to Corporate Communication. Like Accounting, CorComm requires a textbook, but these are the only classes that do so. CorComm's textbook is a light paperback penned by the professor. It's technically a book, but it's actually filled with cases studies. Our first assignment is to read about crisis management—the Tylenol recall many decades ago from which Johnson & Johnson made an amazing recovery—and identify the core reasons the Tylenol crisis was successfully resolved. I read the case and jot down some notes before I see that it's surprisingly already time to meet my study group!

Time flies when you're having…well, I'm not exactly sure why it's flying.

OUR FIRST STUDY GROUP SESSION

I head to Dalton Hall at 4:55. Nelly is biting her nails, looking stressed. Bradley and Dean are talking about politics. Everyone is wondering where Aldo is until he shows up 10 minutes later. "Let's grab dinner to go, and then head upstairs to one of the study rooms," Bradley orders. "Meet upstairs in five minutes."

I order a chicken wrap and some fries. I figure a cold, caffeinated drink won't hurt either, and so I grab a can.

"Hey, Smiley!" Chakira shouts as I'm paying for my goods at the register.

"Hey! How's it going?" I give her a nod and a smile.

"Very *very* well. I'm running off to see my study group right now, but I doubt we can get a room. People are already fighting like greedy real estate developers over study space upstairs."

"You're kidding?" I ask.

"But I wanted to say to you—I'm so very sorry your answer was wrong in Accounting. But don't worry about it. Keep trying." She smiles sympathetically.

She's not even in my section!

"Thanks." I smile back weakly. "I'll be okay."

"I know you will, Smiley." She laughs.

Wow, it really is a fishbowl in here.

I leave the dining hall with my bag of food and head upstairs only to find Nelly at the top of the staircase yelling at another student. The rest of our group is missing in action.

"I put my laptop in that room for a reason!" Nelly shouts at him, her eyes blazing.

"We didn't see your computer in the corner. When we came in, the room looked empty," he counters.

"Well, kindly pack up your belongings and leave," she orders.

"*What?*" he asks incredulously. "You want the five of us to unplug our computers and move? Move where? We're already set up in there with all of our stuff ready to go."

"But I was saving the room for *our* group." Nelly speaks in sharp tones through tight lips. "I was there first. You were second. And the last time I checked, one comes before two, so you lose."

"Unbelievable." He gives up. "This is ridiculous. Un-freaking-believable."

I jump in, feeling bad for him. "Listen, maybe, since you're already set up in the room, our group can just find another place to work?" I look at Nelly.

"No, we cannot," she declares, giving me a look of death.

"It might be easier," I say in a low voice to her. "A gesture of goodwill?"

"Nope." She crosses her arms and won't budge.

I look at the guy with defeat. He sighs and then heads into the study room to deliver the bad news to his group. They'll have to pack up and relocate.

They pile out of the room (cue "Sunrise, Sunset"), giving Nelly and I evil stares as they exit. I make a weak attempt to smile, feeling like a flight attendant standing at the exit apologizing for the extreme air turbulence. *Bub-bye.*

We finally enter the room and Bradley barges in with two large bags of food. "I have to leave by nine. It's our first night of hockey," he says.

Oh yes, hockey.

The School is wild about hockey and encourages students to play for fun on gender specific teams. The women here are especially active in this—the girls have the ice at midnight to practice. You don't have to know how to play hockey. In fact, you don't even have to know how to skate! It's true—the Second Years will actually teach you how to skate. I'm not athletic at all, but the energy is contagious so I purchased a pair of hockey skates at a local store. I can't wait to start, but what's up with the midnight rink time? I'm usually in bed by 11.

Dean explains that he won't play hockey because he has to spend as much time with his wife as possible.

"You're married?" Bradley asks. I'm also surprised Dean didn't mention his wife earlier.

"Two years. She just started law school at Columbia, so not only do we anticipate a possible divorce this year, but we're also officially broke." Dean chuckles nervously after searching our faces for comedic approval.

"Join the club. We're all going to be broke after this year. Where's Aldo?" Bradley looks up, his mouth full of meatballs.

"He's always late for everything, didn't you notice?" Nelly scoffs.

"Different cultures have a different sense of time," Dean explains weakly, his voice trailing as Nelly stares him down.

"We have to get started," Nelly growls, taking charge. "Let's start with Decision Science."

"Wait," says Dean. "Can we spend just a few minutes reviewing the material from today—the assignments we neglected to do? I have a few questions about two of the problems."

"Yeah," I agree. "That sounds good—just five minutes of review before we start the new stuff?"

Nelly fires a contemptuous look. "The material from today was simple—and now it's history. I don't think we should waste any more time discussing it," she argues without room for negotiation.

"I agree," Bradley spats with a full mouth.

"Good point. I guess it *would* be a waste of time," Dean concedes, suddenly having a change of heart.

They all look at me, waiting for me to agree with them. I finally do, realizing that in the few minutes we spent talking about it, we could have actually been discussing today's assignment. It's a lost cause, so I let it go. No sense in wasting any more time.

If I have any questions, I'll have to ask someone else, I guess.

And so will Dean.

MUTUALLY EXCLUSIVE, COLLECTIVELY EXHAUSTIVE

Aldo finally walks in at six o'clock.

"I'm sorry I'm late, everyone," he offers, speaking his English slowly. Nelly looks at her watch, obviously annoyed.

"But I worked on the case," Aldo continues, plugging his cord into the electrical socket, oblivious to Nelly's dramatics. "*And* I finished the spreadsheet."

"For what class?" Bradley asks, excited.

"Decision Science."

Aldo did our homework!

"Yes!" Bradley shouts, poising his hand to high-five Aldo. It takes Aldo a second to recognize this American expression, but he finally smiles and offers an awkward slap of Bradley's hand.

"All right!" Dean and I cheer. Nelly remains silent and stoic. *Maybe someone should drop a handful of termites down her pants, who knows? More importantly, who cares?* I'm ecstatic! Our DecSci homework is done!

Decision Science is a quantitative class focusing on statistical models and technology to make managerial decisions. Tonight's assignment, our first of the term, is a media budget allocation problem. Our goal is to build a spreadsheet model that will optimize the cross-media spending for an electronics company. Basically, we want to find the best way to invest the limited advertising dollars to ensure the highest campaign return on investment (ROI). We'll use the market and media data provided in the case, along with the response and conversion rates for each channel and other buyer behavior patterns, to determine their impact on 'key business metrics' like revenue, profit margins, and costs. The case also provides last year's media spending budget and allocation, so we can make comparisons.

Aldo has prepared a beautiful spreadsheet model with the case data that simply allows us to change the dollars allocated to each media type with the simple tap of a finger on the keyboard. He's even factored in the constraints (for example, the limited budget) and the Excel financial formulas to translate media spending to financial results. We crowd around his computer, calling out different numbers and watching the impact on the bottom line.

"Try $50k for radio, and $100k for online advertising."

"Change $150k from TV to Direct Marketing."

We experiment with different allocations, watching the bottom line escalate, plummet, and then climb again as we alter the mix. Finally, Aldo explains that we don't have to sit around all day plugging in different amounts, hoping to find the optimal mix.

"Just use Excel Solver. It's an add-in file in Excel that will optimize for us," he says.

I use Goal Seek, and sometimes Pivot Tables, but usually not Solver.

"I don't think we should use Crystal Ball for our first assignment. It's too soon. It'll come later in the term, along with Monte Carlo simulation."

"Yeah, the assignments usually start out easy and then progress in terms of difficulty. Same with the cases," Bradley says.

"Right," Dean agrees. "They lay on heavy amounts of work at the beginning, to overwhelm us, but not the hard stuff. They save that for later. I agree, let's not get into Crystal Ball, yet."

Crystal Ball?

I'm sure it's not what I'm thinking—it's not an actual ball used by a fortune-teller to predict our assignments. I think it's actually the risk simulation software I was required to purchase for this class. It's used for forecasting, analyzing risk, and optimizing.

So Aldo uses Solver to find the optimum advertising mix for us. *Great, we're done!* And tonight, when I go back to my room, I absolutely, positively must review the spreadsheet in detail. I don't think I could have built it on my own—we didn't really use spreadsheet modeling at my last job.

"Let's move on to economics," Nelly orders.

Fortunately, Managerial Economics is not new to me. I had this course as an undergraduate business major and I'm familiar with a few of the syllabus topics: demand forecasts over the product life cycle, the industry impact of government regulatory policies, internal transfer pricing, and oligopoly pricing, to name a few. We'll be looking at how the economy affects corporate decisions, and how those economic constraints may change over time.

Our first assignment is a case concerning a regulation program and a fleet of boats. "Elasticity of substitution," Dean says. "Fishermen are facing a limitation on boat days."

"This is a short case—an hour max," Bradley declares.

"It's already 8:00. We could split into subgroups? Some of us can write up the CorComm case and others can run the regression for ManEc? That way we can be out of here before 11?" I suggest.

"I don't think that's a good idea," Nelly counters. "We all need to know what's going on with each assignment."

"Right—so we spend the last hour sharing the knowledge and briefing the other subgroup," I explain.

"No, let's just work on ManEc together—it won't take long—and then we can prep the CorComm together," Bradley agrees with Nelly.

Aldo and Dean don't say anything, so I don't push it. We huddle around Bradley's computer for the next three hours running regressions for the aggravating fleet assignment which proves to be more difficult than memorizing a phone book. Backwards.

Bradley left for two hours to play hockey and was shocked to find us still working on the ManEc assignment when he returned.

The only humor I find in the whole situation is that Nelly manages to use the phrase, "mutually exclusive, collectively exhaustive," at least 10 times over the course of the night, whether she's talking about probability distributions or pizza toppings. It's scary. And is "incentivize" even a word? Or "modularize?" That's her other favorite. We toss around consultant lingo like we're competing on a game show that rewards the contestant who regurgitates the most bogus business jargon in one night. (I catch myself using the word "core" twice, but that's as low as I'll go.)

Finally, after the long struggle, we pull together a satisfactory answer at 11:30 p.m. I'm impressed by their knowledge—Nelly has the business math mastered, Bradley is great with the financials, and Aldo, well, he's an engineering genius as far as I'm concerned. My contribution to the ManEc fleet of boats assignment wasn't strong, so I know I have to take the lead on the CorComm work. Fortunately, I had already jotted down answers to the assignment that we discuss at length while Dean types our answers into a document.

I never make it to hockey. My eyes hurt and my brain is fried right now. Everyone looks pale and spent. We could easily be mistaken for medical school cadavers if it weren't for the periodic groans of frustration. The study room is littered with food containers, crumpled paper, printouts, messy whiteboard scribbles, and 10 paper cups of old coffee. *Time for bed.* I look at my watch.

2:00 a.m.!

We started working at 6:00 p.m.!

I guess it's okay…I mean, it's not going to be like this every night.

Is it?

Oh no! I still have to review the DecSci spreadsheet in detail before tomorrow morning, just to make sure I fully understand what Aldo built for us.

Unfortunately, when I get back to my room, I fall asleep immediately, unable to resist the invitingly warm, plump comfort of my pillow.

CONGRATULATIONS, YOU'RE OPENING TODAY!

The alarm rings at 6:30 a.m. and I jump out of bed to hit the showers. Then I run to the cafeteria only to realize, *I forgot my computer!* I run back to the dorm to get it and then sprint back to the dining hall. I've lost time, so I can't afford a sit-down breakfast but I can grab a banana and some juice before heading to Decision Science.

I arrive with five minutes to spare and begin eating my banana as I start my computer. I'm exhausted, mentally and physically. I must look a mess.

"Feddy, bring your computer to the front and boot up at the podium. I'm going to have you open today," Professor Haven says to me. My classmates gasp in shock.

Open what? A new Bank of America branch in Qatar? A can of peanuts with a giant toy worm waiting to spring out as soon as I pop off the lid? What?

Oh no.

Now I know.

He wants me to "open the case." He wants me to start class, kick off the discussion by sharing my spreadsheet model and answers. I'm being cold-called to the front of the class to present my homework. Side-swipped without any warning. That's despicable, if you ask me. It's our first class! I don't even have my nametag up.

How did he know who I was?

Then I remember Tami's chilling words, "Everyone will know who you are."

A shiver runs down my spine.

I put my banana down and slowly walk to the front of the room. I can hear whispers. My cheeks blush crimson because everyone is watching as I connect my computer to the outlet at the podium. I had no idea I'd be teaching class today. *Who knew?*

Thank heaven for Aldo and his amazing spreadsheet. Let's just pray I can walk through this.

"Well, class, I'm Professor Haven. Welcome to Term One Decision Science," he declares before turning to me. "Feddy, take your seat again. I'll call you back up when we're ready for you."

I willfully return to my seat and try to listen as he explains probability, simulation, and why any of this is relevant in the business world. You would think that I would pay *extra, special* attention given the circumstances, but I'm frozen. I can only think about the inevitable. Who cares about metamodeling and whatever else he's ranting about? I'm about to come face to face with my own doom. *What will I say up there?*

"Okay, that brings us to the homework—Feddy, show us what you've got," Professor Haven says.

"Sure!" I say, pretending to be really excited about spreadsheet modeling. *Spreadsheet models are so cool!* I try to smile confidently as I take my place at the front of the room. The spreadsheet model is projected onto the big screen behind me.

Get it together. Get it together. Get it together.

Professor Haven continues to talk for a few minutes, giving the background information on the case, while I stand there blushing, trying to look upbeat and fearless, nodding as if I actually understand one iota of what he's talking about, waiting for him to address me.

Finally, he does.

"Okay, Feddy," he instructs me. "You're the Marketing Director of this company, you've just finished forecasting and budgeting, and now you're giving your new projections to the executive team at your quarterly meeting."

The executive team?

Professor Haven continues to set the scene. "And sales have been down, budget dollars are tight, so you expect a hostile audience—class, feel free to attack her with questions as though you're the executive team."

Attack me?

"Okay, Feddy, go...you're on!"

Aaaaaand...action!

I clear my throat. "Well, our study group..."

"Your *study group*? I didn't know we had *study groups* at this company?" Haven yells at me. Everyone laughs.

Oops, I dropped out of character.

"I mean, our *team*. My team," I continue when I find my voice. "We...uh...developed this model to optimize our media spending for the next 12 months." *Throw in more business terms.* "The goal, of course, is to maximize the return on our advertising investment. Using historical data, we identified the top five media channels and allocated funds appropriately..." Then I try to mumble some other stuff before I walk the class through the spreadsheet model, piece by piece. Cell B5 is TV, cell B6 is print, etc…

Great, this could go on forever! I'll just keep tediously walking through the model until the class…er, the executive team…falls asleep.

Unfortunately, Professor Haven deciphers my ingenious plan.

He interrupts me with a few hardcore questions (which I can't answer) and then eventually thanks me and asks me to take my seat.

I'm done! And I'm still alive to talk about it?

He then spends the remaining 15 minutes of class masterfully explaining my critical mistakes from both a quantitative model perspective and a communication standpoint.

Who knew one person could make so many errors in 20 minutes?

Oh well. Live & learn—that's why I'm here. I'm proud that I made it.

Juliet Ann runs up to me after class. "You are so lucky! You got your cold-call out of the way!"

Lucky?

"What do you mean?"

"Now Haven won't call on you until the end of the term," she explains knowledgably. "He's going to call on everyone at least once, so you can relax for awhile."

Yeah, right.

"Not for very long," I assure her. "He'll come after me again."

Of this, I am sure.

LAND OF THE LOST

The first month of class is a complete and total disaster.

It's become frighteningly clear that we've already covered all the business material I learned in four full years of college. I've also been involved in several conversations where I had absolutely no idea what my classmates were talking about. Who knew that oil prices per barrel took a hike recently because of conflict between a militia and the government in Nigeria's delta region, or that South Korea's largest bank reported higher than expected earnings? My new classmates are not only sharp, they're also incredibly well-informed in regard to current international and domestic business events.

I, on the other hand, can barely keep from dozing off during class.

"The argument has inconsequential validity!" Cooper Allwin barked during economics today.

"Actually," Debra responded, "putting non-managerial employees on corporate boards is a matter of substantial consequence—it provides greater corporate governance and better distributes power."

Cooper rolled his eyes. "Great, now *there's* something for my diary!" he said as the rest of our class laughed with him.

Debra sank lower into her seat before others eventually jumped on the 'my-brain-is-bigger-than-yours' train to continue the battle for world classroom domination.

It's frustrating to witness the reduction of strong comments into menial and distracting jokes simply camouflaging a dominant classmate's insecurity. Hearing a woman's voice in class is sometimes like having Stuart Little speak at a Grand Sumo wrestling tournament—it just doesn't happen often, it doesn't command the respect it deserves, and you're a little afraid the speaker might get squashed. But women actually belong in the classroom, and some seem to forget the value of their knowledge, so I make an attempt to listen closely whenever someone new speaks in class.

Besides, it's a welcome relief from listening to the same self-important sharks regurgitate boring and uninspiring business jargon day in and day out in class.

And if someone asks me one more time what my "deliverable" is, I'm going to willingly plunge headfirst into my toilet. Team-basing, value-adding, cycle-timing, beta-loving, benchmarking load of folks around here. I barely have time to learn the real business terms, less the bogus MBA lingo. And right now my only "deliverable" is a good meal, a warm bed, and a wishful five hours of sleep.

I'm nowhere near my deliverable right now as I sit at my desk.

I can barely keep my eyes open as I read my syllabus for ManEc: market power, numerous indifference curves, various utility graphs, and endless homework problems like, "To maximize revenue of La-Z-Boy's newest, designer sofa, what would you set the price at? Total Cost of the designer sofa = $100+5Q+Qpc^2$. What is the demand curve in the segment? What is the optimal allocation of designer and non-designer sofas to each market to maximize profit?" And due tomorrow: *The Choice: A Fable of Free Trade and Protectionism.*

Exasperated, I put the syllabus back on my desk. *Read a whole book in one night? Wonderful.* I should be able to squeeze that in after five hours of classes and four hours of homework, but before the marathon nine-hour study group session. My eyes blur over an article about overpriced IPO stocks and aggregate liquidity risk factors before I retire it for another incomplete assignment, a case about the globalization of the world's largest cosmetics company, L'Oreal. For 45 minutes, I read about the company's acquisition and subsequent expansion of the Kiehl's brand.

At least the cases are somewhat interesting and even the outdated ones have themes relevant to today's business world, if you look hard enough. It's just taking me a long time to understand exactly how to learn from a case, how to rip it apart to understand the problem and then reach the core learning. Rick directed me to a few fabulous websites and books about mastering the art of case analysis last week, but I don't have time to *learn how to learn*. I should have prepped before B-school.

At least I'm enjoying the diversity of the cases so far:

- Norwich Software *(sustaining competitive advantage; diversification)*
- Dodds Paper Company *(value chain; competitive rivalry)*
- Yoplait *(expanding retail options; identifying growth drivers)*
- Virgin Atlantic Airways *(preventing brand erosion; global expansion)*
- Royal Caribbean International *(global consolidation; brand building)*
- Colgate *(new product strategy; investing in market research)*
- Bank of America *(consolidation; analyzing new organizational policies)*
- Monster.com *(funding; lead generation; dynamic growth)*
- Edward Jones *(sustaining a unique strategy in retail brokerage)*
- Chevrolet *(infusing technology into product; operational implications)*
- Harrah's Entertainment Inc. *(rekindling growth; crisis control)*
- Southwest Airlines *(organizational psychology; service differentiation)*
- Intel *(innovation; licensing; organizational complexity)*
- Chrysler *(legal responsibilities; pro-forma analysis; manufacturing issues)*
- King Arthur Flour Co. *(environmental responsibility; incentives; action coaching)*
- Jensen Shoes *(managing internal conflict; cash flow)*
- Mary Kay Cosmetics, Inc. *(strategic positioning; client-focused teamwork)*
- Hotwire.com (online marketing; affiliate programs; low-cost strategy)
- SOFTBANK *(cost/benefit analysis of networks; managing equity)*
- Guidant *(ethical and environmental issues; creating new markets)*

Boyer Candy Co. was my favorite case, not only because they make my favorite, chocolaty retro candy, the infamous Mallo Cup (I went online and bought a entire box to soothe my growling stomach after reading the case), but also because the case revealed a miscellany of key business issues from reviving a brand and managing finances to implementing new management.

Plus, who knew there was a National Confectioners Association?

The cases are interesting, but the horrors with my high-octane classmates and professors are repeated day in and day out, without faltering, only growing in viciousness. Professors are either lost in the private euphoria caused by a precious labyrinth of sophisticated statistics, or they're out to kill. Our entire study group was summoned to the front of the classroom yesterday and forced to stand in a firing line as the professor shot economics questions at us, one by one, while the class watched. I took my place next to the rest of the Dream Team and just prayed it would end. We weren't even blindfolded. The public pressure was excruciating.

It's not just the 100-hour work weeks, the blustery days, the public lashings, and living with the Carringtons that's getting me down—I'm also having serious trouble functioning. I've developed severe migraines. I've gained five pounds around my stomach, possibly from a surge in the stress hormone, cortisol. *Or from the Mallo Cups, who knows.* I look disgusting. I'm not eating right. I haven't exercised since summer. I have dark circles around my eyes. I never talk to my friends from home. I don't know what's playing at the local movie theater, what's on TV, or what books are popular right now. I rarely have time to talk to my parents. I end every night by crying. Our study group never finishes arguing before 2 a.m. Every night is a revival of *12 Angry Men*. Our assignments are always wrong. I've been humiliated in class at least 10 times thus far. I seriously feel like leaving.

And to top it all off, Nelly hates me.

I can't figure her out. At least if I had done something to harm her, I would understand her rage, but I've only been nice to her. I'm calm and respectful in study group—I do my work, rarely disagree with anyone, and I am always punctual—but she's continuously rude to me; and now other people have noticed.

"She really has it in for you, doesn't she?" Aldo asks me one night at dinner after an evening seminar: *Internal Corporate Innovation*.

"Nelly?" I ask, taking off my jacket. The weather has changed dramatically in the last two weeks—it's freezing.

"Yes. She's treating you the same way she treated me at the beginning. She wouldn't let me talk at the meetings and when I finally did speak, she ignored me."

Colletta, his wife, is sitting with us in the dining hall. Colletta is one of the nicest souls I have yet to meet at business school; she hosted an unofficial "Italian Night" last week, opening their home to 15 over-worked and starving friends (like me) with a fabulous feast of *Lasagne Magro*, *Insalata Caprese*, and freshly-baked tomato focaccia. I could only stay for 20 minutes, but she promised to make the home-cooked dinner parties a weekly event.

"Nelly's hostile," Colletta adds in careful English. "Aldo would come home at night really upset with her."

I remember Nelly interrupting and dismissing Aldo constantly. I always stood up for him.

"How did you finally get her to stop?" I ask.

"I didn't care anymore. I decided to stop talking at the meetings. Let her fight with herself," he says.

"But that's terrible—I don't want to just give up!"

"But that's how you stop it. Otherwise, she'll mentally destroy you. Just stay quiet. Invisible. Don't bait her. Next term we won't have to worry about her— she'll be in another study group, maybe even in a different section."

I'd settle for a different planet.

"But I'm not baiting her," I explain.

My plan is to be proactive, not reactive—not just with Nelly, but also in life. I know who I am. Why should I compromise that?

"Let me guess…you're talking about Nelly?" Dean says with syrupy-sweet sympathy, sliding his dinner tray next to mine and joining us at the table. "I can't believe how mean she is to you. Man, everything you say, she just cuts down. You can't even talk in study group."

Thanks for the newsflash.

I can't trust Dean as much as I trust Aldo. I've seen him buddy-buddy with Nelly, kissing her ass several times. He's roguish, but I want to trust him, to give him the benefit of the doubt. "By the way," he adds. "Your presentation was *fantastic* today."

"Thanks."

On the plus side, the intense in-class communications training in CorComm has paid off very nicely. Every presentation we give is recorded, and then while the camera is still rolling, the class provides constructive feedback to the presenter in regard to his or her communication tactics (presentation tools, style, voice, posture, hand gestures, eye contact, and more). Later, the presenter is instructed to watch the video and write a self-evaluation on both the overall presentation and the communication style during the feedback session. It's brutal, watching yourself on video receiving criticism, but it works—I'm inevitably blossoming into a confident public speaker.

"I'm telling you," says Aldo, referring to Nelly. "Just make yourself invisible."

Thanks, but I'm not Casper.

The only thing that distracts me from the severe psychological damage caused by Nelly's terminal terrorizing is my perpetual fear of being cold-called in class.

The School is killing me.

HUNTERS AND GATHERERS

"I'm still not getting the hang of cold-calls," I say to Juliet Ann, Tempestt, and Sookie at our weekly lunch. "The message distorts and my mind freezes."

The four of us have become fast friends, which is funny because we have completely different personalities, backgrounds, and business goals—plus our ages span a decade. Juliet Ann is nurturing, wise and protective, organized in both life and profession, and impassioned to have her own consulting firm for small businesses. She's less interested in B-school politics and more interested in finding the good seeds in the bunch to help her make a difference in the community. Sookie is still the young, Hollywood-bound energyball; and the crystal ball of all B-school gossip. Tempestt...well, Tempestt has earned the well-deserved nickname "Queen Tempestt" and her plans are nothing short of taking over the world. Although she suffers from delusions of grandeur, deep down (think deeper) she's only human and shares our fears.

The one thing we all have in common right now is that we're tired and overworked; and frankly, I don't know how I would survive without them.

"Ironic, isn't it? Considering women may have actually invented language," Juliet Ann says about my fear of cold-calling.

"Really?"

"Men were out hunting and using non-verbal language. Women needed a way to communicate in the dark caves where they lived with their children. Verbal communication was a survival tactic," she explains expertly.

Apparently, I have more in common with my ancestors than just hunched shoulders and unwanted hair—we both need language for survival, mine is just of the cold-calling variety.

"But why, then, are men talking so much more in class?" Sookie asks. "And weren't there studies that showed boys were more likely to raise their hands and talk out in class than girls?"

"They seem more comfortable and confident," I add. You don't have to be a military sharp shooter to see it.

"We're not as egalitarian as we'd like to believe," says Juliet Ann.

"Maybe it's sheer numbers?" Sookie asks positively. "Technically, there *are* more men in the classroom, so maybe it just seems as though they're talking more?"

Juliet Ann shakes her head, somehow managing to keep her beautiful dancer's neck gracefully long. "The people who speak in class were probably encouraged to do so as children—the environment fostered their confidence," she rationalizes. "Or perhaps certain personalities have a biological tendency to be cautious, irregardless of gender."

"Maybe men are just more extroverted?" Sookie offers.

Juliet Ann reasons, "But I don't think most women are introverted—you can't generalize. But perhaps some people are more goal-oriented and less self-conscious while speaking?"

We could have an enlightening two-hour discussion about nature versus nurture and class participation. "But at least I've noticed the professors making the effort to bring more women into the class discussions," I say positively. "But then again…" I pause at the realization I'd come full circle. "Their efforts are those horrible cold-calls I dread!"

Sookie laughs.

"Either way, it's affecting my learning," I continue. "I'm too petrified in class to concentrate."

"It must be incredibly difficult for the English-as-a-second-language crowd?" Sookie asks.

"I have the utmost respect for those folks! They do a better job of speaking in class than I do," I confess, thinking of Jin, a student from China who often sits next to me in class. He participates regularly but has asked for my help with idioms and clichés. I like being his portable translator, explaining phrases like "sweating bullets" to him, so he can laugh with the rest of us. In turn, Jin is teaching me about Chinese business etiquette—always accept and offer gifts with two hands, remember the number four has connotations with death, and treat a business card with the utmost respect by never hiding it in a folder or bag upon receipt.

"I think it's my learning style that's really the problem—I'm too visual," I continue. "Remember those Barsch tests we took as kids to determine our learning styles?"

They don't remember.

"Visual, auditory, kinesthetic?" I remind them.

"Yeah, I remember those!" Sookie exclaims, stuffing a cheese croissant into her mouth.

Juliet Ann wrinkles her eyebrows and adjusts her glasses. "I can't remember my score…"

"Learning is an evolving discovery process." Tempestt yawns while nonchalantly flipping through a magazine, although I suspect she is more interested than she appears. "We're a mix of different learning styles—you should know that by now," she continues disinterestedly.

"But I know that I'm a strong *visual* learner—I have to *see* things to understand them. A verbal explanation, or class discussion, won't go as far with me as a printed document—just let me read something. Or take notes. I'm always scrambling to take notes in class, do something tactile, but it's virtually impossible."

"No one takes notes. I had to give that up," Sookie agrees. "I don't even download them anymore."

Juliet Ann thinks for a moment. "An auditory learner definitely has an easier time here—listening and extensive talking are primary."

She continues, "What I find most frustrating is the number of men who shamelessly interrupt in class—and the scary fact that those people dominate the classroom. Without diversity, we'll all eventually be rude!" She gives an exasperated chuckle.

"I'm vocal so I don't have a problem talking in class," Tempestt gloats, closing the magazine, looking relaxed after yet another night of luxuriating in her dorm temple. "Just yesterday I told Kevin Meister his ideas were garbage."

Juliet Ann shoots her a disapproving look. "Well they were!" Tempestt continues. "Regurgitated rubbish…and I have *no* trouble speaking my mind about it."

It's true. There have been days when Tempestt hasn't even read the case and I'm shocked to see her actively participating in class. Half is information she was able to absorb just from listening to the discussion, and the other half is total bull.

"I can't do much about changing my learning style now," I explain. "Fortunately, I do have *some* auditory learning in me—at least I like listening to lectures."

"But it's mostly discussions here, not lectures," Juliet Ann reminds me.

"I'll take what I can get."

"At least Second Year is more hands-on, more learning through experience," she adds.

"Thank God!"

"I can't wait for Second Year," Sookie chimes and suddenly we're lost in private, blissful dreams of Second Year until Suresh interrupts by plopping down next to Sookie.

"I hear there's less cold-calling Second Year, too. Fewer fear tactics as teaching methods," he adds casually while munching an energy bar.

"It's less of a boot camp." Sookie nods, letting her cheek rest in the palm of her hand as she props her arm on the table.

I offer a weak smile and push my mashed potatoes around on the plate. The whole intimidation tactic of using embarrassment as punishment isn't working for me. It's prevalent here, but fortunately there are a few professors who don't employ it. I absolutely cannot learn when I'm nervous or scared, nor do I think one style of teaching works for everyone.

"Just pretend you own the classroom," Suresh says, shrugging his shoulders. "Communication is a status symbol," he explains. "Talk less, or hesitantly, they'll think you have less power. Talk more—interrupt a little—and they'll just assume you're at a higher status."

"But is status already dictating communication style, or is communication style dictating status?" Juliet Ann challenges with a smile.

"In the classroom, it's the latter. It's all about perception here. Do you want to control your status, or do you want to let your classmates decide it for you?" he asks me.

"Of course I want to be in control! But I have to tackle the cold-calls before I can even *think* about managing my classmates. And I'm getting there, I'm adapting to the professors' style, but I'm just not really learning as much as I could be along the way…" I admit.

"I feel that, too." Juliet Ann nods, putting a comforting hand on my forearm. "We're all just grateful to survive, to pass."

"I just wish I had known that my style was different *before* I came here."

Juliet Ann nods again. "If we had greater diversity of learning styles, then perhaps we'd have a greater diversity of teaching styles." She pauses. "Or maybe it's the other way around?"

It's a catch 22.

I unzip my backpack to pull out reinforcements for the troops.

"Here," I say, tossing candy to them. "Have a Mallo Cup."

❄   ❄   ❄   ❄

The next morning I wake up with a new game plan—to actually raise my hand and speak in class. Rick told me about the Rule of Three: never talk more than three times in one class, but talk at least once over three days of classes. I head to class fully charged and take my seat near the front, ready to go.

9:35 a.m., 04 seconds

Say something. Anything. Say it now. Speak now or forever hold your…now! Say it. Say what? I don't even have anything good to say. Think. Okay, I just thought of something easy to say, so I just need to go for it and talk. I can't. What if it sounds dumb? What if my voice cracks? Who cares—just speak. No, wait, someone else just spoke. Shit. But I have a good comment to share. Do I raise my hand or just blurt it out? For the love of God, just say it! Oh no, wait…what? Noooo! Someone else just took _my_ comment! He just said what I was going to say and everyone loved it! I was going to say that! Really, I was! The professor is praising someone else for _my_ comment. Urgh! Okay, back to square one, think of something new to say. Think. Think. Think. Okay, got it. Just raise your hand, no forget about that, just blurt it out—and that way if it sounds bad then only half the class, the half sitting behind me, will know that it actually came from me. Just say it. Say it. Okay, the timing is almost perfect. Just one more second. Right now. Go! Noooo! Someone just changed the subject! Wait-stop-rewind. Go back! Shit. One swift, tangent comment and now the entire discussion has taken a tidal wave turn toward a different direction. My comment is now as obsolete as my laptop. Like me in business school, it will simply have no relevance. Its poetic beauty will be lost and it will only appear to be a desperate attempt to "get in" with a lame comment. Crap. "Feddy, what do you think?" Professor Beatty asks me. The class turns toward me. I freeze.

I have no idea what he was just talking about.

9:35 a.m., 59 seconds

BIG GIRLS DO CRY

"Please tell me it gets better," I beg of Rick the next day after failing to dazzle in class, yet again. I peel off my jacket, wet from the freezing afternoon rain, and glance out the window at the gloomy clouds. *Another dark and stormy day here.*

He laughs into the phone. "Just a little, but especially Second Year."

"So I've heard."

"You'll be fine."

"Maybe."

"Albert Einstein didn't talk until he was four years old."

"Thanks, but I've got a few years on him," I remind him.

"Just pull out your competitive streak."

"I can't just summon it like that."

He laughs. "You don't have to go medieval. Just muster some righteous MBA indignation."

"Can't I just be the quiet, confident type?"

"You might come across as passive."

"I kind of like being humble with bouts of melodramatic insecurity—that's me. I mean, it sucks here right now, but it'll pass. You know I feel good inside—happy with who I am, proud, secure—I just don't have to shout it out from the rooftops."

He laughs. "Trust me, I know…"

"I would never have survived at your school, though," I tell him. At least 50% of his grade revolves around class participation. I'm relieved to have the opportunity to increase my grades through good, old-fashioned written homework and exams.

"You would have been fine," he assures me. "Did you know that at some business schools you can actually skip class?"

"I heard that about Wharton, but I don't know if it's true." The thought of being able to skip class unnoticed by the professor is unfathomable to Rick and I. No way.

There are differences among all the B-school programs, especially around study groups and the class participation/homework/exams grading mix. As mentioned, Rick doesn't have mandatory study groups like I do; the level of operations and business science in my program astounds him. "Why do you have to know so much about simulation? And why are you required to take Capital Markets, shouldn't that be an elective?" he often asks, though he's amused by my swift 'weighted average cost of capital' calculations. And oral presentations are a way of life here; it's common to have at least one student presentation in each class, yet it's not common in Rick's program.

"What else is going on?" he asks.

I think for a moment. "Well…The School is up in arms about the new *Business Week* rankings."

He's confused. "But you're #3 in the world?"

"I know," I explain, "But we're one slot lower than last year, that's the problem."

"Ahh…" He understands.

"There was a barrage of emails from the staff yesterday explaining the drop," I continue in bored monotones, "and the dorm is abuzz with defensive excuses and opinions. I'm over it." I yawn.

He laughs. "It's the same at every business school—'Rankings don't matter, but we're wildly ecstatic about the high scores and insanely pissed off at the erroneous low ones. But really, we assure you, everything is fine, and we'll get to the bottom of it.'"

I laugh. "Exactly! Rankings always matter to some extent."

"Understandable."

"But nothing is without error."

I cradle the phone with my shoulder as I change into a warmer shirt. "How's the interviewing going?" I ask. While I'm fretting over classes and prepping to interview for summer internships, he's enjoying life as a Second Year student interviewing for a full-time job.

"Not bad. Three tomorrow, all investment banks. I have a second round with Goldman, and I may even interview with Bain next week."

"That's fantastic!"

"Thanks—I'll call you after the interviews tomorrow. Will you be around?"

"I'm free between 3:45 and 4:00."

"Perfect, I'll take it."

Great, a whopping15 minutes for love.

"Hey—" he adds.

"What?"

"You're doing fine…" He pauses. "Just don't forget that."

I'm smiling now. "Thanks for not letting me forget."

Later that night, after yet another tumultuous study group meeting, I head back to my dorm feeling beat and ready for bed. Before I can unlock my door, I hear the familiar sounds of crying. *Time to finally seek out the source.* First, I walk down the hallway and pause at Steven's door. He's definitely crying in there, but there's another soft cry coming from elsewhere. I keep walking, finally stopping at Olivia Golodner's door. *Bingo.*

I knock on the door. There's shuffling before she opens the door, surprised to see me.

"Hey, Olivia—I was just heading back to my room and thought I'd stop in to say hi."

Her eyes are red and puffy. "Come on in. Sorry it's a mess in here," she says. "No time to clean, you know?"

"You should see my room. They're one step away from putting the police tape around it."

She laughs.

I try to keep things really light and cheerful with the small talk. No need to ask her what's wrong (I already know), but eventually she talks about it—she's stressed out, exhausted, and not doing very well. *Gee, sounds familiar.* Olivia feels unprepared in class and overwhelmed by the ridiculously heavy workload.

"I feel like I'm just skimming the surface of every subject—and cold-calls are my only study motivator now." She mindlessly folds a soggy tissue in half. "This work overload must be part of a bigger plan…but I just don't see it," she cries. "This isn't really what I envisioned."

"But at least now you can masterfully dissect a balance sheet!" I jokingly remind her of the B-school benefits, hoping to lighten her spirits. The School has knocked us both out in the first round, inviting me to share my own misery with Olivia so we can eventually have a good laugh about it.

I also tell her about Watery Eye Syndrome, a term that Sookie and I have created to describe that irresistible urge to cry at the most inappropriate moments—in class, in study group, while answering tough interview questions, in the professor's office. We've all felt the waterworks, or rapidly and desperately blinked to freeze tears brimming dangerously close to the lash-line. *Please don't let me cry, please don't let me cry.*

Olivia laughs and says, "So I'm not alone?" before we share more embarrassing Watery Eye Syndrome moments.

"It's getting late," I finally say. "I have to head out, but do you want to have lunch tomorrow?"

"I can't—meetings," Olivia explains.

"Well…stop by my room, Olivia, if you ever need to talk."

"I will," she assures me.

We hug goodbye and I head back to my room to read more about discounted cash flows and internal rates of return.

CHAPTER 6

MY NET WORTH

(First Year: Go on, I Dare You)

Ready? On your mark. Get set. GO!

6:30 a.m.: Rise & shine, shower, and find clean clothes

7:00 a.m.: Finish last-minute assignment details on Excel spreadsheet

7:30 a.m.: Rehearse oral presentation in mirror (eye contact needs work)

8:00 a.m.: Pick up cold breakfast and zoom to class, spill cereal on laptop

8:15 a.m.: Sit in class for four hours, shake with fear of possible nerve-racking cold-call

10:00 a.m.: Give awkward presentation and answer menacing questions

12:15 p.m.: Fight long and vicious cafeteria lines, pop Pepcid

1:00 p.m.: Find tiny bathroom, change into powersuit, hit funny bone on sink, drop portfolio in toilet

1:10 p.m.: Sit in hot and claustrophobic waiting area, rehearse interview answers

1:30 p.m.: Go to nerve-racking job interview #1, make complete fool of myself

2:00 p.m.: Spend 15 minutes rehashing all critical mistakes made in interview

2:15 p.m.: Enter interview #2, have encore performance of interview #1

2:45 p.m.: Change clothes & continue self-bashing of critical mistakes made in interview #2

3:00 p.m.: Various meetings—financial aid office, career services, volunteer work

4:00 p.m.: Miscellaneous errands—drop off car, pick up dry-cleaning, fix toilet, pay bills, and clean

5:30 p.m.: Cook mac & cheese dinner without milk and begin homework

7:00 p.m.: Head back to Main House to meet with grouchy and tired study group

8:00 p.m.: Study group breaks into horrendous argument over assignments

11:00 p.m.: Group assignments finally completed, but presentation still looming

12:00 a.m.: Presentation with Power Point slides is finally done!

12:15 a.m.: Speaking roles have been designated, presentation rehearsals begin (eye contact still bad)

1:00 a.m.: Head home to finish my homework—56 accounting problems, 12 chapters of reading

2:00 a.m.: Can't finish homework, go to sleep tossing and turning with stress

6:30 a.m.: Rise & shine, shower, and find clean clothes

Now why didn't they put that in the brochure?

IT'S NEVER TOO SOON TO PANIC

Well, it's official. I'm getting a tutor.

It's not really as humiliating as it seems. Some Second Year students have volunteered to tutor First Years right before exams. I've decided to work with a tutor specifically for Decision Science.

Kurt Roberts.

I've never had a tutor before in my life. I've always been the one doing the tutoring, so this is a big change for me, but not one I'm afraid to take. These are desperate times, folks.

Our first meeting is during lunch—a quick 15-minute introduction—in the dining hall.

"So Feddy, you're a First Year who has summoned me to be your tutor?" His no-nonsense military mechanics are a little frightening, but I'm willing to risk it because I need someone to whip me into shape and Kurt's the perfect person to do it—a bulky, six-foot-tall former Marine. "And you would like assistance with Decision Science, correct?" he asks.

"Yes, desperately!"

"Well, I'm also a Teacher's Assistant in DecSci (*He's a genius!*), so I'm sure I can help you. But why do you think you need help?"

Why do I need help?

"I'm barely able to function here, Kurt," I confess, offering too much information and fighting Watery Eye Syndrome. "I'm so tired that some days I can't get out of bed, let alone add 2 + 2, I miss my family, my boyfriend, my *life*, and this person in my study group is making my life miserable, but I have no idea why, I'm thinking about dropping out, I can't take it here anymore, what in the world was I thinking coming here, somebody should have stopped me, I can't believe I'm stuck in this hell-hole, no way I can make it out alive…"

I can't stop.

He silently stares at me with surprised eyes as I continue telling him everything for a long-winded 10 minutes.

When I'm finished, he pauses considerably, clears his throat, and then speaks slowly with pleasant equanimity, "Well, Feddy, first and foremost, I'm sorry you are experiencing such tribulation. I wouldn't wish that on anyone. Second, rest assured Term One is the toughest time you will experience in graduate school, and possibly in your life. Things will get better. And third, what I really meant when I asked the question was…why do you think you need help *with Decision Science*? Is there a particular homework assignment you didn't quite understand?"

Oh.

I blush.

"Yes, um, sorry to ramble, I didn't know what you meant, but um, yes, to answer your question."

"Yes?"

"It's not that I can't follow a particular assignment, it's that I can't follow *any* of them. These quantitative operations are new for me. We do the problems in study group, thank God, because I could never do an entire problem on my own. Then I go back to my room and try to figure out how we did it. I can barely understand it with the answer right in front of me. And I don't want to let my study group down. I try to carry my weight elsewhere, to make up for my Decision Science handicap, but I'd love to help them more with DecSci, if I can."

"And you want help preparing for the exam, too?" Kurt asks.

"I'd just like to keep from failing my first exam, if that's possible. I just need a foundation, a really solid foundation, to help me to do the basic assignments with my group."

"There's nothing in this class that you can't do," he assures me. "If I compartmentalize the work for you, you'll see that it's logical and quite manageable." He continues, "What makes life difficult in business school is not the actual work itself—I really believe anyone can do it—it's the unbearable constraints that are placed upon you as you try to accomplish your goals. The lack of sleep, the marathon study sessions, the arduous burden of homework, projects, and impromptu presentations for multiple classes, the severe deficiency of unrestricted time for exercise, the inability to sustain proper nourishment, the emotional duress, separation from friends and family, the deadlines, the examinations, the personalities, the recruiting season, the rivalry—the list is extensive but these are the elements that create an environment that fosters our erroneous belief that we cannot succeed here."

Exactly!

"If I had just a few hours, just a little time where I actually felt alert and rested, to sit down and read all of the DecSci data, or if I had a text book of some sort, then I think—I *know*—I would understand it."

"Not only would you understand it, you would *master* it," he says confidently.

"Well, um—I don't know about that." I laugh.

"No seriously, you would. 99% of the people here would. But the question is, *How well can you master the content within the constraints created to simulate the grueling business environment?* Investment bankers, and even some consultants, are accustomed to this lifestyle, but even they eventually become overwhelmed here. And The School purposely makes it that way—they double, even triple, the regular business load."

"It's torture."

"But it will make you stronger and increase your resilience to the demands of the business world. And The School knows this. And they also know you can do it. It's just training."

"But who cares if I can pull an all-nighter if I can't make simple business decisions because I'm too tired to learn anything?"

"Well, that's why you're here with me. You're trying to reconcile your emotional and psychological strengths with your business acumen, right? Put them together, master them all, and you become what the school wants to produce."

An android? A Stepford MBA?

"The best," he states. "And that's what you've paid them to do."

"Don't remind me!" I put my head down on the table.

HELLO MOTHER, HELLO FATHER...

The following week, I decide to spend five minutes of precious free time drafting a letter to my parents, who are probably wondering what has happened to me. I do my best to sound chipper in the letter:

Dear Mom and Dad,

I have not slept in two days.
And I have not been outside for four.
My stomach is growling, but the memory of the missed meal is long gone. The con-crete ground feels cold as I lie on the floor of my 10' X 9' dormitory cell surrounded by paper garbage while I try to prepare for a nine-hour meeting that will most likely conclude in combative emotional exhaustion. If this day ends at all, it will end in scarring humiliation. My vision is blurry, concentration is impossible, and my body is exhibiting the ill-looking signs of undernourishment. The reflection in the mirror is unrecognizable to me and when I walk down the hall, I hear others crying because of the days we share—days filled with fear tactics bordering on psy-chological abuse. Forget about dining with family, talking to loved ones, reading a magazine, going for a walk, or enjoying the simple things in life such as eating or bathing. There is simply no time for life. The physical exhaustion from sleepless nights is debilitating, and for the next two years, each day will be the carbon copy of an ineffable nightmare. I don't know what the most terrifying thought is right now: that I have to get up in the morning and do it all over again, that I may col-lapse at any given moment, or that I willfully paid an astonishing $100,000 to be here.

Realizing the letter may actually cause more panic than reassurance (I briefly picture my parents charging into the dean's office), I crumple up the letter and head to my 10 p.m. study group session.

TAKE ME TO YOUR LEADER

"All I'm saying is that business school is bringing out deep-seeded emotions. As a result, I'm reduced to ridiculous child-like behavior," Sookie declares with the type of fervor that starts revolutions. "It's from sheer exhaustion—they're brainwashing us with the sleep deprivation!"

Guess that explains why I'm still here.

"I agree," I say to her, thinking about my own previously dormant, but now blossoming, emotions. Business school proves that insecurity is officially part of my genetic code, but I never noticed it in my previous life as a mere professional, never doubted my abilities. "It's a conspiracy."

"But 50% of the student body was juvenile *before* coming here," Tempestt reminds us.

Suresh and Juliet Ann squeeze their dinner trays onto our round table in the dining hall, which is currently decorated in vibrant green, yellow, and red paper streamers celebrating the largest country in South America. It's Brazilian Night at The School.

"Brainwashing? You mean unethical persuasion tactics used for mind control to hinder rational or logical thought?" Suresh asks, biting into his *Empadinas de Queijo*, which looks vaguely like a cheese-filled pastry.

"Exactly!" Sookie shouts, enthusiasm raising her body one inch from the couch. "Think about it, what do the boot camp tactics at business school resemble? Anyone?" Before we can answer she blurts out, "Military and cult tactics! Yep, break us down and build us back up again…"

Tempestt stirs her Brazilian black beans, labeled *Feijoada* on tonight's menu. "We're not exactly marching and chanting," she says.

Suresh laughs. "Maybe it's a Jedi mind trick?"

"And when does the Stockholm Syndrome kick in?" I joke.

Juliet Ann reaches for her banana pie and turns toward Sookie. "But I know what you mean, Sookie," she says empathetically. "The isolation and intimidation are oppressive."

Sookie nods as we prepare to go to Holt Auditorium for a special lecture on Rio de Janeiro's economy and the future of Brazil's currency, the *real*.

I finish my *Agua de Coco* (coconut water) and tip my tray into the trashcan. Maybe Sookie has a point? Is team-based learning really just "group think?" Hmm. The insurmountable stress combined with little time for sleep or nourishment. A bombardment of endless activities and new experiences. Complete exhaustion. Total immersion into this life. No time for families or loved ones. Continuous repetition of material.

All brainwashing, perhaps?

Who knows?

I'm too tired to figure it out.

KNOCK, KNOCK

The next night I decide to visit Nelly. I knock softly.

Here goes nothing.

She opens the door, visibly annoyed at the intrusion, and returns to her desk.

"Can I come in?" I ask her.

"Yes, of course. But I'm really busy. Accounting."

"I know. Who knew there were so many metal manufacturers with accounting problems?" I laugh, referring to our latest assignment set in a steel factory.

She doesn't laugh.

She doesn't even look at me. So I sit on the bed near her desk and get right to the point.

"Nelly, if I've done something to upset you, I'd like to fix it. Please tell me what it is." I've decided to take the friendly approach. Start fresh.

"What are you talking about?" she barks.

It's like talking to Helen Keller before Anne Sullivan stepped in.

"Well…it seems like you're mad at me. In study group? Sometimes?"

Crap, why am I so passive?

"Nope," she says. "No idea what you're talking about."

We sit for a few seconds in silence; I watch the cold rain through the window; she pretends to read her computer screen.

"Is there anything I can do to make things better?"

"I have no idea what you're talking about," she repeats. "Everything's fine."

She's not going to meet me half way. I finally say good-bye and leave with little acknowledgement from her.

Well, that sucked.

But at least I tried.

<u>SWORN INTO OFFICE</u>

"He swears at you?" Sookie's mouth falls open in exaggerated shock.

"Bradley? Well, yeah, it's usually Nelly who swears at us, but last night he said, 'I have no idea what the f*** you're talking about!' when I mentioned I could add graphics to his spreadsheet, if he needed help. Then Nelly just started laughing like the Wicked Witch of the West when she realized I'd been humiliated by someone other than her," I say.

"Is your room…*vibrating?*" Tempestt interrupts, taking a seat on my dorm room floor.

"Yeah, whenever they play music in the lounge, my room shakes."

"I cannot believe those jerks—swearing like that." Juliet Ann frowns from my desk chair. She has little tolerance for people like Bradley.

"He apologized later…" I explain.

"They shouldn't do it in the first place! That's not the norm—I hope you know that. I can't imagine talking to my study group that way."

"Me neither!" Sookie agrees, crossing her legs on the edge of my bed. "It's definitely not like that in my group."

"I think Nelly's evil ways are spreading to the rest of my study group," I explain.

"That's not right."

"You shouldn't take it," urges Juliet Ann.

"Yes, I'm now the star of my very own after-school special: *B-School Bullies*. I'm not fighting, or acting defensively—I just numbly exist at this point and Nelly still attacks me. Worse, the disrespect is contagious."

"Bullies try to make themselves feel powerful by picking on others," Juliet Ann explains knowledgeably. "They try to get what they want by influencing others. It sounds like she's bullying all of you, but in different ways. She's manipulative with them, and malicious with you."

I suddenly find it humorous that we are indeed talking about a 28-year-old professional woman, not a child.

"Jealousy is the number one motivator of bullies," Tempestt adds.

Sookie jumps into a karate position. "You need a bodyguard…like a movie star!" She moves her arms in a mock self-defense move, then sits. "Or you can just ignore Nelly? The term's almost over."

"It's hard to ignore her when we're locked in a room together for 45 hours a week and my learning depends on our interaction. Besides, this place is a fishbowl."

I'd have an easier time ignoring Godzilla taking a bite of my car.

DESPERATE TIMES

I've hit rock bottom.

I don't know what else to do but schedule a meeting with Tami from the Student Affairs Office. It's another first—I've never gone to the administration before in my life. Not even last week, when I received yet another parking ticket. (Apparently, they double the fine for "repeat offenders," my new label.) I now owe a whopping $100 for parking for five minutes in the loading zone without my hazard lights! *Loading zone?* Please! There's no loading of anything. And we're on 20 acres of open countryside. It's a moneymaking scam, if you ask me.

I've agreed *not* to mention Nelly's name to Tami. I just want advice on how to approach the situation and I want it to be known that a nameless classmate is severely interfering with my quality of life here at business school, to the point that I am considering dropping out.

"This person is bullying you," Tami explains after hearing my story. "Who is it?"

"I'd rather not say—I just want to know what to do about the verbal and psychological abuse. I've already tried talking to this person, and to the group."

"This person interrupts you, rejects your ideas, ridicules you, and demeans you...are you sure you can't tell me who it is?" she pleads.

Oh boy. This is uncomfortable.

"No, I don't want to say," I assure her repeatedly, fidgeting with my umbrella.

"Okay. Who's in your group? Just tell me that."

I hesitate. Tami has become a gossip-hungry teenager.

"I can just look up the names if you don't tell me..." Tami singsongs.

"Fine...Bradley, Nelly, Dean, and Aldo."

"Oh, it can't be Bradley you're talking about—he's such a fun guy!" she says, caring less about my problem and more about the guessing game.

Then, I make the fatal flaw of referring to my bully as a "she." Tami doesn't miss a beat.

"So it's Nelly!" Tami exclaims. "I knew it! Wow, she looks like a bitch. I really don't know if I can help you."

Great.

I explain to her that I'm not the only one who feels this way about Nelly in the group and Tami finally offers some advice. "Maybe that's just her personality. Talk to the other members of your group," she says. "If you can get them on your side, then you can outnumber her. And you are not going to drop out. Absolutely not."

Thanks.

Foolishly, I take her advice and talk to Dean and Aldo with no success. Aldo is uncomfortable from the start. He's not confrontational—although he agrees with me, he doesn't want to approach Nelly at all. Dean is even worse. He can't believe I went to Student Affairs. I remind him that he was the one who suggested I go there for advice in the first place, and that I only went to get help for everyone's benefit. Dean wants to gloss everything over—he can't be tarnished with this.

In fact, he becomes much closer to Nelly in the following weeks, and talks to me less and less. Dean also told Nelly that I went to Student Affairs. I don't know this for a fact, but judging from the sharp increase in her torture treatments, I'm willing to bet on it.

I head to the dining hall for lunch, only to come face to face with Nelly as she recklessly turns away from the coffee machine while I walk by. She turns too quickly, without looking, and her arm hits me. Her cup spirals through the air, crashing on the ground in front of us, splashing coffee on the floor and on Mishra, an innocent student bystander. *Nooooo! What a mess!* Instinctively, I grab some napkins to wipe the floor and salvage Mishra's soggy ColeHaan's.

Suede. Yikes.

"Mishra, I'm so sorry about your shoes!"

Nelly says nothing.

Mishra walks away to undoubtedly try to salvage her shoes.

Humbling kneeling on the dirty cafeteria floor, surrounded by wet, brown napkins, I frantically clean up Nelly's coffee. I look up to see Nelly hovering over me like a wicked stepsister with her hands on her hips.

Apparently she has Alzheimer's disease because she's forgotten that this is her mess.

Nelly rolls her eyes in annoyed disgust and sighs loudly before pivoting on her pointy heals and marching off, leaving me on the floor.

Gee, thanks for the help.

I stop wiping for a minute and just sit in the soggy mess of coffee and grime, listening to the hailstorm tapping on the roof. *This floor is gross.*

Suddenly I'm acutely aware of my place in this world—not just literally on the ground at this moment, but here, at business school.

I've reached an all-time low.

SANCTUARY

Rick's place is my only sanctuary. Every Saturday, like this one, if the weather permits, I still drive to Cambridge to visit him at Harvard. The drive is soothing—traffic is a pleasure because it's a small tie to the pulse of life outside of school. I crank my music and by the time I hit the Massachusetts border, some of my stress has subsided. When I maneuver my car into the Harvard parking lot, there's undeniably a smile on my face.

We've developed quite a routine, similar to the one we had before I started business school. He exercises at the Harvard gym, Shad Hall, every Saturday morning before we go to the dining hall for breakfast. They have the best dining facility I have ever seen in my life—a full bar of succulent fruit, Belgian waffles with all the toppings, eggs made-to-order, perfectly seasoned potatoes, plus countless other delights for my palate. Happily stuffed, we then spend the afternoon doing homework before heading out for a wild Saturday night either alone or with his classmates—Grafton Street being the pub of choice lately.

I treasure our Saturdays together and by Sunday afternoon it takes all of my emotional strength to leave. Every week it gets harder and harder. Rick's concerned because he sees the desperation in my eyes and that it's killing me. Once again, I feel like a child—my emotions rising as though I have mommy and daddy separation anxiety. *What's happening to me? I'm an adult. Get a grip.*

I wrap my arms around him as we say good-bye at my car in the HBS parking lot after another great weekend. I've loaded my bag in the trunk.

"I don't want to go," I say.

"I know, I don't want you to go, either."

"I'll miss you so much."

"Do you have to go?"

I nod.

"I can't wait until next weekend."

I smile. "Me, too." Then kiss him good-bye.

We hug for a while, silently standing in the parking lot until he reluctantly releases his arms so I can make the inevitable trek back to campus.

But I don't let go. I don't want to.

He tries to break free, laughing, but I hug tighter.

"Don't make me go back there!" I moan, laughing, squeezing him hard, not wanting to end the hug. "It's terrible there! I can't go back! And I won't! Just try and make me!"

He continues laughing and trying to pry my arms from his body but I won't let go. I keep my grip, but release my body weight against him, sliding down his body so he has to hold me up. We almost fall to the ground.

"No! I don't want to go! Please!" I wail, with exaggerated desperation.

"Feddy!" he says.

I suddenly stand upright, loosen my hug, and look him in the eye. We're both smiling.

"Love ya!" I say.

"Love ya, too." He laughs as I get in the car and he waves while I drive away.

He knows I wasn't really joking in the parking lot.

I want to drop out of business school.

THEY'RE DROPPING LIKE FLIES

"Did you hear?" Sookie asks Juliet Ann and me on one of our chilly, October evening walks to the library. "Augusta dropped out!"

"What?" I'm shivering.

"No!"

Augusta is the third person to drop out. Considering it's only Term One, and we only have 200 students, this is shocking.

Sookie skips ahead, calling over her shoulder to us. "Yep. First Andrew, because he hated it and wanted to go back to banking. Then Mason, because he couldn't keep up with the work, and now Augusta."

Sookie explains that Augusta had a terrible study group that accused her of cheating by sharing homework assignments with other study groups—a common integrated learning approach. The Academic Board found her innocent after an investigation, but was she was so repulsed by the treatment from her study group that she decided to leave.

If you learn anything in business school, it's that you absolutely, positively, must have a decent study group, especially for Term One.

Achoooo!

"Bless you," Sookie says when I sneeze.

"You're not getting sick, are you?" Juliet Ann looks at me, fear on her face.

"No, no I'm fine. Just allergies."

She has reason to be alarmed. There's no sniffling or sneezing at B-school. We simply can't afford to get sick. There's no time. Sure it will happen to all of us at one point or another, but it's best to just sit tight and pray it happens over the holiday break.

Juliet Ann hands me two vitamin C tablets.

❋   ❋   ❋   ❋

I sit through the next week of classes with a groggy head full of incoherent thoughts, but at least I don't have the flu. This is actually how I am every day.

I can't keep my head up, but that doesn't stop me from developing pricing forecasts for Foster Farms, calculating the market value of an unlevered firm with $2.5 million of EBIT, determining the number of hypothetical cumulative voting shares I need to elect a new director at Ford, creating a strategic inventory for Marks & Spencer, building a public relations plan for Make-A-Wish Foundation, testing a new product concept for Campbell Soup Company, predicting the CEO's next move during a ruthless struggle for ownership at a family-run company, and deciding the fate of Mr. Johnson's manufacturing company after he's faced with poor capacity planning and unmotivated employees.

Ahhhh…the wonderful simulated world of business case analysis.

A murky Saturday marks a full day of classes before we begin our consulting projects. Today we listened to a guest speaker during lunch—a consultant from one of the top consulting firms—tell us about his glamorous, yet hectic, life as a consultant. It was interesting until he glanced around the room looking at our name cards for a "name I can pronounce," as he put it, before finally calling on Mike Clarkson. Later, one of my classmates told me that my "eyebrows were distracting" during my oral presentation. (I told her I'd try to work on that, but *thanks* for the valuable criticism.) And then the professor gave more priceless feedback that I sounded "too girlish" during my delivery. *I wasn't exactly sure what was wrong with that, but oh well.*

At least it's not as bad as last week when our communications professor asked for a volunteer to role-play a CEO in a classroom activity. The professor said, "I need someone who *looks* like a CEO," and then proceeded to walk right past me after meeting my gaze. Relief and disappointment simultaneously washed over me.

What exactly does a CEO look like anyway?

I'D RATHER BE AT RIKERS

I dial the phone and tears spring into my eyes when my mom answers.

"Feddy!" she exclaims and then I hear her yell to my dad, "It's Feddy!"

"Honey, aren't you in study group right now?"

"I'm on a 15-minute break."

At this point, my mom should be accustomed to this routine. For the past two weeks, I've uncommonly called four times. The topic is always the same.

I'm going to drop out of business school.

"Things aren't getting better, dear?" she asks over the clings and clangs of dishes in the kitchen sink. They've just finished dinner.

"They are getting worse, Ma. I hate it here. I don't think I can go on." The floodgates open and I start bawling.

"No, no, no, honey, don't say that, please," she begs. "You're doing so well. We know you can do it." She's familiar with the pep talk.

"You don't understand." I'm sobbing so hard I can barely talk. "I can't...keep...up...with the work. I'm...trying...so hard. I...never sleep. I'm...not...learning...anything. At least...if I leave now...I won't...lose all of my money."

"Oh, honey."

"Mom, you don't...understand. They're like zombies here. We...walk...around like zombies. Everyone is so tired." If I wasn't crying so hard, I'd tell her a story about one of my classmates, Dale, an Investment Banker. Dale said he was walking down the hall at 4 a.m. to slide his homework under the professor's office door after working for 46 hours straight to meet the deadline. As he sluggishly trudged to the office with his last scrap of energy, he glanced down to find his shoe untied. He stopped and just stared at his shoe for a few seconds thinking—*holy crap, I'm actually too freaking tired to bend down to tie my own freaking shoe*—before slowly continuing on.

"I'd rather be in prison," I plead.

"No, you wouldn't!" my mom assures me.

"Yes, I would! At least in jail I could just lie in my room, reading. And I'd get to go outside at least once a day. And I'd have three meals..." I am so emotional that I truly believe I'd rather be in jail.

My dad gets on the phone. I know it's serious when she calls in the reinforcement, my father.

"What's going on, kid?" he asks. "I heard you're thinking about quitting?"

All of a sudden I feel foolish, calling them like this, acting like an unhappy kid at school. But that doesn't stop me.

"Dad, you don't understand," I cry, feeling the heat of frustration reddening my cheeks. "The School is killing me. I seriously cannot take it here any more. It's not worth it. I don't care about the job, the salary, marketing, or any of it any more. Business makes me sick right now. And these people...*THESE PEOPLE*..." I start to cry again, not recognizing my voice, so desperate and high.

"But you've made friends there," he reasons on cue. "And remember, you're surrounded by overachievers who feel compelled to perpetually prove themselves. They doubt their abilities—emotionally, they can't afford to be unsuccessful. You don't realize it now, but you possess more confidence than they do. They'll never be able to enjoy life and success the way you do."

"I'm not enjoying anything!"

"Feddy," he continues. "If you leave now, you might regret it. You are surviving just like everyone else. You're up there with people who have been doing this for years, and they're having trouble with it, too. You're going to be okay."

"But two more years? I'll crack. They're eating me alive. And I don't want to be like them. I'm not hyper-competitive. Or cutthroat. I don't have that instinct," I wail.

"Feddy, competition isn't a bad thing. You can be competitive without killing your enemy. It's okay to fight for yourself."

"But it's not just competitive…it's…insane…the workload."

"It's boot camp. They're just testing you right now. It will only get easier, I promise you."

I don't say anything because I'm not completely convinced. I honestly don't think I can make it.

Worse, I don't even know if I want to try anymore.

I finally tell him this and he's silent. "You don't understand—I've been defeated! The School has won!"

At last, he speaks softly, "If you don't even want to try anymore…" He exhales slowly. "Then maybe you're right—maybe you should come home then," he says reluctantly.

My mom gets on the phone. I think it's been hard on her to hear me crying all the time. "Honey, your dad and I talked last night. We agreed that maybe our pep talks just aren't the answer. We've never seen you so miserable. If you truly want to leave business school, maybe that's the best decision."

What?

I can't believe what I'm hearing. *They've finally caved?* After all these weeks of giving me motivational speeches, they've finally decided to throw in the towel. That's it. I'm finished.

"Nothing we say is making you feel better. It's torture at this point. We don't want you to leave school, but maybe that's the best option now? You'll be happier," she says, trying to hide her disappointment.

I'm free.

I can leave.

Suddenly I feel happy—like a huge weight has been lifted from my shoulders. I didn't need their approval to leave, but I needed their support to make the decision easier. I feel better with the consensus. It's foolish and unnatural for one person to endure this much self-inflicted emotional trauma. People say that quitting is the easy way out, but sometimes walking away is much more complicated.

Unfortunately, I have to get back to my study group.

I dry my eyes, we say our good-byes, and I promise to call them tomorrow at the same time to finish the discussion.

I run to the study lounge, hoping no one can tell I've been crying.

WARNING: CONTENTS FLAMMABLE UNDER PRESSURE

How do you react under stress? Have you heard the excuse, "Oh, I was just stressed out, sorry," offered after some horrible, irrational action? People always say, "He's just stressed, he didn't mean it," as though being "stressed" justifies having emotional outbursts, underperforming, or treating others cruelly. We seem to think that stress, if not managed properly, causes us to act in ways not typical of our normal behavior, and causes us to do things that we would never (gasp!) dream of doing in our natural, non-stressed state. But I don't think stress makes you do things you wouldn't normally do. Stress doesn't overpower the real you—stress reveals you. The true marks of your personality are fundamental.

"Where the hell were you?" Nelly snaps. Aldo and Dean are in the room, too.

Nice language.

"I needed a few minutes in my room," I explain.

"We need you in *here*."

"I know. And I'm *here*. And I'll be *here* until all hours of the night, as long as you need me, like always. I just needed a quick break." I'm so drained.

"No one else takes breaks!"

"I'm sorry—it was only 15 minutes."

I'm getting mad now. I'm not taking advantage of the situation and I resent her implications. I've never let the group down—I'm *always* here on time, and I *always* stay until the very end.

We spend an average of nine hours together in this room every weeknight. That's a whopping 360 study group hours since school started two months ago. I've only missed *one hour total*, and that was just during the last two weeks to call my parents. Aldo is 10 minutes late for every session; Dean has a consulting business on the side that sometimes takes him away from study group; and Bradley has hockey for two hours every week. I've never cared—it's never bothered me—and to my knowledge Nelly has never confronted them. We're a team—no one is slacking.

This is freaking ridiculous. I'm so sick of being her kickball.

"Nelly, I went to make a phone call. *That's it.* Let it go. Bradley's at hockey right now—no one cares. Let's get back to work."

She explodes.

I don't mean literally. That would have been easier to clean up. I mean, she starts yelling at me like she's the headmistress of the *Nelly Nettor School for Bad Girls* and apparently I've been very *very* bad.

She's yelling so loudly, I can't comprehend what she's saying. It's that frozen feeling I get when I'm cold-called. Except it's not fear that's paralyzing me, it's shock. My mouth hangs open as she continues to yell from her shiny, red face. Watery Eye Syndrome strikes me uncontrollably. *I can't believe this is happening to me.* She's preying on me because she knows I will never fight back. Attacking the weak.

Am I so worthless that I warrant so little respect from this woman?

"Don't bring Bradley into it…he's at hockey…that's a school function…we're talking about you…do you hear me…you need to be here for every damn minute…no one else takes a bloody break…" she yells for seconds that register an eternity.

I was only gone for 15 minutes.

I want to justify what she's saying, apologize for something. Anything. But I simply can't make sense of it all. If I was gone for long periods of time, or not carrying my weight, or being irresponsible, I would understand her complaints. But it's not like that. There's no excuse for her yelling. Every single move I make, no matter how subtle, angers her.

Then it hits me.

I can't win.

And I want to leave this hellhole now more than ever.

She finally finishes yelling at me, grabs her bag, and leaves. She had told us earlier that she had to leave early. *How ironic.*

I'm left standing there in silence with Dean and Aldo, trying to compose myself as the tears stream for the second time tonight.

Dean finally speaks.

"That was the most despicable thing I have ever witnessed. That was *so* uncalled for!" he says.

Aldo just shakes his head. "I cannot believe that."

I was just waiting for her head to spin around.

"She's just stressed," Dean tries to explain. "But she shouldn't have exploded like that…I can't believe she yelled. You didn't even do anything!" He seems genuinely stunned, possibly more shaken than I am.

Aldo continues shaking his head, dumbfounded.

"Then why didn't you two say anything?" I finally ask them, crying.

"It happened so fast!" Dean says.

Aldo speaks softly, "Why don't you take some time to rest in your room and come back later?" He hands me a napkin.

"No, I want to stay. I'll be fine in a few minutes." I run to the bathroom to clean up, barely looking at my reflection with swollen red eyes. Knowing that I'm quitting business school soon is the only cosmic force that will give me the power to survive tonight.

I bravely return to the room to continue working on a case about Whole Foods Market, Inc., where all hiring is team-based and requires a two-thirds majority vote.

"I'm going to talk to her tomorrow," Dean says. "She had no right to yell at you like that."

"No, don't say anything."

"Well, I bet she'll apologize to you tomorrow."

"I'm not holding my breath."

"I think it's important for you to be at all the meetings, and she just wanted you to be here, but she could have communicated it differently," Aldo says.

"But I am here!" I explain, not wanting to defend myself again. "You know that I'm always here—that's ridiculous." I look directly at him.

He nods. "You're right."

Dean agrees. "Nelly overreacted. It's just stress," he assures me again. "We're all under enormous stress—it affects our brain chemistry. Everyone's acting crazy." He twirls his index finger in the air around his ear. "Loco."

Right. As if that makes me feel any better.

"I would never yell at her."

And perhaps that's exactly why she yelled at me.

"I told you to stay away from her," Aldo reminds me and we sit in silence for a few minutes.

Eventually, the shock wears off and we get back to work. I'm plagued by flashbacks and feel miserable. She's confirmed my place at the bottom of the food chain.

What do I care? I'm leaving. I'm jumping off the Titanic. *And good, I hope The School and Nelly will live happily ever after together.*

I head back to my room at 2 a.m.

That night, I don't cry myself to sleep.

My eyes are completely dried out.

CUZ BREAKING DOWN IS HARD TO DO…

Oh no! I'm late to class. A horrible nightmare kept me up all night, but that was nothing compared to the frightening realization this morning that it wasn't a dream—it's my life.

I grab my gloves and run out the door, opting to walk outside instead of taking the creepy tunnels because it's quicker. *Hurry. Hurry. Hurry.* I look down at my feet—*oops! My socks don't match. Shit.* I exit the dorm and take the path in front of the Main House, my breath crystallizing in the frosty air.

Do I have my laptop? Check. Portfolio? Check. Student ID? Check. Keys? Oh no, I forgot my keys! I've locked myself out of my dorm room. *Ugh!* No time to worry. *Keep it moving. Keep it moving*—ahhhhhhhhh!

My butt hits the hard sheet of ice covering the pavement. I've slipped. The pain flares up my lower back.

You've got to be kidding me.

You've got to freaking be kidding me.

I lie there defeated, sprawled flat on my back, staring quietly at the beautiful blue sky. *When was the last time I had a moment of peace like this?* I can move, but I don't want to. A tear springs from my right eye. *Just perfect.*

"Hey, lady! You okay?"

I turn my head to see a group of maintenance workers running toward me, alarmed. They were supposed to de-ice the path this morning to prevent any potential lawsuits.

"Oh, yeah, I'm fine!" I yell to them and jump up much to their relief.

I have to get to class.

I suddenly feel a sharp pain in my right hip. *Crap.*

No time. Hurry.

Like Quasimodo, I hurriedly limp up the stairs to the Main House for sanctuary, hoping to make it to class in time. I see two of my classmates laughing at me from the landing. *I'm okay, thanks for asking.* I storm past them and hobble down the dark hallway; it's early and the administration offices are still closed.

I feel the pain crawling up my thigh, and the anger boiling through my body, flushing my cheeks. *I hate it here. The cold-calls, cliques, parking tickets, distracting eyebrows, my vibrating dorm room, the Coopers of the world. I'm tired of being tired, being embarrassed all the time, dealing with the DNA-coded arrogance of my classmates, not looking like a CEO, not having the right name, realizing that the cafeteria workers are my favorite people here, regretting my decision, suffocating my femininity, building spreadsheet models, letting Nelly walk on me, searching for Dean's backbone, being sworn at, missing my family, crying, not being tough, wondering the meaning of it all, constantly questioning what the hell I'm doing here…*

What the hell __am__ I doing here?

My eyes fill with water.

In anger, I suddenly stop and throw my backpack down the empty hall before leaning against the wall to catch my breath—my chest is heaving. I bend forward to put my hands on my knees and stare at the ground.

Screw it all. This is isn't what I came here for.

I grab my backpack and start walking back to the dorm.

It's over. I give up. I've had enough.

Then I see her.

Right there, clear as day, staring at me with happy eyes and a beautiful face. Annabelle Hall Smith.

She's smiling at me from a large, black and white graduation photo, one of a hundred that line the hallway. I walk closer to the photograph, putting my face just inches away from the glass, and use my fingertip to carefully wipe the dust from her face. There she is, wearing a conservative skirt-suit in a framed photo taken only a few decades ago, glowing proudly in the center of the first row, easily singled out because she is surrounded by fifty men. And why shouldn't she be smiling?

She was the first woman to graduate from our business school.

Damn.

I stare at her for a few minutes and then head to class.

I'M NOT MACHO!

"You are not weak!" Sookie tells me firmly. We are sitting with Juliet Ann and Tempestt in my dorm room, homebound because of an autumn snowstorm. I just told them the Nelly story—reliving it was hell.

"But I'm definitely renting the basement of the food chain," I argue.

"You are not! And even if you were," Juliet Ann clarifies, "Nelly would soon learn that if one group dies, the others suffer. Kill off one population in the sequence and you're disturbing the balance of the *entire* food chain. Each one is dependent on the other for survival."

"Great…if I die, she dies. Comforting."

Sookie frowns and scrutinizes me while crossing her arms across her chest. "You're not a Type A personality," she decides. "That's your problem."

Type A's dominate our student population. Type A personalities can be competitive, hurried, impatient perfectionists (generally speaking, of course) who can be very aggressive. Type B personalities might be more laid back, content, calm and rational.

"You're Type B," she continues, "which means you'll live a lot longer than our stressed classmates who may be prone to heart attacks…but you'll just be miserable in the meantime."

"But if I'm Type B, doesn't that mean I'm generally more relaxed about things and happy with life in general? And by that reasoning, shouldn't I be happier here at business school than I am?"

Sookie arches an eyebrow. "Hmm, good point."

"No one is a perfect Type A or Type B—we're a mixture of each," Juliet Ann explains.

"Except Nelly. She's a *special* type." I try to laugh but groan in frustration. "She's just so…so…*tight*. Everything about her is wound so tight, like she might crack at any moment. The severe hair, the clenched jaw, the tense shoulders, the critical tongue, the perpetual anxiousness, the dark, stiff suits…I just wish she would *relax a little*."

"Nelly hasn't discovered that she doesn't have to assimilate to some archaic stereotype, or disgrace other women, to be successful," Juliet Ann rationalizes. "In fact, if more people understood this, we could all just *relax a little*." She puts her arm around my shoulder. "The people here are an extraordinary bunch, but they get really insecure about it. Sometimes they have to ridicule others to establish their own worth. They don't even realize they're doing it. A touch of narcissism, a touch of ambivalence, a little anger…it's a dangerous combination in a personality."

I hug my knees to my chin while sitting on the corner of my bed. "Why do they have to be like that? Hard-edged, emotionless, tough, stoic, exercise-obsessed…it's not normal."

"These people are unbelievable." Sookie shakes her head. "Nelly could have talked to you rationally instead of attacking you!"

"It's a learning experience," Juliet Ann reasons. "Let it shape your behavior by identifying who you *don't* want to be."

"I'm just not…" I search for the right word. "I'm just not…*macho*."

Sookie roars with laugh. "Like that's a shocker!"

Juliet Ann chuckles. "Thank God! I mean, you're a woman, so it would actually be a problem if you had unusually high levels of testosterone. And the world needs a balance of hormones, so we need you here."

Glad someone does. I smile at them.

Tempestt has been silent this whole time, sitting in a chair, filing her nails, oblivious to our conversation.

Or so I thought.

We turn to stare at her. She slowly looks up, then returns to filing her nails.

"Do you love yourself?" she asks me.

"What?" *That's a bizarre question.*

"Do you love and respect yourself?"

"Well…yeah. Of course!"

"Do you show love and respect for others?" she asks again.

What? "Yeah, all the time, you know that."

"Well, then, if you respect yourself, and you clearly respect others." She stops filing to think. "Then there is absolutely no reason you shouldn't get the respect YOU deserve." She stares at me. "Go out there and get your respect, then!"

She returns to filing her nails.

"And Feddy," she adds, reading my thoughts. "It's not egotistical to demand respect."

THE ID, THE EGO, AND THE SUPEREGO

"My guess is that you're smart and capable. You probably worked hard, had a good job with a nice quality of life before you came here?" Kurt asks me. "I'm also willing to bet that you're accustomed to success?"

Maybe a moderate level—but that's it.

"Sometimes?" I admit.

"No, really…it's okay, admit it. You wouldn't be here if it wasn't true. What I'm trying to get at is this: students always face the same problem when they come to business school—they're accustomed to being *the best*, the *smartest*. Then they have trouble accepting a different role when they get here. They're like Olympic athletes in a room full of Gold Medalists, searching for glory," he explains in his choppy military style.

"Whoa—wait a minute. I understand what you're saying, but I never *ever* thought I was the best or smartest in a room! Trust me, I don't have *that* type of adjustment problem here."

Worry that I'm no longer the smartest person in the class? Ha!

"But you might," he counters. "Just in a different way. You're not the stereo-typical "I'm better than everyone else" type, someone who comes to business school and expects to be worshiped, expects to be the best, and has trouble with reality. That's one breed. But there are other, less stereotypical types who suffer from the same affliction…maybe, for example, your difficulty rests with realizing you aren't as smart as you thought."

I'm not even as smart as I think? Oh Lord, this is bad…

"Think about it," he continues. "You probably never had a tutor before? Never settled at the bottom end of the class? Never gave it your all, only to fail? Never tried repeatedly to learn something but just couldn't grasp it? If you didn't do well in a class when you were younger, it was probably just because you got a little lazy. But you had control. You knew deep down that you'd come out on top. You knew you were intelligent—that's what kept you going. But you come here, and now you're faced with doubts. It's no longer easy…the stakes are higher and the bar has been raised. Even with all of your effort, you still don't feel you can do it. Worse, you're not getting any validation of your intelligence. You rec-ognize that you are not the best, and that's okay because you never thought you were the best in the first place, but now you also realize that success—any social or academic morsel of it—isn't going to come as easily as it has in the past for you. And that's terrifying. Terrifying and exposing."

Thanks for the ego boost, Kurt.

My sad face reveals my thoughts.

"Feddy." He smiles. "I'm not saying that you're not smart," he offers oblig-ingly. "Not in the least. I'm merely explaining that this is the intricate process your mind is trying to work through—this is what you may be feeling that's get-ting you down. Later on, you'll see things more clearly."

"And then I'll be happier?"

"Presumably so."

His authoritative charisma has a way of making me believe every word.

He continues, "Some people—CEOs, Gold Medalists, whatever—will work twice as hard to succeed above everyone else when they get to business school to once again regain their position at the top. Ivy Scholar status, for example. That's how they resolve their issues with coming here and not being the best from day one. They have to find equilibrium again, and for them it's at the top with the highest honor. They simply won't accept anything else, so they establish domi-nance again. Others, however, are quitters—they just give up, stop playing the game. They hold onto their elite status from a previous life, before B-school, and act as though they don't care about anything here because it's beneath them. Their ambivalence hides their fears of no longer being the best. Denial, if you will. They wear a shield—*I can't be a loser because guess what? I'm not playing the game.* And then there's another group—the most dangerous group—that is overcome by insecurity. They consciously devalue other people, belittling others into shame, thereby—in their own minds—increasing their own status. They rationalize: *if there's someone lower than me, then at least I'm not the worst, and now I'm one step closer to being the best!* They're only interested in their own welfare and gratification—they lose a sense of morality and fairness."

Hmm…a few people like that come to mind.

"You haven't completely given up, Feddy" he continues. "But you're close to accepting defeat. But why? Don't give up because you're not the best—that's weak. Get it together," he orders. "Just work hard to do what means the most to you. Find your own morsel of success, even if it's different from what others have carved out, and take what you came here to achieve. Don't lose sight of that."

Why did I come here?

I'm shocked to realize that it's been a long time since I've thought about it. I've just been going with the flow, trying to survive each day, losing track of my end goal, and forgetting the zest that drove me to B-school in the first place. *What happened to that passion?*

What happened to that person?

THE GOOD, THE 'BRAD,' AND THE UGLY

Bradley comes to see me.

I'm shocked when I open my dorm room door. *Bradley?*

"Hi," he says. "Can we talk?"

"Sure, come on in." I open the door wider for him to enter and he takes a seat in my chair. I plop on the bed, moving tomorrow's case, *The Rise of Kmart Corporation,* aside.

"I heard about what happened with you and Nelly. That wasn't right."

"I know. I'm trying to forget it."

"No one else in the group feels that way, I hope you know that. I think she just lost it when she heard that you were thinking about getting a tutor."

"What?" I ask, confused.

"She thought that we would be slaving away all night while you would be working with your tutor, possibly working toward Ivy Scholar, and getting better grades than us."

Ivy Scholar? Sure, right after I'm crowned Miss Teen USA.

I almost choke on my Tootsie Roll. Now I understand.

"Bradley," I explain. "I'm not working with the tutor so I can do *better* than the study group. I'm working with him because…I don't want to fail."

Bradley looks shocked.

"What?"

"I've never failed anything before. And I don't want to bring the group down. But I don't want anyone to carry me, either." I can't believe the group didn't notice this. I should have told them. "Not only that"—I decide to come clean—"I'm thinking about quitting business school."

He's shocked again. "I had absolutely no idea that you were considering quitting. I don't think anyone else in the group did, either."

"I'm trying to work through it now, but it's not looking good."

"I thought about quitting at the beginning, too. It sucked," he admits. "But you would regret leaving."

We talk openly for a few minutes. I explain how I've been struggling. He explains that he feels the same way, and apologizes for not realizing how unhappy I was.

"Please let me know if you ever want to talk, Feddy," Bradley says before he leaves.

"Thanks, Bradley."

Maybe he's not so bad after all.

THE SLINGS AND ARROWS OF OUTRAGEOUS FORTUNE

The next day, I find myself eating with Morteza in the Starbucks Dining Hall, marking the first time in my life I have ever had lunch with a professor. These lunches, a common occurrence on campus, represent the prevalent faculty/student interaction at The School.

"It would be beneficial to offer a course simply explaining all the financial jargon," I say, half-jokingly, when Morteza asks for my feedback.

He laughs with a wide, warm smile that comes effortlessly and often. "You're absorbing more than you realize along the way." He takes a sip of coffee from a blue and white mug emblazoned with The School's logo. "The School requires that you graduate with a comprehension of useful financial data even if you're not pursuing a career in finance—how to read income statements, calculate return, understand debt ratios and inventory turnover. They know this is an important criterion that separates a weak manager from a successful one. You'd be surprised at how many managers don't understand basic finance."

I wipe the corner of my mouth with a wrinkled paper napkin. "It's valuable knowing how to challenge the numbers, to recognize biases in reporting," I hear myself saying.

He nods, finishing his bite. "Absolutely. If you don't understand the numbers, you lack the power or knowledge to question the numbers that are presented to you."

In true professor fashion, Morteza talks for 15 minutes of the benefits of sharing financial knowledge throughout an organization before politely asking about my business school experience thus far.

"It's certainly pushing me to new limits," I confess, polishing off a piece of broccoli quiche. "And I've found an interesting, new awareness of business."

He raises his eyebrows. "That begs for a question…"

"For example"—I turn toward him with my full attention—"now when I look at a company's product, I can see their strategy. The Razors and Blades Business Model—a.k.a. the bait and hook? When I seek expensive razor blades, ink cartridges, cell phone air time, electric toothbrush heads, video games…I know the company is making a high margin on these consumable pieces after selling the main product at a discount to bait people." I turn my fork over in my hand and glance at my strawberry cheesecake. "And the same with licensing—I realize now how some of the biggest brands make a fortune by licensing their names or selling their technology or software—which is cheap to reproduce—using restrictions that prohibit sharing and consequently increase sales." I dive into the graham cracker crust with my fork. "And likewise, I recognize why some of these models are now being challenged."

"King Gillette didn't actually give away the razors to sell the blades initially…but that's another story." He chuckles.

We talk for a few minutes about different business strategies—low cost versus differentiation, the struggle for market power, and the factors that make a market attractive. We even talk about the raw materials costs in an accounting case from last week.

I seriously cannot believe I can carry this conversation.

He smiles and finally says, "Well, don't push yourself too hard, especially when mid-terms explode next week."

I shiver at his graphic.

"And if you feel like you're not learning as much as you'd hoped, I assure you it will all fall into place eventually—as you can probably tell from this conversation." He reaches for his fork and pauses. "Business school is mostly about acquiring a valuable *skill-set* that can be used throughout your professional life. Much of that skill-set is based on problem solving—a tactic that can be used anywhere and everywhere. Try not to get saddled by the weight of the details while you're here."

He takes a forkful of vegetable rice before continuing, "Business really is a combination of art and science." He leans back in his chair and tells me a story about Six Flags amusement park. "One of the indoor rides received a high number of customer complaints—relative to those for other rides—in regard to the long queue times. In response, Six Flags brought in a series of technicians, consultants, and operations specialists to increase the speed of the ride or reduce the waiting time...their solutions were too time-consuming and costly." He leans forward to reach his coffee. "A psychologist finally solved the problem. Having a strong grasp on human nature, he proposed simply putting mirrors in the waiting area—television wasn't feasible—to engage and distract the patrons while they waited. Subsequently, complaints reduced dramatically and it cost Six Flags less that $1,000 to solve the problem."

"The specialists were trying to solve the wrong problem—the patrons were simply bored in line. There was nothing wrong with the ride?"

"Right." He nods. "Business is certainly about solving problems. But it's mostly about first *identifying* the correct problem...and then keeping an open mind while seeking a solution or pursuing an opportunity."

Morteza's advice first resonates with several recent homework assignments; and second, with my experience here at business school. I really don't want to miss any opportunities.

Have I been chasing the wrong problems?
And have I truly been keeping an open mind?

❄   ❄   ❄   ❄

The following weeks present themselves as a beautiful transformation right before my eyes. We have our first DecSci mid-term, which goes off marginally well—surprisingly, I didn't fail it. The best part is the party in Dalton Hall that the Second Years throw for us immediately after the exam, a time-honored tradition to offer an encouraging congratulations. My other exams also go better than expected—apparently I'm much better at writing than speaking; my final grades will certainly thank me for that.

There's a gradual comfort developing between the business methodologies and me. I never thought there'd be a time when I could easily calculate the present value of a growing perpetual annuity (nor do I ever remember wanting to!); or a time when I could prepare a marketing strategy for a new toy; or analyze Virgin Atlantic's brand identity. I have some pride in knowing that when someone talks about a burn rate, a balance sheet, a leveraged buyout, a P/E ratio, a proprietary asset, or an ROI calculation, I can very well follow along and contribute.

Don't get me wrong, it's far from paradise and our study group will probably never talk again after business school; and our work, although better, is still under par. But there's a different dynamic in our study group. There's less tension. And once in awhile, if you listen closely, you can actually catch us laughing. Bradley respects me in the study group sessions, and our group has a new system that seems to work for dividing the course load. I'm responsible for accounting, which I then share with the rest of the team, and they work on DecSci, which they, in turn, share with me. The rest of the work is divided equally. We are teaching and learning from one another, which I now understand is the primary benefit of having a study group in the first place.

Nelly never mentions "the yelling fiasco" again. She repeatedly declines my requests to talk, conveniently blaming her "hectic schedule," until I finally corner her privately at a table in the study lounge.

"You treated me horribly."

She rolls her eyes, but refuses to speak.

That doesn't stop me. "If you were smart, you'd get a head start and think twice about how badly you treat people—otherwise you'll learn the hard way."

"Is that a threat?" She glares at me.

"No, it's a promise. What goes around comes around," I say bravely. "And I do know one thing. I will *never* allow what you did to happen again." I swing my backpack onto my shoulder. "At least not to me."

Glad to know my confidence is gaining strength again.

I walk out with my head held high as a group of jovial students enters the lounge to find a dumbfounded Nelly sitting alone at the table with her small, speechless mouth hanging to the ground. I feel proud, but certain that I haven't heard the last from her.

Fortunately, things move so fast at business school that eventually Nelly becomes lower and lower on my list of priorities, as does quitting school. They aren't conscious decisions, but rather I am sucked into an uncontrollable whirlwind of time constraints that leaves little time for anything but academics.

Simple translation: I am running out of time to be miserable.

Nelly backs off, but of course that doesn't stop her from making an occasional derogatory comment at my expense. I just ignore her (Suresh, forever quoting *The Art of War*, summed it up perfectly one night: "Hence to fight and conquer in all your battles is not supreme excellence—supreme excellence consists in breaking the enemy's resistance without fighting.") and to my surprise I notice that even Bradley talks to Nelly less frequently. I certainly don't need Bradley to fight my battles, but it is nice to feel the group working less under Nelly's tyranny. Needless to say, no one broaches the possibility of our study group voluntarily working together in the upcoming terms. It is simply understood that our group will dissolve after Term One.

In the meantime, I'm just enjoying our new degree of blissful normalcy.

"It is a new world!" Sookie said exuberantly this morning, raising her hands to the sky, mimicking a blissed-out Gwyneth Paltrow in *Shakespeare in Love*.

"Yes, Sookie, it is."

CHAPTER 7

---　✳　---

ATTRACTIVE
INDUSTRIES

(The Social Life: Bulls, Bears, Sugar Daddies & other Personal Assets)

"It was dark in the study room except for the glowing light of the fluorescent light bulb hanging over the table. The only smell was of the gyros sandwich and a side salad from the cafeteria growing stale in its plastic take-out container. She had black circles under her eyes larger than Stephen Hawking's black holes and was hypnotized by the glare from her laptop screen as she incomprehensibly read the same sentence for the 3rd time. It was just the two of them in the room. He sat across from her, trying to remember the last time he had showered. Were these the clothes he had on yesterday? It was 2 a.m. and they had been in the room for eight hours straight. Their music was the hum of their laptop computers working on electric power. The walls, closing in, provided a vomit-yellow backdrop. They glanced at each other with blank, zombie-eyes, drunk with a lack-of-sleep stupor. Funny, he had never thought her attractive before, but now she looked absolutely radiant. Strange, she thought, his crooked teeth and poofy hair are oddly appealing, why hadn't I noticed? Their hands touch as they reach for the same paper cup of cold coffee…"

OUR FIRST DANCE AND OTHER DISASTERS

"You are cordially invited to attend the Annual Fall Fling Dance…"

I took the plunge and bought my Fall Fling ticket from our proud social chair-person who was seated at a corner table in the dining hall selling tickets. Rick's not available tonight, so I told Sookie I would go with her. Term One has allowed for a roaring social life equivalent to that of a Benedictine Monk, but I've managed to squeeze in a few fun things between classes. These social events—if you can call them that—have been happening simultaneously to the infamous classroom and study group terrors of Term One.

So far, weekly cocktail parties in Dalton Hall (sponsored by The School) and unofficial Thursday pub nights (a late-night ritual at every B-school) with bar games and hot wings have been the primary social events. I stopped going to pub night the minute I saw one of our professors (*hey, don't mind me, I'm cool like the rest of the gang—you can trust me*) trying to recapture his youth by mingling with the students near the bar. I guess there's one in every faculty crop.

Anyway, the dance is only two streets away in a quaint, fairytale-inspired (or fairytale-*inspiring*—it's pretty old) cottage that I'm pleasantly surprised can host more than 50 people.

What to wear? What to wear?

I look into my small closet for the thousandth time. I've been living in jeans, boots, and fleece for months—I don't even remember what my body shape looks like.

Oh, yeah. That's right. I'm an endomorph. It all horrifically comes back to me when I put on my dress.

"Ahhhh!" I scream when I look in the mirror.

"What's wrong? Are you okay?" It's Sookie, barging into my room, alarmed.

I point to my reflection in the mirror. "Apparently, I'm part of a bizarre alien experiment. They've secretly replaced my body with that of an 80 year old man." *Which isn't a bad thing, except I'm not 80, and I'm not a man.*

She laughs and relaxes. "You look great! What are you talking about? You had me worried—I heard you scream before I could knock. Relax—you look beauti-ful."

"Thanks, Sookie." I adjust the zipper on the back of my blue satin dress. It feels a little snug (okay, it's like a sausage casing) around the waist. I like my body, but I just can't believe the drastic changes in it since I've started school. *This can't be healthy.*

Sookie is wearing a classic black cocktail dress. "You look fantastic, Sookie!"

"Yeah, well, you never know who you might meet…"

"Sookie, we know *exactly* who we'll meet. We know everyone in our class," I remind her.

"Don't depress me—I'm nervous as it is. I'm a chatterbox, but I actually clam up at these awful things. I don't do well at dances."

Who would have thought that at our age we'd be facing Molly Ringwald-esque school dance social pressure?

"Sookie, you are one of the friendliest people at this school. You will be fine—better than fine—and it will be so much fun! I'll be right by your side. And it's not like we'll do anything dorky like…like…become wall-flowers stuck at the dessert table all night!"

❄   ❄   ❄   ❄

As soon as we arrive at the cottage, the first thing Sookie and I do is head straight to the dessert table to gorge ourselves. She's trying to figure out how to gracefully eat an overstuffed chocolate éclair while I'm cramming a raspberry tart into my mouth. It's been 20 minutes since we've arrived, and so far we've only talked to each other.

We're not budging. I've secured prime real estate near the dessert table. I can actually stand with my back against the wall and successfully put my drink on the corner of the table, thereby avoiding any potentially embarrassing social moments of having to maneuver a drink in one hand while trying to eat finger food off of a plate with the other.

"Oh my God! He's coming over here," Sookie mutters under her breath to me. She's also secured a lovely position next to me with her back against the wall. (I can hand Sookie her drink when she needs it.)

"Who?" I ask.

"Suresh!"

Oh no. Suresh is slowly but surely becoming one of our good friends, but that certainly doesn't excuse his thwarting "Who's Your Daddy?" or "Ride the Pony" dance moves. Spaghetti-Arms-Kumar has been eyeing us the whole night from the small dance area, trying to engage us into his private and painfully awkward dance fever. He took to the floor a few minutes ago with classic Britney Spears—no one else was on the dance floor, but that didn't stop Suresh. *Boy, can that guy move!*

He gyrates toward us. All it takes is three minutes and 15 square feet of dance floor to convert any handsome intellectual into a floundering, one-man dance machine.

"It's all so very, *very* sad," Sookie whispers.

"Hello, ladies!" Suresh says as he glides over to us, still moving his arms and hips in a dancing motion. "Or should I call you—*Priscillas, Queens of the Desserts?*" He glances at the dessert table.

Sookie and I roll our eyes. He laughs at his own joke, still dancing.

"Looks like you're having fun, Suresh?" I finally say.

He snaps his fingers. "Yep. This is my second gin & tonic in twenty minutes. Given my height, weight, and tolerance threshold, I've established my optimal rate of drinking. And if my calculations are correct,"—he looks at his watch—"I should be totally tanked in three and a half minutes."

Sookie and I can't help but laugh. "It's good to have goals," she says to him.

Aw, he really is kind of cute, if you think about it. (Warning: by cute I mean Jonathan Lipnicki "the human head weighs eight pounds" kind of cute, and I mean for Sookie, not for me.)

Within a few minutes, largely due to Suresh's social magnetism, our circle of three grows to 10 and we're fully entrenched in business school social activity. *So this is what it's like?* We start dancing and Tempestt joins us.

"The odds are good...but the goods are odd," she whispers to Sookie and me, referring to the male to female ratio.

"But I can't believe how many people have already coupled up!" I nod toward Chakira and Jay Malone grinding on the dance floor. *Looks like Suresh isn't the only one with a liquor goal.* I want to look away, but I can't.

In addition to the couples, the regular cliques are glued together in tight circles. They've morphed and mutated since orientation week, but the foundations are unaffected. It's fascinating to see which masses survived and floated to the surface after the water settled. Social boundaries have been established, and each family has its own hierarchy of sorts. There's now a group of *Proper Bostonians* under the reign of charismatic Cooper Allwin—they're a golden, squash-playing pack secretly called *The Imposters* by the rest of the class simply because no one wants to surrender to the idea that this unexceptional group is the best we have to offer for the coveted *Beautiful People* title. There's also a keg party group (Bradley's new posse) responsible for our spontaneous dorm parties, and an extreme mountain biking and hiking group led by Adam Bartlett.

Everyone has a place now, whether it's in a group or in noticeable solitude. Our social fates have been sealed.

By eleven o'clock, I've exhausted all of my physical energy (dancing and smiling) and mental energy (small talk). Sookie is ready to go, too, but it's still early by the standards of this crowd and we agree to try to sneak out inconspicuously as to not be labeled, "boring girls who stand by the dessert table all night and then leave early." Gossip at a small school can be vicious.

"Just walk the perimeter of the room," I instruct Sookie.

We inch our way around the room to the front door. The key is to exit swiftly and quietly, drawing as little attention to us as possible. We've crammed into the little foyer to put on our jackets.

"I can't open the door!" I shout to her, fumbling with the handle. It's this darn old cottage with the original lock that the big bad wolf used to contain Little Red Riding Hood—right before he ate her.

"What do you mean you *can't* open the door?" Sookie panics.

"It's stuck!"

"What?"

"I can't turn the knob."

"Is it locked?"

"No, I checked. It's just stuck." I am desperately trying to pull the door with all my weight.

Horror strikes. We hear the *The Imposters* coming toward us in a large drunken group. No!

Sookie pushes me out of the way and grabs the door. No luck. It doesn't budge. I can't believe we're locked in this wretched dance. Sookie finally puts both hands on the knob and leans back. I stand behind her, ready with support. The door flings open with a loud pop! Unfortunately, neither one of us expects the impact, and Sookie falls into me, pushing me down to the ground and landing on top of me.

Someone yells, "Hey!" and Sookie and I instinctively turn around to look. We're temporarily blinded by a flash of white light accompanied by a familiar clicking sound.

It's the class photographer! He's just snapped a picture of Sookie and I trying to escape the dance, sprawled out on the floor. When my eyes adjust, I can see everyone looking at us.

"Leaving so early?" Nelly taunts, laughing as she sips her Kendall Jackson Chardonnay—Bo Standish, her boy-toy du jour, by her side.

"No need to rush off ladies, but you might want to check the fraternity party down the street? You might have better luck there," Bo scoffs, showing his solidarity with Nelly.

Bo Standish: classmates award him too many points for being an empty-headed Neanderthal, too few deductions for being obnoxious.

"And they might enjoy your show," Nelly adds with false pity, laughing with *The Imposters.*

Sookie and I run out, at first mortified, but then giggling. It's really quite funny, if you think about it.

At least it is until five days later when we make our debut in the social section of the school newspaper—a messy heap of bodies on the floor with open mouths and bugged eyes underneath the caption, "You Can Run But You Can't Hide!"

THE NEW NEMESIS

Is it wrong of me to find slight comfort in knowing that Nelly has a nemesis?

The new nemesis is Stellah Severs, a pretty blonde who is in *The Imposters* by default. In a perverse way, this new adversary justifies my ill relationship with Nelly—the weight of our problem may rest more with Nelly than initially realized. It doesn't surprise me in the least that she has an antagonistic relationship with someone else, and I'm certainly more than willing to share her wrath with someone else.

There's an interesting, but not uncommon, social phenomenon happening with *The Imposter*s lately. They seem to have split into two mini-*Imposters* groups, with Stellah in one and Nelly in the other.

"It's reminiscent of high school. People are scrambling for identity...and cliques provide comfort and security," Juliet Ann explains the barrage of cliques at B-school. "But eventually that security is threatened. Animosity among the various groups is inevitable."

"It's only a matter of time before they start killing each other," Tempestt rationalizes.

Juliet Ann, Tempestt, and I are innocently sitting in the auditorium, waiting for a lecture, when I notice Nelly and her posse sitting three rows in front of me. Stellah tries to walk through Nelly's aisle. "Excuse me," she says politely to Nelly and crew as she squeezes to get to her seat at the far end of the aisle. Nelly smiles sweetly and makes room for Stellah to pass.

And then I see it.

The universal finger-in-the-mouth gagging gesture made popular by valley girls decades ago. Nelly turns to her friend Heidi and makes the international barfing gesture after Stellah walks by. Heidi laughs and then returns the gesture. They are pretending to be sick.

And they are both making me sick. Oh, ladies, grow up and stick together, will ya.
Then the possibilities jump into my head.
Nelly has a weakness.
Stellah.
I am certain it has something to do with Bo Standish, because Bo and Stellah are often seen together. *Oh ladies, not over a guy!*
Stellah could crush Nelly socially, hands down. Oh, the limitless possibilities for ruining Nelly, the bad seed who has made my life a living hell. I have brief thoughts about exposing Nelly, leaving her friendless without her cushy inner circle.

Wait! Stop it!
Embarrassed by my fleeting thoughts, I mentally return to the lecture. Sweet revenge has never been my modus operandi and I don't want to star now. Plus, who has time for social politics?
I decide to just silently enjoy the satisfaction of this new knowledge hoping that maybe, for once, I will be able to sleep peacefully tonight.
A girl can only dream.

CLASSROOM HIGH JINKS

"I'm just glad it wasn't me," Sookie jokes. We've been talking about the latest CorComm drama revolving around the controversial case of a breast implant manufacturer. Today, we were bombarded by Professor Scheples, who vaguely reminds me of the Nutty Professor, holding a microphone to our faces as we unassumingly walked into class. In true investigative reporting fashion, he blasted questions while a cameraman took video. Talk about being caught off-guard!
"You say the implant materials are safe? Then why do all of your customers have identical symptoms?" he pestered Juliet Ann as she innocently walked into class.
Fortunately, I had arrived early.
Before she could answer, he moved on to the next person entering the classroom. "What do you have to say about the 400,000-person class action lawsuit?"
"No comment," the student replied, shielding his face.
"Is that all you have to say to the people, '*no comment?*'"
To the next student: "How do you sleep with yourself at night?"

Each student was stunned by the greeting—some played along and joked, some answered seriously, some tried to run, others were just shocked. When class started, we talked about the ethics of the case and making the right business decisions from the beginning, or recovering from the wrong ones; and the moral obligations corporations have to humankind. After extensive discussions, we delved into communication intricacies, thereby launching the media relations portion of CorComm.

"I kind of liked the dramatics!" I find myself saying as we exit the dining hall after lunch. "They had a strong impact."

"It does add diversity to the teaching," Juliet Ann agrees.

"It's so much easier for me to retain the information." I pull my scarf tighter to stop the freezing wind from giving my face a freshly slapped look.

Tempestt brushes lint off her Delaine-Merino shearling jacket before wrapping a silk scarf around her neck. "Enough with the fakes. I can't wait to have my first *real* media interview. I already have my outfit picked out."

"Great, now all you need is a corporate scandal," Sookie teases as we exit the dorm.

"Forget it. I'm not going down like that. I've worked too hard."

"I'm not either, but for different reasons."

"I want my first interview to be for recognition of something meaningful, something I can be proud of, a legacy for my children," Tempestt says proudly. *A little surprising coming from Tempestt-most-likely-to-start-a-scandal-Nandi, but impressive, nonetheless.*

"I'd like to be honored for making a difference in the world, paving the way for thousands of other women in entertainment," Sookie adds animatedly, speaking with her hands.

Juliet Ann's eyes twinkle. "Hmm...it would be nice to be interviewed about receiving a community award...or for giving back to my old neighborhood...or donating a building or library to a local school..."

"Or a nice piece about your consulting company helping small businesses?" I remind her.

"I'd also like to be recognized for being a role model to other women trailblazing through business, expanding previous notions of business, and opening doors never dreamed of!" I explode, smiling.

"Like Kay Koplovitz?" Juliet Ann offers.

"Rose Marie Bravo," Tempestt adds. "Chief Executive at Burberry."

"Or Muriel Siebert, Abby Joseph Cohen...Anne Mulcahy, Meg Whitman, Andrea Jung, Marjorie Scardino...Oprah Winfrey..." Sookie quickly rattles off.

"We'll take the world by storm," Tempestt says assuredly. "But first things first—our dinner reservation is for 8:30. Hustle, ladies!"

We run relentlessly at lightening speed, giggling and shielding one another along the way, to persevere through the gusts of icy wind trying to hold us back.

But we make it.

THE TALENT(LESS) SHOW

Is this the Gong Show? Please, somebody gong these people. Tempestt, Juliet Ann and I are sitting in Holt Auditorium, watching what's loosely called the Annual Student Talent Show. Tonight's Master of Ceremonies, Bradley Berger IV (shocker!), announced the first event as though he was introducing the next match for World Wrestling Entertainment, which as it turns out, isn't too far off because the first event is an eating contest. *The Glutton Bowl?*

"Come on down!" Bradley roars as six of our largest classmates thunder onto the stage and take their seats at a table loaded with buffalo wings.

"Ready? On your mark, get set, go!" Bradley yells and the crowd starts to cheer as the contestants stuff their faces.

"Isn't that MaryAnne up there?" Tempestt asks me.

"Yep." MaryAnne is the only female to partake in the contest. *Perhaps I should feel more proud than I do?*

"This is absolutely, positively disgusting," Tempestt says, not able to pry her eyes away from the action.

Juliet Ann and I can hardly hear her above the rowdy and roaring crowd.

"And we have a winner!" Bradley screams after the buzzer and approaches Lawrence, the new champion, to raise his arm in victory. Lawrence has barbeque sauce covering his face and shirt.

I start to applaud, but I'm a little confused. I'm definitely amused, but I have to be honest, this really wasn't what I expected for a business school function. I thought maybe some music, some singing, acting—I don't know.

Tim Burke, Bradley's best B-school pal, takes the microphone.

"Ladies and Gentlemen! It's time for the one, the only, the infamous...Bradley Berger!" The crowd roars. Bradley bows to the audience. "Tonight, for the first time this year, Bradley Berger will attempt the death-defying, never before seen at business school, hold onto the edge of your seats folks...Nipples of Fire!"

Nipples of Fire? Whose?

Memory is such a fragile cognitive function of the brain. There are certain events in life that we hope to remember forever despite the challenges we face as memory recollection becomes more difficult with time. Likewise, there are certain events in life that, as much as we hope to forget them, we cannot erase from our memories.

I am willing to undergo severe central intelligence brainwashing tactics to erase this one. Hook me up to the electrodes, if you have to.

Bradley Berger set his nipples on fire with a match and some brandy. Don't ask me too many questions. The whole event only took three seconds because the flames extinguished quickly. One second, he's pouring some brandy into a glass, the next, it's on fire; and before I know it, he's suctioned the glass miraculously onto his exposed nipple after ripping off his shirt. Then he repeats the process with nipple number two. He stands there with two brandy glasses stuck on his naked breasts, raising his arms in a victory cheer as the crowd goes wild.

Bradley Berger and the flaming nips?

"I'm entering next year's Talent Show," Tempestt vows.

"Going to light your nipples on fire?" I joke, causing Juliet Ann to laugh.

"No! I have *real* talent."

"You can light your nipples on fire *while* eating buffalo wings?" I kid.

"No! Next year, I'm going to sing at this thing," Tempestt vows.

"Bring it on, girl!"

The events marginally improve to reveal some true talent, but we leave early and head downtown to Mr. Lee's for some Chinese take-out, still talking about Bradley's nipples of fire.

Ouch!

BABY BOOM

"But if you *were* thinking about kids…what are you thinking?" I ask Sookie at lunch while I desperately try to calculate the net present value of a perpetuity before my next class.

"Same as everyone else. Finish B-school first. Work for one to three years. Have babies in my late twenties, early to mid-thirties and on. Possibly take time off to raise them, maybe not, depending on my situation," she says, crossing her legs underneath her on the chair.

We're talking babies because Rona, a single classmate from Russia, is eight months pregnant. If anyone can do it, she can, but it's a tough rarity at The School.

"The married male students have babies. But most of the female married students don't," I say.

"They will right after business school. One to three years. Watch." She nods knowingly.

"My Alumni Mentor just had her baby," I say, referring to Delilah's email last week about the birth of healthy Quentin. "She graduated a few years ago."

"I can't wait to have babies!" Juliet Ann says, surprising both Sookie and I because she's in her late thirties and we incorrectly assumed she preferred to be childless.

She laughs. "Don't look at me like that. Business school isn't *delaying* my childbearing. I planned to have them at this age," Juliet Ann chastises. "It's common now. Did you know that more than 500,000 women over the age of 35 have babies every year in the U.S. alone? So don't be so shocked. Besides, Ashton feels the same way."

Ashton?

"You have a boyfriend?" Sookie shrieks, leaning toward Juliet Ann.

"Good Lord, I'm a feminist, not a doorknob! Yes, I have a boyfriend whom I love very much."

We're dumbfounded.

"How long have you been together?" I ask.

"Three years. He's a photographer back in New York—we met at a friend's art gallery." She takes a bite of her grilled chicken and avocado sandwich and continues talking after swallowing, "There were other things I wanted to accomplish first, but motherhood is at the top. And think about what a great position I'll be in now?" She opens a bag of chips. "I'll be a great role model for her...I'll be able to financially support her...I can give her a better quality of life. And I wouldn't have it any other way—I want to give her the best."

"I say go for it! I'm with you." I stir my macaroni and cheese. "I read about this organization that was going to start running ads showing an upside down baby bottle shaped like an hourglass dripping milk instead of sand, reminding women that their child-bearing time is running out," I say.

"You're kidding!" Juliet Ann eyes widen.

"Nope. Fortunately, some women's organization stepped in to block it."

"But I do believe that conception becomes harder as you age," Sookie says.

"I guess someone forgot to tell Rona!" I joke.

"There were more women over 40 having babies in 1960 than there are now!" Juliet Ann says. "And I think a lot of it had to do with them not being told that they were too old. They wanted big families, so they just kept going and going..."

Sookie laces her hands behind her head. "How close are we to men having the babies for us?"

"Light years."

"It would be like an ectopic pregnancy and he'd have to take female hormones," Juliet Ann explains. "Not a pretty site."

I grimace. "Maybe it's better to leave that stuff to us?"

"Birth, careers, family—it's all yours!" Sookie shouts.

Yes, it's all ours.

"But do you actually want it all?" she continues, pretending to hold a microphone to Juliet Ann.

"The answer is yes. I just want more support for the choices we make," Juliet Ann speaks into the mock mike.

I reach into the air, pretending to grab the microphone. "I haven't decided how long I'll stay home with my children when I have them, but if I do stay home, one option is to work from home, even if it's part-time," I add. "It's really just nice having the choice—the possibility to have it all and to share it with my family."

Juliet Ann nods. "Education allows you a certain level of security and options—especially an MBA."

"And the marketer in me really wishes that motherhood was branded a little better because it deserves so much more respect in our business society," I continue before Sookie retires her "microphone."

"I heard that if we added up all the work that a mother does—chauffeur, psychologist, teacher—and assigned a salary to each of her jobs, her annual income would easily amount to a $500,000!" Sookie says.

Juliet Ann nods. "If motherhood got the respect it deserved, think about the possibilities for both stay-at-home mothers *and* professional mothers?"

✳   ✳   ✳   ✳

Fortunately, Rona's baby arrives safely and in good health. Rona is granted a few weeks to recoup, but keeps up with the course work at the hospital until she returns to campus, completely caught up and ready to go. In fact, she's performing better than ½ the student body at this point.

A few days later, a second classmate announces that she, too, is pregnant and due during Spring Break.

THE TOY COMPANY

Today we are meeting with the client for our consulting project—the sole proprietress of a small company that makes popular teddy bears, Teddy Babies.

"Last year, my company sold 50,000 bears. Earlier this year, I secured a spot on QVC television, but couldn't meet the demand generated from the phone calls," Joannie Mulligan explains to us. She needs help forecasting demand for her product, improving the marketing and distribution, and managing the operations.

Basically, she needs a business plan; she's never had one.

Our study group is relieved to have such a unique company for our consulting project. The toy business offers us an interesting, but mammoth, industry. Other groups are working with software or healthcare companies—we're working with a stuffed animal manufacturer. Plus, Joannie seems nice.

At least at first.

We meet with her weekly and talk daily for the next two months, working diligently to chart Teddy Babies' operations flow, and to develop an affordable online marketing plan. Joannie's sitting on a virtual goldmine and we want to see her tap into its full potential. Unfortunately, Joannie isn't interested in our opinions (I caught her studying a crack in the wall during one of our sessions) and appears resistant to change although she doesn't exactly disagree with our advice. She's just coy enough for me to suspect that she has a secret—one that I'm afraid she'll only reveal during our final presentation at the end of the year.

Ironically, the assignment is actually a blessing in disguise for our study group; we're bonding together as we futilely try to please Joannie.

After all, the project is worth 50% of our grade for this class.

THERE'S NO PLACE LIKE HOME

I'm so excited! Amy Holt is coming to visit me for a fun-packed 24 hours and the year's most popular football game against Harvard. I haven't seen her since my bon voyage party at work, so I'm bursting with feeling when I see her.

We hug for a long time.

"I've missed seeing you so much," I say emotionally. "I'm so glad you're here." My eyes water.

"Wow." Amy laughs. "What are they doing to you at this place?"

"It's a nightmare."

"I hardly recognize you. I mean, I knew from our phone calls how unhappy you were, but...I didn't realize it was this bad!" She's concerned.

"It's bad," I confirm and the tears start to fall.

We go for an early pizza lunch and I brief her on all the bad stuff that's been happening at The School. With hindsight bias, some of it actually seems humorous. Perhaps it's a defense mechanism to preserve my sanity, or maybe it's because I'm so happy to see Amy, but I can actually poke fun at my own misery.

"You're always happy. You'll rebound," she assures me and encourages me to stick with it. She won't let me quit.

For the next hour, I'm normal. Amy's my precious link to the real world, so alive and free. *Oh, to be free...*I can't get enough of the stories. It's like a warm visit home, a window to another world—the real world. *I miss my life.*

I miss the real world.

"Oh—and I have something else to tell you..." Amy hesitates and grimaces.

"Yeah?" I ask with some concern.

"Well...it's about Davey." Amy pauses.

The Sales Rep from my old department? "Yeah?"

She takes a deep breath. "After you left the company he told everyone that the two of you slept together."

Oh, now I remember—the real world totally sucks!

"What!?" I scream and feel the blush on my face.

"I know..." She nods.

"It's not true!"

"I know..." She nods again.

"I mean, he was in sales and I was in marketing." I feel queasy. "We had a few group lunches together, of course, but..."

"I know, I know, I know. I told everyone the truth, don't worry. But I thought you should know."

"That creep!" Everyone will believe him.

"Ugh. Tell me about it. Same old story, you know how it is at work. If you're a woman, there's a 70% chance you have a big, fat rumor attached to your head."

"But I don't like that crap—especially if it's about me, and *especially* if it's false! It's all so...*unnerving.*" I feel sick.

"Sexual politics and gender games—just be glad you're tucked safely away at business school," she says.

I smile at the irony of her statement and she eventually pulls me out of my shock-induced mental paralysis by reminding me that Davey is a complete loser with a deep inferiority complex.

Amy then gives me the cute details of her baby niece and the latest news on the daycare industry to change the subject. Amy's dream is to leave insurance and open a chain of evening childcare centers in the Northeast. She's still a part-time MBA student at a local college (she calls it the five-year-plan) which works well for her because it allows her to maintain her sizable income, keep her brain active over a longer period of time, and apply new MBA knowledge directly to her job. "It's a constantly evolving learning process, which I love, but woman am I tired!" she admits before briefing me on the high jinks of our friends.

The gang is doing well, "same old, same old," and another friend just returned from a six-month consulting assignment at the Bank of New York in Singapore where she worked on a fund for retail investors. "She's thinking about permanently moving there next year, but right now she's on another assignment in Brazil and then one in California in four months. Oh, and I almost forgot!" Amy puts her hands on her cheeks. "Big news…Gary got engaged!"

"No!" I shriek as our second pizza arrives. "Tell me *everything*."

An hour later, after she's divulged every detail of my life-as-I-knew-it back home, we catch the football game and then float with the crowds to several rowdy college bars.

WINTER CARNIVAL

It's time for the annual Winter Carnival! Each November, The School hosts a corporate sponsored, student-run, weekend celebration of winter sports, complete with a slalom skiing competition, snowboarding, family events, and a snow-sculpting contest. Hundreds of skiers from the world's best business schools participate—Dartmouth, INSEAD, Boston College, University of Chicago, Columbia, UCLA, Harvard, NYU, Wharton, and Yale. And this year's corporate sponsors include a local brewery, a major investment bank, a large global consulting firm, and a beverage company.

"Basically, eet's three days of freezing your ass off during the day and then warming up with thee bottle at night!" jokes Chakira. "Eet's one long party!"

She's right. Sookie and I fight off frostbite watching the events on the first day at the major ski slope near campus. Thankfully, it warms up the second day. Unfortunately, it's also warm enough to foster rain and it pours all day. People are skiing in trash bags. But that night we party it up at The Ice House (a legendary house occupied by five Second Years). It's pretty crazy at The Ice House—all the drinking—with Bradley leading his posse into zealously pumping the keg, and *The Imposters* huddled near the fireplace, looking aloof, probably daydreaming about tomorrow's early morning squash match, but it's great to meet people from the other schools. Sookie hits it off with a snowboarder from London Business School.

"Wow—he's amazing!" she passionately tells me later. "I love his Hugh Grant accent. And he's coming here next year on exchange!"

The School has exchange programs with the other major business schools in London, Paris, Germany, Spain and other parts of the globe. We can go virtually any where in the world for one term Second Year.

"Where are the women?" Tempestt asks, looking around the party, promenading toward us like a peacock waiting for the paparazzi. "I see plenty of men from the other schools, but no women. Just the wives of the visiting students."

"They were smart, they stayed home. Would you want to be around all these drunk men?" Juliet Ann frowns. She's had enough of the drinking.

"Have a hot chocolate instead of a beer—maybe that'll cheer you up!" Suresh chimes in, joining our group by the fireplace. This guy is everywhere.

"Hey, Sookie," he adds. "You look cold, I got you some hot chocolate." He hands her a Styrofoam cup.

Juliet Ann, Tempestt and I exchange glances. I got you some hot chocolate? Looks like someone has a crush on dear old Sookie...

Sookie's cheeks redden. "Uh, thanks, Suresh, but it doesn't really go with my beer."

"No problem—I'll drink it. I just wanted to come over and say thanks for working on that pro-forma with me on Wednesday. It's not every night you pull an all-nighter."

An all-nighter with Suresh? We look at Sookie again, but she carefully refuses to make eye contact with us. "Not a big deal, don't worry about it," she says to Suresh. He eventually walks back to his friends on the couch.

We pounce on Sookie. "Pro-forma-ing all night with Suresh?" Tempestt teases. "My, my."

I choke on my laugh. "Is that what the kids are calling it nowadays?"

"You seem to have made quite an impression on him!" Juliet Ann smiles, politely stifling her laughter.

Tempestt can't stop. "Must have been your *ass*-et allocation?"

"Stop it!" Sookie is blushing. "It's not like that! He's a friend, that's it. We worked on the Kmart pro-forma last week. End of story." We look at her in silence, not believing her. "No, really, I would tell you if it were more than that. He's not my type. And besides, I definitely didn't come to school for some random hook-up, who needs the extra stress?"

We laugh even harder. Sookie is the flirtiest of us all.

Feigning frustration, she defends herself. "Hey! Listen—I'm liberated. I'll sleep with whomever I want to sleep with! But he's just a friend. Really."

"But what about your Hugh Grant guy?" Tempestt asks.

Sookie changes the subject—fortunately to something just as juicy. "Did you hear about Cooper Allwin and Catherine Parker?"

"What happened?"

"Well, she's been waiting on him hand and foot, even doing his laundry—"

"Is that true?" I ask in disbelief, skeptical of these rumors about someone as intelligent as Catherine.

"There's nothing wrong with doing stuff for your guy!" Sookie says. "At least there's nothing wrong if you're in love and you treat each other with equal respect, but everyone knows Cooper takes advantage of her. He won't even admit that she's his girlfriend, and he treats her terribly, from what I've heard. And today they broke up! He dumped her for no apparent reason, just boredom!"

"She's better off!" Tempestt says then shakes her head and sighs. "It's starting early this year…"

"What?" we ask in unison.

"Thanksgiving Break-up," Tempestt explains. "Come out of your caves, girls. Surely you know that Thanksgiving Break is the time when most First Years *expire* their relationships from home and consequently begin dating new and exciting classmates only to realize months later that they've made a huge mistake? Thanksgiving Break is known as *Thanksgiving Break-up*. It happens all over the world."

"I don't think they have Thanksgiving outside the USA," I remind her.

"Did you hear about Evan Yajon?" Sookie interjects, excitedly remembering a new tidbit of gossip.

"I heard that one today!" Juliet Ann covers her mouth.

"What?" I ask in confusion.

"Married!" Sookie practically shouts.

"What!? But he's *dating* Eleanor Beaselly!"

"Exactly! Can you believe it? He has a wife back home in New York. Well, they're not exactly married, but they've been living together for years and he recently proposed to her. Eleanor found out and is fuming."

"Poor Eleanor!"

"MBA...Married But Available? Tsk. Tsk. She's better off without him!" Tempestt declares for the second time tonight.

"Those MBA types!" I joke.

"MBA women can only date MBA men," Tempestt retorts. "Other men are too insecure to marry a six-figure-earning Ivy Leaguer. We're doomed to this small gene pool. And even then, the pool gets smaller, because when some of these Wall Street banker types decide to retire their johnsons and settle down, they're more interested in marrying a teacher from Greenwich who will stay at home and raise the kiddies."

"Not true!" says Sookie, putting her right hand on her hip. "I've met a lot of men who are really impressed with what we're doing."

"Yeah, they see it as a free ticket!" Tempestt says.

"No, I don't even mean that. I just mean that they like to see women succeed."

"Whatever." Tempestt laughs.

"My boyfriend is actually supportive, but it might be a rarity," Juliet Ann says.

"And Rick is very secure with what I do," I agree. "He loves it. And he'd love it even if I decided to do something else—he's supportive either way."

"Rick's fabulous, but he's not a typical MBA type. He's excluded from this pool," Tempestt dismisses Rick.

"Well, thank you." I smile.

"I would never date an MBA," Tempestt states. "A Sultan, yes. A President, yes. An MBA, no." We roll our eyes. *Queen Tempestt.*

"Not having much luck on the dating scene are you?" I ask her.

"No," she admits with a scowl.

Sookie laughs and angles her chin toward the air in a debonair stance. "'The men who resent my success won't give me the time of day. And the men who respect my success won't give me the time of night!'" She quotes Sarah Paulson's character from *Down With Love.*

Then she tilts her red, plastic cup, letting the last drop of beer fall into her mouth. "But something like 50% of all female MBA students meet their husbands in business school."

"That's absolutely untrue! Where did you hear that?" I ask.

"I don't know, hearsay. But look at our class. They're like rabbits!"

"They've just got cabin fever. They'll come to their senses after graduation."

"I bet at least 10% of our women marry classmates," Sookie says.

"At this rate, maybe," I agree.

"I can't think of a single student here that I would date, male *or* female," Tempestt adds, making us all laugh.

A few weeks later, Sookie begins dating Cooper Allwin's best friend—Alec Spreen, the slipperiest of snakes.

MBA GOGGLING

Juliet Ann, Tempestt and I are going to stage an intervention to knock some sense into Sookie who has been "MBA goggling" for the last few weeks while dating Alec, the unofficial Vice President of *The Imposters*. It happens to all of us, even to strong, empowered women like Sookie—it's a byproduct of total immersion into The School mixed with a sequence of events fueled by alcohol. The dating pool is so limited that men who once repulsed you begin to look like prime dating material. In reality, your standards are just lower.

"Can we save her?" Juliet Ann asks.

"She can only save herself," I answer.

Fortunately, we don't have to intervene because Alec does us the honor himself and proves what a prick he is, saving us the trouble.

"What a jerk! We dated for weeks and he told everyone we were 'just friends,'" Sookie fumes. "Just friends? Give me a break!"

"He really did like you," I assure her. *As much as he could like anyone besides himself, of course.* I don't really have all the details on their relationship—Sookie was cagey about the whole thing.

"And I pretended to like those boring finance stories. Why? Why? Why?" She pulls at her hair near the scalp above her ears and swings her head left to right.

"Beware of the man who has pictures of himself in his convertible framed around his bedroom..." Juliet Ann warns.

"What's wrong with that?" Tempestt asks. "I like a man who likes himself."

Juliet Ann rolls her eyes.

"And he was always correcting my grammar," Sookie rants. "I hated that! And those stupid tech toys—that stupid grammarian always had to have the latest gadgets, smaller and better than everyone else's..." she rages.

We allow Sookie to vent for as long as she needs to. She broke up with Alec this morning after he made the fatal mistake of commenting that women were not meant to work in finance. He even spewed some bogus comment about women not having the 'biology' to do anything quantitative.

"Gee, and I really thought we had made *so much* progress since the 1950's," Juliet Ann adds sarcastically.

Sookie is a strong woman who was one stitch short of becoming a doormat. It can happen to anyone here and we're just thankful she came to her senses.

TROUBLE IN PARADISE

"Ashton broke up with me," Juliet Ann tells me one afternoon when I stop by her room, wondering about her absence at our lunchtime speaker event, "Managing Peak Performers." It was interesting—a prominent business coach taught us how to match specific managerial strategies to particular types of workers, a practice "guaranteed to motivate the growing number of workers who have mentally checked-out" at the office.

I give Juliet Ann a big hug and she explains that Ashton is upset because she doesn't have time for him. "We haven't seen each other in weeks," she says, gently putting aside an article, "Overview of Foreign Exchange Markets."

"Does he feel threatened by your success?" I ask her, knowing this can be a common problem in such relationships.

She shakes her head. "No, that's not it, he's not threatened. He was happy for me. We saw it as an investment into our future. He's supportive."

"He's just floored by how much time school is taking away from our relationship…and when we do talk, we always fight because I'm stressed out and crabby."

Ashton is a good guy, sweet and caring. I've met him a couple of times since discovering Juliet Ann had a boyfriend and his love for her is apparent, but relationships are difficult here.

"The School takes a toll on every part of life."

"I wonder if it would have been different if he had moved here with me instead of staying in New York? Or maybe it would be easier if he was in business…"

"No! He may have been bored here—it's not exactly a metropolis—and grown resentful. And it's good he's an artist to your business mind—he complements you…"

"He's my best friend."

"Does he worry that you won't have time for him later on? Or time for a family in the future?" This is another common concern with spouses and partners.

"No, it's just school."

"Then that's a good thing! This means it's just The School that's temporarily causing the strain, but it will be different next term, next year, and especially after graduation. The old Juliet Ann will be back."

"I'm worn out." She looks at me, her normally relaxed face suddenly full of stress and vulnerability. "I didn't have to come here, you know. I had a nice job, a good income, challenging work, a great boyfriend, terrific friends, my beloved apartment, my old neighborhood, my favorite Greek restaurant two blocks away…and I left all of it? FOR WHAT?"

Whoa, hold on.

"For what?" I ask incredulously. "For YOU."

I sit next to her on the bed. "You came here to make a better life for yourself and to make a difference in the world. You'll be able to share the knowledge you've acquired. You're proving your independence." I reassure her. "This degree and this knowledge is something that no one can take away from you."

She smiles. "Thanks for reminding me." She grabs my hand. "Really."

"And you should talk to Aaron—I bet he'll have some words of relationship wisdom," I add.

Aaron Jeffries is one of our friends, a married classmate from California. His wife of five years, Sadie, opted to stay on the West Coast rather than quit her job during Aaron's two years at business school. The long-distance plan, although not the norm, is working really well for them.

I try to reassure Juliet Ann for the next hour and she seems to feel better. She loves Ashton and wants it to work. The break-up isn't final; there's hope that if he can just hang on for a few more months, until she finishes First Year, things will be better.

Later that night, I call Rick for our usual chat.

"Are we heading for a break up? I mean, graduate school isn't exactly an aphrodisiac." *More like a surprise visit from your grandparents during a hot date.*

"Well," he contemplates and I can tell he's smiling. "Unless there's something you're not telling me, I think we're okay. We've been together for so many years, it's not like we just started dating."

"True."

"It might be difficult for a newer relationship to survive this, but we see each other almost every weekend," he reminds me. "And neither one of us has had to give up a life somewhere else or relocate for the other, or anything stressful like that."

I start to think about the non-MBA spouses, mostly women, who have accompanied their husbands here, some giving up careers to do so. 25% of our class is married. The School is great—they've set up programs for partners. The spouses have grouped together into a small but strong community. But Colletta, Aldo's wife, said that the international spouses don't really have a strong outlet because the strong partner community is mostly American, so she sticks mostly with the Italian crowd on campus. I have friends who went with their husbands to larger, metropolitan business schools who say that the school provides few, if any, family or partner activities, but it doesn't really matter because there are so many things to do in the city. But here, your social life depends on The School.

"But think about all the married couples, long-term couples, and the families that *successfully* make it through B-school—just look in the alumni book. It's tough, but couples make it through. *Thousands* of them."

"Good point." I hear myself agreeing before we say our goodnights.

He's right, I think after hanging up the phone. When I look at the statistics, it's clear that relationships more often than not survive B-school despite the sensationalism of break ups.

I just hope I can stay on the right side of those stats.

CAVIAR & BUBBLY

This weekend, I'm going to see Rick for Harvard's early holiday party, Holidazzle, in Boston.

"This is magnificent!" I'm in awe as we enter the grand lobby of what appears to be a palace—a cathedral with crystal chandeliers and marble columns—filled with stunning HBS students in tuxedos and sequined gowns.

"It's beautiful," Rick says, admiring the ornamental architecture. "And so are you." He takes my coat.

"Thanks." I blush and smile. "Not too bad yourself, I might add."

"Let's grab some champagne?"

"Sounds good."

We move to one of the champagne reception areas and order two glasses when his classmate, James, approaches us.

"Hey, Ricker, what's up?"

"Hey, James! You know Feddy, right?"

"Hi Feddy—yes, we've met. And I've seen you in the dorm. How are you?"

"Terrific. Are you performing tonight? Rick said you're part of an a cappella group?"

He's flushed. "Naw. I mean, yes, I'm part of the group, but no, we're not performing tonight. But you can catch us next weekend in the dorm, we're performing at a cocktail party. And we have a CD out."

"I didn't know you had CD!" Rick says.

"I have an extra copy, I'll drop it off to you."

"I wish I had that talent. I can't carry a tune in the shower!" I admit.

"You should try it anyway. It's such a tension reliever," he says and explains that singing produces endorphins and triggers the release of hydrocortisone, an anti-stress hormone.

So that's the secret? I curse myself for all those years of goofing off in music class as a kid.

"Rick! Over here!" Ronin calls to us.

"Good seeing you guys." James waves goodbye as Ronin approaches.

Ronin Bersonn. MBA extraordinaire.

"Rick, I *nailed* the Goldman interview last week! They'll probably call me on Monday with the offer. How did you do?"

Mistletoe, champagne, yuletide, and cutthroat competition...

"Pretty well, I met with four of them on Wednesday. Do you know Feddy?"

Ronin initially looks distracted by the notion of taking a millisecond to acknowledge me, but then forces an enormous, albeit fake, grin as he takes my hand to kiss (not shake!). I expect him to say, *Enchanted evening, my lady.*

"Wonderful to have the pleasure of meeting you, Feddy."

"Likewise." I don't know what else to say. His confidence is scary.

He drops my hand. "So Rick, really, how did you do? With Goldman?"

"I think I did well. I'll find out next week like everyone else."

"How many job offers do you have so far?" Ronin asks Rick. Unbelievable— it's a holiday party and this guy is asking Rick rude, personal questions. People in business school seem to temporarily lose their manners when it comes to grades, salaries, and job offers.

Back off!

"I've received five so far. Four banking, one tech. Basically, everything that I've interviewed for," Ronin continues.

Arrogance, party of one—your table is ready.

"So how many job offers do you have?" he challenges Rick again.

"I've received quite a few that I'm proud of," Rick answers politely. He has enough panache not to talk about it tonight, here with me at the holiday party, but he secretly smiles at me because we know he's received many offers thus far. I'm so proud of him.

"Rick's a great guy," Ronin says, turning toward me when he realizes that Rick isn't caving. Wow—and to think I wasn't really sure how I felt about Rick until Ronin revealed this astonishing conclusion.

"Yes, he is!" I agree.

"Hey, Rick, you're coming to St. Thomas with us, right? Spring break?"

Before Rick can answer, Ronin eyes someone more interesting than us and darts to the other side of the room. Rick and I laugh. *Adios, Ronin!*

"There are some people I want you to meet," Rick says and leads us to the bottom of the grand staircase and into a group of classmates laughing and talking about embarrassing classroom experiences. He introduces me to Lisa Marini, the director of a nonprofit breast cancer research program, Judy LaFortune, a healthcare consultant, and another friend, Kyle, who manages an NFL team owned by his father, Big Rick. We also see Ned, the executive at Johnson & Johnson, and Jerome, the publishing magnate, both good friends. Throughout the night, Rick continues to introduce me to other classmates; he makes an effort to make me feel included.

"See him? Right over there?" Rick points to a mob in the corner.

I can't believe it's him! "He just won the Silver Medal, didn't he?" I love ice-skating.

"Yep. And over there, see that guy? His father rules most of Morocco. And there's Artie, the union organizer. And that woman over there—she's the fashion executive I told you about." Last month, Rick and his classmates compassionately and voluntarily held an auction to raise money for this particular classmate's mother, who had recently been diagnosed with a rare brain tumor.

Overall, the mix of Rick's friends is still predominantly of single white males in finance, peppered with a little diversity. He also has a nice combination of Beautiful People and Mere Mortal friends, which makes socializing pleasantly tolerable. "James approached me recently about starting a company," Rick reveals, taking my hand on the dance floor. "Online personality tests."

"Really?" I'm curious.

"I'm going to talk to him more this week, but I'd like to run the details by you—to see what you think?" He looks at me and reconsiders. "But not tonight. Later. For now, let's just relax and have some fun."

I smile. "Don't have to ask me twice…"

I walk on air as we dance and socialize for hours, letting the B-school stress fade into a distant memory.

WOLVES ARE THE NEW SHARKS

"Forget sharks—these guys are wolves!" Sookie says animatedly as we sit in Aaron Jeffries' spacious living room.

Aaron has a beautiful off-campus condo and we relish the novelty of a comfy home with multiple rooms, a kitchen sink, and modern bathroom fixtures. It's heaven compared to the dorm. Aaron, on the other hand, envies our dorm life—camaraderie in the lounges, brainstorming in the study rooms, easy access to classmates, and proximity to all the facilities. "You try driving 15 miles at 2 a.m. during a snow storm," he argues. *Good point.*

It's Friday night—we've rented a movie, *The Corporation*, and ordered a pizza to go with the Indian take-out Suresh brought with him. We're talking about (what else?) our lovable classmates.

"But wolves usually don't attack humans," I remind Sookie of the differences between wolves and our classmates.

"You know, wolves have a highly sophisticated social organization," Suresh explains.

"*Sophisticated?* Then you're surely not talking about our class," Juliet Ann jokes.

He shakes his head. "No, seriously, wolves have a delicate, yet complex, social structure. It's absolutely critical they maintain a stable social environment and it's vital for them to form strong attachments."

"You mean packs? Or cliques? In that case, you *are* talking about our class," Sookie says.

"Wolves are very much like our classmates, if you think about it. Wolves need a stable environment to balance their social behavioral patterns, otherwise social instability and extreme emotional distress prevail," Suresh says.

"Total chaos?"

"Complete." He nods. "They become angry, vocal, destructive, and uncooperative. They turn on one another."

"Yes, I'm beginning to see the similarities…" I nod, thinking of our class.

"It's based on perspective," Aaron adds. "Hunters might see wolves as aggressive and destructive, but biologists might describe wolves as friendly animals."

"Most likely, the disparity in the two views occurs because hunters are witnessing the wolves during times of severe social disruption—hunters, themselves, actually causing this social breakdown. Biologists have a different effect on the wolves' environment, and consequently see the wolves differently during those calmer circumstances," Suresh explains. "Much like our classmates."

"What about jackals and dogs?" I ask as the movie starts to play.

❅   ❅   ❅   ❅

"I think I'm done with classes," Sookie jokes from behind the steering wheel as we drive back to campus in her Volkswagen Beetle. "I'm ready to graduate already. Enough is enough!"

"Me, too," I agree, adjusting my seatbelt in the backseat.

"Looks good, Feddy," Suresh says, unzipping his bag and turning around from the passenger's seat to hand me a printout of a Marketing presentation I had asked him to proofread last night.

"No major mistakes?" I ask.

"Nooooo…but does it bother you that your name is misspelled?" he asks with jovial curiosity, pointing to the first page.

"No!" I groan. "Spellcheck always changes it to Fedora. I missed it—I'll change it right away."

He laughs. "It's only on the first slide. Otherwise, it's fantastic. You really have a strong grasp on distributing new retail products and estimating direct-marketing costs."

I smile. "It's my specialty."

Sookie continues, "I mean, if you think about it, at this point, I'm only attending class for the entertainment value of hearing Professor Goldstein shriek 'This is outrageous economics!' every time his marginal revenue equals his marginal cost."

"You should have seen him trying to explain Game Theory—I thought he was going to orgasm." I put the presentation into my bag.

Juliet Ann lifts her head from the backseat headrest and sleepily adds, "What about Judge Judy?" referring to our Organizational Management professor who often turns the classroom into a courtroom with her persistent badgering and dramatics.

"She's smart, but a little overzealous, too," I say. "And I think Professor Haven has a gambling problem—he relates every statistic or probability to gambling! Somebody take that guy to Vegas."

Suresh agrees, "I loved the quote he used last week, 'The less you bet, the more you lose when you win.' That was classic."

"Cooper and *The Imposters* are all the classroom entertainment I can take," I joke sarcastically. "The only thing worse is the consultants who won't shut up. Experts about everything?" I roll my eyes. "Please!"

"Jack of all trades, master of none?" Sookie jokes.

"Yeah, try telling them that..."

Juliet Ann is wide-awake. "Did you see the way Cooper and Alec refused to present their spreadsheet in ManEc?" She reaches for her bottled water.

"Cooper said the case was 'too easy' and not worth explaining—and then he said to our class, 'If you don't understand it, then you probably shouldn't be here in the first place.'"

"No!" Sookie squeals.

"Yeah, and then he spent the next 20 minutes talking about his linear program designed for zero-sum games."

"Professor Baker battled it out with him for awhile and then finally shut him up," Juliet Ann adds. "Good thing, because I'm not paying to hear a jerk like Cooper talk about his prisoner's dilemma all day. Everyone knows he would be the last to cooperate, anyway."

"When are you ladies going to realize that we're not all Coopers?" Suresh makes a case.

"As soon as you realize we're not all Mirandas," Sookie says referring to *Sex and the City*.

"I'm so far from Miranda," I admit.

"Wait, wasn't Miranda a lawyer?" he asks.

"Different career, same stereotype," Juliet Ann explains.

"I never thought of you as a group of Mirandas! You're nice. Confident, but nice," Suresh says to us.

"And we never thought of you as a Cooper. But there are a lot of them here," Sookie says.

"I think that will change soon," Suresh assures.

I laugh. "I hope so. It's unnatural to have this many under one roof."

"I don't walk into a room two minutes after my ego," Suresh says openly. "My goal is to get an MBA, learn something I can take back to my job, and meet great people. Simple. I don't feel the desire to establish world dominance; I won't destroy our natural resources; I don't want to steal anyone's money. And I don't want to compete with you, as a person or as a gender."

"Maybe you're an international version of Cooper?" Sookie questions.

"What's it like to be an international student, Suresh?" I ask.

"It's a Zen-like retreat of unparalleled ecstasy."

I smirk. "No, seriously?"

"Well…it's great because I speak English fluently," Suresh explains, "but it's not so great for some friends I have here who don't speak English very well. Assimilation barriers can be tough." He opens a can of 7UP. "I'm comfortable speaking in class, but many of my friends from overseas have difficulty with class participation and networking." He takes a drink and lets the carbonation work its way through his body before continuing, "It's not easy for other cultures to be as direct as some Americans are. And even if you speak the language, it's challenging to penetrate social groups or sports."

Juliet Ann laughs. "What, fraternity parties and drunk skiing aren't what an international student has in mind?"

"Not quite. I was actually hoping for *more* beer pong, to be honest. 10 hours a week never seems to be enough…"

We laugh before he continues sincerely, "Being international adds a layer of complexity to landing a job in the states. Not to mention an anthology of paperwork…" He searches for the cup holder for his can. "And if international students aren't properly adjusting and integrating into the program, then domestic students aren't getting the global experience they're expecting, either—and no one wins."

Suresh turns to face the backseat. "On the plus side, being an international student sometimes fosters special treatment from the faculty and staff, some leeway on assignments or cold-calls." He pauses, raises his left eyebrow into a debonair arc, and pulls up the collar of his shirt before continuing in a charmingly deep voice, "And of course"—he smiles—"the international card is great for picking up the sexy ladies…"

We laugh and Juliet Ann nearly chokes on her drink.

"Okay, Casanova, keep it under wraps until we get back to campus," Sookie urges him with a smile.

CHAPTER 8

———— ✳ ————

TRICKS OF THE TRADE

(Job Hunting: Cutthroat Criminals of Interviewing and Recruiting)

"Can you give us an example of a product that you think is marketed poorly?" he asks.

I have a few thoughts about how to answer this interview question; and I decide to go with a product that has been on my mind for a while.

It's a risk that quickly becomes a disaster.

"Moist Wipes for the bathroom," I answer confidently, referring to a new product from a giant toilet paper company.

"You mean…the toilet paper companion?" one of them asks me slowly.

I hate these over-powering interviews where two executives from the consumer products company simultaneously interview me. They are on one side of the table, I am on the other. "Good cop, bad cop" has quickly become "bad cop, bad cop." They look at me with furrowed eyebrows and tight lips.

"Yes, it's a moist towelette," I continue. "The product first appeared as a toilet paper companion, but recent packaging now boasts other confusing, contradictory uses—everything from soothing hemorrhoids to cleaning up hands and face while on-the-go. They're competing with—"

"Wait," one interviewer interrupts. "They're marketing a single product as toilet paper but also to clean the face?" He starts to laugh. His partner smirks. I blush.

"Well…they must have been worried about cannibalization of their own toilet paper products so they're advertising other benefits, but yes—that's the problem, the marketing associations are off. It will be interesting to see how the company continues to position or extend the product in the market, and how they'll circumscribe the current product," I say.

"So," says the other interviewer, not hearing a word I've said, "they actually expect people to use it on their faces or to soothe hemorrhoids? That's absolutely disgusting!"

They laugh unabashedly.

Great, I've lost them to the visuals.

"Yes, but it really is a terrific product with great versatility," I say louder. "New product in a current market, good distribution, good brand, but the positioning hasn't been clearly defined yet..." I want to talk marketing.

It doesn't matter. They're not interested anymore. I never get to talk about the segmented consumer market, limited SKUs, price-points, distribution, coupons to drive traffic, or the new print ad.

They are smug and I am tired of the games at this point. Tired of their attempts to intimidate me, their fake smiles, their over-confident body language, their stupid questions about how to market green potato chips after a hypothetical mix-up at the plant.

The interview is over. "Hemorrhoids" and "toilet paper" are never, ever, to be mentioned in an interview. Part of me is mad that I even mentioned something so ridiculous. *The toilet paper companion!?*

But the other half of me remembers that I was genuinely interested in the marketing of this product and thought they would be mature enough to discuss the sanitation benefits of moist wipes which, incidentally, are predicted to grow to a whopping $1.3 billion next year! Will they be watching when moist wipes enter the baby, anti-bacterial, camping gear, feminine hygiene, athletic, travel, body cleansing, cosmetic, deodorant, and household disinfectant markets?

I close the door as I leave—I've been dismissed—and stop in the hallway to shut my eyes for a second and catch my breath. I am mortified, but finally manage to compose myself and proceed down the hall.

Half way down the hall I hear them erupt into loud laughter. I stop in my tracks.

My dignity is gone.

REASON FOR BEING

At business school, it all comes down to one thing in the end.

Employment.

The recruiting season is a time unsurpassed in its importance and competitiveness. It takes on a life of its own during Term One, pulsating through our class like the plague, squeezing the last drops of self-assurance from our bodies, savagely revealing the Mr. Hydes among us, and uncouthly stealing precious time from our already congested schedules. I wish I could save myself or help others, but its sheer force takes me by surprise even though I graciously and unassumingly invite it into my world.

It starts so innocently with a simple resume.

"Your resume is comprehensive—that's one strength. But you might want to use SAR," Nicole says to me as she helps me to prepare my resume for recruiting season. Preparation begins during Term One, although 70% of the interviewing actually takes place in Term Two, right after the holiday break.

Nicole Rivera is my Second Year mentor who has returned to the U.S. for a mini reprieve from her exchange studies in Paris. Her timing is perfect for me—interviewing preparations started last week, thereby completing the trilogy of B-school terror: study group nightmares, awkward social events, and demanding interview prep.

Not only is Nicole one of the most brilliant and respected students on campus, but also she's being recruited by both the major consumer products companies and the consulting firms. She's also The School's unofficial Healthcare Ambassador, having pioneered a new movement to bring biotech and pharmaceutical companies to campus for lectures and recruiting. I also heard she was working to reduce the use of pesticides in the water used to make soft drinks in India.

I didn't expect her to be so approachable, but she is.

"SARS?" I ask. *The atypical pneumonia in Asia?*

"SAR. Situation. Action. Results," she explains. "A resume is a profile of your professional history, yes, but it's also much more than that. It's a personality profile, too. It's a synopsis of who you are, what you've done, where you've been, but most importantly—what you're capable of doing in the future."

She picks up a pen and begins to edit my resume. "Here," she says. "You have clearly identified this entry level position on your resume, right? And I have no doubt that you mastered this function, but tell us a story. What's your story?"

Cinderella? Love & War? National Lampoon's Vacation?

"What were some of the problems you solved in that first job? What was the situation? How did you improve the situation, eradicate problems? And what were the results of your efforts? Situation. Action. Results," she continues. "Recruiting companies want assurance that you can identify and then successfully work through complex business situations."

I pause for a second. "Well, I identified a flaw in our client billing system—a problem in operations that was wasting time—and I eventually devised a new system for the department to use," I offer.

"Perfect!" Nicole says, excited. "What were the efficiencies? What resources did you save? You mentioned time—what about money? Let's quantify it."

"I have no idea how much money I saved the company!"

"That's okay. We can figure it out. All of the data should be truthful, but you don't have to remember every penny, you just have to prove that you can work through the thought process. Blow your own horn. Estimate the hours spent on the old system, the lost productivity, the opportunity costs, the wages, then think about the new system—hours, labor, and money saved."

"Administrative costs, too. I moved the system from paper to computer."

"Great!" She grabs the pen again and starts to write. "So let's add a bullet here to tell your story. 'Identified source of cost efficiency in $2M billing operations.' You need more numbers in your resume—it should be a nice mix of text and numbers. 'Analyzed key cost drivers to reengineer administrative process. Developed progressive technology system. Achieved X reduction in operating costs.' When you determine the savings, just replace X with the number."

God, she's good.

"Then, during your interview, if it comes up, you may want to mention the strategic implications of your story—competitive advantages, additional scale economies, value chain implications. And make sure they know that the new system you developed is still being used by the company today."

"I will." I hear myself agreeing, secretly wishing she could go with me to my interviews. You know, as my very own Tony Robbins.

"Use parallelism. And action words," she continues. I'm relieved that I'm familiar with these terms.

"You're fine," she says, looking at me, packing up her bag. "Keep up the good work. Send me the next draft of your resume and I'll proof it for you. And if you need anything, *anything at all*, please call me. Here." She gives me her card. "I want you to check in and let me know that you're okay. I know it's tough here."

'Tough' makes it sound easier than it is. I take the card. "Thanks, Nicole," I smile, thrilled to find a friend like her.

"And if interviewing gets you down—*and trust me it will*—just remember one key phrase." She puts her backpack on her shoulder. "Recite it at any time necessary before, during, or after your interview."

A secret slogan? A cure-all expression? A miracle phrase about to be revealed? "What's is it?" I plead desperately.

She pauses to smile for dramatic effect.

"SCREW THEM ALL!" she says with gusto, punching her fist toward the sky and then laughing, causing me to laugh, too.

Yes, *screw them all.*

Now, if only it were that easy…

DRESS REHEARSAL

I head to the Career Services office for my mock interview.

It's a bomb.

"Estimate the total number of gas stations in Oklahoma City," Jennifer Evers, the Assistant Director of Career Services asks me as she pretends to be a hard-nosed recruiter from a consulting company.

What a bizarre question! It has nothing to do with my professional experience or personality. I'm confused. I stare at my resume to collect my thoughts for a few seconds, then glance out the window. *Another gray, snowy day—that's a shocker.*

"Feddy?" Jennifer looks at me from across the table in her office.

"I'm sorry—I'm just not sure what the relevance of this question is?"

"Oh," she puts down my resume. "I'm sorry, I didn't realize that you've never had a consulting interview before. No problem. We'll back up a bit."

"I'm in marketing, not consulting."

"Well, sometimes the marketing recruiters will ask similar questions, so it's always good to be prepared. This type of question is very common in MBA interviews—it's simply a test of your ability to structure a logical thought process and work with numbers. It's different than the other case interviews in that it provides very little information. But don't just randomly guess an answer," she warns. "Think and work through it. If you're consistent, you'll be correct."

"You mean I should *estimate intelligently.*"

"Right—start with an estimate of the Oklahoma population…"

"Then segment it," I interrupt her, catching on. "Estimate the size of the market, the number of people, number of cars, amount of gas needed. Then estimate the amount of gas an average station can supply to a customer…" I nod repeatedly. *I know. I know.*

"Exactly!"

"Got it."

"Are you familiar with the different types of case interviews? If not, you should absolutely attend JP's career seminar tomorrow at noon in Girard. It's the classroom near the cafeteria."

Not even Wolverine could stop me from going. I need all the interviewing help I can get.

"I'll definitely attend," I assure her.

"And I saw on your resume that you conducted some marketing research at one of your previous jobs?"

"Yeah, it was just a customer satisfaction survey early in my career."

"What kind of survey? What kind of statistical model? What tracking program did you use? What were the conclusions? How did you communicate the results to the company? How did you convert the results into action? How did you apply that action? What impact did it have on the company?"

Oh boy.

"These are the types of interviewing questions you should expect," Jennifer looks at me sympathetically, then smiles. "And it's always a good idea to watch the SuperBowl commercials; you can usually expect a question or two about those during the season—what worked, what didn't."

My future depends on talking animals and girls in bikinis drinking light beer?

"Oh and before I forget, JP wanted me to let you know that your resume paper is too cheap."

I can't even get the paper selection right?

"We keep thirty copies of your resume on file. But the stock of paper you submitted to us is a lower, cheaper grade. And it shows. Recruiters won't like it. Just invest in a higher bond of paper and resubmit you resume to us," Jennifer says kindly, trying to be nice. "We just want to make sure you look good."

Nicer paper. Got it.

"Sure—absolutely. I'll buy new paper this weekend."

"Let's just call it a day for now. We can meet again next week to practice interviewing again." She hands my resume back to me with another sympathetic smile.

Harry Potter's invisibility cloak would be good right about now.

"Sounds good," I smile, grabbing my portfolio to exit her office, somewhat embarrassed because I'm sure she's just realized who the weakest candidate is in the entire history of this elite business school.

Me.

THE HOSTILE MAKEOVER

"Can you believe this propaganda? Mind numbing, pointless propaganda," Juliet Ann whispers. She's fed up with JP's career seminar, which is where we are right now. "They say our offers depend on how well we perform in the interviews, but they give us the answers to the questions beforehand. So this means our performance is actually based on acting ability? I'm confused, is this a business interview or an audition for *Days of Our Lives?*"

"Shhhh...he's on a roll," Sookie whispers back from the other side of me, barely swallowing her laughter.

JP Suavaire is speaking from the professor's podium to a packed house at his career seminar that is a cross between a pep rally and a scare tactic.

"You are fortunate because you have two choices," JP says. "One, you can *memorize* the frameworks, or two, you can have them *tattooed* onto your forearms. The choice is yours, but unless you have Popeye's arms with enough surface area to hold Rand McNally's entire collection of world maps, I suggest you either start eating your spinach...or simply opt to memorize the models," JP explains.

I still can't shake the feeling he doesn't like us.

"You should be able to recite the Five Forces in your sleep, the Value Chain under FBI interrogation, the product matrix in Latin. Mind the five P's of marketing, the three C's of strategy, and all the P's and Q's you can remember from finishing school to land a summer internship."

I hope he doesn't give us the 'if you look good, we look good' speech.

"People—it's not rocket science for NASA. It's an interview. Of course, it's a once in a lifetime interview to determine your professional destiny...true...but it's still *just* an interview."

Oh, the drama.

"And we are here to support you every step of the way..."

Here it comes.

"Because if The School looks good, you look good. And if you look good, The School looks good. What do I mean by that? If we produce the best and the brightest for the recruiters, then they'll want more. And this starts a chain of events. Recruiters will come to associate our school with the best and the brightest—that's you, presumably—and our reputation for excellence will grow strong. Likewise, your affiliation with our school will provide *you* with a reputation for being the best and the brightest. And you will earn the most coveted jobs. It's a win-win situation for everyone in the relationship."

"We're fully aware that The School has more riding on us doing well than we do. Namely monies to keep The School running..." Juliet Ann mumbles.

"So we've reviewed the different interviewing formats, you've submitted your resumes for the resume book, and you have the recruiting schedules," JP summarizes as he prepares to end the seminar. "Now, you're ready to go get that internship. (*Grab that dough!*) Participate in mock interviews, submit multiple resumes, and practice, practice, practice. No one leaves here alive without an internship. Take care and God bless."

No one leaves here alive?

Twenty students storm JP, bombarding him with questions. He appears annoyed by, but accustomed to, this routine; he masterfully shoots answers from his machine-gun mouth, silencing even the most talkative students one by one, dead in their tracks—all while barely looking up from his overhead projector. He's heard it all before, no doubt—the desperate cry of the student body trying to use him to secure the most prestigious internships.

If you think things were difficult *before* recruiting season—perhaps you were starting to relax a little thinking that the B-school stress had reached its peak—think again.

That was only the warm up.

HOMOGENEITY ROCKS

"I feel...*uncomfortable*." I squirm in my dark, wool suit and tug at my white collar as I stare in the mirror. "This isn't me. I don't feel right in these clothes." We're in my room searching for the perfect interviewing outfit.

"Your suit makes a statement, it says something," Sookie assures me.

"Yeah, it says: I'm uptight, lack creativity, and forgot to unclench my butt muscles this morning." *Not exactly the look I was going for.*

Sookie laughs. "It's not that bad. You look like everyone else now—you fit in."

"But I'm not like everyone else."

"True...but you do want a crumb of assimilation. Play the game now, and let loose later," she advises.

Conservative suits and crisp shirts in a limited palette of business-appropriate colors, perfectly polished shoes (heels not too high for fear of being considered alluring and not too flat for fear of being too diminutive), no jewelry but a classic silver watch, matronly beige pantyhose, hair rigidly slicked into a headache-causing ponytail or unremarkable chignon...this repressed femininity is stifling!

"I'm a girl!"

She twirls like a ballerina on my rug, trying to sell me her smile.

"A girl who has to dress like a man for 20 minutes, that's all," she reminds me. "It's only during recruiting season. After the interview you can crawl into your pink pajamas again."

"At this point Victorian Era inhibition would be less oppressive." I unbutton the top of my shirt to prevent spontaneous strangulation. "Or jeans and a cute tee? Or even a nice dress?"

"Is it a navy blue dress?" Sookie asks.

"No," I admit, thinking about this beautiful peach number in my closet.

She shakes her head.

"Okay, but I'm letting my hair down!" I defiantly release the tension in my elastic hair band and shake my hair loose, suddenly feeling free. "There!" I mess up my hair. "I'm keeping my hair *wild*! To remind me of my roots," I explain. "Er...no pun intended, of course."

Sookie laughs and then feigns shock by putting her hands on her cheeks and forming an "O" with her mouth. "No, not the hair! People will think you've got personality!"

"No, not that!"

I'm seriously vowing to wear something unconventional, albeit comfortable, to the interviews tomorrow—something that reflects my personality. If more people did the same then maybe it wouldn't seem so unusual—a bright color wouldn't render me un-hirable, a large necklace wouldn't label me excessive—and then we wouldn't have to look like we're going to a funeral or facing a gender identity crisis.

The whole interviewing process is more rigid than the American dating process. There's a monotonous checklist of mandatory rapid-fire talking points followed by some forced conversation. It's grueling and unrelenting and confusing...and it's over in 15 minutes. Quite anticlimactic if you consider how long it takes to get to the interview in the first place.

The process for summer internship interviewing goes something like this:

- Students submit resumes for the Career Services Resume Book that recruiting companies purchase, leaf through, and select candidates to interview from. These candidates are the elite "Closed List" group, the envy of MBAs everywhere.

- Students are provided with a list of the companies coming to campus to interview. If you would like to meet with a recruiting company, and you are <u>not</u> selected as a precious Closed List candidate, you can still secure an interview but it will cost you. You are instructed to use your "interviewing points" (each student is allotted 50 points) to "buy" an interview. The highest bidders get the interviews.

- Students aren't the only ones selling themselves. Each company describes how wonderful their organization is via a short presentation ("See Jane happy at work") before providing not only a free lunch, but also complimentary company goodies. (Cheerios from General Mills, Oreos from Kraft, Mr. Bubble bubble bath from Playtex, a six-pack of Mt. Dew from Pepsi, lotions and perfumes from Avon—it's a brand bash!)

- Bad news: The interviewing schedule will be publicly displayed (even the Closed List!) on the Career Services website each day. This means that everyone short of the Associated Press will know exactly who's interviewing when and with whom.

- If you successfully make it though the "first round" of interviewing, you will be invited back for the coveted "second round." After the second round, you may also be invited to visit the company at their corporate headquarters (but most of the wining and dining comes next year, when we begin interviewing for full-time jobs). Then, you are either accepted or rejected.

- Summer internship salaries generally range from $10,000 to $50,000. For three months of work.

Rick has prepped me a little, especially for the daily barrage of ad naseum, "Did you get Closed Listed?" inquiries from prying classmates. He didn't have a summer internship last summer (his condensed program worked throughout the summer), but he is now interviewing for a permanent position. In June, he'll graduate and start work full-time; and I'll start my summer internship. So our interviewing schedules overlap, but my interviewing process revolves around marketing (consumer product companies, food companies, advertising agencies, marketing research and marketing consulting firms) while his revolves around finance (investment banks, financial services, investment management, and corporate finance). He's also considering interviewing with consulting firms, especially

those where his financial skills can be utilized—for example, in a mergers &
acquisitions group. There's an etiquette involved, though. It's a delicate process.

There are generally three areas of recruiting:

1. Marketing

2. Consulting

3. Investment Banking/Finance

Traditionally (and I use this term loosely), more than 50% of the class accepts
offers in finance or consulting, but career opportunities are broad; there's the
technology sector, general management in manufacturing, healthcare, biotech,
and various entrepreneurial ventures. Nonprofit can apply to all the areas, if you
look hard enough. And most of your recruiting efforts will be done through the
school—on campus interviewing, recommendations from professors, and links
with the alumni network. If the economy tightens the job market, then MBAs
have to get a little creative and pursue opportunities outside of business school,
the same way mere mortals do—namely through traditional executive search
firms, online job banks, and other professional networks. There's also an inverse
correlation between B-school applications and the state of the economy, which
subsequently increases the academic competition during the down times.

JP explained that most of the job interviews are "case interviews." This simply
means you can expect the interviewer to give you a case (a description of a business quandary) similar to a real-world consulting predicament. Some of the cases
provide little information and test your logic, others test your ability to decipher
the key elements from too much detail or test your knowledge of basic business
frameworks.

Each type of case requires a unique approach, and apparently if you learn these
various approaches, you will be one step closer to a job. Career Services teaches us
how to answer the most common case questions (basically they give us the
answers). And all recruiting companies conspiratorially use the same formats, so
we just have to rehearse and deliver the goods during the interview.

The problem is, I don't know if I have the confidence or the memory to
deliver a Peoples Choice performance even though JP said it will become second
nature if I "practice, practice, practice." There are just a few things we have to
keep in mind—poise, articulation, confidence, wardrobe, friendliness, energy,
drive, sincerity, decisiveness, lifetime achievement, resume facts, personal goals,
complex business models, and the structured solutions for each type of business
case.

JP reviewed common interview questions with us today:

- *An electronics company experienced an 18% growth in sales for the last three quarters, but suffers from declining profits during that period. Why?*

- *How much money could Wendy's save by eliminating it's offering of free ketchup packets?*

- *What is the estimated value of a taxi medallion in Washington DC?*

- *How does a brokerage firm determine the number of branches it should maintain each year?*

- *What marketing-related issues should be considered before a toy company develops a new doll?*

- *Help a major flour company determine whether or not it should continue operating globally.*

- *With the given details, determine the profitability of this new line of frozen food business and the size of the market.*

- *A major publisher is considering purchasing a magazine with 40,000 subscribers. What is the value of this acquisition to the publisher?*

Now, all I have to do is follow the paint-by-numbers framework JP provided, and "practice, practice, practice" until interviewing becomes second nature.

PRACTICE MAKES IMPERFECT

I have been practicing my tush off and none of it is becoming second nature to me. It's not even third or fourth nature.

In fact, I'm one step closer to developing extra-sensory perception (ESP) as an instinct than I am to having case-interviewing come naturally to me—it's that bad.

I can't figure out if my problem is the loss of brain cells due to sleep deprivation, my inability to bullshit (gross handicap at B-school), or the overwhelming altered sense of perception I have when interviewing—as though I'm watching someone else. I either see myself failing the interview, or I feel like I'm watching a *Saturday Night Live* skit that pokes fun at my life. All of sudden, the whole experience seems so ridiculous—cookie cutter answers to questions that divulge nothing about who I am. And I still don't understanding the purpose of some of the questions; this doubt creates an unbearable temptation to just run out of the room during my interviews.

Plus, I'm forced to watch malicious classmates with low emotional intelligence ace the interviews, and to my disbelief, secure the jobs. Juliet Ann explained yesterday that it's one of the major fallacies of business school to assume that the best candidate is the one who actually gets the job—interviewing often imitates life.

My only satisfaction has been knowing that eventually the good guys do indeed land internships, slowly but surely. It's only pre-recruiting season at The School, so interviews are sparse until next term when recruiting season actually reaches its climax, but there are a few offers floating around. Sookie is the first to get an offer, but unfortunately not in Hollywood movie production—she's routinely typecast into her old profession despite her efforts to make a change, but she's vowed to keep trying. Juliet Ann is on the yellow-brick, large-firm consulting road and is inches away from an offer; she needs this top-tiered consulting experience with the big guns before she can start her own consulting firm for small businesses. "Occupational hazard," she calls it. And Rick is having a high level of interviewing success at Harvard. He's received several full-time offers from banks, money managers, and two top-tiered consulting firms. Rick says that interviewing is so competitive this year that recruiters actually ran out of rooms on campus and had to rent hotel rooms to conduct interviews. It wasn't unusual to see 50 candidates lining the hotel hallway, waiting to interview. On the plus side, Rick and I were wined and dined and pampered by one of the consulting companies trying to recruit him last Saturday night at the Copley Plaza Hotel in Boston. *Ah, the MBA life!*

Tempestt, on the other hand, is interviewing for anything under our gabled, Ivy League roof—even that Chief Technology Officer position at Enterprise Rent-A-Car in Anchorage, Alaska. Forget that she has trouble charging her cell phone, has never owned a car, and shivers when grabbing a soda from the cafeteria cooler. Qualifications (or possessing genuine interest in the job) mean little to her. It's no surprise that she hasn't found a match. "If they don't want *me* then I don't want *them!*" she chants repeatedly after each ding and then rushes back to her dorm room to meditate before her next manicure.

Fortunately, my friends feel the same way I do about interviewing and we constantly encourage one another while privately sharing our horrific interviewing chronicles. Sookie usually offers a humorous light by quoting *Wall Street*: "The main thing about money, Bud, is that it makes you do things you don't want to do."

That explains a lot.

THE DEATH OF TERM ONE (R.I.P)

Interviewing provides an unmanageable diversion from classes and other obligations in December. My life has become an overwrought noose of classes, presentations, study group meetings and interviews that is choking the life out of me.

And last week, our study group gave our final teddy bear presentation to Joannie. She shocked us by saying, "Thanks, but I've decided to move out of the toy market, and into motorcycle seats." I visualized all of our work flushing down a porcelain toilet as she proudly told us about the glamorous, fast-paced world of motorcycle seats for pets—her true passion. The professor was unforgiving (toward us, not her) despite our attempt to explain that Joannie gave us zilch to work with and wasn't focused. He pushed back saying that we could have used market data to make assumptions or approached him for help. He had a point—we weren't exactly proactive. We should have relied less on uncooperative Joannie, and more on our expertise. We passed the class but we made the other teams look like child prodigy chess champs.

Fortunately, final exams weren't as painful. Study rooms were more difficult to secure during the week prior to exams, and people seemed more grouchy than usual, but when you've been through as much as we have, exams seemed like a vacation (at a minimum security prison) this week. It was hard to muster up an ounce of interest. We were only as motivated as a patient visiting the doctor for an obligatory annual check-up: *please just do it quickly and painlessly*. But at least my study group was in the numb, post-Nelly tantrum stage, and there weren't any shockers on the anti-climactic exams; most took 2–6 hours, and two were take-home finals.

Exams, however, gave birth to a remarkable academic circle of life—completion of exams signaled the death of Term One, which in turn meant a heavenly delivery called *holiday break*. Oh God, I couldn't wait to get home for Christmas. After my last exam, I ran outside and dramatically collapsed into 14 inches of snow to make snow angels with Juliet Ann.

And that's where I am now—lying in the snow, basking in glorious relief, feeling the cold air paint my cheeks a rosy shine.

"Yeehaw!" I yell to the sky.

I'm free! I'm free!

I want to kiss the ground like a prisoner released after a long (mistaken identity/pre-DNA testing) sentence. Looking around, I'm suddenly remarkably appreciative of the beauty of nature—the ground, the trees, the wildlife…

Never, ever again will I take this for granted. I will worship nature from now on. I'll become a freaking mountain guide if I have to. I'll take hikes, photographs, learn about the trees and the baby animals, maybe even rescue a few.

I breathe in the fresh, cold air, suddenly remembering the last time I felt this exhilarated…

One year ago.

After my admissions interview.

Ha.

"Hasta la vista, Term One!" Sookie yells, running out to join us for snow angels.

Suresh throws a snowball at her from the dorm steps, hitting her smack on the top of the head. Sookie shrieks and Suresh hides behind a mound of snow.

Oh boy, this could get ugly.

"Guys, I really don't think we should—"

Crap! A wet snowball just hit my forehead.

*Well, if you can't beat 'em, join 'em…*I secure my glove and reach for a particularly large lump of fresh snow.

❄   ❄   ❄   ❄

A few days later, I head home to Arizona for holiday fun with my mom and dad who incidentally don't recognize me at the airport. "We'll fix you up in no time," they vow with concerned glances before pampering me for 15 glorious days with home-cooked food, Christmas gifts, and unconditional relaxation…

Until I reluctantly return to school in January.

RETURN TO PARADISE: TERM TWO

I could pull the fire alarm?

I'm thinking of ways to interrupt my Corporate Strategy class because I'm fairly certain that Professor Flanders is going to cold-call me within the next five minutes.

Term Two of First Year has been a whirlwind of classes and job interviews, but it has been remarkably easier because of a new study group and new classes:

- Managerial Accounting (thank God I don't have Professor Plank)
- Corporate Finance
- Global Business Policy and Strategy
- Business Law
- Online Strategy
- Advanced Communication
- Marketing Research
- Operations

Plus, I'm still floating on some residual bliss from my shocking Term One grades: *all Passes!* I thought there was a greater chance of East Antarctica defrosting than of that happening, so I'm taking a few days to revel in the small pleasure. Maybe there's hope for Term Two, after all.

Unfortunately, the old cold-calling tactics have returned for an encore.

I watch Professor Flanders pace the room as he talks about merger and acquisition strategies at Nestle.

Or I could just walk out—pretend like I'm going to the bathroom and never come back?

My thoughts are interrupted when the door flings open and a disheveled, shabbily dressed man with melting snowflakes on his hat storms into the classroom in a rage. I almost dive under the table, adrenaline rushing through my body and turning my face crimson. Everyone is stunned and scared—*what's going on?*

Professor Flanders looks frightened. *Does the intruder have a gun?*

"Do you know what you've done to me?" the intruder screams to the class.

My heart is racing.

"Where am I to go?" He holds up a pink slip. "This! This? I give you 15 years of service and you give me this? Do you know what your precious merger means to me? Do you? I'm a father, a husband, a provider—and now I am nothing. You have taken my life away from me," the intruder cries.

At this point I realize what's going on, so does most of the class. Today's case discussion delved into strategic changes that resulted in thousands of employees being laid off. We talked about the financials, the economies of scale, the leverage, but we didn't talk about the human factor.

Until now.

The distraught 'ex-employee' continues to expressively lament, touching all of us emotionally, and finally departs the room, dejected, only to return smiling a few minutes later for a round of applause after Professor Flanders explains to our class that the 'ex-employee' is really an undergraduate drama student he hired to play the part. Flanders didn't want us to forget what *really* happens in a merger, outside of the boardroom.

We spend the rest of the class, and for many of us, the rest of our careers, never forgetting the meaningful disruption.

Or his face.

MILLIONAIRE MADNESS

I lightly tap on the window and mouth the words "Help me" to the ground-skeeper as he walks past the building, crushing 14 inches of snow under his heavy boots. Unfortunately, he doesn't see me. No one is going to slip me a cake with tools baked into it.

I'm stuck here.

For the last 48 hours, we've been participating in a computer simulation strategy game monitored by real executives and management consultants who have volunteered to be our advisors. Each study group represents an executive team, and we compete against the other teams as we manage companies through years of simulated operations using strategy paradigms. At each phase of the game, extra uncertainties, crises, and conflicts are added to test our analytical skills. By the 16th hour, our group suffered an emotional meltdown.

I guess it could be worse. I could be locked in this study room with my old study group instead of my new one.

For Term Two, I'm grouped with four sharp men, all very cordial and respectful. Unfortunately, two are particularly hyper-competitive with one another and possess polar opposite business minds. Simon has a gentle, conservative approach to resolution; Joseph aggressively takes risks despite the consequences.

"You're not thinking about the suppliers," Simon rationalizes.

"It's a *game*, Simon, why not risk it all?" Joseph counters.

"It's also a test of conscience…and it's our grade."

"I'm not going to cower away from change!"

"So you want to risk productivity and profitability?" Simon asks.

"The new platform will reap those rewards! How do you expect to manage a company without taking risks?"

"I'm not afraid of making bold, educated decisions, but I refuse to purposely sabotage our revenue structure for one erratic deal!"

"Fine—we'll just keep *breaking even* until everyone dies of boredom!" Joseph yells.

So this is why the game is called Millionaire Madness.

The argument unfolds over several hours and silences the rest of us, crippling our game playing. It ends with Joseph storming out of the room, vowing to *never* return. I stifle a yawn as the Consulting Consultant (technically, that's what he is today) immediately enters our study room to offer his priceless expertise: "The show must go on," he says proudly—which is truly great advice as our team continues through the simulation for two straight days.

It's now our 48th hour of Millionaire Madness and our team is currently in last place, but at least Joseph came back to exchange humble apologies with Simon. The proud Consulting Consultant couldn't stop smiling during the reunion he facilitated. We now have five minutes before the end of the game to make a crucial business decision that will affect the entire simulated industry and seal the fate of our company.

We decide to risk it all.

❄   ❄   ❄   ❄

Our last place trophy is a consolation joke at the closing ceremony, but at least I feel good when the Consulting Consultant takes me aside and says he has seen few people in his career who hold as much emotional intelligence as I do. Read: I'm the only one in our group who didn't crack.

"I've seen worse," I say to him and wink.

If he only knew.

BUSINESSBOTS

"I'm tired of seeing women forced to act like men," Juliet Ann declares, joining us for a gab session in my room, speaking a frustration we've all felt.

"But women are the new men, haven't you heard?" Sookie jokes, putting her hands near the heater for extra warmth.

"Men are great and all, but the last time I checked I wasn't one and I can't continue to act like one. When will more women come here so I can stop acting like a man for just a few minutes?"

I push aside my Samsung case, lean back on my favorite pillow and get comfortable in the corner of my bed. Samsung will just have to wait for me to develop the perfect response to large-scale Chinese entry into the electronics industry.

"Forget the gender issue—I think we're all just turning into emotionless MBA robots clad in dark suits! Only our hair is more severe than our expressions."

Sookie stands and stiffens her arms, waddling across my room like Robot from *Lost in Space.* "Look at me," she says methodically. "I can answer 60 complex business questions in 45 seconds…I'll be your VP in two years…danger, danger!"

Juliet Ann and I crack up before she contemplates, "Hmm…a robot that obeys all commands and basically does the work no one else wants to do?"

"Hey—just like us!" Sookie laughs, returning to her seat on my bed.

"Businessbots," I joke. "That's what we are." I open a bakery box of egg-custard tarts, pineapple buns, and sesame balls sitting on top of my mini-fridge (Chinese desserts left over from The School's Chinese New Year celebration yesterday).

"I really don't want to act like a robot to continue to succeed in business," Juliet Ann admits.

"Think of it as a stepping stone," I offer, reminding her of the advice that both she and Sookie have dispensed repeatedly to me when needed. "How can business truly represent you if you don't participate in it? You have to be part of the system before you can change it."

Sookie shrugs her shoulders. "I can see why women don't want to be in business—my mentor told me that she was mistaken for a prostitute at a business meeting in Asia a few years ago. Granted it was a small town, but still…she was asked to sit in another room while 'the men' conducted business." Sookie jumps abruptly from the bed. "Almost forgot! Bye, gals! Gotta run." She grabs her back backpack and heads toward the door. "Suresh and I are working on a strategy for a leveraged buyout. It's due tomorrow."

"Bye!" I call out. "Have fun with Suresh." I wink at her knowingly, but her frown, forces me to contritely add, "Just kidding."

Once she's gone, I turn to Juliet Ann. "I feel your pain. I'm sick of the MBA stereotype, sick of playing businessman…"

"When do women get to change the dynamic at business school rather than conform to it?" Juliet Ann says. "It's changing, and thankfully there's progress, but I want it to move faster and stronger."

"Young women have an aversion to business—"

"It's not just business school," she continues. "Careers are still modeled after those of males who have wives to care for the children and home. It's certainly not an equal playing field."

Where are the women?

"I guess I don't understand why women would be willing to sacrifice their financial freedom? It's the power to do anything you want, whenever you want."

"When can we just *be ourselves*, irregardless of gender, without the pressure of having to fit into an undemonstrative stereotype?" Juliet Ann continues her thoughts.

"Again, when more women come here."

FRANKENSTEIN MBAs

The next day, I face my own demons.

"How did the interview go?"

"Did you make it to the second round?"

"Did they offer you the job?"

"How many people got offers from that company?"

"Did you accept the offer?"

"What's the summer salary?"

"What city are they putting you in?"

"What brand will you be working on?"

"Why on earth do you want to work for them?"

They've cornered me in the mailroom. I was innocently getting my mail, casually leafing through my L.L. Bean catalog, when a classmate standing next to me asked one simple question that eventually led to a bombardment of questions from others about my interviewing status. They're not just curious, they're judging. They're not just ill-mannered, they're ruthless. They're not just classmates, they're monsters. And they're coming at me from everywhere, surrounding me in a tight semi-circle. I lean my back against the wall of metal mailboxes, trying to escape. "Please, I just want to get my mail in peace. I mean you no harm!" I plead, frightened, but the questions continue. Their faces are now only inches from mine and I can feel the heat from their breath as they fire questions. I have no place to go. There are 5, 10, 15, 20 of them now. Hoping to crawl away, I slide down to the floor.

I'm on the ground now, but I still can't go anywhere. I just sit in a defeated heap on the floor, while they continue to yell.

"Why did she get the offer?"
"She doesn't even know how many gas stations are in Oklahoma!"
"Did you hear she actually talked about toilet paper during an interview?"
"And she thought the Value Chain was a discount menu at McDonald's!"
"Interviewing against her for a job is like interviewing against Homer Simpson!"

Ha! Hahahahahahaha! Hahahahahahahaha. They continue to laugh as I look up at them helplessly while their faces crowd over me. Nelly, Bo, Cooper, Chakira, Bradley, Dean, and countless others. Wait—is that Professor Haven in the group? And JP Suavaire? And...*the cafeteria cook?* What's *he* doing here? Their laughs grow louder. I cover my ears. Please make it go away! I can't breathe. I've got to get out of here...

Beep Beep Beep Beep Beep.

My alarm clock goes off.

I wake up from the nightmare, instantly jolting upright in bed. I look around the room. I'm alone, warm and safe in my own cot.

Sweet relief—it was just my egocentric paranoia.

There are no evil classmate monsters suffocating me with nosey questions.

Or are there?

WHAT HAPPENS ON SPRING BREAK STAYS ON SPRING BREAK

While some of us are still slaving over the interviewing process, Rick is caught in an enviable mountain of offers and facing his toughest decision: choosing the right job.

So many job offers, so little time.

"I've developed a spreadsheet model," he confesses.

I raise my eyebrows.

"And...a decision tree," he hesitantly adds.

I don't say anything.

"What?" he asks defensively, knowing what I'm thinking. "They're viable tools!" he justifies. "We use them for business decisions so why shouldn't I use them for major life choices?"

A spreadsheet to help him chose a job?

"Well...did it help?" I ask.

"In a scientific, unemotional way, yes..." He laughs.

"You could factor in utility?" I suggest, doubtfully. *If western mathematical principles can't solve it, maybe there's no hope...*

"I did—but I'm still not happy with the outcome. All signs point to taking a job in investment banking, but I can't get James's idea out of my head, despite the risk."

Rick and I have talked endlessly about the possibility of Rick starting a new company with James. Over the past few months, Rick has divulged all the details to me—the proposal is for an internet company that focuses on online personality tests. Customers take tests—some for fun or entertainment, some for legitimate evaluation, like an IQ test—and marketers can use the data to target advertising. James wants to start raising money for the company now; he needs Rick's answer in a few days. James has offered Rick the role of Chief Financial Officer and Co-Founder.

"Why wouldn't you do it?" I encourage him. "No obligations, no responsibilities, perhaps now's the time to take risks? 10 years down the road you may not be able to," I remind him.

We've had this conversation every day for the last week.

"True..." He runs his hands through his hair. "And when I come back from Spring Break, I'll have my final answer—I'll have time to think. And then James and I can discuss venture capital."

Spring Break!

An oasis of academic amnesty granted to both undeserving and deserving academics alike—a timely buoy in the overwhelming scholastic sea.

Rick is literally sailing away tomorrow to St. Thomas with seven classmates.

Unfortunately, my Spring Break doesn't overlap with Rick's this March. I'll be heading home to Arizona when he returns from St. Thomas. Most of my classmates will be traveling the world—sailing the British Virgin Islands, climbing Kilimanjaro, discovering the rainforests of Central America, hiking in Machu Picchu, and trekking through African safaris.

I, however, will be escaping to a treasured sanctuary so vital that my very existence depends on it: my bedroom.

Not even a kiss from a handsome prince will be able to wake me from the deep slumber on my comfy, gingham bedspread in the suburbs. Not too exciting, I know, but I have to listen to my body. And right now it's sending me a Code-Red-Emergency signal to get some rest and relaxation before it collapses.

Rick and I talk for hours about his career decision. He seems tired—probably from his daily 5 a.m. crew sessions, which he loves despite the unfathomably chilly morning sessions on the Charles River. I tell him some good news: Juliet

Ann and Ashton patched things up. Apparently Aaron Jeffries gave her some great advice, "Don't do anything," and that seemed to work.

"We just took a step back," Juliet Ann explained to me last week. "Aaron was right, we needed to get back to the basics. Business school is only temporary, so we're not going to stress out about it anymore. We just reminded ourselves that we're two people—completely whole and independent—who choose to be together because we enjoy one another. We're best friends with tremendous respect for one another and we don't want to lose that."

The way I see it, if a relationship can survive business school—the long distance, the frustration, the time constraints, the temptation, the relocation—it will ultimately grow stronger in its ability to survive at least 50% of what life has to offer.

And I didn't need a spreadsheet to figure that out.

DOUBLE SECRET PROBATION

Oh boy, are we in trouble. Recruiting season isn't going so well and The School is on a tirade. JP has called a special meeting in Holt Auditorium for all First Years.

"Are you trying your best?" JP rants. "Look in the mirror tonight, if you can, and ask yourself, *Am I trying my best*? In fact, look at your neighbor right now and ask, *Are you trying your best*?"

No one moves.

"Or," JP continues, "are you *purposely* trying to sabotage your chances for success?"

Yeah, sure, I'm purposely trying to sabotage my chances for an internship. I've invested six figures, sacrificed family and relationships, endured endless nights of stress, and forgone two years in a rapidly evolving career to purposely screw up an internship opportunity. You caught me!

"Have we not prepared you for the interviewing process? Have we not trained you? Do you not have all the tools you need?" JP yells.

Sounds like somebody's cranky and needs a nap...

"Here is the list of complaints I have received most recently from recruiters." JP pulls an index card from his jacket. "*Students smelled like smoke or perfume, students look sleepy, students not prepared, student wore white socks...*" he continues reading from a list, pausing only to glance at us with a raised eyebrow.

White socks?

I don't know what's worse—that a student would wear white socks, or that a recruiter would list that as a complaint.

JP continues to rant and when he finally asks what he can do to increase our enthusiasm, everyone complains about the unbearable workload.

"How about a little sleep?"

"And who has time to prepare for interviews?"

"We're running on empty!"

"Thees is reediculous!" Chakira shouts. "I smoke—so I smell like smoke. I get nervous so I smoke. But my performance is good. Even with no sleep and all the stress, I do well."

"The professors aren't helping," someone else calls out.

"I agree. The academic work appears to be increasing during the recruiting season, not decreasing. So each day it's a struggle—do the homework but risk a flawed interview, or prepare for the interview but risk a failing grade."

"The professors will not cut us slack!"

I speak loudly from the back of the room. "I don't know what the procedure was in the previous years, but this year they've added two or three courses to the First Year schedule—but that doesn't necessarily guarantee that the administration and faculty have properly adjusted the workload to accommodate for these new classes."

"They've just added more courses to our schedule, but haven't reduced the assignments!" Sookie agrees.

"There just isn't any *time* to prepare for interviews."

"Forget about preparing for interviews, most of us can't stay awake in class."

More people chime in and the lecture becomes an open forum. *Revolt of the masses!* Surprisingly, our complaints work—JP appears sympathetic.

"Okay," JP finally agrees. "Most of you have looked peaked lately…I'll talk to the faculty."

I guess the 'you look good, we look good' mentality finally worked. In the weeks following the discussion with JP, the professors seem to lighten up. Of course, for them, lightening up is equivalent to the Queen of England selecting biscuits instead of scones at teatime. But still, point noted. And the Career Services Office increases the frequency of the motivating emails to the students, reminding us of what a fantastic job we are doing and giving us the outstanding placement statistics.

And then it happened.

I got an offer.

WHO, ME?

I had finally made peace that my professional destiny did not include an internship, but I never gave up. I just relaxed a little. In fact, it was actually when I stopped stressing out about it that the first opportunity came. And once you have the security of one offer in your pocket, it improves your performance in other interviews and the offers start rolling in.

Well, in my case, they didn't exactly *roll* in (it was more like a slow crawl), but I received a couple, nonetheless.

What really helped was Rick. One of his classmates worked for an advertising agency and offered to secure a marketing position for me after our phone interview. Another one of his classmates recently accepted an operations position for a major theme park and offered to 'see what she could do,' if I was interested. The security of these potential opportunities gave me confidence. I just relaxed a little knowing that I had potential leads.

But nothing truly diminished the sickening, mounting anticipation of waiting to hear back from a company—the thick tension that grew tight in my stomach as I dialed my voicemail to hear the verdict from a recent interview, or my fingers quivering as time stood still when I opened an email from a company recruiter, knowing that one call or one email would change my fate. And each day I had to relieve the chaotic, emotional bundle of anxiousness and nerves, infinitely rising and falling through my system, wreaking havoc on my body. Waiting for the verdict was almost as stressful as the interview itself.

Almost.

Except for an interview like the one I have today with a premier global giant.

I walk into the Kingsbury-Kutter interview wearing my best suit. The recruiter, Justin Gonzalez, is a handsome man in his mid-thirties, dressed in a blue button-down shirt and khakis. *No powersuit? Nice!* I like it better when the interviewers appear in human form.

"Hi, Mr. Gonzalez," I say, firmly shaking his hand with direct eye contact (another Hostile Makeover tactic).

"Call me Justin. And please excuse me—I caught a cold on the flight over here."

I like that he has a cold. I mean, I don't *like* that he has a cold, but I like that he's confident admitting he has a cold. In business, some consider it a weakness to admit so much as a sniffle. I appreciate his humility, and the cold doesn't distract from his sharpness during the interview. Such poise must come with experience.

"Tell me what you know about our company." He leans back and spreads his arms.

MBA interviews don't start with expected questions like, "Tell me about yourself," or "What are your strengths?" They're much trickier and usually get right to the gut-wrenching punch. And even my answers to seemingly innocent questions will be under intense psychological scrutiny.

I remember to breathe before I spill my knowledge of the company. Located in the Midwest, Kingsbury-Kutter is the royalty of packaged-dessert companies, the biggest in the world with over $7 billion in retail sales each year. Frozen, ready-to-eat, shelf mix, foodservice, you name it, they've baked it. And if you've been in a grocery store, recently baked a cake, had lunch on an airplane, dined in a cafeteria, grabbed a snack at a convenience store, or used the basement vending machine—you've eaten Kingsbury-Kutter. They're king of the yummy kingdom of sweet, delicious, baked goods from which childhood memories are made.

I talk about their competitors: General Mills, Pillsbury, and Nabisco; Hostess, Little Debbie, and Entenmann's, among many others in each segment. Abbreviation is critical because Kingsbury-Kutter has three major lines of business, each one worthy of its own discussion. I have to strike an intricate balance—keep it simple but touch on the key points of each line.

"Tell me how you would improve the marketing of our new Butterscotch Truffle Brownie."

Good thing I eat those rich suckers.

I rattle off an answer, carefully offering improvements without insulting their current process or marketing. *Don't let him trap me.* It's too easy to accidentally mention my opinion on another issue or product, thereby giving spark to a fire of new questions. Recruiters can jump on those opportunities. I answer directly, leaving little room for deviation to unexpected topics. He catches me off-guard twice, but I'm able to recover. He tests my marketing knowledge, my financial acumen with a quantitative breakeven analysis, my strategic vision, my knowledge of the industry, and then selects key points from my resume upon which to drill. Recruiters are usually specific, so it's pertinent to know everything on your resume. You absolutely must be able to expand on every bullet point. *Situation, action, results.* And sometimes they'll throw you a curve ball and challenge the business decisions you've boasted about on your resume. If you increased corporate sales by one million, they'll argue, "Why not two million?" They don't truly disagree with your decisions, but they want to hear the rationale behind your actions, and they want to see the fire in your eyes as you talk about it. They also want assurance that you want to work for them, and only them, but it's important not to shame other companies in the process. *Strike a balance in all of your moves, anticipating the opponent's next move.*

I'm more impressed with Justin than he probably is with me. I respect that he didn't go through the canned interview process, but chose an integrated approach to get a better picture of my personality; I've dedicated my life to marketing—I'm not playing games. He smiles when we say goodbye.

I don't have a great feeling, but I have a *good* feeling, and at this point that's success.

✳   ✳   ✳   ✳

The following week, I learn that one of my classmates, Blanchard Fong, received the offer from Justin. She's great, but the irony is that she interviewed with Kingsbury-Kutter on a whim. She's not even seeking a marketing job; she's trying to leave marketing to pursue consulting. "Career switching" becomes a sport when the market it tough: I-bankers take consulting jobs, consultants take marketing jobs, and some take anything they can get.

But a few days later I receive a surprise phone call from Justin.

"Hi Feddy, this is Justin Gonzalez. From Kingsbury-Kutter?"

I'm a little groggy this morning because there was yet another lounge party last night and the music rocked my room until 3 a.m. Plus, Rick and I spent Saturday night in Newport, Rhode Island, at another Harvard Business School function—the annual Newport Ball at the RoseCliff mansion. And while lying in bed this morning, I desperately tried to finish a Factory Physics assignment on capacity planning, throughput rates, and cycle times for a Tapioca plant in Singapore.

"Hi Justin, how are you?" I manage to compose my professional courtesy. *Justin!?*

"Do you have few minutes?"

And a lifetime.

"Absolutely! I'm heading to class, but I have 15 minutes."

"Great, because I wanted to talk to you about the Assistant Marketing Manager internship…you may have heard that we offered the position to one of your classmates?"

"Yes, Blanchard."

"Right! She had experience marketing consumer food products, which, as you can imagine, is valuable to this role."

"She's a great candidate, I'm sure." *Is he looking for more reassurance of Blanchard's perfect candidacy? It's quite humiliating.*

"Yes, she is, but I was really impressed by you, too. Your experience wasn't as extensive, but your personality is perfect for our corporate culture."

Oh, now I get it. How nice is this? He's calling to explain why I didn't get the offer. I'm impressed—he didn't have to do that.

"Thanks, Justin. It was a pleasure to meet you, too. Kingsbury-Kutter was my first choice, so of course I was disappointed, but thanks for the interviewing opportunity."

"Well, that's what I'm calling about. Would you still be interested in working for us?"

What?

"Of course," I answer with questioning hesitation.

"Blanchard has declined our offer. You were next on our list, so I'm calling to offer you the position. The summer internship is yours—if you're still interested?"

Still interested? Is the Archbishop interested in becoming the Pope?

Okay, now I know I should be the consummate professional, thank him for his confidence in me, and then ask for time to consider the offer.

But I don't want to play games, and I already know the salary range, and I just told him that Kingsbury-Kutter was my first choice, so I can't very well act aloof. Technically it was offered to someone else first, which is yet another blow to my ego, but I have to keep what's left of my pride in check. The experience of this particularly prestigious internship will be incredibly valuable to my career; no one will care about my runner-up status. At the end of the day, it's all the same on your resume. This is an extraordinary opportunity to work with one of the best companies in the world, doing what I love with smart, genuine, Midwestern folks; and Justin is so nice.

I'm so freaking ecstatic I can hardly contain myself.

"Yes!"

"Great! It's not official until you sign the papers. I'll FedEx them. I know you have to go to class now, so I'll call you tomorrow to discuss the details of the position—salary, perks, logistics, etcetera." I can tell he's smiling through his voice, probably happy that I'm so happy.

"Perfect."

"How about 12:30 your time then?" he asks and I agree. "If you choose not to accept the position, we are not going to offer it to anyone else. We knew we were going to offer you the job, but I thought you might like to know that Blanchard also recommended you for the position when I last spoke with her."

How nice! I congratulated Blanchard yesterday—while sitting at a management innovation lecture—and told her how much I had wanted to work for Kingsbury-Kutter. She must have passed along the info. *Sweet!*

"Justin—thanks so much for everything. Really."

"We're glad to have you. I think you'll like it here."

"I'm sure I will!" I burst.

"Well, review the terms first. And we'll talk soon," he says with a little laugh. My glee is contagious.

After we say good-bye, I immediately call Rick as I sprint to class.

His voicemail greets me. "Hi, this is Rick, I'm not available right now but please leave your message…"

"Rick!!" I yell into the phone. "I got it! Call me! I got an offer from Kingsbury-Kutter! I'm a summer int—"

Beeeeep.

Oops, I spoke before the beep? No problem, I have plenty of enthusiasm to repeat myself. "Rick!! Guess what?" I yell into the phone again, leaving a complete message. We'll talk tonight, I'm sure. I can't wait to share my excitement with him. And with my Mom & Dad. And with my classmates. And with the media. And with the entire freaking world. Yahoo!

Finally.

A glimmer of hope in this dark business school world.

For the first time, I smile all the way to class.

BETRAYAL BY JOB OFFER

I walk over to Juliet Ann's room, only to find her sitting on her bed, furiously whispering to Sookie, who is sitting in a chair, and to Tempestt, who is sitting on the floor in one of her many Hatha yoga poses.

"Stay calm. Learn from his mistake," Tempestt offers in her wiser-than-thou voice. "Then tell him to screw off!"

"What's going on?" I ask taking a seat on the floor next to Sookie, thinking this pertains to Juliet Ann's recent McKinsey interview.

Sookie grabs my arm and whispers, "Al Wheelen stole a job from Juliet Ann!"

"What?" *How does one steal a job?*

"I was offered an internship at Bagger Hampton in Boston," Juliet Ann speaks with a tired voice. Bagger Hampton isn't the typical MBA playground—it's a full service marketing and creative agency. "The people I interviewed with were incredible—friendly, smart, genuine. They won me over and I was seriously considering accepting the internship, even though it wasn't consulting. But I wasn't sure."

"Of course not. You wanted to take some time to think about it." I understand. Most students don't accept immediately.

"Exactly! I wanted to weigh the pros and cons, do my own personal SWOT (strengths/weaknesses/opportunities/threats), and then maybe visit their headquarters. Or at least talk with more people from Bagger before I committed," she explains diplomatically.

"Absolutely!"

"No one really knows much about them, they're new to the recruiting circuit—everyone is still trying to feel them out," Sookie assures.

"Well, I made the mistake of talking to Al. I didn't think anything of it, we're friends. I told him about my offer. And I told him about my thought process, my hesitation."

"Oh no," I say, recognizing where this is going.

"Yep. I didn't know that he wanted to work for Bagger, so I underestimated his competitiveness."

"Competitiveness isn't the right word," Sookie says. "It's jealousy."

"Anyway, he actually *called* Bagger," Juliet Ann says to me. "And he told the head recruiter that I *wasn't really interested* in the position, that I *wasn't committed*, that I was undecided, blah blah blah, and that *he*, however, was indeed very committed and would accept the job *immediately* if offered."

"No!" I'm disgusted.

"Uh huh."

"Desperate and pathetic," Tempestt says, stretching her right arm above her head.

"What happened? Did they give him the job? And how did you find out?"

"He told me! He came to me last night and said, 'I know you'll find out sooner or later, but I wanted to let you know that I called Bagger today,' and he told me the whole story. I didn't know what to say."

"He told you because he knew you'd find out."

"Or the Shakespearean-like guilt was driving him mad."

"I never trusted that guy," I say. "Last week, I caught him reading my email when I left my laptop unattended in the study lounge."

"No!" Sookie and Juliet Ann shriek.

I nod vigorously. "Caught him red-handed, sitting at my computer, reading a personal email."

"You didn't say anything?" Tempestt asks.

"It happened so fast, and it wasn't until after he left that I realized what had happened. The people here never cease to amaze me—I just chalked it up to yet another crappy thing from the soulless student body. Nothing phases me."

"I know what you mean. In the real world, this behavior would shock you, but here…well, it's somewhat common," Juliet Ann says sadly. She's disappointed in Al.

"Did you talk to Bagger?" I ask.

"They called me this morning—I've become pretty friendly with one of the recruiters, Leslie, and she called me this morning on the hush hush. She was professional and friendly, but her whole attitude was just—*what in the world is going on over at your school?* She couldn't believe that another classmate would do that. She assured me that my offer still stood firm, and that they had removed Al's name from their candidate list. They wouldn't consider hiring someone like him."

"That's good."

"Yeah, but I'm just shaken up. I don't even want to look at him."

"Then don't," Tempestt orders. "Mind your business, go on with your life, ignore him. He doesn't deserve your attention. He's harmed you and our school's reputation," she says.

"Or forgive him," I add. "Understand why he did what he did—he's insecure and desperate. An internship means more to him than personal relationships? He's pathetic, but we can't expect people to not make mistakes—that's unreasonable. Learn from his mistake, but don't torment yourself. Forgive him. You'll feel better."

"Yeah," Juliet Ann says, dejected. "I'll forgive him. Then ignore him. But I can't forget." She pauses. "Who the hell can you trust at this place?"

We look at each other but say nothing.

LADIES AND GENTLEMEN, ELVIS HAS LEFT THE BUILDING

I choke on my Cajun crawfish (it's New Orleans night in the dining hall) when I open the letter from Kingsbury-Kutter explaining the details of my impending internship.

Is this a typo?

The summer salary is more than I made in six months at my last job!

I frantically stuff the letter into my backpack when I see Tempestt approaching the table.

"What are you blushing about?" Tempestt eyes me suspiciously as she places her tray next to mine and takes a seat.

No more student loans, a new car, fabulous gifts for my family, a new library at The School named after me...

"The Crawfish is really good," I say, nodding vigorously.

She throws me a dubious glance, but drops it when Sookie and Suresh arrive. "I won't miss this place—New York can't come soon enough!" Tempestt grunts. She's heading to Calvin Klein for the summer to work as a strategist. "First, a full spa day at Bliss 57 with a deep sea detox, oxygen blast, and a ginger rub massage. Then, dinner at Shun Lee. I can almost *taste* the steamed lobster with garlic....mmmmm..." She closes her eyes.

There's no place like home. There's no place like home.

"And don't forget Marguerite's party. It's that first weekend we arrive," Juliet Ann reminds her, taking a seat next to Sookie.

Tempestt and Juliet Ann will be living together in NYC for the summer. After much deliberation, Juliet Ann finally accepted an internship at Bain & Company, thereby marking her debut into the consulting world and putting her one baby-step closer to launching her boutique consultancy. Sookie is heading to California to work as a Marketing Associate directly for a Vice President at Walt Disney Studios. Both Juliet Ann and Sookie accepted pay-cuts from their pre-business school salaries, but think it's a small price to pay to follow their professional dreams. *Pay-cuts!? How much were they making before B-school?*

Aaron Jeffries will be a Brand Manager for Tide laundry detergent at Procter & Gamble in Cincinnati, Ohio. And Suresh will continue in private equity at the London office of Lehman Brothers after a three-week independent field study in Nepal with Sookie, who is coincidentally also enrolled in the field study program.

The School offers nonprofit international field studies in more than 25 countries; it's a chance for students to spend three weeks of summer studying overseas markets while consulting for international nonprofits. The assignments include: creating an operations plan for a hospital in Africa, restructuring administration at a national park near Mount Everest, developing programs to introduce students to social entrepreneurship in Warsaw, or creating a strategy for business expansion into the United Kingdom. Sookie and Suresh will be in Katmandu helping a children's hospital find resources to serve the poor.

"I passed on the field study thing," Tempestt says. "Students had to write a marketing plan for Gobar in Delhi last summer, so no thanks."

"Gobar?" Sookie asks.

"It's one of India's most valuable resources!" Suresh answers. "It's used as fuel."

"It's *cow dung*," Tempestt reveals flatly. "No thank you." She pinches her nose in disgust. "Eww!"

I think of the Buddha shrine in her dorm room and her daily meditations for world peace and inner harmony. *So much for her quest for enlightenment.*

"How was Rick's graduation?" Juliet Ann asks, reaching for a saltshaker.

Sookie cracks a crawfish shell. "Oh that's right, it was last weekend!" she says excitedly. "Tell us *everything*…"

"It was incredible!" I gush. "Spectacular. Amazing. Outdoors on a beautiful, sunny day," I say between attempts to eat my crawfish. "The ceremony only took two hours, but I got to spend quality time with his family. And Alan Greenspan was the commencement speaker…"

"Wow!" Sookie blurts out.

"I know—and the reception was elegant under enormous white tents. They served green mango and cashew salad, and shrimp with avocado salsa. And cohort competitiveness seemed under control for the day, which is always nice."

"What did Rick decide to do for a job?" Suresh asks, placing an extra piece of Cajun cornbread on Sookie's plate. "I know you like this stuff," he says to her.

"Big news!" I scream.

"Rick decided to start his own business?" Sookie asks excitedly, and then quickly whispers to Suresh about the cornbread, "Thanks, I'll eat it later."

"Yes! He's starting his own business!"

"Congratulations!" Sookie squeals.

"Good choice!" Suresh says, smiling. "I didn't think he'd do it—but I'm glad he did. Tell him he's an inspiration to us all."

"Me, too." Juliet Ann nods. "Good for him!"

"Does he know how difficult it is to start a business?" Tempestt retorts. "Only 2% are successful."

Everyone groans.

"Entrepreneurship is an opportunity," Juliet Ann assures. "It's an exploration. And for some, it's a gift. Why shouldn't he try it now?"

"It's a calculated risk, not an imprudent one," Suresh agrees.

I wipe my hands from the buttery oil. "That's how we felt. This is a point in his life when he has the resources, the network, the education, and the opportunity. If you think about it, it's less of a risk right now than it will be at any other point in his life—especially with a family or mortgage in the future."

"That's what business school is about—opening doors for chances of a lifetime," Sookie agrees.

So Rick is going to be an entrepreneur.

He's not going to be a consultant or an investment banker—he'll be working with James, after all. Sure, it's bold, but why have it any other way? It's certainly the most surprising decision, that's for sure—this opportunity wasn't even a seed of thought before business school. Now, he's working with James to build a viable revenue model and secure their first round of funding.

After two hours of New Orleans crawfish and chatter, my friends and I finally say our goodbyes for the summer. It's officially over. I just slaved through my last excruciating First Year final exam; and I even found a minute yesterday to say goodbye and congratulations to my favorite Second Years, Kurt, my tutor, and Nicole, my mentor, who are graduating and heading to Chicago and Georgia respectively for consulting jobs. I reminded them that I couldn't have survived First Year without them, hugged them for too long, and then promised to keep in touch.

Now it's just goodbye to my own classmates and I'm done.

After dinner, Sookie and I share a Watery Eye Syndrome moment saying goodbye; Juliet Ann and I can't stop hugging. Suresh promises to keep in touch. Tempestt explains that it's nothing personal, but she'll be "extremely busy" this summer and we shouldn't expect to hear from her too often unless she needs something. This makes me tear up even more.

There's also a powerful, residual sentiment amongst us from sharing this life-changing experience. We're emotionally exhausted, but relieved—proud of the accomplishment, but honestly just glad the most grueling and terrifying academic year of our lives is dead. And now, as the disbelief evaporates, we can finally relish the long-awaited finale.

First Year is over.

I made it.

I actually did it.

I don't know who's more shocked: me, the faculty, the administration, my friends, my classmates, Rick, my family, or the Channel 7 News Team—but without realizing it, by God, I seem to have miraculously made it through First Year!

Back in Butler Hall, Room #121, I zip my suitcase and shut the window in the now-vacant room. I close the door for the last time, smiling as I glance back, hoping for a wave of pleasant nostalgia to flow over me.

Nope.

Nothing.
Except peace.
It's over. I'm ready to move on. And there's no way in hell I'd do it again.

❄   ❄   ❄   ❄

That night I board my flight and head west.
Midwest, that is.

SECOND YEAR

CHAPTER 9

※

RISK VS. REWARD

(A Whole New World: Second Year Splendor)

I sit on the old couch, pick up the nearest magazine, and flip through 20 pages of glossy advertisements for five minutes before I toss it onto the coffee table and turn on the T.V. I channel surf, stopping at only the most outrageous programs, until I hear the microwave beep summoning me to the kitchen— my lunch is ready. I return to the couch to eat my lasagna in peace until my next class. My work is done for today. I know exactly what meetings I have tonight; and everything is in its place. I even know what I'm doing this weekend, and it's actually something I may enjoy.

I stop eating.

T.V, a magazine, weekend plans…and peace?

What in the world is going on?

Oh yeah…

I think it might be this wonderful thing they call Second Year.

HOT FUN IN THE SUMMERTIME

Viva la internship! I had one of the best summers of my life. Kingsbury-Kutter treated me like a queen. First, they housed me in a beautiful high-rise apartment (rent included!) smack in the middle of the city. Then, my days were spent eating cake and attending professional events. ("Let them eat cake!" I always like to say.)

KK assigned me to the Cakes Division, and my summer job was to launch a new cake product.

Yep.

Cake.

I walked through the door into a whole new world of caloric cake and cookie tastings. Imagine my surprise the first week when the VP of Marketing, Jeb, took me to the "KK Kitchens," an entire floor of conference rooms converted into workable kitchens. The cooks stationed in the kitchens had the sole responsibility each week of baking new concoctions developed by marketing. We walked into a "kitchen" and I saw 30 batches of cookies sitting on the table.

Heaven!

"Take one cookie from each batch, taste it, swallow it or spit it into a cup, and then choose your favorites," Jeb instructed me. "We're looking for the ultimate mix of chocolate chips in a cookie. We'll test the cakes this afternoon."

I put on my most serious face and carefully crunched a peanut butter chocolate chip cookie.

Mmm...delicious.

I gave Jeb an approving nod. Quite honestly, I didn't think there was such a thing as a bad cookie, so perhaps I wasn't the best judge.

And why would anyone ever spit it out? In fact, I might have another.

We progressed to chocolate chip butterscotch, chocolate chip oatmeal, chocolate chip fudge...and 25 cookies later, in a frantic mouth-stuffing scene that would rival Lucille Ball at the candy conveyor belt, I suddenly felt queasy.

"Why don't you head back," Jeb suggested. "You're looking a little pale."

"Right." I nodded. "Excuse me."

Billy, a fellow Assistant Marketing Manager who joined us at the tasting, laughed as I ran out of the kitchen. "You didn't actually *eat* all of those cookies, did you?"

"No! Of course not!" I called to him.

Inhaled is more like it. Where's the bathroom?

I was sick for the first two days of my internship, but that didn't stop me from plowing through the program.

The summer was an interesting melting pot of various top-tier MBA interns from around the world, living, socializing, and working together. The well-oiled Kingsbury-Kutter machine dedicated an entire internal team to expertly develop our summer internship program. Every night, there was a party, concert, fashion show, art exhibit, or extravagant social gathering for the interns. In addition, the company awarded all employees with Friday afternoons off, free breakfasts every other Monday, and a beautiful corporate headquarters with two cafeterias, a salon, a small store, and a gas station in the parking lot! It was also interesting to note that the group of interns reflected the usual cast of lovable business school personalities: Attila the Hun, Einstein, Little Hitler, Bill Gates, American Psycho, Mother Theresa, Queen Elizabeth, Martin Luther King, Jr., and the regular Ivy League types I like to refer to as "The Skulls." So I really didn't have to worry about missing the old bunch from school—they were born again as Kingsbury-Kutter interns.

Jeb was fantastic to work for—so brilliant—and he championed me through the work; I learned about volume forecasting, ACNielsen, competitive research, and worked directly with the advertising agency, DDB in Chicago, to develop a new TV commercial for cupcakes. Jeb also gave me some valuable advice: *The best managers are the ones who spend the entire day networking with colleagues, talking about their business. They know everything that's going on.* It seemed like pretty reasonable advice so I spent my summer days talking to everyone from VPs to shelf stockers about my cake business and how to improve it.

To my surprise, I used quite a bit of my B-school knowledge (who knew?), especially marketing and strategy. And executives were frequently accessible—Kingsbury-Kutter arranged for the interns to have lunch with the CEO, and Jeb and I went to a barbeque at the Vice President's lake house. Most importantly, and I don't mean to sound hokey here, the people were just so *incredibly nice.* I didn't want the summer to end; but eventually Kingsbury-Kutter chartered a boat during our final week and sent us on a farewell cruise with champagne and lobster. The summer was sweet perfection. Well, compared to First Year it was.

And on an exciting note, Rick's world had officially rocked.

We talked every day over the summer. In June, Rick and James moved into an apartment together in Boston, christened the company with a name (Emode) and recruited local MIT graduates to join the company, bringing the head count to an impressive 17 employees. Rick did everything from scoping out office space in Cambridge during the day, to building a business plan with James into the wee hours of the night. But he loved it—I had never seen him that excited—especially because Emode had secured $9 million in venture capital. I couldn't even fathom that much money. It came mostly from a Series A round with August Capital, a few angel investors, and even Harvard professors and psychologists who believed in the company enough to invest in it. In July, Rick and I spent a weekend in nearby Chicago celebrating his new business venture and the arrival of my final First Year grades—all Passes with one High Pass!

The fabulous summer days of extravagant Kingsbury-Kutter parties and delicious cake tastings flew.

10 pounds and three cavities later, the summer came to an end.

PUTTIN' ON THE RITZ

So far, Second Year is off to a phenomenal start. Sookie and I have secured the luxury penthouse of graduate school living!

Figuratively speaking, of course.

It's actually the top floor of a prehistoric duplex owned by the Catholic Student Center. Neither of us is affiliated with the church next door, but I plan to be on my best behavior anyway because an enormous stain-glassed image of Jesus shines directly through a window over my bed. We have three bedrooms, a bathroom, a kitchen, a washer and dryer, and a living room. But the pièce de résistance?

Our new apartment is only one street away from The School!

Heck, we could even sled to class during the grueling winter months if we wanted to. And we're close to our friends: Tempestt, Suresh, and Juliet Ann are renting a large house one mile from campus. Of course, Sookie and I have a standing dinner invitation at their house every Thursday evening, beginning tonight.

❊   ❊   ❊   ❊

"Second Year rocks!" Sookie declares while passing a bowl of peppery green beans across the table at our first official Thursday night gathering. "First, we get to choose our own classes." She counts on each finger. "Second, study groups are only needed for projects. Third, we actually have time for a social life—not that I really have much of one anyway…fourth, I have time to exercise and volunteer now."

I reach for a serving spoon. "And everyone I talk to seems to have had the 'internship of a lifetime'—imagine that!" I roll my eyes referring to the bulk of our classmates who have been eager to brag about how they built the "most incredible spreadsheets in the history of the universe" over the summer, received obscenely generous full-time job offers on the spot from their CEO's, and collected first-of-a-kind "best employee in the world" awards.

Juliet Ann laughs. "They never let their guard down. Even if they had miserable summers, they'd still gloss it over." She hands a platter of baked chicken
breasts to Tempestt.

"What are you taking this term?" Suresh asks me, taking a roll from the breadbasket while passing it to Sookie.

"Oh, I've got a great schedule: Medical Management, Advanced Organizational Management, Marketing New Products, Statistics, Effective Teamwork,
and International Business."

"I'm in Statistics, too," he says.

"10:45 with Professor Sadeghi?"

"Yep!" He scoops mashed potatoes onto his plate.

"And I'll be volunteering for Junior Achievement all year," I add. "Aaron Jeffries and I are Co-Presidents this year."

Sookie jumps in. "I've got Financial Reporting, Derivative Securities Valua-
tion, and Advanced Corporate Finance. Plus, International Marketing Strategy.
Suresh, I think you're in most of those?" Suresh nods.

"Strategic Business Management, Competitive Industry Analysis, Leadership,
and Entrepreneurship," Juliet Ann rattles off as she heads back to the kitchen.
"And I have Marketing New Products, too," she calls.

"I've got Effective Teamwork and Organizational Management," Tempestt
adds, not lifting a finger to help with the serving of the meal. "And I also have
Strategic Business Relationships…and Presentation Skills."

"What's the Medical class?" Suresh asks me. "Sounds interesting."

"Medical Management? It's awesome!" I lick a small dab of mashed potatoes
off my thumb. "It's a joint class with the medical school—basically a consulting
project under the supervision of the professor and a surgeon. I'll be matched with
a med student and together we'll be working with the local hospital to develop
plans for a breast cancer clinic."

"A real clinic?" he asks, impressed.

I nod.

"I wish I had signed up for that one," Juliet Ann admits, returning to her seat
with a shaker of salt and a pile of napkins. "I ran out of time."

"I'll definitely let you know how it goes," I offer as we continue sharing
internship tales.

I'd heard it all before, but Sookie recaps her California summer stories, including several movie premiers and celebrity sightings. Juliet Ann and Tempestt had a
terrific summer in NYC. Juliet Ann worked 70-hour consulting weeks but
enjoyed the expected lavish internship perks and dinners. Tempestt remained

unusually mum about her internship, but Juliet Ann later explained that Calvin Klein released Tempestt early from her responsibilities due to "personal and creative differences." *They give pink slips at internships?*

Suresh and Sookie also describe their amazing field study in Nepal working at the children's' hospital. "It really made me question my life," Sookie reflects. "The clutter in it, the insignificant, petty problems, the things I'm ridiculously enslaved to, the meaning of it all."

Suresh nods, putting his hands into an exaggerated prayer position and closing his eyes. "It was a fulfilling, life-changing experience, my little, un-wise MBAs."

Sookie slaps him playfully on the arm and shrieks, "It was!"

"Ouch!" He rubs his arm in mock pain and laughs.

"Selfless contribution brings true fulfillment," Tempestt adds soberly and grimaces. "You had to go all the way to *Nepal* to figure that out!? I could have told you that!"

Everyone laughs and Suresh picks up his wine glass, prompting all of us to do the same. "Cheers to making extraordinary things happen, moving from success to significance, and to a healthy and prosperous Second Year!" he toasts, winking at Sookie.

"Cheers!"

<u>MAKE GOOD CHOICES</u>

I walk into the classroom ready to rumble. Their expectations will be high, their demands unyielding, their judgments fierce—but I can handle it.

Bring it on.

"Welcome to Greeley Elementary," Miss Coffee-Smith says to me before turning to her classroom of 15 kindergarteners.

Today is my first day volunteering for Junior Achievement at a local elementary school.

Miss Coffee-Smith continues, "Class? I need your attention. Remember I told you we'd be having an extra special visitor today?"

Five little heads nod. "Well, she's here. From Junior Achievement. And she's going to talk to us for the next hour about business so I need you to take your seats on the floor in the reading area." The tykes reluctantly, but obediently, put their toys into wooden cubbyholes and shuffle to the carpeted reading lounge and form a seated semi-circle around the chalkboard. "Junior Achievement is a non-profit education organization dedicated to teaching elementary students about economics, business, and the importance of staying in school," Miss Coffee-Smith continues slowly, emphasizing the 'staying in school' part. Finally, she leads my introduction and hands me the floor.

I move to the opening of the semi-circle and clear my throat. "Uh…hi, kids."

Silence.

"I've been volunteering for Junior Achievement for five years and I'm now Co-President of the Junior Achievement chapter at my school. I raise money for the organization, recruit other volunteers, and volunteer in classrooms like this one," I explain to blank, bored faces.

Free ice cream for everyone?

"Can anyone tell me what business is?" I ask, taking a seat on the floor.

Again, silence. Miss Coffee-Smith's eyes are on me.

"Well, then…does anyone know the difference between a want and a need?" I ask hopefully.

Zilch. I might as well be speaking Latin.

"Who likes lemonade?" I desperately ask.

"Meeeeeee!" they scream and raise their hands. Only a few shake their heads and grimace.

"Who's ever had a lemonade stand?" I ask.

"I had one in my front yard," little Antonia offers.

"Great! And what did you do? Did you sell lemonade?"

"Yeah."

"Why?"

"Because it was hot. And people were thirsty. And my mom and I had fun making it."

I'm actually relieved that making money is not a kindergartener's first thought.

"Did you give away the lemonade for free?"

"No." She smiles shyly and tilts her chin toward her chest.

"Why not?"

She pauses. "I don't know," she says, confused.

"Do people *need* lemonade?" I ask.

"People need water in the lemonade," Daniel shouts.

Hmm…smarty pants.

"What are some examples of other things people need to survive?" I ask, launching into an explanation of a survival "need," like food and shelter, versus a desirable "want." It's more challenging than expected convincing them that television is not a necessity, but I have a few converts.

Every time the children misbehave, Miss Coffee-Smith never yells or gets upset, but reminds them to behave by saying, "Make good choices!" or very subtly, "Are you absolutely *sure* you're making good choices?" It stops the students in their tracks every time.

Interesting behavior modification system—*I wonder if it works with adults?*

I finally explain the concept of business to the class in terms of the lemonade stand.

"So," I conclude, "the money you make from selling lemonade can be used to buy basic survival needs, and to care for your families and community."

"But…" Antonia hesitates, swallowing a question.

I try to encourage her. "Yes?"

"Don't you need some of the money to buy the lemons and make the stand?" *Gosh these kids are good.*

SECOND YEAR ROCKS!

"This is so cool!" I whisper giddily, taking my seat in Holt Auditorium.

Sookie gushes, "I know—I can't believe she's here!"

We're in dreamy awe. Second Year allows us time to attend several guest lectures like this one sponsored by the Women in Business Club. In addition to seeing the most famous businessmen in the world speak this term (the Vice Chairman of the Federal Reserve; the Chairman and CEO of American Express; the CEO of Nissan; the Chairman and CEO of General Electric), we'll also meet several current and former female executives, CEO's, governors and university presidents:

- Andrea Jung (Chairman and CEO, Avon Products Inc.)
- Anne Mulcahy (Chairman and CEO, Xerox Corporation)
- Marion O. Sandler (Chairman of the Board and CEO, Golden West Financial Corporation)
- Caroline Little (CEO and Publisher, Washingtonpost.Newsweek Interactive)
- Ann M. Fudge (Chairman and CEO, Young & Rubicam Inc.)
- Ann S. Moore (Chairman and CEO, Time Inc.)
- Carol Evans (CEO, Working Mother Media)
- Christine Whitman (Governor—New Jersey)
- Judith Rodin (President, University of Pennsylvania)
- Sila Calderon (Governor—Puerto Rico)

- Cynthia Harris (President, Gap)

I can't get over the wonderment of reading a business case and then actually meeting the employees mentioned in it. For example, I don't just read about the manufacturing of Nissan's Altima SE-R—I meet the executives, managers, and manufacturers who build it; I don't just read about The Body Shop's latest social cause—I meet Anita Roddick and ask her questions about it. Plus, we have video-conference lectures every week with other business schools to watch prominent leaders speak from around the world—like Muriel Siebert and Kay Koplovitz.

Sookie, Tempestt, and I have also volunteered to help fundraise the annual "Balancing Life & Work symposium." Basically, we'll be calling corporations and begging for money. In the meantime, Juliet Ann is working hard to develop a separate conference focusing on the environmental and social consequences of business; and yesterday she moderated a WIBC panel of women discussing the growing wealth of women in America. Juliet Ann's personal goal is to eventually eradicate gender-based salary differences. "Why should women make 30% less than men for the *same* work?" she offered with conviction. Likewise, it was fantastic to hear from the number of women on the panel making over $100,000, managing their money, and supporting their families.

Second Year has exceeded all of my expectations. My positive attitude is back—my confidence is soaring. For the first time, I don't feel like the shell of a person I had been whittled down to during First Year. I'm back to being me and it feels good.

What's most amazing is that business school is actually starting to make sense; the workload is more manageable, and the new obstacles seem more important— even the courses seem more relevant. First Year was about priority management and chaos; Second Year is about putting business theory into practice. They're building us back up again. Sometimes I sit in awe after a class, understanding for the first time how I might use some of the new material in the real world. Financial statements, marketing matrices, product life cycles, entry strategies for new products—it all makes sense.

Of course, it's still not a bed of long-stem Ecuadorian roses—unfortunately, the people are the same and some old problems do creep up. I still can't wait to leave business school, but now my motivation stems more from excitement— starting a new life, getting a new job, using my knowledge—and less from running away from my misery. I even managed to attend a forum (Tunes and the Evolution of Music Business Models) with Suresh last week at the Center for

Digital Business. And I was able to attend Emode's launch party in Cambridge last Friday, proudly cheering Rick on as he officially opened Emode for business.

The truth is, although I haven't actually crossed the line of affection into "love" for Second Year, I'm becoming quite "fond" of it. It's like The School and I are in the "courting stage" of a relationship. It's a new beginning—I've forgiven all and I am slowly regaining trust and falling back into The School's warm, inviting embrace.

This year is all about that great stuff in the school brochures—the speakers, courses, events, sports, volunteering, socializing, and most of all just having the precious time to actually enjoy these things; and I don't know how long it will last, but I intend to have some fun while I can.

There's a round of hearty applause as Dean Denton introduces today's guest: a Boston Globe columnist.

"She could be talking about a leaf falling and I'd still be interested," Sookie says as the speaker takes the podium.

"Shhh!" Tempestt hushes from the row behind us. "Some of us are trying to listen."

We frown at her.

"By the way, have you met Professor Grace yet?" Sookie continues before the lights dim and the presentation begins.

AMAZING GRACE

Professor Grace entered confidently and quietly. She didn't tiptoe, she unpretentiously glided into the room, her long red hair perfectly illuminating her young, 40-year-old face. Then she did something that I had yet to witness in a B-school classroom: she asked us to introduce ourselves on the first day of Marketing New Products.

Perhaps just as refreshing was the syllabus for this course. We'll spend the entire term launching a new toothpaste product for Colgate, complete with focus groups, research, a promotions campaign, packaging, and general development. Executives from the company will meet with us on a weekly basis; and Grace will oversee the whole process.

"And I'd like to invite all of you to dinner at my house next month," she requested at the end of our first class. "Significant others and spouses are also invited."

Dinner at a prof's house?

This was common at The School, but I had never actually done it.

❄   ❄   ❄   ❄

Four weeks later, Juliet Ann and I head to Professor Grace's modest, but beautiful, country home in Vermont. 10 students are huddled around a small bonfire in the backyard. Grace's husband and teenage children—a son and a daughter—join us and distribute marshmallows on sticks. *S'mores!*

Most of the small talk revolves around classes and projects, and how fast the term is moving. A few students ask Professor Grace canned marketing questions that she answers politely before steering the conversation toward a new direction.

"What are you planning to do, Feddy?" she asks me in her soothingly peaceful signature voice.

I'm being cold-called?

"Marketing management," I answer, stuffing a melting marshmallow into my mouth, my cheeks blushing from the heat of the fire.

"No, I mean, what do you want *to do*?" she repeats with slightly more fervor.

Sell pre-packaged desserts to grocery store chains? Eat frosting for a living? Make at least $100k annually? That doesn't sound right...

"What legacy do you want to leave behind?" she continues when I don't answer immediately.

A chocolate cookie with pecans?

"Success, knowledge, reputation for fairness—something that will help others. A happy family," I answer.

Professor Grace smiles before launching into a lengthy discussion about business philanthropy. "Life doesn't always allow us time to remember to give back to society." She leans back softly in her chair, relaxed. "We spend ample time thinking about earning money, but less time considering how to use the money in positive ways."

I feel it's a good time to tell the group about my work developing a breast cancer clinic with the local hospital and my volunteer work with Junior Achievement. Professor Grace seems impressed.

Juliet Ann talks about her idea, too. "I plan to develop a consulting business to help small companies—especially minority-based ones."

"Adam and I are starting a fundraising company. It's a merchant shopping network that will contribute cash to schools and nonprofits," Daniel, another classmate, interjects.

"Excellent!"

"I'm taking my daughter's entire class on a hiking trip this summer," Jeff adds, figuring it counts for something, and it does, but everyone laughs.

Professor Grace puts her marshmallow stick near the fire, every move having a quiet finesse. "Well, I hope all of you recognize the great opportunities offered from business school"—she removes her blackened marshmallow from the fire— "and support themes of giving and caring in the future." She lowers her voice, making it sound faintly like an order. "And I presume everyone will be attending tomorrow's Annual Nonprofit Auction?" she gently reminds us, referring to a student and faculty auction where fun activities such as fishing, cooking, and dancing lessons with professors are sold. The money raised pays for the housing expenses of First Year students who choose nonprofit summer internships without income.

I'm going to the auction but I'm left to ponder Professor Grace's question about my legacy. It reminds me of an alumna I met over the summer who started a social entrepreneurship company dedicated to reforming education. An "edupreneur" was how she described herself as I listened in awe to her stories about bringing investors together for a social mission.

Am I making a difference like that? Have I even thought about it?

"Dinner's ready!" the teenage daughter calls from the doorway.

"By the way, how's interviewing coming along?" Professor Grace asks me as we're ushered into the house.

MBA FOR HIRE

Oh yeah, I almost forgot.

Remember the horrendous interviewing process last year for the coveted summer internships? You know, where classmates were selling their souls, drawing blood from unsuspecting cohorts, and bartering with their first-born children?

It's baaaack...

And it's worse than ever.

It seems like just yesterday we were interviewing for our internships and yet here we are, scrambling to gather our full-time destinies. Recruiting season starts much earlier in Second Year—I can practically hear Sookie jokingly recite, "'It's all about the bucks, kid. The rest is conversation,'" from *Wall Street*, as we schlep to our first interview.

Classrooms are once again filled with nervous students sitting uncomfortably in business suits, waiting to negotiate their corporate lives after class, while professors wrestle unsuccessfully for their attention. The interviewing process is similar to last year's internship process, but the stakes are much higher—like a marriage versus a summer fling. This is permanent.

Well, semi-permanent.

Families will be uprooted, houses will be built, offices will be decorated. It's an emotional and long-term professional investment not to be taken lightly.

On the one hand, it opens new doors to new worlds for many people—a chance to explore cities and exciting jobs. On the other hand, recruiting season creates a twisted sense of desperation that forces classmates to choose jobs previously considered inappropriate simply because students don't want to be branded "jobless and hopeless" at graduation.

I thank God for Kingsbury-Kutter every night.

They've awarded me with a false sense of invincibility and a hefty blanket of comfort: a full-time job offer.

I'm 99% sure that I'm going to accept their full-time offer of $100,000 with a $20,000 signing bonus. Kingsbury-Kutter is even willing to splurge for my relocation costs—movers, packers, temporary housing, and the costs associated with selling my house if I had had one.

They've given me until spring to decide. *Oh glorious Kingsbury-Kutter!* Now I won't have to go through the interviewing madness with the rest of my classmates this year; I'll just complete a few, obligatory safety-net interviews.

"*You* got an offer! Where?" Jonas, my classmate, asks when he overhears me talking to Juliet Ann in the hallway after class.

Why does he seem so surprised?

I tell him a few details as we stand huddled in the hallway.

He grimaces. "I would never work in that wretched pit of a city," he says.

Awww, how sweet...

Then something occurs to me.

"Have you ever actually been there?" I boldly ask him, not willing to let him deflate my excitement so easily.

He stammers. "Uh, well, no...I've never been there...but it just doesn't *seem* like it would be fun."

He's never even been there? Get over yourself!

I'm fed up.

"You know what, Jonas? It's actually *okay* to congratulate another classmate on her accomplishments. It's *okay* to be happy for me. And guess what?" I feign shock. "It won't kill you!"

Juliet Ann's eyes bug out as she grabs my arm and leads me away before Jonas can offer a retort.

She giggles. "Feddy—I can't believe you!" she mockingly reprimands, then whispers, "I wish I had said it!" and we laugh.

I'm distracted when Issy Bettencourt breezes past, her long blonde hair trailing her regal, upright stature.

"ISSY!" I yell down the hall, but she doesn't stop.

Is she avoiding me?

"I'll call you later, Juliet Ann." I excuse myself to run after Issy.

"Issy!" I yell louder, finally reaching her. "What happened?"

"Oh, Feddy…" She looks uncomfortable but doesn't stop walking. "I'm so sorry."

"Issy, I went out on a limb for you—" I'm not happy, but I'm out of breath.

"I know. And that was so sweet. Really." She makes an artificial pout. "It's just that…well…I decided to go with a consulting offer instead. Sorry about that."

That's it?

I keep a brisk pace next to her. "Issy—what do you mean 'sorry about that?' I put my professional reputation at risk for you. I made a promise to the President of the division! I'm looking pretty bad right now. I trusted you."

Last week, Issy, a First Year student and recent *Imposters* recruit, came to me and told me that it was her absolute "dream" to work for Kingsbury-Kutter for her summer internship and wondered if I could help out by putting in a good word for her.

Sure, I assured her.

Anything for a schoolmate.

At dinner with the President of Kingsbury-Kutter's largest division two nights ago, I made a plea for Issy. The President was hesitant. She looked me straight in the eye and asked, "Are you *sure* Issy Bettencourt wants to work for us? She's only our third choice."

"Yes," I promised.

"Because I'd hate to offer it to her and have her decline," the President warned me.

"But it's her *dream*," I assured the President.

So imagine my horror when I heard yesterday that Issy had declined the offer.

Issy stops and shrugs her shoulders. "I said I was sorry."

Right.

She walks away.

LIGHTS! CAMERA! NO ACTION!

Why is she pointing the camera at me like that?
That's my bad side!

"Hold still," Jennifer from Career Services instructs me. "There…right there…perfect." I see my face projected onto a TV screen.

Here I am again, on yet another interview. But this is a first—a teleconference interview. *Ah, the marvels of technology. No need to get on an airplane and fly half-way across the country to interview. Now we just do it via satellite.*

My humiliating interview is actually going to be televised!

"I'm going to leave, and in a few minutes you'll see the company representative appear on the screen. Speak clearly into the microphone so the two of you can communicate and view one another."

"Okay, thanks."

Maybe if I'm stumped on a question I can just blame it on static interference—*I'm sorry, you're cutting out, can you repeat that?*

I'm fiddling ridiculously with the top button on my suit when the representative beams in, catching me off-guard.

"Oh! Hi!" I blush.

She gets right to business. "You're our Marketing Director and you need an additional $100,000 to launch our newest product—elf costumes for basketball players—but you've already maxed the budget. So what do you cut first?"

Elf costumes?

"I'm sorry, you seem to be cutting out—can you repeat that?"

STOP THE INSANITY

"I'm done interviewing," I tell Aaron Jeffries and Juliet Ann at lunch in early October. The School has officially deemed this week Interview Commitment Week—no classes, just interviews and loads of stress. "What's the point?" I continue. "I'm 99% sure I'm going to Kingsbury-Kutter, and I've already interviewed with three safety-net companies. And I'm not excited about any of the jobs anymore; now I just want to truly enjoy my last year here, if possible."

Is that too much to ask? In truth, I'm hoping for more time to dedicate to the two things that bring me the most joy right now: my Colgate project with Professor Grace and my work with the medical school. And I'm happy to report that although interviewing is a complete nightmare on the nerves, I've actually faired quite well and secured a few second-round invites.

But I still want out.

"You should keep interviewing anyway!" Aaron Jeffries urges me. "Get as many offers as you can, then you'll have more negotiating leverage. 70% of the jobs are obtained during Interview Commitment Week."

Easy for him to say, he's received multiple offers and is often selected by companies as a coveted Closed List candidate. In the end, he finally decided to accept a Marketing Manager position at Ben & Jerry's in Vermont, the state where he plans to eventually open a bed & breakfast with Sadie, instead of a brand management position at Dairy Queen's headquarters.

"I'm not interviewing anymore, either," Juliet Ann reveals.

"You're going to Bain?"

"Yep. I won't miss the stress of interviewing, but I will miss the pampering a little…" She laughs. "The fancy dinners, the concert tickets, the basketball games, the nights at the Royalton Hotel…"

"Me, too," Aaron agrees.

"I did have another consulting offer," Juliet Ann admits. "And when I told Bain, they increased my starting salary. But if you're really not interested in other companies, Feddy, why waste your time?"

Exactly. Why waste my time?

That's it. I'm officially DONE with interviewing.

No more stressful nights waiting for "the call."

Good-bye, good riddance, see you never.

"I can't wait to tell Rick the good news," I say to Juliet Ann and Aaron. Rick mentioned he has some big news for me, too.

APPARENTLY INSANITY RUNS IN THE FAMILY

I laugh into the phone. "I'm sorry, Rick," I talk between laughs. "For a second there I thought you said you were *moving to California!*" I laugh louder. *Can you imagine?*

But he's not laughing.

"I did," he says.

"California, California?" I stop laughing now. "The one on the West Coast?"

"Yep. That's the one."

"On the Pacific Ocean?"

"Yes, Feddy," he says, slightly annoyed. "I think we've clearly established that we're indeed talking about the same California."

"Just checking. But how? *Why!?*"

"Remember I told you that our investors were from San Francisco?"

"Vaguely."

"I tell you everything! I gave you these details months ago!"

"Okay—but *months ago* the details didn't seem as important as they do right now!"

"August Capital wants us out in California."

"Shouldn't we talk about this first?"

"There's not much of a choice. We have to move the company this summer if we want to survive."

"California or bust?"

"Something like that."

Long distance love from the Midwest to New England seemed manageable for a year. *But California?*

"What do you want to do?" he finally asks me.

"That's a strange question, isn't it?"

"No."

"Well, what are you talking about then?" I ask.

"Do you want to come out with me?"

"I already have an offer at Kingsbury-Kutter."

"But this changes things."

Hmm…this is probably one of those scenarios that is actually a lot easier if you're married.

"Yes, it does change things, Rick."

"I just figured you'd come out with me—interview for a job in California. Or maybe stay in the Midwest as we originally planned for a year and then eventually move to California?"

"I don't know, Rick."

"Feddy…if it was reversed, and you were starting a company, I would definitely move any place you had to go. In fact, our next stop in life will be for you," he vows

I don't have any reason not to believe him. But…

"Let me just think about things for awhile," I say before heading to class.

WHEN IT RAINS, IT POURS

I walk into Advanced Organizational Management and almost puke.

There, in this tiny classroom, sitting in the center row, three seats from the left, is Nelly.

Out of all the classrooms in the world, she had to walk into mine.

I quietly take my seat in the last row and contemplate dropping the class. It's a mid-term, mini-course that lasts only two months. There are only 14 of us in here, so we're bound to have interaction. I can't avoid her.

Screw it. I'm staying.

No one can stop me from learning about cultural, organizational, and economic contexts of management. It's a girl's right!

And besides, I'm too busy worrying about bigger and better things to give Nelly the attention she seeks.

I'm working like a dog with Allegra, the medical student I've been matched with, to design the operational queue for the breast cancer clinic; we're in the process of interviewing the hospital employees and patients. And the new toothpaste for Colgate is coming along well. We conducted focus groups in Boston last week; and now we're pricing a sampling program and developing incentives to retailers for prime shelf space. These projects give me purpose, a focus on more important issues. *Who cares about Nelly?*

Lizbeth, another classmate, takes a seat next to me and immediately begins to rattle off the obligatory complaints concerning the "astonishing number of interviews" she's been summoned for, and how she "can't possibly find the time."

I roll my eyes as Lizbeth continues her Jobapalooza brag-fest; and Stephen Earleson can't resist turning around to join our conversation.

"You got an interview with Mercer?" Stephen asks with barely controlled envy.

There's an undeniable, suffocating sense of panic overtaking our graduating class as we approach our final months of interviewing. Insecurity and competitiveness fall out of their sheep's clothing; casual or seemingly innocent inquiries about a fellow classmate's interviewing status are desperate, thinly-veiled wails for self-validation.

"Yes," Lizbeth confirms, raising her chin slightly, knowing it's killing Stephen. "And they gave me an offer." She plunges the dagger. "But I don't even want to work for them." She sighs dramatically, pausing before digging the dagger deeper. "And I haven't a clue how to tell them the bad news…"

"You could send a flower-gram?" I suggest.

Lizbeth gives me the look of death. I shrug my shoulders. "What? It might make the blow easier for them, don't you think?"

Rachel Adams, Vice President of our class, enters and sits next to Stephen. Not able to soar above his insecurity any longer, Stephen bluntly asks Rachel how many job offers she has.

Rachel, unfazed by Stephen's abruptness, casually reports that she is going to be a Marketing Director at the Smithsonian, in Washington DC, after spending the summer developing a fund for art endowment in Boston. Lizbeth feigns lack of interest, but Stephen and I are interested.

I listen carefully and admiringly, completely moved by Rachel's dedication and professional courage. Rachel is really making her mark in the world with a bold and meaningful entrepreneurial venture.

A moral pang jolts through my head: *Should I be doing something like that?*

Professor Botticello enters, saving me from having to embarrassingly reveal to my classmates that I have no idea where I'm going to work, where I'm going to live, and whether or not my relationship will survive my boyfriend moving 3,000 miles away from me.

And oh yeah, I won't exactly be *saving* the world, but I'll certainly be changing it.

One chocolate chip at a time?

TRIPLE X

"I'm going to die." Sookie blushes to a shade of ripe tomato.

"You are not going to die of embarrassment!" I reassure her despite my private doubts.

It's bad.

While innocently checking email to prevent succumbing to irreversible catatonia during a repetitious pricing analysis in her Corporate Finance class, Sookie inadvertently became prey to one of the oldest and dirtiest email high jinks of all time.

"So I opened the email, thinking it's from my friend." Sookie relives the classroom nightmare for us as we sit in our living room. "And I didn't realize that the volume on my computer was set to maximum, and the next thing I know…" She pauses, obviously verklempt, but Tempestt and I can barely contain our laughter. We know what comes next—it's all over school.

"My computer shouts: HEY GUYS, I'M WATCHING PORN OVER HERE!"

We break into hysterics.

"Don't laugh! I'm mortified!" Sookie pleads, throwing her face into her hands to hide. "Totally and utterly humiliated. We had to stop class."

"So were you watching porn?" Tempestt asks nonchalantly while wrapping a silver Pashmina over her jacket.

"What? No! It was a joke—just an email with an embarrassing sound byte sent to me as a joke."

"Just asking."

"Eventually you'll laugh about this," I offer.

"Yeah, when I'm applying for AARP benefits…"

"The next 30 years will fly!" I nod assuredly.

"So what did you finally do?" Tempestt begs.

"The class laughed and Professor Finley said (Sookie imitates Finley's stoic voice), 'Well, Miss Wong, continue watching your pornography or kindly turn it off and return to our slightly less provocative financial model. The choice is yours, but I assure you that only one of those subjects will be on the final exam.'"

Sookie shakes her head in defeat as Tempestt and I hold back our laughter. "Then, this afternoon I went to Finley's office to formally apologize for the disruption."

"He's probably laughing on the inside. He'll get over it."

Sookie rolls her eyes.

"My friend at Yale burped during one of her job interviews," I share.

"My cousin in Chicago tucked her skirt into the back of her pantyhose right before a presentation to an audience of 200," Tempestt adds.

"I know someone who meant to write the word 'count' in an email to her project team, but accidentally omitted the 'o' in haste." *Totally not necessary to mention it was me. Absolutely irrelevant.*

Sookie smiles and gives in. "My old roommate who's now at Northwestern once called the wrong company to accept a job offer," she shares. "She worked for the company for six months rather than admit her mistake."

"Oh! And remember last week when Collin fell down the mailroom stairs?" Tempestt asks excitedly.

"That's right!" I nod. "See? It's old news now—and next week you'll be old news, too!" I exclaim. "Someone else's misfortune will replace yours as the gossip of the week."

"Right…" Sookie says pensively. "Now all I need is a major social mishap to happen to another poor, unsuspecting soul."

"You just might have to take matters into your own hands…" Tempestt smiles mischievously.

BUSINESS IS BAD FOR BUSINESS?

"I'm really getting tired of fighting the MBA stereotype and listening to chronic business-bashing," Juliet Ann says in the dining hall the next day. "Sometimes we have to wrestle the system, sometimes classmates, sometimes coworkers, and now the media." She plops her lunch tray onto the table. "I'm exhausted!"

Several anti-business magazine articles were published recently, including a few that savagely attack business schools. Constructively criticizing the MBA curriculum in search of reform is one thing, but it's another to attack the entire species of MBAs.

"The media perpetuates the image," I agree, thinking of the lack of business-women on film or TV and the wicked stereotypes of either gender that often appear.

Sookie frowns. "Why is it okay to bash some groups but not others?"

I shrug my shoulders. "Certain minorities are just more popular than others. Likewise for some professions, I guess."

"I mean, the arrogance at B-school is sometimes overwhelming, but the intentions aren't always bad," Sookie argues.

I have to agree. One thing that surprised me when I came here was the number of people (yes, even the pompous ones who drive me insane) who were actually more concerned with hard work, corporate governance, and volunteer efforts. But that's not the stereotype you see in the media.

"Crap!" I scream when I open the letter I brought with me from the mailroom.

"What is it?" Juliet Ann asks.

"It's a letter…from Kingsbury-Kutter." I scan the page. "They want me to sign my final offer letter. Today."

Sookie and Juliet Ann exchange glances. "Haven't you told them you're not going?" Sookie asks, confused.

I shake my head. "Not yet."

"So you're not sure?" Juliet Ann asks gently.

"No. Not about anything." I put the letter into my bag, signaling to the group that I don't want to talk about it.

"But at least things are changing for the better," Sookie reminds Juliet Ann, returning to the subject of MBA diversity. "Look at the percentages of minorities and ethnicities here now. Companies are increasing their mentoring programs and encouraging female enrollment in B-school, supporting the work/life balance…"

"I don't think it's changing fast enough," I say. I've read the other reports. "We need more women here." I search for my vitamin on the lunch tray. "Medical and law schools are at least 50% women, which reflects the general population, but business school is nowhere near that stat. We're lucky to get 27%."

"More women at business school means greater economic power and influence for women in the future," Juliet Ann agrees.

"So why aren't more women here? Especially because alums seem really happy with their decisions to go to business school?" Sookie asks. "It doesn't make sense."

"Because they don't understand the opportunities," I say.

Tempestt opens her eyes. She has been silently—and dramatically—meditating at the end of the table, nurturing her surprisingly spiritual side. "The yin and yang are not balanced here at business school," she decides in her holy voice. "Our survival depends on our adaptability and our ability to either transform life or to construct stability. It's not a male/female issue, it's an energy issue. Diversity. We need a balance to create one another, to control one another, to make proper decisions, to give us foresight, and to help us to understand challenges. The yang balances the yin and each one has elements of the other." She then returns to meditating.

I roll my eyes before uttering, "Namaste."

Meditating, shopping, and enjoying spa treatments? Tempestt is the only person I know who hasn't altered her lifestyle for business school.

"But we need more diversity at B-school to actually *attract* more diversity so we're stuck," Juliet Ann continues.

"Well, I like the idea of bringing more women to The School, especially professors," I say, looking at my watch before quickly jumping up from the lunch table.

"Oops—gotta run."

I have an interview.

BACK IN THE SADDLE AGAIN

Sometimes I lovingly reminisce about those 10 precious minutes three weeks ago when I had officially decided to stop interviewing. *Ah, the good old minutes.*

One minute, I'm a jolly Second Year student, looking forward to the comfort of a cushy six-figure job at a top global company, coasting through the recruiting season, sleeping a sweet eight hours a night knowing that all is well in Relationship Land.

The next minute, I'm left with the white elephant of business school gifts—a nagging conscience, questions, indecision, an unclear future, interviewing nightmares, relationship blips and peer pressure.

I knew Second Year was too good to be true.

Lately, I've been trying to test the California job market with an interview here and there, but I haven't officially decided to move, yet. Rick and I are still in negotiations, but even if I don't go to California, I'm not sure if I want to sell consumer food products in the Midwest, either.

So that's where I am in the decision-making process.

Nowhere.

But now there's another unexpected issue on my mind, another complex layer topping my life: I've been thinking more about business philanthropy and finding meaning in my education.

This worries my parents, of course. Like normal parents, they have been enjoying the peaceful sleep induced by the comfort of knowing that their only child is only seven months away from graduating an Ivy League business school. Suddenly, I've given them cause for concern although they would never admit it to me.

"Well, what do you *think* you want to do?" my mom asks me on the phone.

"I'm not sure, that's the problem."

My dad is on the third line. "She wants to join one of those MBA enterprise companies—go around the world working in Estonia or Thailand," he says, referring to those organizations that encourage MBA's to help small businesses in developing countries.

"I'm not sure if I want to do that either," I confess.

My dad sighs. "Business school has provided you with too many opportunities and now you're confused?" he asks with a touch of fatherly sarcasm.

"Well, I hadn't thought of it that way…but yeah, I guess so. That's part of it. Mostly, I just want to do something meaningful."

Brief silence.

"Take the Kingsbury-Kutter job for at least a year," my dad urges. "You can pay your business school tuition, gain valuable experience for your resume, and then move onto something else later."

"We don't want you to waste your education!" my mom pleads.

"Ma, I won't waste it!" I assure them, laughing. "Don't worry, I just want to do something that I feel good about, nothing crazy."

My mom breathes a sigh of relief.

"And thanks for the care-package," I continue. "Sookie and I ate the cookies and watched three of the movies already."

"I'll keep sending them until you come home for Christmas. It's the final countdown, honey—you're almost done!" my mom cheers.

"Thank God!" I say, secretly wishing I had more time to figure out my future.

My parents ask me a few questions about Rick and California. They're protectively excited about the prospect of me moving closer to Arizona, but they only support it if it's a career decision that I truly want to make independent of the relationship. I also tell them about The Ritz-Carlton employee recognition program I designed for Advanced Organizational Management. My dad then asks me grueling questions about exams and job interviews before they promise to call me next Sunday, as usual.

"Love you!" we yell into the phone before hanging up.

Then I turn on my computer to check my chaotic interviewing schedule for the upcoming week.

A PROFESSIONAL IDENTITY CRISIS?

"We just finished developing the operations plan for the new Breast Cancer Clinic," I excitedly tell Juliet Ann, as we walk across campus. I haven't felt this invigorated in a long time. "Allegra and I presented it to the doctor this morning!"

"Congrats!" she says over the crispy autumn leaves crunching under our feet.

"And I really like working with the medical students. Every move they make seems so...so *consequential*," I add dreamily.

She raises an eyebrow. "So you're switching to Med School?"

"No way!" I shout, quickly coming back from the clouds. "They've got their own med school drama just like we do at business school!" I open the front door and we walk upstairs to my apartment. "I just want to do more with my life."

She nods supportively. "You want to do more significant things with your business degree?"

"Exactly!"

"You want to reconcile (A) loving what you do for a living with (B) turning your philanthropic ideals into actions?" she asks, taking off her jacket.

My eyes widen. "Exactly!" I exclaim again, surprised that she understands so well.

"I went through the same thing," she explains.

"That's why you're starting your own consulting business?"

She nods. "I can't see myself doing anything else."

I plop down on the couch and she sits in the chair across from me. "I'm having what I like to call a "professional identity crisis." I just spent my whole professional life working toward something and now I'm not sure what I want to do!? It's ridiculous."

"95% of the working population has doubts, don't be so hard on yourself." She kicks off her shoes.

"I've just replaced all of my old problems with larger, more significant ones this year."

"Better than the trivial, petty ones of First Year," she jokes.

"True…"

"You can start over in California," she suggests.

"Don't remind me."

"It's an adventure!"

"It just caught me by surprise."

"How are things with Rick?"

"Okay, I think. We're not talking as much lately—he's busy with Emode and I'm interviewing. But I'll see him this weekend."

"Still unsure about California?"

"Yeah," I admit. "It's a big commitment. Sometimes I don't know if he realizes that."

She sighs sympathetically. "Did you tell him that?"

"I've tried."

"If he's taking you for granted, it's probably only temporarily—he really loves you." She untwists the elastic in her hair to relax her ponytail. "And anything you wanted to do in the Midwest with your business degree, you can do in California, right? You don't have to sacrifice that."

"True, again. Maybe it's a blessing in disguise." I get up to stretch and walk toward the kitchen. "Want something to drink?"

"Only if it's the hard stuff, otherwise water will do."

I laugh. "Speaking of the hard stuff, I heard pub night was pretty crazy last night?"

"I couldn't go," she calls to me from the living room, "but Sookie said we missed a big one. Second Year guys were pathetically plastered all over the First Year women."

"Me Tarzan, you Jane?"

She laughs. "As expected. It's the obligatory blooming of more mini-romances that end as soon as they begin."

I hand Juliet Ann a glass of water and resume my position on the couch.

"And we'll have a new surge of romances after November," I remind her.

"Of course! Thanksgiving Break-up. Out with the old, in with the new." She rolls her eyes. "But we'll also see more engagements and marriages this year."

"Sookie told me that Jamie Waverly and Kennedy Livingston got engaged last week."

"And there were three engagements over the summer," Juliet Ann reminds me.

"And we'll probably have more proposals over the holiday break."

She sets the glass on the coffee table and relaxes onto a pillow. "Events will be sprouting until the end of the year—engagements, and marriages, and pregnancies, and births…"

"And graduation!" I add.

Can't forget about graduation.

WHAT'S LOVE GOT TO DO WITH IT?

He stops eating. "And why do you feel guilty again?"

"I don't know…you know…" I falter. Rick and I are eating lunch at Cheesecake Factory. My grilled chicken sandwich could feed an army.

"No, I don't know." His voice is full of irritation. "And that's why I'm asking."

Check please?

"It's just…well, I worked so hard to get here, and now, well, I'll just be following you to California. Maybe it's not putting my full potential to use?"

He removes his napkin from his lap and puts it on the table. "Your full potential? We've been together for years, Feddy. And now we're starting a life together. We'll both be working hard for the next few years—no one is stopping you. I love you, so to hear you say that you feel *guilty* for building a life with me is ridiculous."

"It's a little more complicated than that."

"Is this because we're not married?"

"Maybe. I don't know. I'm not ready to get married either, but you never actually said that you really wanted to me to move to California with you—it was all just so business-like—and that's making it hard. There seemed to be no emotion on your part, no enthusiasm, just business." I put my hands in my lap. "It wasn't exactly a *joint* decision to go to California. I'm a follower."

"You are anything but that! And you *know* I want you to come to California," he says rudely, shaking his head in disbelief. "This is what people who love each other do! They make *sacrifices*."

I smile weakly. "It's hard to explain. I love you and I want to be with you, but it's just that I can't shake this 'I'm following my man around the country' feeling that makes me think I'm disappointing my entire generation, like I'm willing to give up my own dreams to follow yours."

"But you're not giving up your dreams! You can do it all in California—and you said you've always wanted to try the West Coast anyway—now's your chance!"

"And I honestly want to do it, because I love you so much, but I'll need to shake this nagging feeling first. I want to move for the right reasons so we'll both be happy."

"But you know I'd move for you, wherever you wanted to go," he reminds me.

"I believe that you think that right now," I say.

"You don't believe me!?" He raises his voice.

I motion with my hand for him to calm down. "I believe it is your whole-hearted intention, yes, but realistically we have no way of proving it until it actually happens. It's easier said than done."

He sighs in frustration. "Maybe you should go to Kingsbury-Kutter then. Or wherever you want to go when you figure it out." He tightens his lips. "That way you can make your own decisions and feel good about not having to sacrifice for me or anyone else."

I shake my head. "I'm not selfish. Don't make me sound that way."

"Well, then, I don't know what to tell you. I'm not exactly feeling so hot right now knowing that you feel *guilty* for being with me and that I may be responsible for the potential demise of your gender—"

"I didn't say that!" At this point I regret telling him my feelings. He feels awful, and I feel worse.

He exhales loudly, rubbing his forehead to soothe what I imagine is a growing headache. "I know," he finally admits softly. "I know, Feddy."

"Would you like to try our Fabulous Chocolate Mousse Cake for dessert?" the waiter interrupts, sidling up to the table. "It's enough for two and very, very romantic." He winks suggestively.

"No thanks," Rick says. "Just the check."

LOSING IS FOR LOSERS?

"Sometimes you have to accept not being the best," Professor Grace tells me in her office one day when I reveal that I did not secure a job interview I desired.

What kind of advice is that? I feel 100 times worse after hearing it.

"Thanks," I mumble, looking out her window to see the winter storm clouds rolling in. *A dagger in my shoulder would hurt less...*

She smiles serenely at me from across the desk in her office. "It's a valuable mechanism for coping with life," she assures me while arranging papers into a folder. "And yet it can still motivate you to achieve greatness."

She swivels her chair to face me. "You're a solid individual with healthy self-esteem. I know this despite your expansive self-deprecating humor—you wouldn't be where you are today otherwise," she adds before I can object. "When you're strong, your disposition relies less on your environment, less on always being the best, and more on who you are inside. When you're at peace with not always winning or being the best, when you see each situation as an opportunity to learn from someone who might know more than you, it's growth potential. Always strive for excellence, of course, but use each opportunity as a platform for growth. And at the end of the day, you're not taking a sad "loss" to bed, you're not holding grudges, there's no residual anger—it simply registers as another extraordinary life experience. Because inside you know your strengths and who you really are."

"It's not always a win or lose situation," I say, understanding.

She smiles, quietly adding, "And greatness is not always synonymous with winning."

"Thanks for the advice."

"Anytime."

I grab my backpack and head to Organizational Management, reminding myself that 99% of students usually have jobs before graduation. I'm okay as long as I can avoid my nosey classmates who pester me relentlessly with questions about my job interviews. I usually tell them to "check CNN for my interviewing progress report" and that shuts them up for a few days.

And things have become more complicated at The School. The magnificent "courting period" with The School has evolved into a full-fledged "break-up." Our love affair ended before it even began. I can't even finish writing my personal vision statement for Effective Teamwork (the "development plan for my life" as Professor Goldsmith calls it). The School even hired business coaches to help with our personal progress. *Where do I want to be in 10 years? Who knows?* I'm confused.

Last year, I wrestled with the challenges of a new environment, but those seem meaningless in contrast to this year's problems. Now I'm sparring with my professional future—my relationship, my legacy, and my conscience. Most students are struggling with choosing the right job or negotiating vesting schedules for their stock options, but I'm not even on the launch pad. Forget about deciding what job I want, first I have to decide what I want to do.

And all I know right now is that I don't want to fall into some career stereotype, either professionally or personally, but yet I still want the MBA to be the catalyst of my next move. I just don't know how to reconcile the two.

Last year, my biggest concern was The School.

This year, it's my life.

BUILDING BLOCKS (AGES THREE AND UP)

"And so, the Building Blocks theory involving both formal and informal workgroups has both creativity and leadership consequences," I say to the class, concluding my Advanced Organizational Management presentation.

Thank God it's over.

"Any questions?" I ask my classmates.

Raise your hands and I'll scream.

Nelly raises her hand.

Ah, my favorite aversive stimulus.

"Yes, Nelly?" Professor Botticello asks her.

"Yeah, I just don't get it," she addresses me from her seat.

I stand silently at the front of the room. *Doesn't get what? The philosophy behind basic human compassion? How to remove the stick from her...*

"I don't think what you're saying makes sense," she continues. "The Building Blocks theory? It doesn't make sense."

I'm prepared to confidently defend myself, but Professor Botticello is eagerly on the defensive and beats me to it. "Nelly, the core thinking is figuratively based on the scientific and fundamental building blocks of matter. From a business perspective, internal group formation has a direct impact on decision-making, productivity, problem solving, and organizational influence. This is based on several studies..."

For the next thirty minutes, Professor Botticello delivers an exhausting, research-based explanation.

Phew—hard to argue with that.

"Now do you understand?" he finally asks her.

Nelly looks embarrassed and nods as she sinks into her seat. Someone should have told her to never, *ever* argue with the professor if you don't have your facts straight; because unbeknownst to Nelly, the Building Blocks theory that she claimed "didn't make sense," the backbone theory of my presentation, was indeed penned by none other than Professor Botticello himself.

"Thanks, Feddy," Professor Botticello says at the conclusion of class. "Excellent work."

I blush with pride, but resist glancing at Nelly.

I'm still in awe of the daily access the students have to the most distinguished authors and researchers in the world, usually right under our noses as professors.

I smile a thank you to Botticello and take my seat, silently reminding myself that for every Nelly there are a thousand wonderful Juliet Ann's and Sookie's.

THREE'S COMPANY

"Remember Hugh Grant?" Sookie asks mischievously while we prepare to head home for Christmas, the final holiday break of our business school lives.

I think for a minute. "The British guy you were hanging on at Winter Carnival last year?"

She frowns. "I wouldn't necessarily call it 'hanging,' but yes. Him."

Put a bell on her head and she could have been a Christmas tree ornament.

"Draped?" I ask teasingly.

"Anyway," Sookie continues, ignoring me, "he's moving in with us in January!"

Us? Us who?

"What!?" I stop zipping my suitcase.

"He's coming on exchange from London Business School!"

"What!?" I repeat.

"We've been emailing for the past year...I told him about our place...and the extra room...and he mentioned he was looking for housing..."

A guy? In our small apartment?

"Sookie, I don't think so!"

"He's really, really nice! And sweet!"

Men's underwear in the laundry room, more annoying phone calls and messages, more dirty dishes...

"It's just for Term Two," she assures me. "Our last term here!"

No more pajama mornings on the couch, no more panty hose and bras hanging in the shower, no more running from the bathroom to my bedroom in just a towel...

"And we could use the money..." she reminds me.

Cha-ching.

Hmm.

"Please, please say it's okay?" She blinks her big brown eyes.

I sigh, finally conceding. "Okay."

"Thanks!" Sookie bounces off the walls, hugging me as she rocks us from side to side. "He'll be moving in right after our holiday break—in January. And don't worry—he absolutely, positively won't be a third wheel or anything!"

No, but will I?

CHAPTER 10

❋

TAKING STOCK OF YOUR INVESTMENTS

(The Final Term: Finding Meaning in It All)

"I'm flying to California for three interviews on Monday, coming back on Tuesday, meeting Rick in Massachusetts on Wednesday, spending a few days with his family, heading out with my old, pre-MBA friends on Friday, going out with business school friends on Saturday, going to a wedding on Sunday, and oh yeah, squeezing in 70 hours of homework and miscellaneous projects," I say to Sookie as we discuss our Spring Break plans over lunch.

My schedule doesn't faze us.

If fact, it sounds easy.

I look at my cases for tomorrow: *Mt. Dew's New Creative* and *Process Redesign for Procter & Gamble's CoverGirl Cosmetics.*

Hmm…that should take all of 20 minutes.

OUR BOARDER

Hugh Grant's name is Finneas.

And he's not as bad as the nightmare I envisioned. In fact, he's quite delightful and charming.

"I'm in love!" Sookie tells me after Finneas's first week. "He's wonderful!" she gushes.

I've never seen Sookie this happy.

Well, except for last term when she aced her Corporate Finance exam.

There's definitely something in the air between the two of them, but they're keeping a tight lid on it. However, a roommate can sense these things, especially when I see them sitting dangerously close to one another on the couch, spending weekends together, or laughing from behind closed doors into all hours of the night. (I don't mind the noise—it's a thousand times better than the musical earthquakes from Butler Lounge.)

And I actually like having Finneas around for our final term of business school. He's not the uppity, Oxford-bred stereotype at all—in fact, he's quite shy and sweet—and we have lengthy kitchen conversations about life, religion, and the unfair treatment of women in the media. Plus, he reluctantly gives me a fun dose of Royal tabloid gossip when I pester him for it.

"The British are quite different from Americans," Finneas explains to us one night at dinner, homebound after yet another January storm delivers eight inches of snow.

"In what way?" Sookie asks, pouring water from a glass pitcher into my glass.

Finneas rests his fork on his plate and finishes his bite. "Americans are quite lovely, actually. There's a cheeriness about them that's quite contagious and I like that. And we share a common language which is convenient despite some bits having different meaning."

His verbal formality never ceases to amuse me. "But isn't business etiquette different?" I ask.

He pauses to consider the differences. "Well, the famous American enthusiasm may not translate quite as well overseas, nor would certain aggressive selling tactics." He takes the pitcher from Sookie. "And we use humor quite often."

"If you can call sarcasm humor!" Sookie teases.

I cut a slice of French bread, adding, "Or the art of understatement."

"Ouch!" Finneas smiles, securing a tuft of light brown hair behind his left ear. "At least in England *we* can have business lunches in pubs, don't forget. It's quite nice, actually." He passes the blackberry spinach salad to Sookie. "And overall I think I'm quite happy with my assimilation here—especially with the abominable and perpetual snowstorms."

"Mmm...speaking of snow, snowboarding tomorrow at three, Finneas?" Sookie reminds him.

His eyes brighten. "Three it is."

"Oh, Feddy." Sookie wipes a crouton crumb from the corner of her bottom lip. "Before I forget, Kingsbury-Kutter called for you yesterday. Call them back *immediately.*" She reaches for her water.

They're like relentless hounds over there. It's only January, for Pete's sake.

"I'll call them after class tomorrow," I assure her, brushing it off with a nervous smile.

For the next 45 minutes we linger over dinner while talking about classes. Finneas and I will be spending a lot of time together this term because we have an identical course load: Information Technology, Digital Strategies, Corporate Governance, Nonprofit Management, Product Positioning, Leadership, and Brand Management. Sookie has Taxation, Investments, Business in Asia, and Supply Chain Management among others.

"Sookie reveals that you've had quite a challenging time at business school?" Finneas asks empathetically, his blue eyes full of warm concern.

This brings a blush to my cheeks. I glare at Sookie who shrugs her shoulders and smiles sheepishly.

"I'm sorry. I didn't intend to embarrass you," he says.

"Yeah, well, it's not *that* bad…" I try to explain to Finneas.

Sookie clears her throat.

"Okay! Okay!" I humbly admit. "There may have been some…uh, *emotional trauma* that may have, well, *disrupted* my regular cognitive process and chipped away at my psychological dynamic a little."

"Ha!" Sookie laughs dismissively. "She's completely miserable, Finneas!"

"But Second Year has been much better than First Year!" I remind her, refraining from blurting that my grades last term were the best they've ever been. "I'm definitely not experiencing the same trepidation."

"It's never easy, I understand," Finneas interjects and reaches toward the rack for a bottle of dessert wine. "I took a detour from the darkest reaches of my mind to put it all into perspective last year."

The darkest reaches? Yes, that's what I have! Deep, dark reaches.

"What did you do?" I ask him.

"Well," he contemplates while opening a bottle of V. Sattui's Angelica, "I continuously reminded myself of my purpose—what I hoped to accomplish in business school, what I could do with the degree in the future, and such."

I love that Finneas carries a pure perspective—he's still seduced by the bewitching charm of The School, but not yet tainted by its power—but I still find myself saying, "That sounds too easy."

"True, it was difficult at first," he continues, "but eventually those thoughts left little time for rubbish like social politics or wallowing in my sorrows." He pours wine into three goblets. "Perhaps we have to make room in our lives for the good things, and sometimes that requires quite a bit of mental reorganization."

"I feel like I've finally made room for the 'good things,' but now I don't know what the 'good things' are anymore," I explain.

"It's quite unrealistic to expect to know immediately what you want to change in the world, and then to know exactly *how* you want to change it. Perhaps allow yourself more time to work it out? No sense in harming yourself with torment."

"But we're graduating in a few months," I remind him.

"Well..." he searches for an answer. "This could warrant a lifetime effort—there's no rush. It's an evolution of sorts." He smiles and lifts his wine glass.

"Ad astra per aspera," he toasts in Latin.

"Cheers!" Sookie chimes, clinking her glass against Finn's and then mine.

"Cheers!" I echo, thankful to have them around for the final B-school stretch.

✳ ✳ ✳ ✳

That night, I search online to find a loose translation of Finn's toast—ad astra per aspera—which turns out to be wholly appropriate for not only business school but also for the enormity of life.

"It's a hard road to the stars."

I HEARD YOU THE FIRST TIME!

Term Two of our Second Year is like the last week of college—a carefree campus full of problems suddenly sedated with an impassive and blissfully remedial "Who cares?"

Likewise, the days are passing like minutes; and if I can be bold for one of those minutes, I'll also admit that classes and business calculations have become even easier than they were last term. Likewise, this term has allowed me to develop a friendship threesome with my roommates. Sookie and I spend our free time skiing or swimming in the indoor pool, if we're not attending parties or dinners; and almost all of my academic time is spent with Finneas as we prepare reports and presentations for our classes. Last night, we stayed up until 1 a.m. rehearsing a skit for our Leadership class, role-playing two senior executives trying to negotiate better rates on chocolate shipments for Nestle. We spent most of the night laughing, making fun of Professor Leidershtot, and debating American versus European chocolate; surprisingly, our hard work rewarded us with a great performance in class this morning.

Finneas and Sookie also seem to be growing closer, spending every weekend snowboarding; they frequently let me tag along because Rick has been Mr. Big Workaholic lately. And in February, Finneas, who seems to spend every waking moment volunteering, encouraged us to spend a weekend working with him at a women's shelter in Boston—he said generosity would invigorate us and force us to get "outside of our heads." He was right—working with carpenters and engineers to build a new lobby for the shelter turned out to be the most glorious and inspiring retreat from B-school pressures, yet.

By "B-school pressures" I mean recruiting, which is, by far, the main technical stress of this final term.

Still undecided, I've been spending my valuable lunch hours attending "Guess Who's Coming to Campus?" speaker sessions with alums who now have successful, but varied, careers: a booming board game business, product management for Jamba Juice, marketing for Nestle, secondary interests in private equity…you name it, an alumna has done it. And every week I scope the recruiting companies on campus because I'm still involved in the cutthroat interviewing process. This week's list of companies include:

- Boston Consulting Group
- The Walt Disney Company
- Gillette
- Pfizer
- John Deere
- American Express
- Microsoft
- Aetna
- Merrill Lynch
- Saks Fifth Avenue
- Putnam Investments
- General Electric
- Dell
- Citigroup
- PricewaterhouseCooper

Second Year recruiting season also welcomes a series of corporate-sponsored events open to the student masses—GE Capital hosted a cocktail party; Bain hosted a reception with hors d'oeuvres at the posh La Folie restaurant; Goldman Sachs provided an open bar at a local winery last week; and General Mills will sponsor a Boston harbor cruise in May. The events have common, powerfully hypnotic themes, "Come work with the best!" or "Think beyond your dreams—join us!" The companies spend generous resources wooing job candidates with decadent parties, but don't be fooled—true pleasure of enjoyment is not allowed. Even the most casual events are opportunities for corporate representatives to scrutinize your every move—attire, humor, posture, wit, group dynamic, ability to sell…you have to be "on." I'm attending as many events as I can; my cheeks ache from chronic smiling, and my voice is hoarse, but I'm hoping my quest will eventually enlighten me.

Unfortunately, I still haven't found my "niche" as we say in marketing.

It's hard to find chatter about anything besides recruiting within a 10-mile radius of The School. The offers are pouring in for my classmates and Tami and JP have been our daily cheerleaders. Most offers are for the traditional and stereo-typical MBA roles—investment banking, consulting, and marketing. As usual, those seeking non-traditional careers have to get a little more creative. One of my classmates, Lisa Girard, revealed to me that she had a terrible time securing a job at a low-paying nonprofit simply because they were reluctant to hire "an MBA." It's not the first time I've heard of people discriminating against MBAs—some corporations won't even interview us. Their prejudice simply powers the stereo-type.

Other students, however, continue to unabashedly boast recent victories. I'm usually too busy with my internal struggles over my career to care about the exter-nal social pressures that are mounting, but sometimes they're overwhelming. For-tunately, I have a stock of responses I frequently use to fend off the braggarts in the mailroom, in the classroom, in the dining hall, at parties, in the bathroom, and anywhere else classmates may unsuspectingly corner me with the bloated and swanky particulars of their latest conquests:

"Your *twelfth* job offer? WOW, that's great!" [Smile.]
"$150,000? Congrats—that's AWESOME." [Drop jaw. Hand to cheek.]
"250 people reporting to you? *Including* a Vice President!? Wonderful!"
"A $30K bonus simply for *accepting* the job? Fantastic!"
"And free health insurance for a year? Super!" [Shake head in awe.]

But that's nothing compared to what's happening right now in the dining hall.

Tempestt has erupted into tears.

"Why are you crying?" Juliet Ann asks sympathetically over today's lunch special: vegetable, deep-dish pizza.

Tempestt dabs the outer corners of her eyes with a paper napkin. "I just"—she shakes her head in disbelief—"can't believe how much *money* they're going to be paying me!" She blows her nose loudly.

Tempestt received an offer this morning from a small online consulting company in New York.

Juliet Ann and I exchange "you've got to be kidding" glances. Sookie and Suresh are having a private conversation at the other end of the table, completely (and luckily) oblivious to the dramatics.

"Congratulations," I say as Tempestt continues to hyperventilate. "But I still don't understand why you're crying?"

She wails louder, "Don't you get it? If the company goes public next year, I'll be"—she pauses to catch her breath—"a millionaire!"

Tempestt is crying because she's going to be rich? Whaa!

"I just can't believe this is happening to me!" she howls, releasing the waterworks. "I grew up poor! And now I'll probably be richer than all of you!" She blows her nose again between Lucille Ball-like sobs.

Just when you thought you'd seen everything at business school.

Stifling our laughs, Juliet Ann and I resign to hugging Tempestt with surprisingly sincere congratulations—in a strange way, it's hard not to be happy for her.

When my nausea subsides, and the weeping drowns to a low moan, I seize the opportunity to check my voicemail messages.

There's a call from Rick reminding me that he's flying to San Francisco this weekend to look at apartments and office space. I haven't talked to him since last Sunday.

Wow, has it really been a week?

We seem to talk less during the week, but I still see Rick on the weekends; and it's nice because I have more time to emotionally support him when he vents about the tribulations of a start-up. He's stressed beyond capacity—he's busy adding yet another source of revenue to Emode's business model, managing an uncooperative and greedy Human Resources Director, dealing with an emotionally unpredictable COO, and evaluating an unexpected buyout offer they recently received from a rival company. On top of that, he's struggling to manage Emode's 3,000-mile move to California. 24 hours a day are not enough for him.

The second message is from The School's surprisingly pleasant Facilities Manager, reminding me that I have $400 of unpaid parking tickets, which, if left unpaid, could result in my failure to graduate.

Delete.

The third message is from Kingsbury-Kutter. *Yikes.* It's the Recruiting Assistant. "Please be aware that the deadline for your job offer is fast approaching. We anxiously await to hear from you at your earliest convenience—"

I delete the message before prompted to do so, feeling hot around the collar. It's the third voicemail from them this month.

"Are you feeling well?" Finneas ask me, sliding his tray next to mine.

"Yeah, yeah, I'm fine." I turn the phone over in my hand.

He's not convinced. "Let's have dinner tonight—before we finish Corporate Governance—and we can talk. It can't be that bad?"

"You're right. It's not that bad," I agree, trying to smile. "But dinner sounds great."

I've become a master at the art of ignoring the humongous issues looming over my head like a blossoming monsoon ready to erupt.

Maybe I need another distraction…

GLAD I GOT TO KNOW YOU, STAY COOL, AND KEEP IN TOUCH

Do they give Pulitzers for yearbooks?

Who cares—I'm thrilled!

I've just volunteered to be Co-editor of the yearbook!

It's my goal to ensure that every student has at least one picture in the yearbook and today is my first meeting with the other Co-editor with whom I will be working side-by-side, day-by-day, for the next three grueling months. I can't wait—we'll be huddled in the yearbook room editing and cutting away until the wee hours of the night under tight yearbook guidelines. Maybe we can order pizza, blast the music, perhaps even bring in some movies and make a party out of it—girls' night!

I swing open the door to the yearbook room.

The doves stop singing, the flowers wilt, animals crawl into the ground, and dark clouds sweep overhead.

"What are you doing here?" Nelly shouts at me.

"I'm…I'm the new Co-editor."

"Well then, grab a photo and get started. We don't have all day." She motions to the chair across the table and points to the messy pile of photos in front of her.

"W-w-what are you doing here?" I ask, frozen, and unassumingly invite her sarcasm.

"Well, Feddy, you see, I'm under house-arrest for a series of brutal crimes against cafeteria food. My punishment is to spend eternity locked in this ridiculously small room creating yearbooks with you." She rolls her eyes. "What do you *think*!? I'm Co-editor!"

"Right. Co-editor. With me. In this room," I say numbly.

"Very good." She turns her words slowly. "And these are pho-*tos*. And this is a *computer*. With more pho-*tos* on it. And this is a pen…"

"Got it," I interrupt.

The door shuts behind me, locking us into our cell.

My own private prison.

❄   ❄   ❄   ❄

"Cheers" Finneas chimes, clinking his glass against mine.

"Cheers," I echo, taking a drink.

We're in our apartment celebrating a successful website launch for our Digital Strategies class. Unfortunately, Sookie has an evening class and can't join us for the living room celebration; I'm simply glad to be anywhere but the yearbook room.

I put my beer on the table, sink into the couch, and glance at my watch. "Well, Finneas, we have 10 minutes to celebrate before we have to start Nonprofit Management."

"Ah, yes, the marketing plan." He nods. "I shall savor these few precious moments…"

I laugh and reach for my backpack on the floor, pulling the heavy bag onto the couch next to me.

"Is something wrong?" he asks after a brief silence.

Realizing that I may have zoned out for a minute, I quickly respond, "No, why do you ask?"

He raises his eyebrows. "Is it Rick?"

I sigh and stop unzipping my bag. "Maybe a little."

"Because he's not around?"

"And some other stuff, yeah."

"He loves you, you know."

I search for the zipper on my bag again. "I know."

Finneas folds his hands and leans forward in his chair, letting his elbows rest on his knees. "The earliest stages of his new business will be the most difficult. If he had time for you in the past, he will certainly make time for you in the future. Don't let the relationship slip away…"

I explain, "A lot has changed this year—it took me by surprise."

"Life is about sacrifices."

I suddenly wonder if men face similar dilemmas at business school, having to make sacrifices for their wives' careers like this. "Sometimes I wonder if men have it easier at B-school," I admit.

Finneas laughs. "Trust me, we have our own set of problems." He relaxes back into his chair. "We sometimes put undue burden on our shoulders, carry the extra weight, refuse to ask for help, and then feel guilty about major sacrifices or missed opportunities. Then we suffer in silence, often seeking solace in a bottle." He smiles to let me know he's kidding and tilts his head to the left, allowing a flock of hair to fall over his eye. 'It's quite a sad tale, really."

"Sounds like you've got a lot to look forward to?" I smirk.

"I'll let you know."

We laugh and he closes his eyes for a minute and opens them before continuing, "My chief fear is not so much that the grass is greener, but that there are major sacrifices in life and you have to take responsibility for those decisions whether you are happy or not…"

"You feel like life is happening to you more so than you are choosing what happens?" I ask after a brief pause.

His eyes widen. "Yes, precisely." But his voice trails and he suddenly looks out the window. "Do you think this snow will ever subside?"

Did someone switch to the Weather Channel?

Understanding he may wish to change topics, I nod and stare at the drizzling snow with him.

Then I spread my body on the couch and spoon my backpack while lying on my side. "Have your views toward business changed recently?" I ask tentatively.

"Yes, I'm afraid, they have," he confides. "It's impossible not to be affected, wouldn't you agree?"

A soul who understands me? "Yes," I say excitedly, suddenly sitting. "It's like, business doesn't excite me the way it has in the past—I'm more critical, especially of marketing to kids. Now, when a company launches a new product, I'm thinking about whether or not consumers really need that product, whether they can afford it, whether the product is healthy, whether we've used too many resource to make it…"

He nods. "And I find it appalling that our society is quite a disposable culture. The days of not wasting are long gone." He reaches for his beer, changing tones. "But, if the knowledge one has acquired is indeed this new ability to challenge business practices and to think analytically…perhaps this is a truly beneficial skill to own?" he reminds me.

"True, albeit just different from what I planned to learn at business school…" I turn to face him.

"It's quite all right to take away a learning that is different from what everyone else is gathering—that's how you'll change the world."

"To each his own, even in education," I agree, suddenly remembering Morteza's words from last year about business school providing a life-long *skill-set.*

Finneas remains silent as the corners of his mouth turn upward and his eyes pleasantly gaze at me.

Our 10 minutes have expired.

"Ready for Nonprofit Management?" I finally ask, unzipping my bag.

His blue eyes sparkle. "Straight away."

I'll TAKE JOBLESS, HOMELESS, AND AIMLESS FOR $400, ALEX

"Cheers to your impending graduation!" Rick toasts over dinner at Fazio's Ristorante & Pizzeria. "Three more months!"

We're trying to regain some amount of normalcy in our relationship. *Operation Emotional Avoidance.*

"Yes!" I joke, clinking my wine glass against his. "Cheers to being jobless, homeless, and aimless at graduation! Yipee!"

"Feddy!" he chastises.

"Hey, at least I'm a good sport," I remind him.

"It's not like you don't have opportunities—and you don't have to decide your entire future right now, just a few immediate things."

"Oh, contraire. Do you know how humiliating it is to hear all of my class-mates repeatedly talk about their exciting post-graduation plans? It's like the rest of the world stops moving!"

He nods. "Unfortunately, I do remember."

"Whether I want to or not, I know *exactly* how many job offers each classmate has—complete with salary, signing bonus, stock options, and retirement benefits. I can't even enter the dining hall without someone bamboozling me with their latest relocation details." I sip my water. "And conversations with my classmates have been reduced to having only one of two motives: one, to provide a forum for my classmate to reveal how 'absolutely amazing' his or her latest job offer is, or two, to reveal that I am the big loser who doesn't know where she is going to work. I don't want to hear any more of the details—salaries, office space, perks, benefits—I don't care! I just want to put a bag over my head, hide in a corner, and be left alone," I say.

"Half of them are lying, you know." He breaks off a piece of garlic bread in the basket.

Wow, this almost feels like Rick and I are back to normal.

"They're just as confused as you are," he continues. "They'll take jobs they don't really want for a year and then wake up one day and wonder, 'What the heck am I doing with my life?' and go through the same thing you are right now. Technically, you're ahead of schedule."

"Right on time for my quarter life crisis. Perfect." I laugh.

He raises his left eyebrow accusingly.

"I know, I know," I concede, taking the breadbasket he hands to me. "It's just hard to make life decisions with people constantly bombarding me with their nosey questions."

"Ignore them."

"I'm trying." I smile, not wanting him to feel concerned. "But don't worry about me—I'll decide what to do with my life soon. I just got thrown off my uncomplicated path for a minute."

"A detour?"

"Exactly!"

Definitely a nice, normal conversation…

The waiter arrives with two plates of Chicken Parmesan.

"And JP gave an encouraging career services presentation on Wednesday," I continue as we begin our meals. "He said that 65% of our class has accepted full-time job offers already but fewer are in banking or consulting; there are more entrepreneurial ventures than in previous years."

He laughs. "I hope they know what they're getting themselves into…"

Rick has been working like a maniac managing one Emode crisis after another.

"So what did you decide?" he asks.

"This Chicken Parmesan is definitely delicious!" I confirm with my mouth full, and cut into a second piece.

"No! Not about the chicken…about California and us," he says in even tones.

Oh, that.

"Yes, about California," I repeat. (Repetition is a clever conversation-stalling tactic I learned in my communications class.)

"Yes, about California," he also repeats, slightly annoyed.

God, I hate these dual MBA conversations.

I clear my throat. "Well, what are you thinking—given how things have been lately?"

"I don't know."

"It would be nice if we could talk it out—make a decision together—instead of all of it resting on my shoulders—"

"But I thought you wanted to make your own decisions?"

"I do," I explain. "But that doesn't mean we shouldn't share opinions. I could really use your support with the decision. Some encouragement, at least."

"Have you told Kingsbury-Kutter, yet?"

"No—but it's not about them. I don't think I'll be going there either way." My fork lingers over my baked potato as I wait for the comfort of my defense mechanism (my wandering mind) to take over. "I can't see you next weekend; it's Admitted Students Weekend," I randomly remind him.

"I'll be in California anyway, remember?"

"If things were a little better between us, the decision probably wouldn't be so difficult," I finally admit bluntly.

"It's not that hard."

"But it is!"

And so begins a rousing night of entertainment—the spin cycle of arguments followed by the blame game.

So much for normalcy tonight.

ADMITTED STUDENTS WEEKEND

Having missed Admitted Students Weekend last March because I was knee-deep in study group politics, bad grades, and social anxiety, I have decided to participate in this year's festivities—an exhausting two days of barbeques, cocktail parties, dinners, lectures, student panels, tours, and parties for recently-accepted students who need a "gentle nudge" when deciding whether to attend The School.

"More like a gentle push off a cliff," Juliet Ann jokes as we enter the Main House, wiping our boots on the carpet while pulling off our heavy jackets and gloves.

We've volunteered to work the official Welcome Booth, meeting and greeting admitted students as they arrive. Tami has instructed all volunteers to be themselves—friendly, cordial, excited, and positive, but mostly honest. I refrain from telling Tami that if I were to be "honest" with the prospective students, 50% would run home crying to mommy, turn on the gas, and stick their heads in an oven.

But I am, after all, trying to make peace with my journey—and I really want more people to come here—so I've agreed to help with the soft recruiting and be on my best behavior.

Most of the time.

"Why should I go to *your* school?" a large man bellows as he charges toward the Welcome Booth where Juliet Ann and I are waiting to hand him a weekend agenda, a school coffee mug, a bag of chocolates emblazoned with the school logo, and a packet of miscellaneous brochures explaining why our program is the best in the world.

Students applying to business school are motivated to be on their best behavior, but apparently students already admitted have nothing to lose.

"Tell me why I should go to your school!" Big Mouth repeats impatiently.

Because we're probably the only school that accepted you? Because it's the lesser of all the evil programs? Because it will bring you to your knees and knock the ego right out of you?

"You'll soon find out!" I say with a smile and hand him a brochure. "You can read our latest statistics—we're ranked the 4th best business school in the country and 8th in the world; 100% of last year's class had jobs by graduation. But the students and alums will give you a candid perspective of the program—talk to them and I guarantee you won't hear a bad word." I smile again.

He opens his mouth to challenge me, but I cut him off by saying, "Hello, thanks for making it to New Hampshire for the weekend!" to the next person in line. Eventually, Big Mouth moves on and Juliet Ann and I spend the next four hours smiling and distributing chocolates. Most of the people are nice and have intelligent questions (and kudos to them for commuting in 21 inches of snow), but there are a few other Big Mouths with rude, arrogant tones. They think they'd be doing The School a favor by attending. Someone should remind them that there are 10,000 hopefuls just waiting to take an open spot at this business school.

At the end of the day, Juliet Ann and I head downtown to Malley's pub for cocktail hour.

❊   ❊   ❊   ❊

"No!" Sookie shrieks and spills the foam from the top of her beer glass.

"I don't believe it," I say, unraveling the scarf from my neck, glad to be inside where it's warm.

Tempestt nods. "It's true," she assures.

"Lauren Heffenberger did *not* sleep with an admitted student!" I yell over the crowded bar. "No way." I shake my head.

"Yes, she did—and it's not a bad thing!" Tempestt argues.

"It is if you're a Second Year and he's a prospective student visiting the campus for Admitted Students Weekend!" Sookie jokes as we stand at the bar. "Can you imagine what he must think? Come to our school—get your MBA and get laid! How's *that* for a marketing campaign!?"

"Gives new meaning to the phrase welcome wagon." Tempestt laughs as a huge crowd storms the door and the bar becomes packed to capacity.

"Tami would be *so* proud," Sookie adds with a giggle.

"Of course she would!" Tempestt agrees. "So would the whole administration—Lauren just doubled our annual application rate! Not to mention potential endowment…"

"Listen, Lauren can sleep with whomever she desires, any weekend she desires. But it's just a rumor. Let's not jump to conclusions," I say.

Sookie and Tempestt laugh harder. "Please!" Sookie says. "Lighten up!"

"I don't like spreading rumors—especially about women. We need all the support we can get." I put my empty glass on the bar.

"You do have a point," Tempestt agrees. "Last month everyone was talking about that drunk First Year who paraded naked at Jason's house party."

Sookie nods. "Ellyn Fitz."

"But I heard it wasn't even true—she was actually out of town that weekend!" Tempestt says.

"*Precisely*," I confirm. "It wasn't true, but everyone believed it. And everyone talked about what an irresponsible decision it was on her part, but no one—*no one*—mentioned what jerks the guys were for not covering her up! The idea that those *gentlemen* didn't take *any* responsibility for helping her infuriated me.

"Good God, even rumors favor men," Tempestt says, finishing her beer. "On second thought—forget everything I said about Lauren." She puts two dollars on the bar and whispers, "Somebody help me, I sound more and more like Juliet Ann every day..."

"Don't tell Juliet Ann about this latest rumor," I say, thinking of Juliet Ann's protective nature and disdain for fraternity-type rumors. I instinctively strain my neck to look out the window to confirm she's still outside, shivering on her phone in front of the bar.

"Oh my God, she'd freak out!" Sookie agrees. "She's already upset about that faculty comment."

"What faculty comment?" Tempestt asks.

I push my body onto a recently vacated barstool. "A frustrated professor was talking about minority students who need academic help and someone overheard him say, 'Well then *they* shouldn't be here!' referring to the minorities."

Tempestt's jaw drops. "That happened here?" she yells over the noise.

"No, not here. Some other East Coast business school—can't remember which one," I yell back.

"That's just as bad as Daniel Teski and Christopher Sousa," Tempestt says, referring to two of our classmates who were reprimanded by the administration last week for using hand signals to rate the attractiveness of female students as they entered classrooms.

"I'm looking for Bridgette but I can't find her..." Sookie interrupts, scanning the bar, referring to her First Year mentee. "I told her I'd introduce her to you guys."

"At least you *have* a mentee," I say with envy. "I didn't get one this year—Tami told me there were too few women."

"That sucks! I love being a mentor," Sookie says.

"Don't you love being a Second Year, watching all of the First Years painfully squirm their way through a dreadful and sickening year?" Tempestt laughs.

"You're a pillar of support as a mentor, aren't you?" I joke, feeling sorry for her mentee.

A large crowd passes by from which Suresh emerges.

"Hello, ladies!" he says, putting his palm over the top of his beer glass to keep it from spilling as the crowd continues to squeeze by.

"Hi, Suresh," we say in unison.

"Nice job in Corporate Governance today!" he says to me.

I blush a little. "Oh, thanks."

Tempestt and Sookie perk up. "What happened?" Tempestt asks, raising her eyebrows. "Do tell, Miss Feddy."

"She told Cooper off!" Suresh shouts.

Sookie laughs. "Well, it's about time someone did!"

"I wouldn't exactly say that I 'told him off.'"

"What are you talking about? You bulldozed him into a lifeless mound of dirt!" Suresh assures me.

"Well…I get very *protective* of marketing. He had it coming," I explain, then turn toward Sookie and Tempestt. "Cooper was delivering one of his long-winded, academy-award winning schpeals about how great investment banking is and how marketing is for weaklings who don't like to work."

"And Feddy told him that if he had one ounce of creativity in his body that he wouldn't be a banker in the first place," Suresh boasts.

Sookie laughs. "You didn't?"

"I hope you *did*," Tempestt urges.

"I did." I smile to confirm. "But I really hate having to stoop to his level." I unzip my sweater a few notches as the body heat rises in the bar. "And now *The Imposters* really dislike me and may *never* talk to me again. Oh no!" I wipe a fake tear from my right eye.

The group plays along and pretends to pout, too. "We should all be so lucky!" Tempestt says.

Sookie tries to grab a napkin from the bar but can't reach. "Cooper has been gloating all week about his new offer. He wants to make sure that everyone knows he received the most coveted I-banking offer at The School, the best job out there."

Suresh hands her a napkin. "Correction—Cooper's getting the best job *for him,* not the best job out there."

"In his eyes, they're synonymous," I say.

"How's Rick?" Tempestt asks me.

"Fine!" I answer a little too loudly and defensively. Tempestt and Sookie exchange glances.

"Everything okay?" Sookie asks.

"Yeah, yeah, fine. He's in California right now, checking out the area. I'm going to see him next weekend." A big, fake grin dominates my face. I'll tell Sookie the truth later.

"He doesn't seem to be around lately," Tempestt pressures, squinting her eyes to read my reaction carefully.

Suresh clears his throat. "He's a busy guy with a busy business! Did you hear about Evan's new job? He's going to be a buyer for Saks Fifth Avenue."

To my relief, Suresh has changed the subject. Apparently fashion is more exciting than my relationship because Sookie and Tempestt ravenously pump Suresh for details about our classmate's new job while I zone out, thinking about Rick.

I haven't talked to Rick this week, have I?

"Hey, where's Finneas?" Sookie asks at the precise moment Finneas makes his way through the crowd to the bar.

"Finneas!" Suresh cheers.

"We were just wondering about you!" Sookie hugs him.

"Sorry I'm late," Finneas says to the group, but looks at me with apologetic eyes as Sookie unravels his scarf. I look away before he can search my eyes, trying to figure the quickest way to escape.

Truth be told, I've been avoiding Finneas for days. We had a potentially disastrous encounter five nights ago and I've been making up lame excuses to avoid him.

Last Friday night, hoping to salvage the rest of the weekend, Finneas and I stayed home to finish our Brand Management presentation on Mercedes-Benz. The trouble began as we worked until midnight on the floor of my bedroom, amidst a messy pile of marketing books, notebooks, computers, and crumpled printouts of our presentation drafts.

"If we draw a perception map on slide four—" I sigh.

"We won't have room for the brand scorecard," Finneas finishes my sentence.

"Exactly!" I nod as I change the slide layout on my laptop for the hundredth time, lying on my stomach as I type.

He runs a hand through his hair in frustration and grabs a marketing text, flipping to the chapter on brand equity; he rolls onto his back, holding the book mid-air as he continues to read.

"I've got it!" He jolts upright, smiling. "We'll do the pyramid."

"The brand pyramid of resonance?" I ask, excited.

"Yes!"

I practically scream, "Perfect!"

My excitement from being seconds away from completing our presentation completely overshadows the sad fact that I'm ridiculously giddy about a silly marketing pyramid.

"You're a genius!" I say while still lying on the floor, frantically typing the changes to our slide.

He blushes. "Thanks."

Finneas begins to clean the notebooks and papers scattered on the floor around us.
He reaches for a folder near my keyboard at the same time I do. His hand covers
mine and lingers for what feels like an enormous blow of electricity through our
hands.
What on earth was that?
I gasp and pull my hand away as I jolt into a sitting position.
He stares at me wide-eyed and stunned. "I'm so…sorry," he says hesitantly,
undoubtedly as surprised as I am.
"I'm sorry, too…" I echo shakily.
We can't bear to look at one another as we awkwardly scramble to clean my room,
then hurriedly mumble goodnight before scattering away.

Since then, with all the maturity of a fifth-grader, I have successfully avoided
all contact with Finneas. Now, seeing him tonight in the bar, I can feel the stress
rising as he waits for me to make eye contact.

My phone vibrates in my pocket as I try to work out what to do with Finneas.

It's a text message from Kingsbury-Kutter! My head feels hot and my palms
moist. It's another message from Human Resources asking me to call them *imme-*
diately with my decision. They simply can't wait any longer.

Rick, Kingsbury-Kutter, my family, where to live, where to work, what to do…

"You okay?" Sookie asks with concern, reading the discomfort on my face.

"Yeah, yeah I'm fine." I smile and put my phone away, wondering what in the
world I'm going to do and knowing that I am most certainly not fine.

OUT WITH THE NEW, IN WITH THE OLD

My cell phone rings at 8 a.m.

"Hello?" I ask sleepily.

"It's Nelly."

"Up early on a Saturday morning, eh?"

"We have a problem." She ignores me. "People aren't submitting enough photos for the yearbook. Did you make that poster for the mailroom?"

"Yes—I hung a poster on the bulletin board. In addition to the 1,000 email
reminders and 800 classroom announcements."

"The sign's not big enough. We need to make it bigger," she snaps.

I speak slowly as though she's a child. "Okay…well, I'm in Massachusetts
right now trying to spend some overdue quality time with my boyfriend. I won't
be back until tomorrow."

"But it needs to be done today."

My head throbs. "Right…but you see, I'm not in the same *state*. Are you on campus?"

"Yes."

"Can't you just run to the mailroom and fix it with a marker? If not, I'll do it as soon as I return on Monday morning."

"It needs to be done today," she repeats. "You need you to fix it *today*."

Earth to Nelly, come in, Nelly.

"Yes, but again, I'm not *there*," I explain.

"It's urgent."

"But we don't need the pictures today—we've got weeks," I shoot back. "If it's important to you, just fix it today."

ALL GOOD THINGS MUST COME TO AN END

After a few glasses of wine, Rick gets right to the point.

"Is it just me, or do you seem a little aloof tonight?" he asks.

"Yes, I am," I admit.

He sips his wine and then stares into his glass. "This wine is terrific. It reminds me of the stuff I bottled at Kevin's last year."

Silence.

I wait a few more seconds for him to admire his wine and then I continue, "You're not even going to ask me why?"

"Why what?"

"Why I'm being aloof?"

"Okay, why are you being aloof?"

"Do you even care?"

He sighs impatiently. "Yes, Feddy, I care," he says in bored monotones. "That's why I asked you."

"No, you asked because I asked if you were going to ask."

He rolls his eyes. "Whatever."

I drink the last of my wine. "It just seems strange that you wanted to know if I was being aloof, but then started talking about wine. It's confusing." I twirl my fork into the few remaining strands of spaghetti from a dinner I made for us tonight at his apartment. "And it hurts when you dismiss me with a 'whatever' or a sigh. You never used to do that."

"I'm just growing impatient," he states, all business. "Let's just get over it."

Get over it?

"I'm not one of your clients," I remind him, anger burning my cheeks crimson.

"I know you're not," he says, his disinterest angering me even more.

"Then why have you been treating me like one for the last month?" I say, struggling to keep my voice low in his dining room.

Silence.

When he doesn't speak, I put my fork down. "You're turning into one of them, you know."

He looks at me in disgust. "One of what? What are you talking about?"

"One of those"—I choose my next word carefully—"*confident* workaholic business types who grows increasingly impatient with everyone else and then finally resorts to rude one-liners when communicating, as though no one else's opinion matters, as though having compassion is a sign of weakness! Why are you acting this way?"

"I am not one of them." His words are sharp and deliberate.

I look at him but don't speak, silently asking myself the same question that I have been for weeks—*who is this person?* He's Dr. Jekyll and Mr. Hyde—one minute, jovial and lovable, and the next, cold, rude, and business-like.

"Don't," I warn him.

"Don't what?" He asks, in a voice that reveals he's just humoring me.

I look at him with disappointment. "Don't become one of them."

"But I thought you said I was *already* one of them? Which is it then?" He challenges me callously.

I shake my head slowly. "You're right," I say faintly. "Let's just drop it."

We sit for 5 minutes in another round of unbearable silence I don't understand. Finally, I try again.

"What's wrong?"

"Nothing." His eyes avert mine.

Cue the guessing game.

"Are you still mad about our conversation at Fazio's?" I guess.

"Well, yeah, I am."

"You could have just told me, rather than act like nothing was wrong and then shutting down and getting all business-like."

"This is how I am," he says defiantly.

"Well then, you've completely changed since business school."

"I'm still me," he reasons.

"Yeah, but with a joyless alter-ago."

"I've just had a lot on my mind at work lately. And it doesn't exactly seem like you want to be with me anyway, Feddy." And with that statement, he returns to his spaghetti, letting his eyes drift to a small landscape painting on the wall while he becomes emotionally unavailable for the night.

And for the rest of the weekend.

ENOUGH.

On Monday morning, I head to the yearbook room and take a seat across the table from Nelly, almost tripping over her golf clubs.

Another favorite B-school pastime.

"Hey, how was your weekend?" I ask her, feeling less than rejuvenated with overbearing thoughts of my future, Rick, and Kingsbury-Kutter.

She slams a black marker and the infamous cardboard mailroom poster onto the table in front of me.

"Fix it," she says.

"Fix what?"

"Here's the poster. Take the marker. And fix it." Her eyes narrow.

My head throbs. "Are you kidding?"

"You said you would fix it," she remarks.

"But…" I look at her confused. "That was only if you couldn't do it."

"Fix it," she orders.

Red or green kryptonite today? Hard to tell.

"Nook…" I push the marker toward her. "I'm not fixing it. It's your peeve."

I can't believe she brought the poster to me.

"Listen," I continue. "It's not right of you to ask me to fix it when you're here and can do it yourself. This is juvenile."

Silence. No acknowledgement.

"Nelly?"

She buries her head into a yearbook document.

"Nelly?"

No answer.

I don't believe this. "Are you giving me the *SILENT TREATMENT*?"

She jots notes on the paper.

I bite my lower lip to keep from laughing. "Nelly?" I wave my hand in front of her face, trying to get her attention.

Nada.

"Okay." I take a deep breath and rub my forehead. *Think think think.* "Nelly, you can't give me the silent treatment—we've got a yearbook to finish!"

She pushes the marker back toward me.

Silence.

More scribbling.

"This is really quite immature—you can talk to me like an adult, you know."

More feverish scribbling.

"Can you at least look at me?"

She pauses and reaches for a different pen.

"Nelly!" I shout.

Nothing.

"Nelly! Nelly! Nelly!" I chant louder, standing up.

She ignores me.

"NELLY!" I scream hysterically. "This is FREAKING ridiculous! Are you REALLY going to do something this IMMATURE?" I grab my bag and begin stuffing my belongings into it. "You are the epitome of B-school, aren't you, Nelly? You are just everything I hate about this place packaged into a little arrogant nutshell, aren't you? You are the living, breathing, gut-wrenching stereotype that spawns anti-business movements everywhere!"

I zip my bag. "I've been working my ass off, Nelly. And do you know why? BECAUSE I'M NOT LIKE YOU." I grab my sweater. "And because of that I'm being punished. I'm not full of testosterone. I don't seek gratification in putting others down. I don't have anything to prove…I ACTUALLY LIKE MYSELF THE WAY I AM! AND BECAUSE OF THAT, I HAVE TO WORK TWICE AS HARD TO DEAL WITH PEOPLE LIKE YOU DAY IN AND DAY OUT, DISTRACTING ME FROM MY REAL PURPOSE AND MERCILESSLY SUCKING EVERY LAST OUNCE OF MY ENERGY."

I feel the blush of rage creeping through my skin to my face. "I DON'T HAVE TIME FOR YOUR RIDICULOUS PETTINESS! BELIEVE IT OR NOT, I'VE GOT WHOPPERS OF PROBLEMS TO WORRY ABOUT—ENORMOUS, GIGANTIC, REAL PROBLEMS JUST LINED UP AND WAITING FOR ME!" I slide my chair toward the table. "I JUST CAME HERE TO LEARN, NELLY!" I swing by bag onto my shoulder. "IS THAT TOO MUCH TO ASK!? IS IT, NELLY?"

I storm out the door.

Oh God. What's happening to me? I can't believe I just yelled.

Tears of frustration burst from my eyes.

❅   ❅   ❅   ❅

The next morning, feeling penitent, I call her with a very humble and formal apology to which she reluctantly sighs, "whatever," before hanging up.

We avoid one another in the following weeks and somehow manage to finish the yearbook without speaking.

COMPLAINING WON'T STOP THE RAIN FROM FALLING

"I'm so happy that I'm here at business school," Sookie declares to a very shocked Juliet Ann and me over dinner at Brickhouse pizzeria one Thursday night.

How sad. And I really thought she had stopped smoking the crack.

"I'm just in a good mood," Sookie explains. "It's nice to see everything clicking. The Women in Business Club is working hard, every week we meet women who are changing the world, and I have fantastic people in my network now…"

"You sound like a walking advertisement," Juliet Ann says, raising her eyebrows.

"We can swing by the deprogramming center after dinner," I joke.

"Of course there are things I would change, but overall I'm in awe of The School." Sookie pauses dreamily before picking up her pizza slice. "And you know what? I don't want to complain about it any more! In fact, I'm sick of complaining!"

No more complaining? It's easier to imagine a life without air.

"It's not exactly complaining," I say defensively. "We're just *identifying* what's wrong so we can fix it."

"Then let's fix it!"

Sure, right after I replace the Hoover Dam with a band-aid.

"It's up to us to change it!" Sookie charges again.

Definitely placebo pill day.

"Listen," she says, reading both my thoughts and Juliet Ann's expression, "like you, I'm just sick of hearing people degrade the MBA. And I'm sick of lying back and letting The School step all over me. They want to make things better—I don't want to lie around doing nothing, I want to step up and help them to make it a better place."

"So you think the MBA is worth it, then?" Juliet Ann asks.

"Absolutely, it's worth it," Sookie says, taking a bite of her pizza and nodding 15 or 20 times reassuringly.

"But the opportunity cost! And the stress," I remind her.

She rolls her eyes. "What about the network? Contacts at almost every major company in the world. And the possibilities? You can run a nonprofit, start a magazine, launch your clothing line, join a global peace organization, *anything*. 'Women are the architects of society!'"

"Harriet Beecher Stowe?" Juliet Ann asks.

Sookie nods and continues her exuberant plea, "And no matter what we do in life, we'll always have this graduate degree. Don't you want to be able to take care of yourself when you turn 90? And your family?" She turns to Juliet Ann. "And don't you want financial freedom?"

"Of course—and I have it—I just want more women to have easier access to it. Business school needs flexibility," Juliet Ann explains.

Sookie's having fun and we're not.

She's reached the summit of acceptance and understanding, but Juliet Ann and I are still slowly and skeptically climbing the mountain. I'm beginning to share Sookie's sentiments about complaining—I'm tired of being miserable, too—but I'm just having a tougher time getting over the hurdle.

"It's not exactly a slice of heaven," I say, picking up a piece of pizza, not feeling any of her enthusiasm.

"What do you mean?" Sookie asks.

Where do I start?

I return my pizza slice to the paper plate before my first bite. "The School has me right where it wants me. It smoothly lures people in with promises—money, a life of luxury, stability, a golden ticket, business knowledge, independence, prestige—but with a price. I don't just mean tuition or salary, but something bigger. It's that Henry David Thoreau quote, 'The price of anything is the amount of life you have to exchange for it.' A piece of your soul, if you're not careful. But I am. I am careful, and I still had to pay the price." I can't stop. "I was foolish to think that First Year was the harder of the two—the biggest decisions are made now. Without even considering the disastrous, hellish, emotional turmoil of First Year, I will tell you what I'm feeling: confusion. Confusion about where I'm going, professionally and geographically, and how I feel about business, the profession to which I've devoted my entire professional life and that 70% of the country now seems to suddenly despise." I catch my breath on the last word. "But it's too late to turn back. My sense of security, my general outlook on business, has been rattled; but yet I am consumed by a mind that is slowly becoming wired for only business. That's the price I'm paying. I feel guilty about not making a difference in the world; and I wonder if I'll make too many sacrifices, or worse, too few sacrifices, for my personal life." I take a deep breath. "But that's not even including the worst guilt of all—guilt for having any of these feelings because I know business school is an opportunity of a lifetime and I should feel very, very lucky. Instead, I feel like a scorned lover The School has left at the alter." I say emotionally. "The School has won. Don't you get it, Sookie?" I exhale slowly and casually pick up a slice of pizza. "It's over."

I calmly take a bite of pepperoni.

"And last night I caught myself building a spreadsheet model to compare summer vacation packages!" I groan with a small smile and mutter, "Will the madness never end?" before dropping my pizza onto the paper plate.

Silence

"Wow," Sookie finally says.

Juliet Ann sighs. "Phew."

"I'm fine," I say.

Juliet Ann puts her hand on my arm sympathetically. "Hey, I feel the same way. Every morning of every day I question my decision to come here and wonder how to build a career out of the rubble of my life."

"They haven't won!" Sookie tries to rouse me. "Why do you think that? *You're* the one who is going to graduate with the degree! *You'll* have access to more opportunity than most people in the world dream of. *You'll* have independence—you can do whatever you want. And you'll do more for the community than most people I know! So what if you don't know what you want to be when you grow up? Who cares? No one knows—and you'll change your mind a thousand times. But you'll come out on top. Especially with this degree. *They* haven't won. *You've* won."

I sit stoically, melting only a little.

"I get frustrated, too," Juliet Ann admits. "Can you imagine what it would be like if everyone here told the truth?"

Sookie laughs. "We'd hear things like, 'I had 27 interviews but I'm still graduating jobless!' or 'My new jobs sucks but no one else would hire me,' or 'I just got my fifth low-pass and it turns out I may not graduate after all!'"

Juliet Ann laughs and I finally crack a smile.

"Sometimes I remind myself that maybe it's not always a battle," Juliet Ann offers. "And if it is, I don't have to fight it. I think right now you're just burnt out on business. In this environment, you're seeing the most innovative business practices, but you're also seeing the ugly, frustrating side of business. But you know that's not the norm; it's the minority. And it doesn't matter if you're not following a traditional MBA career path."

"What's traditional, anyway?" Sookie interjects.

Juliet Ann nods reassuringly. "Just the very thought that you want to do something 'better' with your life shows that you will. And business school will give you all the resources to do that, no matter how long it takes."

"Remember last month when I was freaking out about my job offer? I wasn't sure if I wanted to work in Hollywood anymore?" Sookie asks me. "And remember what you said to me? You said that it was just my fear that was holding me back—fear of change, fear of success—and you were right!"

"How many times have you reminded me that we all have the power to change our lives? Sometimes you just have to do it in baby steps," Juliet Ann adds.

"You've always told me that it's okay to be scared," Sookie continues. "We don't always know how things are going to turn out, so we shouldn't be attached to an outcome—we should just make the best decisions we can and have faith in the future."

I can't believe anyone ever listened to my advice, let alone is repeating it to me.

"And do you remember what you said to me about my consulting company plans?" Juliet Ann asks.

I wrinkle my eyebrows trying to remember.

"You said, 'Go Big!'" she reminds me.

I said that?

Sookie starts laughing. "You said the same thing to me—GO BIG!"

"And business school will help you tackle the next big thing," Juliet Ann adds, "no matter what you do."

I smile. "Go big," I say softly and then chuckle at my youthful expression.

Suddenly, Suresh barges into the Brickhouse with a group of four rowdy, cheering classmates who head to the bar to order; Suresh spots us and waltzes toward our table with excitement.

"We won!" he shouts, raising his arms in victory.

"You won? You won what?" Juliet Ann asks.

"The VCIC?" Sookie shrieks, then jumps.

"Yeah! We just found out today." He hugs all of us.

"Congratulations! That's incredible!" Juliet Ann and I tumble our sentiments.

Sookie is ecstatic. "We knew you could do it!"

VCIC is the Venture Capital Investment Competition, a fantasy league of venture capital, so to speak. Student teams from all over the country play as firms making investment recommendations to a panel of professional venture capitalists for an undisclosed "cash prize." Suresh has been performing due diligence on companies, analyzing business plans, networking with corporate executives, and preparing term sheets all year.

"I was hoping it would pay off," he admits with a growing smile as he relaxes into a chair. "Not in regard to the money," he's quick to explain, "but the sense of accomplishment."

We loudly applaud his teammates as they approach our table with their drinks.

*   *   *   *

Later in the evening, after several beers, the conversation culminates with the inevitable "value of the MBA" discussion. Suresh offers a different perspective than the usual ROI calculation; he tells a story about his family. "My uncle in India has a dream of having a business. He has the warehouse, the equipment, the funds, even the labor, but still can't operate. Why? Because his town lacks consistent access to electricity! *Electricity!* Can you imagine?" he asks passionately. "My uncle struggles just to turn the lights on, something so simple that we take for granted every day." He unfolds his arms. "Here, we have the resources and the freedom to bring any idea to fruition. That is why I absolutely cannot discount the power of the MBA—I want to use it to help him with his struggles, help my family." He takes a swig of beer and his eyes glisten, showing a surprisingly sentimental side. "We have these opportunities *every single day.*"

After a silent pause to digest his words, Juliet Ann finally releases a low whistle from her breath. "Well, perspectives like that certainly restore my faith in business when I least expect it."

A chorus of nods and "yeahs" trickles from the group.

"Sometimes I lose sight of it, but you're right, Suresh," I say softly. "Business touches every part of the world—and it's an opportunity." I find myself remembering the passion I had before business school; I remember thinking, *I am applying to business school viewing business as such: a challenge. It's not lost on me that if you want to make a change, the best way to start is to learn.*

I put my beer bottle on the table. "Business school forces you to painfully examine your progress in life and your future. It's hard to believe that The School is giving you any direction at all, but it is—sometimes it's just on a different path than what you'd imagined for yourself. It challenges you, but most of the time that's probably a good thing. It just takes time to get used to," I hear myself saying.

Juliet Ann agrees, "The School forces you to examine yourself even when you can't bear to look. You feel confused, but then The School soothes you with a seemingly simple solution: *Change your life, that's all you have to do.* And then, almost cruelly, The School leads you to the erroneous belief that it's actually extremely difficult to do so..."

I lean back in my chair with a moment of truth brewing in my head. "But you know, I'd rather have these obstacles and difficult choices, than not have them at all."

Suresh nods. "Business school is an institution, a machine of minds and business knowledge. It exists as it is, every year. It just exists. It's there. It's mammoth. How you react to it depends on you. It's not altering itself for a single person, it's not personally out to get you, it just exists and watches the people around react to it."

"But arguably the "machine" is better suited to some people," Juliet Ann adds.

"And the mass reactions of the people around it will inevitably change it," Sookie says.

"And maybe that's why we're here?" Suresh reasons.

"Cheers to life!" Sookie says to lift the mood, raising her beer bottle to the ceiling and then downing the last of it.

Suresh chuckles and follows.

❅   ❅   ❅   ❅

Maybe it's the deep conversation, or the mini-breakdown, or the liquor, but I'm feeling peaceful right now—I don't want to be one of those stoic, unhappy people that business sometimes produces. And it's liberating to know that I don't have to be; but I also know that I've got to get it together. Pronto.

WAKE UP AND SMELL THE WORLD

The next day, I begin afresh.

"Thank you for a terrific year. I'll remember all of you for a long time—and I want you to know that I think each and every one of you is destined for something great."

Bernie bends over to moon me before Miss Coffee-Smith harshly reminds him to make good choices.

It's a beautiful day in late April and I am reluctantly saying goodbye to my favorite kindergarteners. "And next year, when you're in first grade with a new Junior Achievement tutor—you'll have just as much fun together as we did. Thanks for a great year and good luck with your lemonade stands!"

"Class, let's say thank you to Feddy for taking the time to help us learn about business." Miss Coffee-Smith leads a loud chorus of "thank you's" from the kids, making my heart melt.

"And now you can go to the tables and continue playing games until Feddy leaves," she instructs, causing the children to scatter from the floor to various tables in the room to play their business games. I watch with a bit of nostalgia before finally making my way to the first table to help a group of children.

"This is for you, Feddy," Antonia says and hands me a sheet of white notebook paper with five nickels and a penny taped to it.

"Why thank you, Antonia," I say.

"That's the money I made from my lemonade stand last week. And you said we can give the money to people we care about, so I want you to have it."

She wants me to have her money.

"I want to be just like you!" She beams.

She wants to be just like me.

I feel a flashflood of images wave over me—Aaron and I receiving an award last week for our work with Junior Achievement, Rick, Sookie, Juliet Ann, Tempestt, the breast cancer clinic, Professor Grace, Morteza, the exciting moments when I received my job offers, the Information Technology exam I aced, the Colgate product we designed, the posh parties with Rick, the Kingsbury-Kutter internship program, the WIBC roundtables, meeting Anita Roddick, late nights at Brickhouse pizzeria with friends, meeting the greatest business minds in the world, the new web portal I built for my Digital Strategies class, California, the world, a new life, my parents pride, Antonia's smiling face…all because of business school.

Oh God, I've been such a fool.

A first-class fool.

❋   ❋   ❋   ❋

After a full day of volunteering and blitzing through a case about Harley-Davidson's brand community, I spontaneously high tail it to Boston, arriving well after 10 p.m. to a very surprised, but delighted, Rick.

Rick.

All I've thought about for the last few hours is Rick—how proud I am of him, how important he is to me, how ridiculous we've been lately. *I'm not letting The School take my relationship, too.*

After vying for the world's worst person award ("No, I was terrible"; "No, I was.") in his apartment, we vow to make it work by spending an emotional two hours putting together an emergency relationship rescue plan.

"I've been horrible," he admits, after we've hashed out our future together. "I don't know what happened to me."

I collapse on the bed next to him. "Me, too."

"Don't let me turn into that person again, consumed with work," he pleads. "It won't happen again."

I laugh. "Well, it probably will, but that's okay—if we catch it, we can work it out before it gets bad."

He had revealed to me earlier that the only reason he didn't beg me to go to California was because he didn't want me to feel pressured as a woman—he knows how important my independence is. But then, when I said that I felt like a follower, he thought his efforts had truly been fruitless because I had backed away emotionally anyway and still felt like a stereotype. Rick just wanted me to choose him of my own freewill, and to realize that in doing so, I was actually opening myself up to more opportunities in life, not shutting them out.

After spending so many years worrying only about our independent selves, it had been easy to fall into the "me first" line of thinking. But now we hope to change. I realize that, in a strange way, the security of my degree awards me independence, but it also allows me to feel good about choosing to be with my best friend. It's my new outlook on this whole experience: I know now that I can stand alone, but I'm *choosing* to share part of my life with someone I love.

Independence makes dependence easier?

I turn toward him. "And I promise to be as committed to us as you are."

He smiles. "I'm not always the bad guy, Feddy."

He really cares. And I know it's a struggle for him to balance the weight of work with our relationship; and to reconcile preconceived notions (however small they may be) about what a family was like when he was growing up versus what our family may be like tomorrow. But he's trying. And he never gives up on us.

I kiss him on the forehead. "I know you're not, Rick."

❆   ❆   ❆   ❆

The following week, Rick moves to San Francisco, but vows to return for my graduation before we start our new lives together on the West Coast (California, incidentally, being much closer to Arizona and to my parents than any other alternative).

As Juliet Ann once said to me about Ashton, "We're best friends with tremendous respect for one another and we don't want to lose that."

And neither did we.

HELP! IS THERE AN MBA IN THE HOUSE?

"It's a grant-making foundation supporting basic global human rights, economic independence, and education," Finneas explains the full-time job he recently accepted in London.

"What will you be doing?" I ask him as we walk across campus with Sookie.

"I'll be the Development Director for the UK."

"Congratulations!" I hug him, relieved that we've accidentally fallen into our old friendship again simply by choosing to ignore the bedroom incident. Time has healed us for the moment.

"I volunteered with them for several years, so this is a great opportunity."

"Finneas was tired of banking," Sookie interjects.

"There's nothing wrong with banking," he quickly justifies as we enter the bagel shop. "I just wasn't fulfilled."

Now he's going to be saving poor people around the world? Wow.

Sookie, floating on a similar cloud of philanthropy, has decided to work for a nonprofit organization called Females in Film as their new Strategic Planning Director. She explained this will give her exposure to female screenwriters, actresses, and studio VP's while easing her conscience somewhat, too.

"He's going to *save the world*!?" I whisper to Sookie while Finneas orders our bagels at the counter.

"I know! Isn't he incredible?" she jokes.

"Are you going to keep seeing him after he goes back to Europe?"

"What?" She looks confused.

"A long-distance relationship?" I suggest.

She laughs. "Well...I think you actually have to *be* in a relationship first before you can have the long-distance variety."

Now I'm confused. "I thought you two were dating?"

"What? No!" she yells.

"Shhh!" I warn, so Finneas won't hear us. "But—?"

She grabs my arm as she leans toward my ear. "I mean, maybe there's something there, but we never defined it...and now he's leaving."

"Really?" I find myself asking with a bit of sadness.

"But we both...I don't know...London's far! And there's not much room in his life for me—why complicate it for him? Plus, he's married."

My mouth drops. "He's married!?"

"To his work, I mean. You've seen him—he works nonstop! I don't want to take him away from that," she explains. "Not that I could..."

"He's too busy saving the world?" I say again jokingly.

She laughs. "Yeah. Tragically romantic, isn't it?"

Finneas returns with our bagels.

"Everything with plain cream cheese?" He hands me my bagel. "And cinnamon raisin with butter?" He gives Sookie her bagel as we head outside to a small table in front of the shop. May has just arrived; mud season has officially ended and the campus is thawing out nicely.

So there's nothing between Sookie and Finneas after all?

"Ready for your presentation tomorrow?" Finneas asks me.

"Absolutely!" I confirm.

Sookie bites her bagel. "What presentation? The cruise line thing?"

"Yeah, we finally finished our brand assessment," I explain, putting on a stodgy, professional voice for fun. "Aaron Jeffries and I teamed up with two other classmates last month to work on a project for Brand Management—a brand assessment of Royal Caribbean Cruises." I exaggeratedly tilt my nose to the air for dramatic effect and continue in my elitist voice, "We conducted a full brand equity scorecard with an industry analysis, a brand inventory, a positioning map, and recommendations for future branding—all of which the cruise line has expressed interested in reading."

Sookie laughs. "Well done. I see they've taught you well!"

"Aaron's giving the actual presentation," I continue in my regular voice. "But it was the most fun I've had on a project all year."

"You sound happy," Finneas says.

"Yeah, it's finally coming together. I've made a few decisions recently."

"She got another job offer!" Sookie blurts out.

Finneas beams. "Congratulations!"

"Thanks." I blush. "It's from the hospital were I worked on a project last term."

"The breast cancer clinic, right?" Sookie asks.

I nod. "They offered me a marketing position in the Women's Comprehensive Health Clinic there."

"When do you start?" Finneas asks.

"Well…"

"She doesn't know if she's taking it," Sookie explains.

"It's a fantastic position, but I'm not staying in this area. I've still got my fingers crossed for other opportunities."

"In California?" he asks.

"Yeah," I say, smiling because this is the first time I can confidently admit that I want to go to California and it finally feels right. The move to California could be a blessing in disguise. "I don't think it will be easy, but it's a chance to pursue an adventure together and see how our relationship holds. There's no pressure, I finally realize, because I always have choices."

"I'm okay graduating without a job," I continue. "I want to find something that's right for me—not a quick fix to impress everyone else. I'm not really one to give in to peer pressure."

Maybe The School hasn't won, after all.

"Inner harmony often projects outward," Finneas says. "If you're happy inside"—he points to his heart—"and at peace, you'll be able to live the life you want on the outside."

"Plus, you'll be closer to me in California! I can visit you in San Francisco, and you can come to L.A." Sookie reminds me.

"And if you can brave the fine UK rain and hail, you're both welcome to visit me in London," Finneas offers.

"Nice to have friends on both continents," I say cramming the last bite of bagel into my mouth.

"Suresh!" Sookie yells suddenly when she sees Suresh walking across the street. "Guys, I've got to talk to Suresh. But I'll see you later back at the apartment?" She jumps up, collecting her paper trash and jacket before running off to catch Suresh.

"Bye!" we call to her as she darts between cars to meet Suresh.

Finneas finishes his orange juice and looks at me. "I guess at the end of it all, we realize what matters most in life and try to work it all out and do the right thing, don't we?" he asks.

I smile at him.

"I'm certainly trying."

PARTING IS SUCH SWEET SORROW

There are more zeroes on this piece of paper than I've ever seen before.

It's my bonus check from Kingsbury-Kutter. An early "thank you" from them in anticipation of my new full-time employment. A little something special in addition to my regular six-figure salary. In addition to my regular benefits. In addition to my generous retirement plan. In addition to my relocation package. In addition to everything else incredible they've ever done for me. My bonus check.

All those zeroes...

I pick up the phone.

"Hi Jeb," I begin.

"Feddy!" He's excited. "Great to hear from you! Can't wait for you to join us in the fall. Don't blame you for taking the summer off first—I did the same thing after business school—but let me know if there's *anything* you need before you come here. Maggie and I would be glad to help," he mentions, referring to his wife.

Urgh. This is going to be harder than I thought.

"Jeb—that's why I'm calling. I'm afraid I've got some bad news," I blurt out. "I won't be joining Kingsbury-Kutter in the Fall."

Silence.

"I wanted you to be the first to know."

"Well..." he says slowly and more professionally. "I'm surprised at your decision, to say the least. Are you absolutely certain you've thought this through? This is a stellar company." He defends Kingsbury-Kutter for several minutes.

"Jeb, my decision is not a reflection on the company, but rather on me."

"Did something happen? Is everything okay?" he asks concerned.

"Yes! Jeb, I'm fine." *Oh God, how do I explain the inner turmoil?* "I'm experiencing a career dilemma right now and I'm not sure if Kingsbury-Kutter is the right choice for me..."

"Oh," he says with a sigh. "I see. You have another offer? Well, I'm sure we can negotiate your salary. I'll talk to Human Resources first thing in the morning."

"No, Jeb, thank you for that offer, but it's not about the money."

"We can change your placement, move you to another department?"

"No. Thank you, that's very nice of you, but Jeb, it's not about another offer. I wasn't calling to negotiate. I just...won't be coming back to Kingsbury-Kutter."

He's completely confused and I can't blame him. "Well, okay then, I guess?" he offers doubtfully.

"I'm sorry. It's hard to explain. After months of careful deliberation, I just don't believe that brand management is the right fit for me at this time. It's not where I want to be right now. And I want to go somewhere were I can be fully committed and give 100% and likewise feel fulfilled."

I promised myself that I wouldn't mention California to Kingsbury-Kutter, mainly because it's not truly the sole reason I'm not going to their company.

"I think you're making a big mistake," he advises. "Kingsbury-Kutter is an excellent career move. And you're virtually guaranteed to reach the next tier in two or three years..."

We continue for several minutes while he tries to convince me I'm making a mistake, especially because it's not really clear to him why I'm leaving. He has 15 solid professional reasons why I should secure my offer with Kingsbury-Kutter. And he's right, but it's that intangible x-factor that he can't compete with, and that I can't explain.

He won't give up and promises to call me tomorrow; and he also asks me to speak with Human Resources before I make a final decision. I politely oblige, but I already know where I stand.

After we hang up, I feel strangely relieved as I slowly tear up the bonus check. *All those zeroes...*

KNOCK, KNOCK...WHO'S THERE? (APPARENTLY OPPORTUNITY)

"It's an organization dedicated to ensuring the development of socially responsible business policies," Professor Grace explains with her natural, tranquil sophistication.

"They're consultants?" I ask.

"For corporate responsibility, yes. They provide companies with the tools they need to make social responsibility a fundamental part of the business—and sometimes they act as liaisons between businesses and civic or public sectors supporting the community and environment. I thought it might be a good fit for you." She hands me a business card. "Plus, they're in California..." Her eyes sparkle above her calmness.

Professionals for Prosperity?

"Here," she continues. "Call this woman. She's the Director of Marketing for PFP and I've already mentioned your name to her." She winks.

"Thanks," I say before heading home to research Professionals for Prosperity.

✳   ✳   ✳   ✳

"They employ more than 10 million workers around the world!" I tell Rick two weeks later while visiting California, which happens to be a beautiful paradise of ocean, land, flowers, sunsets, and gorgeous people. Rick loves the media and technology rich community; and we found a spectacular, over-priced (there's no other kind out there) apartment in lower Pacific Heights that will be available this summer.

To live together or not to live together, that is the next question.

But first things first...

"Basically, PFP goes into companies and give them resources for social responsibility—like training, evaluation methods, technical support, business expertise, research and networks..."

"What are the major issues?" he asks as we get ready to go to dinner.

"Human rights, ethics, corporate governance, community investment—sometimes domestic, sometimes global. They recently worked with Gap, Inc. to improve labor conditions, and last year they worked with Ford—"

"What would you be doing again?" he asks.

"It's exactly what I've been looking for. Marketing and Communications Manager for Women's Initiatives." I search the desk for my hotel key card. "I'd be gathering and communicating research on women in business, putting it into the training modules, and then sharing it with corporations." I grab my sweater and follow him out the door. "I can tell you verbatim what the director told me. 'PFP is trying to develop a comprehensive center around women in the labor force to ensure that women are treated fairly and ethically around the world and to bring awareness to these issues.'" I push the elevator button and continue, "It's not a tangible center, just figurative, more like a one-stop resource hub at PFP." I push my arm into the sleeve of my sweater as we enter the elevator. "I'll be part of the inaugural Women's Initiatives team—developing the center, growing it, and then promoting it." I add excitedly,

Rick smiles. "Sounds different…but interesting. You'd be making a positive impact," he reasons and looks at me. "You feeling good about it?"

"Yeah, I am." I take his hand as we exit the hotel and turn onto Market Street. "I talked to them yesterday. My second interview is on Tuesday—before I fly back—with the President and the VP of Marketing, but they've told me the job is basically mine."

Rick is shocked. "That's awesome!" he gushes.

"This just feels right," I confirm, smiling, and he hugs me.

"I just have a few things to wrap up in New Hampshire—and then we're good to go!"

❅   ❅   ❅   ❅

"Well, you seem to be in good spirits—I presume due to the final countdown?" Professor Grace smiles from her desk while I lean against the doorway to her office.

"Technically, the countdown began on day one of First Year!" I joke and she laughs.

"I heard that PFP offered you the job?"

"Yep, yesterday," I confirm. "It happened so fast—just like everything else here—but it's official: I'm going to California. Thank you." I hand her a box of Godiva chocolates to show my gratitude.

She looks surprised. "Oh, don't thank me—I just put you in contact with them. You did the rest."

"Well then, thanks for the contact."

"So did the MBA meet your expectations?" Professor Grace asks curiously.

"Well…" My voice travels under a long, heavy exhalation that turns into a chuckle. "Yeah, I guess it did," I finally admit. "It just took me awhile to figure things out and appreciate the opportunity again—but I'm not done with the evaluation, yet," I quickly remind her. "Ask me again in a couple of years!"

We laugh as Morteza dips his head into her office. "Feddy! I've been looking for you—I wanted to say good luck and congratulations!" He shakes my hand with the usual business school strength and gusto that we've mastered so well.

I firmly squeeze back. "Thank you. And thanks for explaining assets and liabilities."

He laughs and waves his hand as if to communicate it was nothing. "Use it in good health," he says. "And congratulations on your new job."

Word travels fast at a small school.

"Oh, I'm looking forward to it," I assure him.

"And I just heard that 100% of your class is graduating with a job," Morteza reveals. "But I'm sure that Tami and JP will tell you that this afternoon." He's referring to a farewell meeting we have with the administration in Holt Auditorium at noon; it's our opportunity to officially say goodbye.

He continues mysteriously, "There's one thing that I hope you take away from here besides business acumen—it's the number one indicator of future success in business."

"What is it?" I ask anxiously.

"The ability to talk to anyone comfortably." Morteza emphasizes each word with an animated motion of his index finger. "At *any* level in an organization—assistants, CEOs, cleaning crew, managers, creative, operations, engineers, directors. *That* will bring you success."

Professor Grace nods and leans back in her chair. "And I hope you'll also leave here remembering what's truly important in life," she adds, looking directly into my eyes to guarantee my attention. "*You* have the opportunity to change the world."

"I can't wait," I assure her, truly excited about my future in California, both professionally and personally. I'm feeling pretty good about things right now—I'm ready to grab my future and just go for it.

There's only one thing standing between me and the rest of my life.

Graduation.

CHAPTER 11

FORECASTING

(Graduation)

"Oh my God, is she alright?!"
   "Lay her down! Put her feet up, drink this water."
   "Give her space—back up!—she needs to breathe."
   "I'll run a cold shower for her."
   "Feddy? Fed? Can you hear us? Are you okay?"

I look up. I know I have 20 of my dearest friends and family waiting for me on this sunny, nauseatingly humid graduation day. I also know that I have debilitating heatstroke after wearing the black graduation gown in the record-breaking 95-degree summer weather. My body is burning up, hot to the touch, but I have stopped sweating—a sure sign of its severity. There is nothing left in my stomach and my head would hurt less if a sledge hammer hit it. I will have to miss the post-graduation festivities because surely I will be in the hospital. I think I am going to die.

I can barely make out my mother's voice. "Feddy, honey, your father and I are going to take your guests to the graduation dinner party. Rick is going to stay here with you."

I spend the night in bed with heatstroke, passing out between intervals in the bathroom, while everyone celebrates my glorious achievement with a night out on the town. (I find out later that they had a super time.) The school administration sent an email the next day, apologizing for the unbearable conditions at graduation.

Once again, The School gets the best of me.
Talk about going out with a bang!

INVESTITURE, JUNE 10th, 3 p.m.

It's officially called investiture, but it's really a graduation. And there are two of them—one for the business school, and one for the entire Ivy League college. The program for the business school ceremony reads:

- *Processional March (basically that means we march in looking proud)*
- *Welcome from Dean Denton*
- *Granting of Honorary Degree*
- *Remarks from the Honorary Speaker*
- *Bestowal of Hoods (don't ask)*
- *Presentation of Medals (for what army?)*
- *Scholarship Recognition Ceremony (Ivy Scholars)*
- *Presentation of the Class Gift (I don't remember being consulted)*
- *Student Speaker (notes from our Class President on how easy his job was)*
- *Readings of Historical Documents (naptime)*
- *Recessional (marching with shell-shocked faces as family members bombard us with camera flashes. "Smile, honey!")*

Robert E. Rubin is our honorary graduation speaker (one of the perks of going to B-school: top-tiered graduation speakers), which seems to delight my father to no end, but barely impresses my non-business school friends. I think they were hoping for the President of the United States, or Bill Cosby.

Two things worry me about the ceremony: length that could rival the Academy Awards ceremony, and the frightening ambiguity of the "Bestowal of Hoods." I have flashbacks to the scary Convocation Ceremony rituals that I wish I had never seen.

Ha.

Convocation?

It seems like ages ago. Two years…two very long years.

And now, in just two hours, it will be done.

What's this? A tear of pride? I wipe my right eye with the sleeve of my heavy, black graduation gown.

So here I am. At graduation, listening to Dean Denton congratulate us with as much confidence as when he first greeted us. And there are my parents, sitting with Rick under a nearby birch tree, surrounded by twenty or so friends I've invited to the ceremony—Amy, Gary, friends of the family, the Bergen's, the Rivera's, the Young's, and Rick's family.

Wow, it's hot, isn't it? The heat is debilitating. It must be 95 degrees with 100% humidity today. My black gown is attracting the heat like a magnifying glass—unfortunately, I'm the ant.

Oh God, I'm going to pass out.

I briefly contemplate pouring my bottled water over my head instead of drinking it.

Chakira winks at me from the next row and gives me a thumbs up, which I immediately return. *The Imposters* surround me, sitting expressionless in their metal chairs; even Bradley's Keggers are unusually quiet in the back row because of the oppressive heat. My mind wanders from thoughts of a heatstroke death to a more reasonable fear: there's a actually a small chance I may not graduate today because of some unpaid parking tickets…

My name! They just called my name. And they pronounced it correctly!

I run to the front and collect my diploma, proudly smiling as my dad snaps a photo from the left while I march back to my seat.

It's over?

I barely hear the final, whirlwind moments of the ceremony, or remember the glorious "Pomp and Circumstance" march. "Smile, Feddy!" my friends and family yell like the paparazzi, before we're corralled into tents for chicken skewers, salads, pastries, and wine.

Something's not right. My head is throbbing and I'm sweating profusely. I feel sick and need to sneak off to the bathroom to die.

"God, your face is red!" Jonas yells as I run by.

Thanks for the breaking news.

"Hey—you okay?" another classmate, Deepa, asks with concern.

I just keep running to the bathroom.

Thank God I make it.

I look in the mirror. *Ahhh!* My face is beet red and shiny. I splash cold water on it, then grab a brown paper towel to soak it up. *Still red.* I run the faucet and begin splashing again. Feeling nauseous, I stop and look up at the mirror.

Ahhh!

Nelly is standing at the sink next to mine, washing her hands.

"Hi," I blurt out from surprise.

"Your face is red."

Good, now maybe you can use those clever sleuthing skills to solve that murder on the Orient Express.

"Yeah, I'm overheated," I explain and dab the towel on my forehead.

Okay, now I know she's going to say something rude. Why not? I'm completely exposed. I'm sick, overheated, red, sweaty, miserable, and I look hideous—I'm easy prey.

"It's a thousand degrees out there," she says.

What? Come on, Nelly, let me have it. It would be the perfect ending to my suffering. How about a little, "You look disgusting," or "It's a good thing I'm so physically fit, the heat doesn't affect me at all."

But she refrains.

"I'm overheated and miserable, too," she admits and I pause for a minute to contemplate a deeper meaning in her words that I'm sure she didn't intend.

I turn off the faucet and turn toward her, lingering for a second.

"Good luck to you, Nelly," I finally say.

She smiles sincerely at me. "Good luck to you, too, Feddy." Then she walks out the door.

Now I wish I could say we held hands and pledged our new life-long friendship to one another, but it just didn't happen. And that's okay.

I'll take what I can get.

❋   ❋   ❋   ❋

I can't go back outside into the heat yet, so I decide to take the long route through the empty, air-conditioned Main House before joining my family again.

I feel absolutely horrible—I don't know how I'll be able to celebrate tonight.

Wobbly legs, red face, weakness and all, I slowly trudge down the main hallway with only one destination in mind.

I have to see her one last time.

Scanning the photo-lined wall, I quickly find Annabelle Hall Smith. There she is, still smiling at me from her graduation photo.

I can't believe that soon my own photo will grace the wall, marking both the history and the future of The School. Someone will look at my photo 30 years from now—maybe a family of alumni passing though the hallway, reminiscing with their children; maybe a group of nervous prospective students on tour; maybe a girl just like me, searching for inspiration…

She's the reason I'm here—she stirs something deep inside my heart. I look at Annabelle closely and I'm suddenly moved by one thought: *We've made a difference.*

"I did it," I say to her, kissing my finger and planting it onto her photo, smiling as much as she is.

"We did it."

THE SUN WILL COME OUT, EVEN IN NEW HAMPSHIRE

The next morning gives birth to a glorious strand of sequential events. I feel terrific, mostly because I made it through the night alive.

Rick and I attend the college graduation with my parents on the main campus green. It's brief because the President of the college refrains from identifying the graduate students (medical, business, and engineering) individually. Instead, my school is lumped together as "The Business School" and instructed to rapidly proceed in orderly single file. It's over in 10 minutes.

I catch Aaron Jeffries after the ceremony and say goodbye to him and his wife, Sadie. They're off to Vermont after a month-long Scandinavian summer cruise. I also find Suresh, as usual, surrounded by a crowd of classmates, saying his goodbyes. He sneaks away when he sees me and gives me a big hug. "You never gave up!" he says.

"No, I didn't."

"And that means you never will. I'm so proud of you."

"Thanks, Suresh." His right arm lingers over my shoulders as we walk toward a tent. "Heading back to Lehman?" I ask.

"Yeah, in two days, but only for six months. I don't think I want to work at a big firm anymore—maybe a boutique firm or venture philanthropy. Maybe even head out west for a few years."

"Really?" I raise an eyebrow. "California?"

"Maybe. I have to think a little more about what I want to do now—there's a new twist to the mix." He winks mischievously. "But of course, I'll be making frequent trips back to India."

"Of course." I nod as his family calls for him.

"Duty calls." He motions to his family and slowly walks backwards toward them so he can continue to face me. "Congratulations, Feddy!"

"I'll email you next week!" I call after him, then seek out Juliet Ann and Tempestt who are hovering in the shade of a nearby tree with their respective families.

I meet Tempestt's entire clan from Atlanta—all 50 of them. Cousins, brothers, sisters, lovers, you name it. They're gregarious and exceptionally jovial.

"We're so proud of our Tempy!" her mom bellows, hugging an embarrassed Tempestt. "She's the first one in our family to go to graduate school!"

"Congratulations," I say to all of them and then turn toward Tempestt.

Tempestt glances at the sky. "I can't believe it, but I'm actually going to miss you," she admits with what I think is a sliver of emotion.

"Me, too." I smile and give her a purposely overbearing hug, slyly adding, "*Tempy.*"

"Don't ever repeat that name!" she shrieks, but she's laughing.

"I promise not to. Even when in New York." I hold up my palm to pledge my promise. Sookie and I are planning a trip to NYC to visit Tempestt and Juliet Ann in August.

Juliet Ann finds us and quickly introduces me to her parents, both doctors, and to her younger brother, who just happens to be applying to undergraduate business school this year.

"Don't worry," Juliet Ann lets me know. "I've already warned him about the good *and* the bad…"

Ashton returns with a glass of lemonade for Juliet Ann and gives me a hearty "Congratulations" hug.

I wrap my arms around Juliet Ann. "Thank you for being my best friend here," I say to her.

"I couldn't have done it without you."

I hug her again. "Me neither," I agree. "And I wouldn't have wanted to."

"Did you book your flight to New York?" she asks when we finally release.

"Yeah. I'll send you the details tonight."

"I'll call you tomorrow," she says, waving as I leave to find my family to begin our walk to the Main House.

❄   ❄   ❄   ❄

Trailing behind my parents and Rick, I linger to glare at the mammoth structure of the Main House, a building I have anxiously entered a thousand times.

The School is a palatial cage of ivory pillars and peeling windowpanes that will hurriedly usher in unsuspecting students minutes before the warm grandeur inevitably breaks open this fall to reveal cloaked malevolence. *The better to see you with, my pretty…*

The corners of my mouth turn upward and my eyes narrow as I look at the cement steps brazenly daring me to enter.

Been there, done that.

I trudge past the building and laugh at myself, remembering that it's only in my head—my personification of The School is the only thing keeping it alive.

But I still can't help *The Fall of the House of Usher* from flashing in my thoughts; and I briefly picture the last scene of a sci-fi movie where the evil force meets its fate via the popular "freezes into statue and crumbles into dust" tactic.

I smile at The School, thinking perhaps I've been harder on it than it has been on me.

You don't seem so scary anymore, now that I know your secrets.

Suddenly I'm reminded of a quote: "To forgive is to set the prisoner free...and then discover that the prisoner was you."

I purse my lips together to contain my emotion before glancing at The School with complex, bittersweet affections of raging indignation, creeping adoration, and a very humbling gratefulness.

Then I walk away.

CAN OLD ACQUAINTANCES EVER REALLY BE FORGOTTEN?

I'm smiling as I pack up the last of my clothes, books, and bedding. And even though I'm saving 1/3 of my business school cases (you never know when you might need Purina's frozen TV dinners exit strategy), I can still pack all my things into 10 brown cardboard boxes and have them shipped via UPS. I don't have much, really.

I look around my empty, dusty room, a million memories flooding my head.

Sookie appears in my doorway, her smile brimming with excitement. "Pretty unbelievable, huh? We're done."

"Yep."

"Yahoo! We made it!" she finally whoops and puts her arm around my shoulder, tilting her head against mine as we look around my empty room.

I hug her. "Thanks for helping me get here, Sookie."

"Thank *you*. We should *both* feel proud."

"I do. I do feel proud." I bite my lower lip and reach down to grab one of my boxes. "We set out to do something, and we did it. Very few people can do it— but we did! And tomorrow begins the next journey."

"I can't wait! I figure if I can make it through business school, I can make it through anything! But it's still a little scary..."

"We're ready, Sookie. Ready to move on, ready to start doing things, ready to make things happen."

Rick knocks on my open door. "Almost ready?"

"Umm, no, not yet," I say to him.

"No problem—I'll be in the living room with your parents." He picks up a pair of winter boots sitting on top of a box. "I guess you won't be needed these anymore?" He laughs and heads back into the living room.

"Just five more minutes!" I call after him. "Two more boxes to go. And we're still saying goodbye."

"It's not goodbye, it's *good luck*," Sookie reminds me.

"Right! And I'll call you next week."

"And I'll fly out to see you next month," she promises. "And then New York City!"

"I'll miss you."

"Me, too." She hugs me and we share our final Watery Eye Syndrome moment before she leaves the apartment for the last time. I run to the bathroom window to wave goodbye and I'm stunned to see her getting into Suresh's car.

Why is Sookie getting into Suresh's car?

"Sookie!?" I yell to her.

She smiles mischievously through the open, passenger-side window. "What?" She feigns innocence. "I thought you knew?"

"Sookie!" I yell again, but she only winks as they drive away, honking the horn.

Sookie and Suresh?

For how long?

And where are they going?

I head back to my bedroom, shocked, but easily releasing to a growing smile of acceptance. *They're quite perfect together, now that I think about it.*

With a bit of a startle, Finneas arrives in my doorway to say goodbye. He's catching a flight to London in a few hours.

"I like you and you are fun." He smiles affectionately, handing me a white envelope. "And we have made good friends in that which is quite nice."

"Thanks, Finneas." I take the small envelope and reach for his shoulders to give him a hug.

He responds warmly and his hands linger around my waist for a moment until I look up at him. "Read it later. And be assured that I am only hoping for good things for you," he says.

"And I for you," I manage to say, unable to coherently speak the sudden flood of thoughts pouring into my head.

Perhaps sometimes less is best.

His eyes brighten. "Ring me when you're in London on one of your posh business ventures?"

"Absolutely," I agree, smiling. "And after you've finished saving the world, maybe you can save me from myself?"

Finneas laughs and retreats toward the door, pausing to wave for a moment before he disappears through the frame.

"And don't forget to send chocolate!" I yell after him.

"Will do!" he calls.

Having an uncharacteristically anxious moment (ahem), I feverishly open the envelope before he's more than 10 feet down the hall.

Next to his business card, there is only a single quote on a sheet of white paper.

"Education is not the filling of a pail but the lighting of a fire ~ William Butler Yeats."

I smile to myself, knowing I'll see Finneas again one day.

❄   ❄   ❄   ❄

It's quiet as Rick and I work with my parents to load my boxes into the car. Rick pulls me into the kitchen for a private moment.

"Congratulations!" He kisses me gently.

I return the kiss. "Thanks, Rick."

We hug for a long time, leaning into the corner where the stove meets the counter.

"Thanks for listening to me and encouraging me for the last two years," I whisper into his ear.

"Thank *you* for listening to me and encouraging me through Emode"—he laughs—"whether you wanted to or not!"

Suddenly, I remember something. "Congratulations on reaching 18 million registered users this week!" I release my grip so I can look at his reaction.

His blue-green eyes shine. "Thanks!"

"Not bad for just a few months in the biz?" I don't want his milestone to go unnoticed.

"Not bad," he says modestly with a growing grin. "But it'll be even better when you're out there with me…"

"Soon!"

He squeezes his arms around my shoulders. "I couldn't have done it without you."

"I couldn't have done it without you, Rick," I echo, "and I can't believe it's over!"

As I say those words, two things strike me: one, business school is never really over—it has changed the course of my life and will forever have a seat in my mind; and two, I'm perfectly okay with that.

"I love you," I say to Rick.

"Love you."

❄   ❄   ❄   ❄

During one last trip to my bedroom, I find a manila folder resting on the floor. I open it.

"Dear Ms. Pouideh:

Congratulations! It is with great pleasure and honor that we extend to you an invitation from the Admissions Committee to join us in September…"

It's a copy of my acceptance letter! From two years ago!

"I kept a copy—thought you might like it," comes my mom's voice from the doorway. I turn around to face her.

I feel the corners of my mouth curve upward as I remember the day I received the letter for the first time. "Thank you," I say softly.

She pulls me into an embrace, her eyes filling with tears. "Honey, we are so proud of you!"

My dad returns, dropping an empty cardboard box when he catches us hugging. "Congratulations, honey." He puts his arm around me. "Your mom and I very proud of you."

"We're so happy for you!" My mom dabs her eyes with a tissue. "You're the first woman in my family to get a master's."

I'm overwhelmed with pride knowing that for the rest of my life I can forever maintain that I earned a graduate degree from one of the most prestigious schools in the world.

"We couldn't be happier," my dad confirms, pulling out his video camera for the thousandth time today, beaming a grin wider than I've ever seen before.

My mom puts her arm around me and we smile for the shot.

Mom and dad. The greatest and most extraordinary influences in my life. I really owe everything to them—and I'm just grateful to give them today as one big, loving thank you.

I push a heavy box toward the door with my foot and catch a glimpse of myself in the full-length mirror on my wall.

"Oh my God!" I shriek, putting my hand to my mouth.

"What?" my mom asks.

For the first time in a long time I fearlessly raise my head and smile.

"I'm not blushing!"

CHAPTER 12

---

*

THE ANNUAL REPORT

(Epilogue from the Author)

When someone asks me why I went to business school, I often jokingly reply, "Well...I guess because no one told me I couldn't!"

And there's a beautiful, youthful truth in that statement. I wasn't overly concerned with gender minorities when I applied to business school—I simply wanted to learn and took the next logical step. Of course, this innocence about the obstacles faced in business school sometimes left me side-swiped in my new, sophisticated environment (where was *The Blushing MBA* when I needed it?), but it also worked double duty to help me through adversity—I simply kept charging forward in my own natural way.

I know now that business school is the most powerful step I have ever taken in my life and I will forever gather the wonderful benefits. That is why it is disheartening to learn that some women and girls shy away from business degrees—and that gender-biased educational models will consequently remain a reality, and perpetuate the gender stereotype, until more women enter the arena and pave an easier path for all female business students.

I can't stop encouraging more women to pursue education, to take risks, to make better lives for themselves and for their families. Women are the world's largest economy and almost any related national statistic will show you that women's earnings are on the rise; women earn most of the college and master's degrees granted each year; a growing number of women supply more than 50% of household income; most homes have two incomes and few households remain with a father-only breadwinner; the number of women earning more than

$100,000 has skyrocketed, as has the number of new businesses started by women; and women are embarking on varied business careers and exciting new levels of occupational status.

Perhaps girls do not understand how business knowledge will help them to remain successful in such an emergent world; and how a career in business will offer self-assurance, protection, freedom, and opportunities that will not only improve their lives, but also the lives of their future generations.

It certainly changed my life.

The lessons I eventually learned at business school were not the ones I expected. The world is changing and business is evolving, but I left business school with a greater understanding of life. It's not just about spreadsheets and business models; and I'm certainly not a workaholic obsessed with profit margins as some erroneous stereotype might suggest. I value quality of life, creativity, and personal choices. I've had a varied and fruitful business career that included something as wonderful as writing this book. My family means more to me now than ever and they know it. People deserve respect and I am sensitive to that. I know how to treat people and how I want to be treated, what is right and what is not. Business will always be my valuable livelihood, but most importantly, it allows me the security to focus on the other priorities in my life. The simple, important things are suddenly clear to me. And I cannot lose sight of one thing...

I did not graduate from business school solely a better professional.

I graduated a better human being.

978-0-595-37287-4
0-595-37287-2

Printed in the United States
220753BV00004B/74/A

9 780595 372874